Advance Praise for *The Feathered Bone*

"From the beginning, this story gripped me. Julie Cantrell is a wonderful wordsmith, and *The Feathered Bone* offers deep insight."

—Francine Rivers,
New York Times bestselling author

"Julie Cantrell has done a marvelous job here of telling a story about real people who are confronted with unthinkable loss and hardship, but who rise up from the ashes to become fuller, stronger, and better versions of themselves. *The Feathered Bone* is at once heartbreaking and uplifting, tragic and beautiful. And it is also a book that reminds us that even in our darkest hour, there is still hope, still reason to go on, still reason to forgive, to be alive, and to love."

—David Armand, author of
Harlow and *The Gorge*

"Julie Cantrell is not only a bestselling author, she is also a groundbreaking one. Her latest novel, *The Feathered Bone*, tackles the important topic of human trafficking and how a child abduction impacts the lives of a close-knit community. Through lyrical writing, Cantrell creates a page-turning story of suspense that weighs the strength of faith, forgiveness, and the resilience of the human spirit. *The Feathered Bone* is not to be missed."

—Michael Morris, author of *A Place Called
Wiregrass* and *Man in the Blue Moon*

"Emotionally gripping, *The Feathered Bone* will break your heart, but Julie Cantrell's masterful skill as a wordsmith will not leave you broken. If you believe beauty can emerge from devastation, this story is for you. If you don't, this story is for you."

—Susan Meissner, author of
Secrets of a Charmed Life

"Julie Cantrell does not hesitate to dive in to the deepest places of the heart. She knows it's all there in our fallen world—the good and bad, love and evil, the brokenness and the healing. In *The Feathered Bone* we meet three best friends who believe that their childhood promises will keep them safe, but when tragedy strikes one of them, they all fall. Cantrell's characters ask of us all—what would you do? How do we recover from the worst we can imagine? A stunning story that takes us through tragedy, heartbreak, and ultimately to both courage and redemption."

—PATTI CALLAHAN HENRY, *NEW YORK TIMES* BESTSELLING AUTHOR OF *THE IDEA OF LOVE* AND *THE STORIES WE TELL*

"Only a writer of Julie Cantrell's caliber could craft a story so thoroughly moving. Filled with courage, love, and faith in the most horrifying of situations, *The Feathered Bone* promises to grip you until the last page, and then long after."

—BILLY COFFEY, AUTHOR OF *THE CURSE OF CROW HOLLOW* AND *WHEN MOCKINGBIRDS SING*

"This is my favorite kind of book. The type of story that dismantles your heart and then puts the pieces back together in better working condition. A powerful tale of devastation and redemption. I loved it."

—JAMIE FORD, *NEW YORK TIMES* BESTSELLING AUTHOR OF *HOTEL ON THE CORNER OF BITTER AND SWEET*

"*The Feathered Bone* is a rare find, a beautifully written page-turner that left me stunned and breathless. In Julie Cantrell's masterful hands, the horror of Hurricane Katrina becomes a metaphor for the personal tragedies of lives torn apart and patched back together by the power of faith, courage, and love."

—CASSANDRA KING, AUTHOR OF *THE SUNDAY WIFE*

"What a book with heart. Ms. Cantrell's empathy for the complicated twists and turns of tragedy is woven throughout her new novel. She explores the gray area of simple decisions that come before disaster. This book is by far her best work yet."

—ANN HITE, AWARD-WINNING AUTHOR OF
WHERE THE SOULS GO AND
GHOST ON BLACK MOUNTAIN

"Startling and suspenseful, *The Feathered Bone* zips along with color and action, but doesn't fail to underscore the issues; for instance, questions of faith, and the perpetual domestic guilt that wives and mothers seem always to feel. Julie Cantrell knows how to tell a story."

—LISA HOWORTH, AUTHOR OF *FLYING SHOES*
AND OWNER OF SQUARE BOOKS

"*The Feathered Bone* fulfills every expectation that Julie Cantrell occasioned with *Into the Free* and *When Mountains Move*. It is haunting and hauntingly beautiful, a heart-wrenching story about how one woman, Amanda Salassi, rises from the depths of despair to discover that freedom and miracles do exist. Seeing pure darkness enables her to appreciate the light of love and hope."

—ALLEN MENDENHALL,
SOUTHERN LITERARY REVIEW

"In a journey through the darkest parts of the spirit, Julie Cantrell provides a near handbook for surviving crushing tragedies. Peppered with colorful characters and places and touching on real-life topics, *The Feathered Bone* is a beautifully written, rawly honest look at human frailty and strength, faith and doubt, and the resilience to keep living."

—MARGARET DILLOWAY, AWARD-WINNING
AUTHOR OF *HOW TO BE AN AMERICAN HOUSEWIFE*
AND *SISTERS OF HEART AND SNOW*

"*The Feathered Bone* is a haunting look at humanity. A ferocious tale of failures and flaws and the necessity of forgiving ourselves and one another. A breathless read from the moment young Sarah disappears from the suffocating crowds at New Orleans's Café Du Monde. Julie Cantrell has expertly captured the unrelenting terror and enduring hope of a community transformed by loss."

—KAREN SPEARS ZACHARIAS, AUTHOR OF *BURDY*

"Julie Cantrell, like all brave writers, puts her protagonist Amanda Salassi through unimaginable loss. And like all great heroes, Amanda battles to the brink of her own destruction . . . to be saved, ultimately, by her own enduring faith and love."

—NEIL WHITE, AUTHOR OF
IN THE SANCTUARY OF OUTCASTS

"Powerful and riveting. As a therapist who works with women in destructive marriages I was encouraged to see this topic explored without the 'just try harder' solution many women receive."

—LESLIE VERNICK, COUNSELOR,
RELATIONSHIP COACH, SPEAKER, AND AUTHOR OF
THE EMOTIONALLY DESTRUCTIVE MARRIAGE AND
THE EMOTIONALLY DESTRUCTIVE RELATIONSHIP

"Julie Cantrell confronts the horrors that hide in the shadows of our modern world with love and grace. I read this novel in a great inhalation, and maybe it was the tenacity of her heroine, or the gamut she runs, from awful sadness to revelry and redemption, that kept me clinging to this story of real people in painful circumstances. *The Feathered Bone* reminds us of the value of letting in the light."

—JAMIE KORNEGAY, AUTHOR OF *SOIL* AND
MANAGER OF TURNROW BOOK COMPANY

The Feathered Bone

Julie Cantrell

THOMAS NELSON
Since 1798

Published in Nashville, Tennessee, by Thomas Nelson. Thomas Nelson is a registered trademark of HarperCollins Christian Publishing, Inc.

Published in association with the literary agency of WordServe Literary Group, Ltd., www.wordserveliterary.com.

Interior design by James A. Phinney

Thomas Nelson titles may be purchased in bulk for educational, business, fundraising, or sales promotional use. For information, please e-mail SpecialMarkets@ ThomasNelson.com.

Scripture quotations are taken from the *Holy Bible*, New Living Translation. © 1996, 2004, 2007, 2013 by Tyndale House Foundation. Used by permission of Tyndale House Publishers, Inc., Carol Stream, Illinois 60188. All rights reserved.

The "Beatitudes of a Christian Marriage" are courtesy of the plaque in the Blind River Chapel near Baton Rouge, Louisiana. Author is unknown.

Publisher's Note: This novel is a work of fiction. Names, characters, places, and incidents are either products of the author's imagination or used fictitiously. All characters are fictional, and any similarity to people living or dead is purely coincidental.

Library of Congress Cataloging-in-Publication Data

Cantrell, Julie, 1973-
The feathered bone / Julie Cantrell.
pages ; cm
ISBN 978-0-7180-3762-8 (trade paper)
I. Title.
PS3603.A597F43 2016
813'.6--dc23
2015028781

Printed in the United States of America

16 17 18 19 20 RRD 5 4 3 2 1

For the people of Livingston Parish, no matter where adventure leads me, my story always begins with you.

For Carol, Chris, Gina, and Kerri, you have taught me the power of true "sister friendship."

For Teresa and the entire Murray family, thank you for calling me one of your own. Carry the torch. Pen a happy ending.

For Larry (and Dean), you entered my life at exactly the right season, reminding me we are here to love in spite of, not because of. For that, I owe you "every day by the sun."

And for the students of Still Creek Ranch, you are the bravest spirits I have ever known. Keep fighting for the light.

Part 1

Love is the child of freedom, never that of domination.
—ERICH FROMM

Chapter 1

Friday, October 29, 2004
The Day

A MAGIC MOVES THE DAY AS IF ANYTHING COULD HAPPEN. PERHAPS
it's the pulse of jazz in the air, or the rhythmic churn of the river-
boats, or the warm winds that swoop the levee, but there's a hint
of mystery surrounding us. Something has charged the marrow
walled within my bones. *Pay attention*, it says. And so I do.

It's the week of Halloween—not the best time to bring a sixth-
grade class on a field trip to the Big Easy. But three rain delays
pushed back the date, so here we are in New Orleans, where thick,
milky fog rises from the river like steam. It nearly blocks our view
of a shiny white tugboat and her long string of barges nosing their
way through the coffee-colored currents.

We wait at Mardi Gras World, the famous tourist trap where my
daughter, Ellie, and her classmates have come to learn the history of
carnival season. Unlike the cars that buzz across the Crescent City
Connection, or the boats that linger lazily beneath the bridge, we
are landbound. We're also surrounded by mermaids, each elabo-
rately carved and painted by Blaine Kern's studio artists.

Around the sculptures, a festive crowd filters through. They are
free spirits, wearing rainbow face paint as they scuttle for a better
view of the Mississippi. "A cape?" my friend Beth whispers. "Cute."

"Getting that party started early." Raelynn eyes the most flamboyant tourist before taking a seat beneath the pergola. "Argh, it's wet." She pulls beads around her neck, adjusting the plastic pendant that serves as our admission ticket for the guided tour.

Across the waterfront patio, a brass band pipes through scratchy speakers. Potted palm trees dance in the breeze. From the river, a dull horn bellows, causing our students to roar. The raucous tourist swings by again, her cape whipping wildly, her cheeks all aglitter. While this scene might be expected during Mardi Gras, it's unusual for a Friday morning in October.

My daughter shuffles through the crowd, staying close to her best friend, Sarah. A heavyweight redhead wearing dollar-store fangs jumps in front of them with a deep and masculine "Boo!" Ellie startles, and the jokester jolts away, laughing. This leaves our students wide-eyed, the chaperones on edge.

"Let's go ahead and get the children back inside," Miss Henderson instructs. She is young and not yet burned out from the never-ending demands of public education. Even now she remains pleasant as she taps one of her more rambunctious students on the shoulder, nudging him down from the railing where he's at risk of falling into the dangerous currents.

"Girls?" Beth and I both call for our daughters. In response, Sarah and Ellie skip into line, their arms laced together, their steps in sync. As they prance beneath a strand of purple and green party lights, Sarah's blond hair catches a glow, exaggerating her angelic complexion. Her innocent blue eyes twinkle with a sort of naïve joy not normally associated with raucous Bourbon Street celebrations. I whisper to Beth, "She could model for American Girl dolls."

"They're both beautiful." Raelynn drags behind. "The only problem is, which one will get to marry my Nate?"

"Yuck!" they protest, and Miss Henderson laughs, closing the double doors behind us.

Inside the gift shop, students explore rows of spirit dolls and voodoo pins, while Sarah and Ellie move to the collection of intricate masks. They have just begun to dance in disguise when a shopper steps up from behind. She's older than us. Close to fifty, I'm guessing. At thirty-five, fifty is sounding younger to me by the day.

"They sisters?" She asks this while watching Ellie and Sarah giggle in feathered face gear.

"Might as well be," Beth answers. "Born on the same day. Best friends since birth." She doesn't bother explaining that our girls are without siblings and have learned to rely on one another to fill that role.

"Figures. My daughters wouldn't have been so nice to each other at that age." She looks at me a little too long, and I shift away, adjusting my heavy backpack. It's crammed with first-aid gear and water bottles—just in case.

The woman leans closer. "You're from Walker?" She points to my bright-green shirt, the one Miss Henderson designed. It shows a school bus surrounded by classic New Orleans symbols: Mardi Gras masks, musical notes, and the traditional fleur-de-lis. At the bottom it reads *LP to NOLA 2004*, suggesting we've all traveled more than an hour east from rural Livingston Parish to explore our state's most famous city, "The City That Care Forgot."

I nod. "We're here for a field trip. You?"

"Albany," she says. "You may not remember, but are you a social worker? In Denham Springs? Amanda Salassi?"

My heart sinks. *Is she one of my clients? Why can't I place her?*

I scrape my brain, trying to pull this file—her round face, the gnawed fingernails, the tiny Hungarian hamlet of Albany known for its strawberries and quiet way of life. I draw nothing but blanks.

"You go out on call sometimes, with Sheriff Ardoin?" She keeps her voice low, hesitant.

Chills rise. I remember. She weighed at least a hundred pounds less when I last saw her, but her soft voice, something about that thin smile. "Mrs. Hosh?"

She nods, and we offer one another a warm glance.

"I'm sorry I didn't recognize you. Your hair was a lot longer. And brown."

"Yeah." She says this with a half chuckle, reaching up to feel her short blond crop.

It's all coming back to me now. The tight-knit settlement. The protective way her kinfolk circled, unwilling to let me in. Her late-night calls to my home phone, in secret, asking to talk.

"I want you to know"—she dabs her eye with the back of her finger—"I couldn't have survived it without you. Knowing you cared. And you didn't judge. Getting the others to call me. That helped. More than you can understand. Just knowing they had survived it."

I gesture for Beth to watch the girls. Then I lead Mrs. Hosh to the side. "You're here," I whisper. "You survived it too."

"One breath at a time. That's all I can do."

"That's all you have to do," I tell her, drawing her into a gentle hug. "Just keep breathing."

She holds me close, so tight her shoulder clamps against my throat, but I don't dare pull away. It doesn't matter that we are in a public gift shop, surrounded by chaperones and strangers. Or that my daughter and her friends watch us as they toy with touristy trinkets. All that matters is that this woman, right this moment, needs a hug. So that's what we do. We hug.

After the emotional exchange with Mrs. Hosh, I hurry to catch up with Ellie's class. They are following a cheerful tour guide into the theater, where he instructs us to zip sparkly costumes over our clothes. I grab four hangers, each with a long satin shirt that's been studded with sequins. Ellie chooses turquoise, her favorite color. It works well with her olive complexion and dark curls, which she inherited from Carl's Italian roots. In contrast, Sarah snatches hot pink, a bright anchor to her blond ponytail. Beth and I settle for the leftovers, while Raelynn snags a set for Nate and crew.

"Choose a hat." Beth points to a stand filled with plush velvet caps. We select a few and hurry to the back of the room, where a three-dimensional Mardi Gras mural has been built for photo ops.

Sarah waves her hand like a princess and stands straight. "I'm the Queen of Endymion."

"And I'm the Queen of Bacchus," Ellie adds, bending her knees in a dramatic curtsy. I snap her photo, certain it will make the cut for this year's scrapbook.

Just on the other side of the wall, a café keeps our space swirling with scents of chicory coffee, a temptation that is becoming hard to ignore. "Man, I need a cup of brew," Raelynn admits. She rushes past us with her group of boys, a motley crew of hunters and fishermen who would rather be on a boat or a four-wheeler than anywhere near a city. But they are being good sports, pretending to fight over which one of them gets to wear the pastel pink shirt for the photo.

Before the students get too hyper, the guide takes over again. "All righty. Parents, please put the costumes away while I start the film." He speaks with enthusiasm, dimming the lights.

The students quickly pass the gear while black-and-white images begin to flicker, bringing us back to the early 1800s when Creoles held lavish masquerade balls. Eventually the parties spilled into the boulevards, and revelers began to toss special treats to onlookers. Then came the first floats, lit with flambeaus—an elaborate party-on-wheels.

"When will they pass out the king cake?" Raeylnn asks, causing the students to look our way.

Beth puts her finger to her mouth, the way a mother would tell her child to hush. Then she sweeps soft curls from her forehead, revealing a thin streak of gray at her crown. Raelynn's brightly dyed locks and tattooed wrists mark a stark contrast to Beth's conservative style. And yet we've grown up a tried-but-true trio. The "three amies" as Raelynn likes to call us, a play on her Cajun tongue.

The film ends, and we make our way into the café where our guide begins doling out the cake, a braided sweet dough topped with confectioner's icing and sprinkled with colorful sugar crystals. Miss Henderson prompts, "Do any of you know why we eat king cake?"

Sarah, teacher's pet and usually the first to raise her hand, draws a blank and turns to Ellie for backup. But my daughter, too, seems to have no clue. Either that or she's too shy to answer.

One of the boys shouts his guess. "Some kind of voodoo thing?"

The guide chuckles. "A lot of people do associate New Orleans with voodoo, you're right. And some in these parts still practice, but we're mostly a Roman Catholic culture. So if you grew up in Louisiana, you probably already know the story of the three wise men."

Seeing we are from Walker, a rural sidekick to Baton Rouge and the kind of place that has more steeples than graves, the guide must realize he's safe with this religious topic, even if we are a public school. "Twelve days after Christmas, on January 6, we celebrate the wise men's visit with the Feast of the Epiphany. And we keep the party going all the way through Fat Tuesday, which in French is called . . . what?"

"Mardi Gras!" A handful of students are proud to know the answer.

"That's right. It's the day before Ash Wednesday, which of course launches the Lenten season—when Catholics give up our favorite treats and focus on being good." He laughs before adding, "Well, as good as we can be down here in New Orleans."

Then he steers off course a bit. "I'm sure some of you are Catholic." About half the class raise their hands, including Nate, one of the many CCD kids who has spent his Wednesdays riding the catechism bus to Immaculate Conception. "Anyway, to honor those three wise men, or *kings*, we make the cake round—like a crown—and we only serve it during carnival."

Ellie takes a bite, dusting her lips with green sugar sparkles, just as Nate cheers, "I got the baby!"

"Figures," Sarah says, eyeing the small plastic token in Nate's hands. "He wins everything."

When offered a piece of the dessert, Beth holds her perfectly trim waistline, saying, "I'd better not."

Raelynn then woos the guide into giving her Beth's forsaken slice. "Score!" She turns my way, beaming.

I nibble my cake and stay with the girls as our guide leads us into the massive warehouse—one of many owned by the business-savvy Kern family. Here, they design and decorate floats, while storing the oversized parade trailers.

We are led past giant replicas of everything from anime characters to zoo animals. At our first stop, a woman stands on a ladder, coating a massive sea monster in papier-mâché. Strip by strip, she covers the sculpture with brown craft paper, patiently building a smooth surface for the next round of artists to coat with primer.

"They must not know your trick," Beth says, wafting the air as if she can't bear the odor. She knows I add cinnamon to our glue at home, where Ellie and I are always working on some kind of art project.

"I want this job," Ellie says, now admiring a half-painted prop. The artist dips a thin brush into a pool of pink and drags it across the lips of a goddess.

"Seems like a fun place to work." I roll my fingers through Ellie's dark curls. She tolerates my touch for a second before easing away, moving from childhood through tweendom, closing in much too quickly on the tipping point of thirteen.

"I wish I could draw." Sarah's praise causes my daughter's cheeks to turn pink.

"What do you want to be?" I ask Sarah.

"A missionary," she says. "Somewhere far away. Like what my parents did."

Beth responds with affection, recalling her brief stint in Ghana where she fell in love with Sarah's father—the laid-back Cajun youth minister known only as Preacher.

Before Beth gets too deep in reminiscing, the guide redirects our attention to another artist, this one drawing a corset around a tiny waistline, exaggerating the voluptuous figure. The painter holds a feather and examines her work.

"What do you call that thing she's wearing?" Sarah asks.

Beth stiffens. "We'll talk about that later."

Sarah blows her cheeks and accepts defeat, but the artist turns and with a grim expression says, "It's a corset."

I'd guess she's in her sixties, with thinning gray hair and skin that hasn't seen the sun in decades. Her clothes, wrinkled and paint-stained, give her a look not so different from the homeless men we saw on our way through the city this morning.

"What's the feather for?" Our guide points to the brilliant blue plume in the painter's hand.

After a heavy sigh, the woman grimaces. "Well, a long time ago, women used to wear these corsets under their fancy dresses. Some people called them *stays*. Girls had to start wearing them when they were very young. Maybe eight years old." She looks at Ellie. "How old are you?"

"Twelve," Ellie answers, nibbling her fingernail. It's a habit she's trying to break.

"Twelve," the woman confirms. "So, if you lived in the eighteenth or nineteenth century, you'd be wearing one of these. Your ribs and your lungs and your stomach would all be pinched up tight beneath the stays." She tweaks her face at the thought of it.

"Why?" Sarah asks. Not a speck of hesitation.

"That's the question." The artist smirks. "Why do you think?"

No one comes up with a guess.

"Because women were slaves."

Beth scoffs.

"It's true!" The artist comes closer. "Slaves to fashion. To society. To culture. The men wanted women to have tiny waists, and we gave them what they wanted." She points her feather at our tour guide, the only adult male in the group. "Sometimes, if a man was looking for a wife, he would line up women and wrap his hands around their waists. If his fingers could touch, she might stand a chance."

The girls begin to wrap their midlines, measuring their own worth according to waist size.

The artist notices. "Women were expected to wear these corsets all the time, so they could train their bodies to have this wasp shape."

"Why?" Sarah asks again, leaning in for a closer look.

"Because most women couldn't work, remember? They needed someone to provide for them. Many even slept in these corsets, tightening the straps more and more each day. Some schools would measure their female students, making sure waistlines were shrinking. Like those foot-binding traditions in China. Ever hear of that?"

Ellie looks back at me, her eyes wide with curiosity. "Later," I whisper.

"The things we do to our girls. Torture, I tell you." The painter shakes her head. "Good thing I wasn't alive back then. Put me into one of those things? Might as well wear a straitjacket."

Beth whispers between her teeth, "I'm thinking she could use a little time in a corset."

It's the meanest thing I've ever heard Beth say. I raise one finger, just enough to catch the artist's attention. "I'm still not clear. What's the feather for?"

"Oh yes. I got sidetracked. Sorry." Her eyes light up. "For years, the corset boning was made out of hard, rigid materials. Rods. Reeds. Whalebones. Can you imagine? Being caged into that every day? Even at night?"

Girls peak their brows. Boys shake their heads. Parents sigh.

"But in the late 1800s a man named Edward K. Warren had a store up in Michigan. Dry goods, they called it back then. His customers complained about the whalebone corsets. They were too expensive, too uncomfortable. They didn't seem to hold up. So when Mr. Warren was buying supplies over in Chicago, he noticed a factory that made feather dusters—you know those old-fashioned dusters?" She waves her feather as if dusting the corset. "Y'all ever seen those?"

Miss Henderson promises she'll bring one to class next week.

"Well, anyway, Mr. Warren noticed that the factory threw away big piles of feathers. He thought he might be able to use them to make corsets. And he was right. He patented his idea. Earned himself a fortune. People loved his new featherbone corsets. You know why?"

Blank stares.

So she continues. "They were less expensive, for one thing, but mainly the featherbones allowed women to bend." She bows the feather, demonstrating her claim. "So in a way, Mr. Warren helped women break free from bondage. You see? This was the beginning of their—emancipation—so to speak." She stresses this word. "Anybody know what that means?"

Nate pipes up from the back. "Set them free?"

"Exactly!" The artist's face softens, and a warm smile stretches her mouth. "So when I got this assignment to examine women's fashion, I decided to give these nineteenth-century women some breathing room. Kind of my own little act of rebellion."

She looks at the group of children with a tenderness now, then toward the ceiling where birds flitter between the roof beams, serenading us. "Girls, promise me this. Every time you see a bird flying around with her beautiful feathers, I want you to think of all the women who strapped themselves into corsets against their wishes. Think of all the women who fought to break free from those restraints. And then remind yourselves to never again become slaves. In any way, to anyone. You keep yourselves free. Understand?"

The girls whisper as we leave the woman. "Who would want to look like a wasp anyway?" Ellie asks.

"I'm glad we don't have to live like that. In a cage!" Sarah says. She squirms as she reaches behind her back. "Now if only we could stop wearing these."

They both giggle, and Beth pulls her lips tight, still recovering from our recent shopping trip when we bought the girls their first real bras.

I put my arm around Beth's shoulders. "If only we could slow the world for them," I say. "Keep them young, and safe. And free."

Chapter 2

WE SPEND THE NEXT TWENTY MINUTES EXAMINING ALL SORTS OF floats and props while the birds dart above us. By the time we exit, storm clouds are building. Miss Henderson eyes the sky. "I can't believe it. Three weather cancellations and now it's going to rain on us anyway." She sighs. "We'd better get Gator to drop us at the ferry. I'd hate for the kids to get wet." She waves for the bus driver to head our way.

While we wait, students pose for more photos, many of which will land on their MySpace pages later today. Nate climbs the jester statue, pretending to pick its nose. The entire group of boys follows suit, aiming for the giant nostrils.

In response the girls yell, "Gross!" and share looks of disgust.

I switch gears and plan next week's LSU tailgate. We're all skipping tomorrow's match against Tulane.

"I'll kick in dessert," Raelynn says. "After that Georgia disaster, I should probably make my Good Luck Cupcakes. Maybe some divinity? Pralines?"

"Cupcakes!" My daughter's dimples expose her love for Raelynn's famous buttercream frosting.

"Pralines!" Sarah counters with an equally persuasive grin.

"Both it is." Raelynn is happy to oblige.

"Carl and I will cook up a pot of jambalaya." My friends nod. I pull the heavy backpack from my shoulders, tempted to leave a few of these water bottles behind. "We did gumbo last time, right? Red beans and rice before that?" They nod again.

"We'll do our usual," Beth says. "Drinks, coolers, appetizers." Then she switches back to our plans for today. "I wish I could go with y'all over to the French Quarter. This wedding has been planned for a year, and with their family coming in from out of town I couldn't reschedule the rehearsal." She straightens Sarah's green hair bow.

"It's okay, Mom." Accustomed to life as a youth pastor's kid, Sarah seems unfazed.

"Wedding coordinator. Just another hat." Like Sarah, Beth says this without complaint, fully accepting her role as one of the church anchors. "I have to hurry or I'll be late." She fishes car keys from her purse and offers final instructions to her daughter. "Keep close to Ellie and Mrs. Amanda. And please don't mess with those palm readers. Remember. The tour guide said there's still some crazy voodoo stuff in this city. Eyes open and stay safe."

Both girls react sarcastically, voicing a deep "Voodooooooo" to exaggerate their fake fears.

"Don't worry," I reassure my friend. "I won't let them out of my sight."

"I know you won't." Beth gives each girl a quick peck on the cheek. Then she heads for her car and rushes back to Walker.

Raelynn leans against the wall. "So who was that woman? The one in the gift shop?" She lowers her voice.

"Just an old friend." I look around to make sure Mrs. Hosh is nowhere near.

"She lost her son, didn't she?" Raelynn persists, even though she knows I'd never violate client confidentiality. "Couple years back. Suicide. It was in the paper. If my boys ever did anything like that, you'd have to kill me too. I couldn't handle it."

I sigh. "No one thinks they can survive it. But somehow they do. They have to."

"You still like working with Jay? What do you call it you're doing up there? Forensic something or other?" Raelynn bends to adjust the knee brace she's been wearing for the last two weeks. She slipped at the school cafeteria where she manages the nutrition program.

"Oh, I'm still at my clinic most of the time. Outpatient therapy. Normal family counseling stuff, you know. But yeah, I'm still on contract with the sheriff's department too."

"I never have understood what you're doing with them."

"Like you said, forensic interviewing. Case-by-case basis."

"You mean child abuse?"

"That's only when they need me. Mostly they call me out to counsel people at trauma scenes. Crisis intervention. Your knee okay?"

"No, it's killing me." She rubs it.

"You should sit."

"Yeah. I should." She looks around for a seat, but there's none to be found. "You like it? Forensic whatchamacallit. All that therapy stuff. Going out on suicide scenes. I can't imagine anything worse."

"It's tough. To hear some of the stuff that happens. But it's rewarding too. To help somebody come back to a safe space after trauma. I guess that's why I do it."

"I don't think I could." She winces. It's clear she's in pain.

"Well, it's not what I set out to do either, remember?"

"Yep. You wanted to be the school counselor, right? Work the same hours as Ellie."

"I'm lucky. I manage my clients around Ellie's school schedule, but summers are tricky. And Carl worries when I get called out to a scene. Still not sure how I ended up with that gig."

"Jay, of course." She bumps against me with a playful tease. "Our friendly sheriff. No matter how long you fight it, y'all are gonna end up together. Mark my word."

I swat the air. "You really have to stop, Raelynn. Carl and I have been married fifteen years."

"Yeah, but the only person Carl's ever been in love with is himself."

"Aww, come on. He can be a little too serious, but Carl's a good guy, Raelynn. In fact, he's good at everything. People love him. Even you."

"Hmph." She grimaces. "He's good at everything except being your husband. And that's kind of the most important thing, don't you think?"

This catches me off guard. "Are you talking about my husband or yours?" As soon as I say it, I have regrets. After the last violent attack, Raelynn filed a restraining order against Nate's father, a hardened man who likes to take his anger out on his wife. She steps away from me now, and I follow. "Raelynn?"

She keeps walking down the sidewalk, away from the students.

"Raelynn, I'm sorry. I shouldn't have said that. I didn't mean it the way it sounded." I reach for her shoulder, and she turns toward me.

"Say whatever you want, Amanda. At least I have the sense to draw the line. Might be something you should try. Or else you might find yourself being hit one day."

The way she's talking about my husband draws pain from someplace deep inside. "Why do you hate him so much, Raelynn? Carl's never done anything to you."

She huffs. "You didn't hear a word that lady said in there, did you? About the corsets? The featherbones? Being a slave?"

Before I can answer, my strong-willed friend limps back to Miss Henderson, who greets us with a gentle smile. "I sure have enjoyed having your kids in my class this year," the teacher says. We follow her to the bus. "You three have been friends forever, haven't you?" She includes Beth, even though the third ring of our circus is long gone.

"Since kindergarten," Raelynn tells her, still a little miffed.

"I can see why Nate, Sarah, and Ellie get along so well."

"Yeah, they kind of balance each other. Like us." Raelynn cracks a sarcastic snicker. "A party girl, a diplomat, and a mother hen. Somehow it works."

"I bet I can guess who's who." Miss Henderson looks to me for backup.

I nod and play along. "My mother used to say Beth was born to be a preacher's wife. Even way back when we were kids."

"Half step from a politician's wife," Raelynn snips. "You'll never crack that polished surface."

I smile, remembering Mom's admiration for Beth, the poised spirit of our trio.

"What's Preacher Broussard's real name?" Miss Henderson asks, letting Raelynn's comment slide.

"Humphrey Jr.," I say, smiling.

"See why we call him Preacher?" Raelynn draws laughter all around. We've got friends by the likes of Coon Dog, Crazy Horse, Turtle, and Twirly Earl. Not to mention our bus driver, Gator. If anyone called Preacher by his real name, we'd know they weren't one of us. It's a secret code of sorts, an admission ticket to the inner circles of Livingston Parish, or LP, as locals proudly call it.

"What'd she say about me? Your mom?" Raelynn has a glint in her eye, ready to cause trouble.

"She said you'd do pretty much anything for a party."

"True dat!" Raelynn exaggerates her bayou accent, and I'm glad to see her coming back to good.

"And let me guess." Miss Henderson looks at me and says, "Your mom would say you hold the center of the fleur-de-lis. The steady, stable, sure thing that keeps Raelynn from going overboard and Beth from drying up into an old prune."

"You got it!" I say, wrapping my arm around Raelynn, who is laughing. "Truth is, I wouldn't want to do life without them."

The rain is still nothing more than mist by the time Gator pulls the yellow school bus around for boarding. As the kids climb the steps, they greet the friendly driver with high fives and hellos.

"Gator!" Nate skips the middle step, singing the driver's name. "When you gonna bring your snakes back to school?"

"When you want me?" Gator asks, enjoying the fame he's earned for carting critters into the classrooms and sharing everything he knows about wildlife—which is a heck of a lot.

"Every day," Nate yells. He has already moved to the back of the bus, where he steals a seat next to a girl who seems too shy to stay beside him. She bumps up a couple rows as the rear section fills with boys.

Before we know it, the kids are all seated and we've rounded the block to the New Orleans ferry.

"Perfect timing," Miss Henderson says, grabbing an ice chest as we climb off the bus. "If we hurry, we'll catch the eleven fifteen and have time for a picnic once we reach Algiers."

As we head toward the Canal Street landing, Miss Henderson eyes a paddle-wheeler, docked for afternoon tourists. "I opted for the ferry," she explains. "Figured we'd save both time and money while still getting a ride across the Mississippi."

As we board, the ferry attendant frowns and points to a place for our ice chests. "Over there." His eyes are tired from too many back-and-forths across the water, and it's clear he has spent a lot of time on this boat. Heavy. Slow. Loud.

"Has this ferry ever seen the rest of the river?" I ask. He stares at me, hollow and confused. When I realize he will grant me no answer, we leave our coolers on the lower deck and lead the kids upstairs.

Miss Henderson rounds the bend, pointing to our state flag as it flaps from a dockside pole. The image of the pelican sets a close match to the ones who prowl the waters near the boat. Just as she begins to explain the symbol of motherly sacrifice, the horn sounds. The students scatter to the perimeter of the slick deck. They lean over the handrails as muddy waters churn against the sunken hull.

Raelynn takes a seat in a fiery orange chair. I choose a faded pink one beside her. Along the east bank, high-rises stand in rows like a troop of uniformed sentinels watching our departure. With the fog still blanketing us, our view is haunting. "Looks more like something from an old Sherlock Holmes episode," I say. In the distance the dark spires of St. Louis Cathedral contrast with the hazy white horizon, as if the faithful hope to claim a higher piece of the heavens while others lurk below, concealed in smoke and shadows.

Our trip is brief. Before Raelynn can finish a story about Nate's latest hunting victory, the engine grinds and the boat spins into position, parallel to the west bank. The crewmen toss thick yellow ropes around the oversized posts, securing the craft against the dock which, with its industrial gray piping and heavy-duty weld-work, reminds me of the offshore oil rig where Carl is working another fourteen-and-fourteen.

Just beyond the landing, our group gathers around a bronze statue of jazz trumpeter Louis Armstrong. Miss Henderson begins doling out a few facts about Algiers. As I pass out the brown-bag lunches, she shares stories of floods and a fire that nearly destroyed this rowdy railroad community.

Behind us the quiet streets dispute her tales of seedy juke joints and organized crime. Tree-lined boulevards hold Greek revival cottages, family-run grocery stores, and Gothic-style churches, all anchored by pastel houses and coffee shops. Despite the city's rough past, we see no signs of mobsters in today's Algiers.

While the kids enjoy their sandwiches, Miss Henderson shifts gears. "In class we've been talking about slavery."

Ellie gives me a wounded look, setting down her sandwich. "Her heart's too big for this topic," I whisper to Raelynn, who nods.

"We've learned that in slave times, people were bought and sold. Some were taken away from their families and shipped far away from their homes. And many of them were brought right here to Algiers Point, where they were held in what they called slave pens."

Miss Henderson looks around, as if the scene is clear in her own mind.

"They were crowded together, sometimes as many as a thou-sand people. Men. Women. Even children. All forced to stay behind brick walls where they had to sleep on the ground."

The students, all of whom identify themselves as white, squirm uncomfortably. We live in one of the Florida parishes, a unique zone of Louisiana that has about as much diversity as a can of white beans. The South's history of slavery is a topic we tend to avoid.

The gentle teacher continues, refusing to sugarcoat the lesson. "Can you imagine the sounds? What might we be hearing if the slave pens were still here today?"

"Crying," Ellie says, her hand over her heart.

The teacher nods. Others shout out answers: "yelling," "screaming," "praying."

"Try to think how scared you'd be if someone came and took you away from your family. Locked you up. Sold you to a stranger who was now your owner. Your master."

Raelynn shakes her head. "Why is she telling us this stuff? Can't we just talk about Mardi Gras?" The other parents groan in agreement.

Miss Henderson eyes Raelynn. "It's not pretty stuff." Now she turns to her students. "But it is important to know the facts, even the bad ones. Otherwise, how can we learn from our mistakes? Look around Algiers today. There's no trace of this dark history. Just a statue of a famous musician. If we didn't talk about these things, we'd never know slaves once stood right here, shackled and beaten, waiting to be shipped across the river and sold."

"Who bought them?" Sarah asks. There's a pain in her voice that pinches me.

"That's a very good question. They were sold to a slave trader or to a new master. And for a time, those buyers could have been white or black. A man or a woman. Sitting over there, sipping coffee and placing bids, as if they were buying cotton."

"Or cows," Sarah says indignantly.

"Yes, Sarah." Miss Henderson continues. "And the sad thing

is, this happened right out there on the streets. In the lobbies of the fanciest hotels. If people weren't buying or selling slaves, they were ignoring it completely. As if it were a normal way to behave."

Ellie crosses her arms and says, "So mean." I pull my daughter into a half hug, hoping her spirit can stay this sweet.

"What would you have done if you walked by a slave pen?" Miss Henderson continues to challenge us all. "What if you saw a child on an auction block? Or you heard a person calling out that he had a big, strong man for sale? And behind him stood someone the age of your dad? His hands and feet chained? Or a woman with brown eyes like your mom, only hers are sad and looking to you for help?"

The children shift and gaze anywhere but at their teacher.

"What would you do if you saw a slave today?"

"Call the cops," Ellie says, looking to me for approval. I soften my posture, letting her know I agree.

Sarah rubs her hand across the raised letters of Louis Armstrong's plaque. "Thank goodness there aren't slaves anymore."

Miss Henderson echoes the thought. "Thank goodness." Then she shifts her tone. "Now let's take a quick walk along the levee before we get back on the ferry."

As she leads the class toward the water, her voice carries in the wind. "Can you believe that in some parts of New Orleans, the land is actually below the sea? As much as six feet lower than the ocean!"

Eyes grow wide.

"It's true!" She laughs, enjoying her role as a teacher. "These levees work pretty well, don't you think?"

Students nod, looking out to the river.

"But sometimes the waters rise over the top or even break through the levee walls. Thankfully, that hasn't happened here in a very long time. So what are you waiting for? Go stretch your legs!"

With this, the students dash full-speed, laughing and racing along the levee until they are hustled back onto the ferry for the return trip.

Beside us, an elderly man in a wheelchair waits to board. He stares at Ellie and Sarah, so I pull them to the side to grant him room. Chewing the end of her hair, a young girl, likely his granddaughter, follows as he maneuvers his electric chair into a slot against the lower deck wall.

"My knee has about had enough," Raelynn says, finding a seat. "I'll just wait down here." She sits near the man and the girl, but neither bothers to look her way.

"I've probably got something." I rifle through my backpack until I find the acetaminophen lodged between Band-Aids and Bactine. I pass Raelynn two pills and a bottle of water. Then I leave her on the lower level alongside the grumpy attendee, the old man in his wheelchair, and the girl, who stares sleepily out toward the east bank.

As I reach the upper deck, Sarah leans into the wind, spreads her arms like wings, and yells, "We're free! We're free!"

Chapter 3

By the time we return to the Canal Street landing, the fog has lifted. Humidity remains heavy. With each student assigned a chaperone, we've had more than thirty minutes of free time to explore. Now I grip Ellie's hand on one side, Sarah's on the other, and like a three-piece segment from a recess round of red rover, we string our way through the French Quarter.

Despite the noon hour, the streets of New Orleans are filled with black-lipped vampires and one-eyed pirates, all rushing to a Halloween luncheon. It is sponsored by a local nonprofit, whose banner flies from the historic Presbytère. Werewolves, wizards, and witches stalk beneath the storm clouds, determined to reach their fancy fund-raiser before the sky opens wide with rain. Between them, a trio of priests scuffle through in their clerical garb and Roman collars, trying to make it to the cathedral, not looking all that different from the costumed socialites.

In the distance looms the riverfront stage where we're supposed to meet Ellie's teacher at one o'clock. Sharp. With minutes ticking, I pull the girls, spiraling through various vendors. We've almost made it to the greens of Jackson Square when a ragged fortune-teller reaches from her Bohemian stand and grabs Sarah's arm.

"You look like the kind of girl who knows a little about a lot." The woman eyes Sarah and turns her tiny palm skyward.

Sarah shifts uneasily, and I step in between them, smiling so as not to offend. I pull both girls a safe distance from the truth sayer. Nearby, a card-trick magician has drawn a mass of onlookers who now have us jammed, so despite Beth's instructions to steer clear of the palm readers, there's no quick escape.

The old woman continues the one-sided chat, talking directly to Sarah, as if Ellie and I are not here at all. "You on a school trip? Here to see the zoo? The aquarium? Maybe that bug museum?"

Sarah shakes her head and answers with confidence, "We went to Mardi Gras World and rode the ferry."

"Over to Algiers?" The woman looks out toward the river, her gravelly voice haunting me in a way I cannot quite pin. I want to hear more, as if what she has to say is important. As if it matters.

"Yes, ma'am. You know slaves were sold here? And the levee is the only thing keeping us all from drowning?"

Sarah's enthusiasm lights a spark in the woman's eyes. She laughs, carrying a tint of mystic to her tone. Then she bends to pull a set of chicken bones from her stained knit bag, placing the oddities on the table near her tarot cards and half-melted candles.

Sensing Ellie's interest, I place my hand on her shoulder, a sign of encouragement to help my timid daughter feel brave. It works. "What's that?" She points toward a brightly painted birdcage.

"What, this?" The woman pulls an arched metal cage to the table, her many bangles clanging against her wrists. Inside, a sparrow perches on a twig.

As Sarah leans closer, a spark of sunlight catches the small gold cross attached to her T-shirt. It was a baptism present from her mother. An emblem of faith she wears every day.

The woman gazes at the bird with watery eyes. "He's a sparrow. A Bachman's sparrow is what they call him. My friend found him over on the Northshore. He had a broken wing. You see? Still on the mend."

"Can I hold him?" Ellie asks, her love of nature overcoming any fear.

"Well, I guess so. Just be real gentle." Then she lifts the latch and reaches into the colorful cage. Despite being wild, the sparrow hops onto the woman's finger as if it were a branch. His tail is long and rounded at the tip, darker in color than the rest of his feathers, especially those on his pale white belly and his soft gray face.

Ellie cups her hands to hold him, and he obliges, resting his tiny pink feet against her palm.

"Will he ever fly again?" Sarah asks, strumming her fingers gently across his feathered head. It peeks out between Ellie's thumbs as she holds him securely tucked between both hands.

"Of course," the woman says. "What good is it to have feathers if you don't fly?"

I pet the bird, reaching behind his flattened forehead. Wearing a brown crown, he has a dark line that arches back from his eyes. "He doesn't peck?"

"Not so much now," the woman says, her river accent coming through. "Oh, but when she first brought him to me. Not the case. These birds are kind of shy, like you." She looks at Ellie, who turns hot-pepper red. "They stick low to the ground, even nest in the underbrush. We hardly know they're out there. Except for their song. But now we do just fine. Don't we, little man?"

Sarah takes the bird from Ellie, eager for a turn. "Hello, Sparrow," she says. The bird sings in response.

"Ah, you hear that?" The woman grins. "He sounds good, don't you think?" The sparrow's tone is clear and smooth, a high-pitched call that draws a smile from both girls. And from me.

"The lady at the Mardi Gras place told us they used feathers to make corsets," Sarah tells the truth sayer. "Featherbones, she called them."

"That right?" The woman tugs at her long skirt. Her seat bows beneath her, straining nearly enough to break. "Here," she says, pulling a loose brown feather from the bottom of the birdcage. "Which one of you wants this?" Sarah passes the bird back to Ellie and holds her hand outstretched.

"Your very own feathered bone." The woman cackles, pressing the small wing feather into Sarah's palm. "Take this. From the sparrow. Guard it."

Sarah closes her fingers, clasping the fragile brown feather in her hand. "Guard it?"

"Yes, yes." The woman strokes her own twisted dreadlocks. Piled high as a hive upon her head, the graying weave is so dense I imagine it has been matted for years. "There are those among us who were born to fly. And you, sweet child, are one of those chosen few."

"Me?"

"Yes, you." Her deep-toned laughter causes steely gray pigeons to circle the ancient courtyard.

The crowd begins to thin as the black-hatted magician finishes his act. I nudge the girls, but they're too enchanted to leave the table.

"You see," the woman continues, "feathers—no matter what size or shape or color—are all the same, if you think about it. They're soft. Delicate. But the secret thing about feathers is . . . they are very strong. Am I right?"

The girls both nod, captivated, and I capture the moment on film.

"Of course I'm right." The woman laughs, tossing her head

back in a grand gesture. "A feather may look weak. Vulnerable. But truth is, it's a powerful little thing. Like you girls. And the most magical thing about feathers is . . ." She scoops the sparrow back into her hands. "When they get to do what they're made for, they carry a soul right up into the sky. Set it free. So you see? My friend here is giving you his feather to remind you that you are more than just a pretty little girl. You are strong, a powerful soul. Do what you're made for. Don't believe the lies people tell you about yourself. Then you will fly free too."

Both girls step closer, examining the feather, charmed by the woman's strange message.

Above us the ornate clock of St. Louis Cathedral rings its series of melodic bells, followed by one deep chime that announces the hour. The sacred tone fills the square, spilling out from the triple steeples to roll beyond General Andrew Jackson atop his bronze horse before stretching across the Pontalba Buildings with their iron lace, then echoing above the historic Cabildo and Presbytère neighborhoods of old New Orleans.

In the distance, students gather at our designated meeting spot. I nudge Ellie, adding a quick thanks as I shuffle the girls away from the woman's cluttered cart. I push down knots of guilt for not leaving a tip and focus instead on getting a safe distance before the palm reader convinces the girls they can jump from a rooftop and fly.

"Remember," she calls out behind us, "God's eye is on the sparrow." She erupts again in deep-toned laughter, causing wild green Quaker parrots to scatter with the pigeons. I glance back quickly to see the flock of birds circle as she returns her sparrow to its colorful cage, locking the clasp securely. His sweet song calls out behind us, as if to echo the woman's sage advice: *What good is it to have feathers if you don't fly?*"

As the chimes fade, Miss Henderson holds her right arm straight above her head and sends three quick breaths through her silver whistle. I rush the girls past chatty tour guides, each urging us to rent a horse-drawn carriage draped in beads and flowers. We reach the designated landmark and climb the concrete steps while rhythmic hooves clop through the streets behind us.

I squeeze past a group of nuns discussing All Souls' Day to join six other parent chaperones. Some take quick photos of the Jax Brewery sign. Others show off bargain buys they gleaned during their frantic French Market shopping spree. From the waters, the paddle-wheeler cranks its calliope, and the tunes transport us into another era. Racing past us, the children tackle the incline at record speed, determined to be first to the summit—until the teacher sounds her whistle once more and they swarm to form a line.

"Impressive," I whisper to Raelynn, who has been so busy rummaging through her purse for something sweet she has no idea what I'm talking about. I point toward the orderly queue, in awe of Miss Henderson.

"Teachers." Raelynn rolls her eyes. "Never did like me much."

"They liked you." I offer a gentle giggle to remind Raelynn I'm on her side. "They just didn't like how you couldn't keep your thoughts to yourself."

"Still can't." At a loss for candy, Raelynn plugs a cherry cough drop inside her cheek. The smell of menthol brings me back a year to my mother's final days. I coated her chest with Vick's VapoRub the way she had done for me when I was a child.

Tucking a wild strand of hair behind her ear, Raelynn tilts her head toward Café du Monde. "She'd better let us get beignets 'fore we board that bus."

Of course she says this loud enough for Miss Henderson to hear—a classic Raelynn move that works every time. As if on cue, the students turn toward the famous riverfront café where batches of hot, fried dough draw visitors from around the world. Then she drives her final nail. "They've got a bathroom." And here comes the smile, the one where Raelynn's strong spirit shines through to melt even the most reluctant soul.

Miss Henderson checks her watch, turning toward the row of round white bulbs that trace the café's roofline. Next she eyes Gator's bus, parked parallel, ready for departure. "Does everyone have your buddy?"

The students check in with their partners-for-the-day and nod. "Let's do a head count."

Sarah is first in line, as always. She sends up a clear "One," which is followed by Ellie's "Two," and so forth down the line of jittery grade schoolers until the final student yells, "Twenty-four."

"We have just enough time for a treat. Stay with your buddy and follow me. Parents, would you guide them to the restroom, please? I'm going to rush our order at the to-go counter instead of waiting to be seated. We'll eat on the bus."

Like the students, we do as she says.

"No dillydallying." Miss Henderson almost sings this command.

"Is that even a word?" Raelynn snaps. "Who is this woman? Mary Poppins?"

When the girls pause for a photo, Raelynn allows Nate to move ahead with another parent. Then, with a sideways glance, she asks, "Okay, Amanda. What gives? You've been walking the moon all day."

"The moon?" I laugh.

"Your head's been on some faraway planet. What'd he do now?"

Wind whips my hair across my face, and I pull it away to give Raelynn a direct stare. Without any words, I let her know I'm done talking about Carl.

But she doesn't back down. "For real, Amanda. What's wrong?"

Ellie and Sarah skip ahead a few feet, and I call out to them, "Wait a second, girls." They come to a halt as their last classmate ambles past.

"Helicopter," Ellie whispers to Sarah. Both girls roll their eyes, frustrated with the way I hover. I give Ellie a look, and they continue walking, slowly. Nearby, a man has coated his entire body with gold spray paint. He stands frozen in place on the sidewalk. They stop to watch him as they wait for us to catch up.

"Amanda?" Raelynn pries. "Absolute truth. And absolute trust." She repeats the oath we made when we were ten years old. The three of us climbed into Raelynn's tree house, pricked our fingers, and swore on our own blood. *Absolute truth. And absolute trust.* Now I opt for an easier path.

"I'm just missing my mom, is all."

"Oh, Amanda. I should've realized." Raelynn touches my shoulder in a sisterly way and pulls close. I assure her I'm fine.

"Have you heard from your dad?"

"Nope." I shrug it off.

"Still living down in Florida?"

"Honestly, I have no idea." I lead the way toward the café, hoping she'll give this topic a rest, but when she urges me to say more, I give in. "You already know the story. I was ten the last time I talked to him, the day he moved out."

"Yeah, but didn't you call him? To tell him about your mom?"

"I left him a voicemail, thinking he might want something from the house. He never returned my call. It's been a year. I'm not holding my breath."

"You ever think about looking for your birth parents?"

I fumble with the camera, still strapped around my neck. "I don't know." No matter how hard I try to avoid these tender topics, Raelynn is determined. "Feels like it wouldn't be right. To Mom."

"I still can't believe she's gone," Raelynn says. "For the cancer to have taken her so fast. It's not fair." Then she adds, "I'm sure she would want you to find them."

"Honestly, we never talked about it much, and I never asked."

"Why not?" Raelynn limps more now.

"Maybe I needed it to come from her. I didn't want to hurt her feelings." I don't have to explain. Raelynn knows I've carried a hole in my heart my entire life. No matter how much love my mother gave me after the adoption, even more so after her divorce, I was unwanted, abandoned, and unloved from the start.

We approach the café, where tourists and locals scramble by us. I scan the crowd, something I've done for years, searching the faces for my dull brown eyes or dirt-floor-brown hair, as Carl calls my unruly strands. I find no one with the familiar hitch in my step or the crooked curve of my nose. No one who might be my birth mother.

One road-worn young woman does catch my eye. She is squeezed into a tight, low-cut tank top and a miniskirt that's more than a few sizes too small. With a cocked hip, she brushes against men, dropping temptation their way. Although her smile might be described as captivating, her gaze is heavy, hungry. I am tempted to pull Ellie and Sarah to the side. Come up with something to say to ensure they will never end up like this. *Pay attention, girls. See this woman.* As soon as I think it, I chastise myself, wondering if this street-hardened girl has ever had a mother whisper to her at all.

On the same corner, the old man from the ferry now slumps in his wheelchair. He shoots me a strange look, one that puts me on guard. His wiry hairline recedes nearly six inches back from the mark of his youth, and his teeth are worn down and yellowed, like his eyes. The young girl I assumed to be his granddaughter is nowhere to be seen, but by his side the short-skirted woman, no more than twenty at most, throws me a bold, whatcha-lookin'-at stare. I assume they're together. I turn my head, ashamed.

While I've been lost in a mother's worst fears, Raelynn's focus has been on something else entirely. She drops her arm around my shoulders and gazes toward a handsome saxophone player in front of the café. "NOLA," she says with a grin. "Does a body good."

She doesn't notice my dramatic sigh. The dark-eyed musician has her full attention, performing with his hardscrabble jazz group beneath the boughs of a billowing oak. Peppered hair, cleft chin, Gypsy vibes, he is a beautiful mix of Johnny Depp, George Clooney, and Jared Leto with enough years on him to be fair game for my wild-hearted friend. Sensing the possibility of a tip, he offers Raelynn a flirtatious gaze, pumping his tunes for the travelers who sip café au lait and spill powdered sugar from heaping piles of beignets.

Raelynn tosses another corny line my way. "He's *saxy!*" Then, to make sure I didn't miss the punch line, she nudges me with her elbow. "See what I did there?"

I give her the laugh she's after and turn my attention to the opposite corner. There, three school-age boys tap the sidewalk with rapid rhythms, competing against the lively bucket drummer one block down. Lucky Dog vendors and plein air painters fill the gaps between bartenders, drag queens, and paper boys, making it hard to tell who is in costume for the charity luncheon and who would look a little wacky no matter the day.

Tuning out the chaotic clash of sounds, I follow the girls through the open patio and into the café. The soothing smell of sweet dough and fresh-brewed coffee works wonders. Outside, the clouds build, while inside, an attendant keeps the restroom line moving, ushering the students through as quickly as possible.

"Mo-om." Ellie says this in two syllables, with a hushed tone. I'm flying too close. I'm the only parent standing in line with the kids for the restroom, so I take the hint.

"I'll go see if Miss Henderson needs help with the food." I convince myself we are safe enough here to give them some space. "Hold my pack? You've still got water. The first-aid kit, too, if anyone needs it."

I drop my cumbersome bag and head for the counter, finally able to handle the small space without bumping into people. Behind me, Ellie and Sarah start rock-scissors-paper, giggling at the end of the line. I stop for a second to watch them play the innocent game of chance. Despite being surrounded by all this commotion, they seem completely content within their own simple world. Just the two of them.

After grabbing bags of beignets from the teacher, I make my way across the patio, where the wind tosses paper napkins like tiny white kites. Above us the storm swells, but this hasn't stopped a second line parade from forming on Decatur Street. People young and old pile out from the crowded shops to join the impromptu party. Without warning, umbrellas begin to bob up and down as people dance to the beat of the renegade brass band. Tambourines and trumpets, tubas and trombones sprout from out of nowhere, pulling a song and a story from every side street, every alleyway. Beneath scrolled-iron balconies, folks wave handkerchiefs, some with the fleur-de-lis.

Just as the parade begins to wind away, a white split of lightning jags the dark divide. Thunder announces the downpour, and torrents begin to fall with force. The savory smells of roasted coffee and sugared treats are now replaced by the metallic scent of steam rising from rooftops. Mere feet away, the rain-speckled river rolls on.

"Take a bag," I instruct the students. "We'll eat on the way home."

Hurriedly, one of the moms takes a group to the bus. They scurry ahead as Raelynn looks out toward the Mississippi. "Mark my word. That river's gonna burst right through someday."

"Let's hope not!" I serve the last of the beignets and rush through the rain.

As we reach the bus, Miss Henderson's levee lesson echoes in my mind. *"Here in the bottomlands and bayous, we have built our lives on soggy soil, perched below sea. The water is always eager to regain its domain."* When she said this, we were crossing back to the east bank, cutting across currents too deep, too powerful to tame. Raelynn's not the only one who believes it's only a matter of time before the Mighty Mississippi claims her stake and all of New Orleans washes away.

But not today.

Today, the musicians splash through soggy streets, and the boys remove their tap shoes to run with bare feet. Umbrellas protect the brass from the rain, and the music plays.

And the music plays.

Chapter 4

SIXTEEN, SEVENTEEN . . . MISS HENDERSON COUNTS HEADS AS THE children shake water from their matching green shirts. Strong winds sway the bus as the last student jumps up the steps and Gator snaps the doors shut behind him. He has agreed to drop the parents back at Mardi Gras World, where we've left our personal vehicles for the trip home to Walker. The annoying school district policy kept Raelynn complaining for nearly the entire drive down.

As she slips in to share the front bench, she carps again, "Still don't understand why we can't just ride with the kids. They're so afraid of lawsuits they've lost all common sense."

Miss Henderson lets the comment slide. She claps three times from the adjacent row and the children settle, welcoming relief from the rain.

"Can I have one of those water bottles?" Raelynn asks, already opening her bag of beignets.

I call over to Ellie, trying to salvage my tousled hair. "Pass my backpack, please." Wrinkling my nose does little to dim the over-whelming odors of wet and sweaty tweens.

"Sarah's got it." Ellie turns her attention to the row of friends who are bouncing behind her.

"Whac-a-Mole," I say, pointing to their jarring motions.

Raelynn laughs. "Somebody needs to give them a few bonks to the head!"

"We need a recount." The patient teacher claps three more times before speaking again, finally silencing the sugared crowd. "Does everyone have your buddy?"

Children swap spots and pair off into their designated duos. The organized structure collapsed in the café, where they grabbed bags of beignets before darting toward Gator in the downpour. Soaking and shrieking, they had crammed onto the aging vinyl seats without any regard for partners.

Now, as the last kid finds her mate, Miss Henderson still counts only twenty-three students. Not the twenty-four she is responsible for, the twenty-four she loaded onto the bus this morning, the twenty-four she brought together an hour earlier, warning everyone to stay with their buddy. Now that the children have divided back into pairs, one student remains without a companion. My daughter sits behind me, alone.

"Where's Sarah?" I whisper.

Ellie's wide-eyed expression says it all.

"It's not like them to be separated," I tell Miss Henderson.

Throughout childhood these two girls have lived like twins, sharing everything: sleepovers, birthday parties, homework sessions, summer vacations. Now, as I search the bus, my stomach twists as though I've lost my own daughter. I try not to panic.

"When's the last time you saw her?"

Ellie shrugs. "At the bathroom."

"Where'd she go from there?" Miss Henderson this time.

Ellie narrows her eyes.

"You never saw her after that?" I ask, hoping my voice holds steady.

Ellie shakes her head. The teacher clutches her clipboard.

"I'll run find her," I say.

I dash through the rain without bothering to dodge puddles, but as the seconds spin, Sarah is nowhere to be seen. I scan crowds for a bright-green shirt that matches my own.

"Have you seen a blond girl? Twelve years old? Green shirt?" I shoot out quick questions in every direction, raising my voice to a frantic yell above the pounding rain. "Black backpack? Field trip student?" Folks in the café turn their heads as I dart among the tables. I move toward the restroom where I last laid eyes on Sarah. The man who helped us manage the long line is still here, tucking tips into his pocket with a gap-toothed grin.

"We're missing a student," I tell him, describing Sarah's blue eyes, blond ponytail, green bow.

The man shakes his head and insists he hasn't seen anything out of the ordinary. "Take a look," he says, opening the door between customers to prove the room is empty. My backpack rests against the corner wall. I grab it and question him again.

"She had this backpack," I shout. "She wouldn't have left it."

He tilts his head as if trying to make sense of what I'm saying.

"She was here. In the restroom. Where'd she go?" I'm spewing questions too fast. He shakes his head and draws his shoulders up to his ears, as if he doesn't know anything more than I do.

Frustrated, I rush into the crowded kitchen without asking permission, boosting my voice over singing fry cooks and clanging plates. "Have you seen a blond girl? Sixth grade? Green shirt?"

Many of the employees are first-generation immigrants. With muddled expressions they shoo me, determined to get me out of their kitchen. I don't let them stop me. I search all the way to the trash room, opening the wooden door that leads out to Decatur. Then I turn back toward the fry cooks. Waiters circle through the pick-up line for orders. Again and again I ask. Again and again heads shake. No one has the answer I need.

Panic clenches my jaw tight. Wiping rainwater from my forehead, I slide past piles of dishes, scanning the chaotic space with a frantic intensity. I hurry back into the dining area, slipping a bit on damp tiles. I rush out back to the alley, past ivy-cloaked walls and rain-soaked hedges. I run up the concrete steps to the riverside parking lot. I loop through cars and run to the river, searching the waters, crying out her name.

Still no Sarah.

Winding my way back past the colorful fountain, through the café, and then out to Decatur, I take in every sound. Every sight. *She's got to be here. Where else would she have gone?*

I shout down the sidewalks, screaming her name. A few curious folks turn in confusion, sipping Sazeracs or iced mint juleps beneath the balconies, but most ignore me, carrying on their normal routines as if I'm just another party girl who's had too much to drink.

But this is no stunt, no street show. Sarah is missing, and no one seems to care.

I scan the upper-floor apartments, examining the iron lace verandas that line the sky. I find nothing but ferns, flowers. No Sarah.

The woman with the sparrow! I race past the artists whose sketches have since been protected in plastic, sealed tight against the rain. Here, beneath the spires, the truth sayer's table has been packed away, and she is nowhere to be found.

The cathedral? It's dry in there. I open the heavy doors in haste, hollering, "Sarah?" My hopes rise, remembering the flash of light from her gold pin. *Of course this is where she would have gone. She's got to be here.*

To my right are rows of candles, many lit from prayer. As my voice bangs against the sonorous space, the flames bend around the sound. I call again, "Sarah!" The sanctuary is packed with people seeking shelter from the storm. They begin to whisper, to help me search. I explain my way into the gift shop, my backpack clipping others as I rush through the crowd.

"I'll call Father Murphy," the shopkeeper says as she peers over her glasses to the phone.

I mutter thanks and give her my cell number. She writes it down on the back of a Mother Mary postcard she's pulled from the counter. As she places her call, I don't wait. I continue moving, searching, shouting. Through the cathedral and then back outside. No matter where I look, I cannot find Sarah.

All these umbrellas. It would have been easy to miss her. Maybe she's already back at the bus.

With the rain still heavy, I breathe deeply, trying to calm myself. Jackson Square is quieter now. The streets are nearly empty, but I shout to anyone within sight, calling out for a blond girl. Twelve. Green shirt. Tiny gold cross pinned against her chest.

Still no answers. No Sarah. *Why wouldn't Beth and Preacher let her have a cell phone? Why do they have to be so strict?*

The bus doors open and I pound up the steps, out of breath, hoping to see Sarah sharing my daughter's seat, laughing at me for looking like a drenched dog. But as I top the stairwell, dropping the backpack by Raelynn, it's clear Sarah has not returned.

"She's still not here?" I am panicked.

Miss Henderson's face shines white with fear. She turns to my daughter, and her timbre tightens. "Tell us again. When's the last time you saw Sarah?"

Ellie answers with a nervous voice. "When she went to the bathroom."

"Did you wait for her?" Miss Henderson tries not to sound angry, but the accusation is clear. Ellie abandoned her buddy, the one friend she was accountable for.

"No, ma'am." Ellie's voice quivers, and I squeeze into her seat, pulling her close, trying to say without words that everything will be okay.

"Did you see her after that? Did she get her beignets?" Miss Henderson eyes the bus driver. Gator grows tense behind the wheel. He fidgets with a switch or two as the bus stays parked by the stage.

Ellie answers, even more timidly now. "No, ma'am. I couldn't find her. I went back to the bathroom, but the man said she wasn't there. I thought she was already at the bus with everybody else. You told us to hurry. So I did."

I jump to my daughter's defense. "It's my fault," I insist. "I shouldn't have left them in line. I thought they'd be fine."

Miss Henderson continues the inquisition, trying to remain composed. "So the last time we saw her was at the restroom?"

"Yes, ma'am." Ellie begins to cry. "She was last in line. Right behind me."

"I checked," I insist. "The man even opened the door to prove the room was empty." My heart pounds violently and my throat tenses. "The backpack was there."

Raelynn sits still, her green eyes anchored tight as she watches this scene unfold. For perhaps the first time in her life, she is very quiet.

Miss Henderson presses her forehead into her palm, runs her

hand through her wet hair, and speaks to the class. "Has anyone seen Sarah since you all went to the restroom?"

No one answers.

"Anyone? Surely someone saw her get beignets? Run to the bus?"

Again, silence. The students glance around, trying to gauge each other's expressions.

"I'm going to look again," I announce. "She's got to be there."

"I'm with you," Miss Henderson says, following me out through the folding glass doors. As we move again into the rain, she leans back through the doorway and shouts one last command up the steps to the students, leaving Raelynn at the helm. "Mrs. Melancon is in charge. Stay quiet." Then she looks at Gator. "Don't let anyone off this bus."

Raelynn shouts as the bus doors slam behind us. "Amanda, call Jay!"

Chapter 5

More than ten New Orleans police officers are weaving a web outward from the café where Sarah was last seen. "She was only out of my sight for a few minutes," I tell the investigator, clinging to Ellie. She's shivering, despite the heat.

"A few minutes is all it takes," the investigator says, clicking her pen, ready to take notes. She's interviewing each person separately while her partner tag-teams, hoping to catch any discrepancies as the stories unfold. They want to question Ellie apart from me, but I refuse to move away from my child. For the first time in nearly a year, Ellie doesn't protest. In fact, she clings to me, fear gripping us both.

"So you're friends with Sheriff Ardoin?" With a cropped hairstyle and no makeup, everything about the investigator is matter-of-fact. She speaks with a thick New Orleans Yat accent, not all that different from one found in a New York borough. Nothing like the rural Southern tongue I lapse into when tired or emotional. Like right now.

I nod. "Jay's one of my closest friends. Since kindergarten." When she arches her brows, I don't bother explaining how Jay was elected sheriff at such a young age. It's basically because there's not a person in LP who doesn't admire and respect him.

"And you're the one who called him? The sheriff?"

"Yes, as soon as I realized . . ." I look away and focus on breathing. It's becoming more difficult by the moment. "Then I called Sarah's mother."

"Beth Broussard?"

"Yes, but she didn't answer. I left a voicemail." The words echo within: *"Beth, it's Amanda. Call me. As soon as you can."* Then a second: *"Beth, call me. Please."* And a third: *"Call me!"*

Now my cell phone is ringing, and my hands are shaking. I don't wait for the cop's approval before answering the call. "Beth? Where are you?" I wish I had thought this through. I know better than to give someone this kind of news over the phone.

"I'm still at the church. Why?"

"Is Jay there?"

"Jay? No." Her pitch peaks. "What's wrong?"

"Who's with you?" I try not to reveal alarm.

The investigator's face tightens as she gives me a look of concern.

"I'm in the office. The staff's all here. Why?"

Our church secretary happens to be one of the toughest women I know. I exhale and try to phrase this carefully. "Beth, we're going to be a little late getting back to school."

"You don't sound like yourself, Amanda. What's going on?"

"I'm sure everything is going to be fine. We're just . . ." *How in the world can I say this?*

"You're just what? What's happening?" There's a tinge of panic in her voice.

I can't answer.

"Amanda, tell me." Her volume rises.

Despite my best efforts to stay strong for Ellie, I struggle to hold back tears. "I'm sorry, Beth. I only turned my back for a minute.

Just long enough to help Miss Henderson pass out the beignets. I left Sarah and Ellie together, in line for the bathroom. I thought they'd be fine."

"What are you saying? Where's Sarah?"

"I don't know."

"You don't know? You don't know *what*? Is she okay?"

"I don't know, Beth, I'm sorry. We're looking for her now. We've got the cops and—"

"What do you mean you're looking for her? Where is she, Amanda?" And then much louder, fear-filled: "Where is my daughter? Find her! Find Sarah!"

"Beth, please listen."

The investigator holds out her hand, offering to talk to "the mother."

How many times have I stood on the other side of a trauma, keeping my cool in the midst of chaos? I pass the phone and press my fingers to my temples. The haze lifted hours ago, yet my head feels foggy. As if none of this is really happening. As if it's all a strange show. I'm playing a part, and any minute I'll pass my hat, collect tips from a street-side audience, and we'll all return to reality.

Beside me, the investigator stays steady. She is a square-framed middle-aged woman who talks to Beth without emotion. "I've got two girls myself, ma'am. I can imagine how this must feel. I'll be looking for Sarah as if she were my very own."

From the receiver, nothing. I've seen it time and again—the brain's refusal to accept reality. Beth can't cry or wail or scream because she feels numb.

"Sheriff Ardoin is your friend, right?" As she asks this of Beth, I begin to wonder if we're getting special treatment due to our connection with Jay. Would any other missing child receive such an immediate reaction? Would anyone be looking for Sarah if Jay hadn't made a few calls? "I understand he's on his way to meet you." The investigator lifts her brows, asking me for confirmation.

I nod, repeating Jay's plan to escort Beth and Preacher down to the café.

"He'll get you here as fast as he can, ma'am. Stay on the phone with me until he gets there."

I nod again. It's finally starting to sink in. *Sarah is missing. She is a missing child. This happened on my watch. I was supposed to keep her safe. It's my fault.*

The investigator continues talking to Beth. Raelynn is being questioned in the opposite corner. The rain has stopped, and the café has been quartered off with crime scene tape, much to the dismay of the manager. Tourists, curious and eager for photos, have wrapped the sidewalks and added to the confusion. Around us, officers work the crowds, questioning bystanders and canvassing the streets. "Have you seen this child? Did you notice anything unusual? How long have you been out here? Who do you remember seeing? Who was with you? Where are they now? Did you take any photos, video?"

While I am familiar with the routine, their words hit me in pulses, choppy little bits that barely make sense. In the back, officers are examining footage from the café's security cameras. Someone at headquarters is likely searching the sex offender list. *This can't be happening.*

Explaining the process to Beth again and again, the investigator's sentences arrive in jumbled fragments, as if my mind can no longer comprehend the English language. The more she talks, the less I understand, and I find myself whispering words, repeating phrases as she speaks: *NOPD, state police, Louisiana Clearinghouse for Missing and Exploited Children, National Clearinghouse, NCIC database.*

"The first forty-eight hours are crucial," the investigator says. "The first three hours especially."

I look at my watch. Surely Beth must realize time is ticking. We're creeping much too close to that critical three-hour mark. What Beth may not know, and what I wish I didn't, is that more than 75 percent of abducted children are killed within those first three hours. Sarah's kidnapping simply does not make sense. So these statistics don't rise to the surface. Instead, they build in my brain, a static reminder that things like this sometimes happen. But never to people like us.

"Of course, we'll be working with you and your husband to get as much information as we can." The investigator speaks respectfully but with an authoritative tone, in parsed phrases, giving Beth time to let this hard truth sink in. "The sheriff knows the protocol. He will have to follow it, even though you're friends."

A boat horn sounds, preventing me from hearing Beth's response, but I sense she's questioning the investigator.

"I'm only saying this because you can't take it personally, Mrs. Broussard. It's all part of the process. I'm sure you understand that your daughter's safety is our first concern. If you're on her side, then you're on our side."

Beth yells through the phone, causing the investigator to distance it from her ear.

"Nothing is adding up," I say. "The café was packed. Tell Beth. Tell her. There were people everywhere. Someone saw something. Someone has to know what happened."

I step toward the alley one more time, Ellie at my side. Detectives scour the area, climbing the steps to the parking lot and searching out toward the Mississippi. My stomach twists. *Did she fall into the river?*

"He's there?" The investigator waves me back her way. I hurry. "And he's with your husband?" Another pause. "Okay, Mrs. Broussard. I want you to give the phone to Sheriff Ardoin. That's correct. Yes, ma'am. Thank you."

As Jay takes over from the other end, I continue to scan our surroundings, certain we're all overlooking an obvious clue. At one table Miss Henderson is folded over, her face covered. She is crying. A detective sits with her, pen in hand. Raelynn is also still being questioned, and from the looks of it she's been crying too, a rarity for my thick-skinned friend.

Having finished their interviews, the other moms circle protectively, trying to shield the kids from onlookers. Miss Henderson wipes her eyes and joins her class, giving final instructions before they head home without her.

The café employees have been separated too. No one seems to be protesting, as one of the bilingual waiters serves as an impromptu translator. When a second detective tries to pry Ellie from me, it is all I can do not to lose it. But I stay calm, for my daughter's sake, and convince him to let me keep her in sight.

"You know we have to do this," he explains. He lowers his chin and gives me a sincere eye, as if he genuinely feels bad about it. He puts his hand on my daughter's shoulder, and she retracts. Ellie is crying, rubbing her arms, going back and forth between shock and panic. She gasps for breath.

"Sweetie, they're going to ask you some more questions. They're trying as hard as they can to help us find Sarah. You need to tell them the whole truth. Everything you remember. You won't be in any trouble, no matter what you say. I promise."

Her crying has turned ugly. It's the snot-dripping, wet, messy kind of emotional draining that no one likes to display. Every piece of me is in pain for my child. And for my friend's child. For all of us.

I wipe Ellie's cheeks and draw closer. "I'll be right here, sweetie. You need to go with him. Just far enough away so I can't hear what you're saying. I'm not leaving, I promise. You can keep your eyes on me the whole time."

With this, the hefty male investigator takes Ellie to the far end of the café. She looks behind at me, and with each step my chest caves deeper against my heart.

While Ellie is being questioned, I dial my husband's number. He is fourteen days offshore; it isn't easy to reach him. I've already called three times, but it's not our regular time to talk. Now I try his supervisor, and Carl comes to the phone.

"Amanda?" The concern in his voice reaches me across the Gulf of Mexico.

"Carl, something's wrong."

"What? What is it?"

"We're on that field trip today, with Ellie's class, down in New Orleans. You remember?"

"Yeah. Is she okay?"

"Ellie's safe. Yes, thank goodness. But, Carl, listen. We can't find Sarah."

A long line of silence.

"Carl?"

"What do you mean, Amanda? Where are you?"

"We're still in New Orleans. Café du Monde. Sarah's missing,

Carl. Cops are here. They're questioning everyone. It's serious. We can't find her anywhere."

"That's not possible. What happened?"

I fill my husband in on the timeline, and he asks to speak to Ellie. "She's with the investigator."

"She's not with you?"

What little strength I have now crumbles. "I can see her, Carl. I'm looking right at her. They can't let me interfere with the questioning. You know that." I steady my voice, trying to keep my husband stable.

"Is a lawyer with her? Don't let her answer anything."

"What? Of course not. Why would she need a lawyer? They're questioning all the kids, Carl. They're just trying to—"

"What do you want me to do?" he booms, anxious and tense.

"I don't think there's anything you can do right now, Carl. I just wanted to talk to you. I wanted you to know what's happening. I just wanted to hear your voice."

"I could try to take the chopper home, but it'd be a couple hours at least. Sarah will probably be back before I could get there."

"Carl?" I don't know what I want to say, I just know I don't want him to hang up his phone. I need my husband. I need him. The fight we had before he left for the rig, his violent outburst during which he threw his hammer against the bricks, none of it matters now. I need Carl.

He listens silently.

"I overheard two of the cops. They think this might be tied to a crime ring or something."

"Crime ring? Like the mob?" He sounds skeptical.

"I don't know. One of them mentioned trafficking. Said it's become a real problem down here. He started talking about massage parlors and strip clubs, sleazy places on Bourbon Street. I've seen a little of that in my office. This doesn't fit. It happens to vulnerable girls looking for father figures. Or runaways desperate for shelter. Or addicts needing a fix. I can't imagine someone trying to kidnap a little girl like Sarah. From such a crowded place? With so many chaperones watching? You know she's not one to just follow some stranger out the door. Nothing's adding up."

"Sounds like they're on the wrong track, Amanda. They're wasting time."

"Honestly, Carl, I'm afraid she might have—" I can't say the words. It would make it all too real.

"What? What are you thinking?"

"What if she walked up to see the river? What if she fell in?"

"I thought of that." Silence. Then Carl asks, "Are they searching the water?"

"Not yet. I'm sure they'll call in a dive team at some point." The very idea makes me ill.

"I hate to say it, but that does make more sense." He softens, and my body reacts with a slower pulse, calmer breaths.

"I just keep hoping she'll come strolling in, wondering what all the fuss is about."

"How long has it been, Amanda? Since you saw her?"

I fumble with my watch, an inexpensive Timex Carl gave me when I turned thirty-five last year. He laughed when I unwrapped it, saying, *"Maybe now you'll be on time."*

But with Sarah missing, time has shifted into a strange sort of fluidity. "Almost three hours," I tell him. *How is that possible?* "Beth and Preacher should be here soon."

"Amanda?" Carl's voice takes a serious drop in pitch. "Don't take your eyes off Ellie."

Within an hour Jay arrives with Beth and Preacher. I rush to meet them, but NOPD officers step in between. Mere feet away, a few journalists have joined the scene. They shout questions as photographers squeeze in to capture a mother's worst nightmare. The lens acts as a tool to numb their sensibilities.

"Amanda?" Beth's voice is hoarse. "What is happening? Where's Sarah?" She clings to Preacher, who seems to be holding her together. Her hair is a mess, and mascara traces the tears beneath her reddened eyes. It's the first time I've ever seen Beth express such raw emotion, and the impact hits me full force. *I promised to keep her daughter safe. I was trusted to bring Sarah home.*

The police officer eases back, allowing me to reach my friend. I wrap Beth in a hug and release a sorrowful string of apologies.

Jay gives me a tender look of sympathy. It is all I can do to stay strong.

"Show us," Preacher says to me. "Tell us everything that happened. Where'd you last see her?"

With officers on either side of us, I lead them through every detail of the day. Starting with the moment Beth left our group at Mardi Gras World, they track my story onto the ferry, crossing to Algiers, and then back toward the Central Business District. Then on to the French Quarter, where Sarah was given the feather from the fortune-teller before coming here, to Café du Monde, where I left her in line at the restroom playing rock-scissors-paper with Ellie.

Beth and Preacher do their best to absorb the facts. Facts that make no sense at all. "I shouldn't have left her," Beth says, too numb again to cry. "I should have been here with my child. On her field trip. What was I doing at the church? Why'd I leave her?" Then she shifts, and anger seeps through. "Why did you leave her, Amanda? In New Orleans? What were you thinking? This isn't like you."

"I'm sorry, Beth. It's my fault, I know. I can't understand what could have happened. I'm so sorry."

Beth turns to one of the officers. "The palm reader! Did you find her?"

"Yes, ma'am. We've questioned her. She'll be listed as a person of interest."

"Does she have Sarah? Does she know who does?" Beth shouts out questions, talking her way through her own thoughts. "She's supposed to tell the future, right? Get her to tell us where Sarah is!"

"Anyone else on that list? Any suspects?" Jay asks this one, stepping up as sheriff more than friend, even though we're not in his parish right now.

"We're talking to a lot of folks," the officer says. "We just have to find the right person."

I lean closer to Beth. "She probably got turned around in the crowd. Just went the wrong direction. We'll find her." Maybe if I say this enough, it will come true.

"What can we do?" Somehow Preacher remains rational. But his dark eyes dart in all directions, and he pulses his fingers as if playing an instrument. He's a small-built man with a gentle heart, but I get the sense he could blow at any moment.

"Are you calling in more help? State police? FBI? What's the plan?" Jay again.

As the officer explains the procedure, I step toward Ellie, who has just been released from yet another interrogation. She rushes back to me and accepts my hug. "It's going to be okay. We'll find her." I guide her back to our friends and pull out a chair for her. I do the same for Beth, but she can't sit down. Finally finished with her second interview, Raelynn also joins us at the table, explaining that she'll send Nate back home on the bus with the other kids. They have all been waiting patiently for their driver to carry them back home. "They asked me a lot of questions about Gator," Raelynn tells Jay.

We direct our gaze toward the bus driver, who is being questioned by three officers.

"I'd better get over there." Jay heads Gator's direction as Miss Henderson moves toward us, apologizing every step of the way. She rushes into Beth's arms as much to receive comfort as to give it. The two stand together, sobbing, while the rest of us look away.

"I should have known better than to come to New Orleans." While the teacher weeps, the female investigator offers coffee to Preacher and Beth. They decline, each now taking a seat.

"Why won't they let us leave?" Preacher asks, drumming his palm against the table in nervous pulses. "We need to be out there looking."

Jay finally returns to our group and takes the lead. "All right. Here's what we're going to do. We're going to work with the NOPD. Anything they need. If they want to question us again, we let them. If they tell us to sit, we sit. If they tell us to wait, we wait. And when they tell us we can hit the streets, we hit the streets and join the search. Right now they are in charge. They know their city. We have to trust they'll do a good job. And I believe they will."

Accepting his support, the investigator smiles.

We sit in silence, staring anywhere but at one another. And we wait. Chaos takes shape around us. A million moving parts, all trying to achieve the same goal: find Sarah.

"Can't you make them go away?" Beth stares at the journalists with a spiteful eye. A familiar Baton Rouge reporter by the name of Frank Doucet jams his microphone toward us. "Mrs. Broussard, how did you feel when you were told your daughter had been lost on a school field trip?"

Beth ignores him, so he shouts more questions, hoping one will hook. "Is there any reason to think your daughter simply ran away? Do you know of anyone who might be involved if this is an actual kidnapping? Anyone who might have a grudge against your family? Any enemies?"

"Be glad they're here," Jay says, centered as always. "The coverage will only help."

Placing her hand over her husband's to still him, Beth lowers her head in silent prayer. By contrast, I want to shake my hands at the heavens. *How dare you?*

I run scenes through my mind like the series of images we viewed earlier today on the oversized screen in the Mardi Gras film room. Only there is no well-rehearsed narrator making sense of this sequence. I focus, trying to find clues we're overlooking. *Who was here? Why didn't Sarah come back from that restroom? Why did she leave the backpack? Where in the world can she be?*

Beside me, Ellie twists her hair into knots. "Sarah wouldn't let anybody take her."

"You're right, honey. She wouldn't." I pull Ellie's hand into mine, feeling both gratitude to have my child with me and guilt that Beth's hand cannot reach Sarah's.

Beth lifts her head. "Ellie, you know her better than anyone. Where do you think she is?"

My daughter glances out to Decatur, then over to the broad-limbed oak where the jazz band no longer plays, then back toward the colorful alley. She turns toward the now-vacant takeout window, then toward the rear of the café where she last saw Sarah standing in line for the restroom. The rest of us follow Ellie's stares and try to reason along with her.

"Honestly, Mrs. Beth," Ellie whispers, "I have no idea."

Chapter 6

Sunday, October 31, 2004
Halloween

OUR BATON ROUGE NEWS REPORTER, FRANK DOUCET, IS UPDATING us from the television screen. A New Orleans station shares his footage here in the hotel lobby. "Sarah Broussard was last seen day before yesterday, when her sixth-grade class took a field trip to New Orleans. Friday at approximately 1:30 p.m., she waited in line for the restroom at Café du Monde. That was the last time Sarah's classmates saw their friend. Today the Livingston Parish School Board, ignoring the advice of legal counsel, has sent their entire fleet of buses to New Orleans, carrying full loads of LP volunteers who are determined to find Sarah. The school district's superintendent is with us now. Sir, what's the latest on the search?"

The superintendent is a family friend, a lifelong member of our church, and a well-respected leader with the parish Rotary. "We're doing all we can to find Sarah," he says. "We've filled every seat on every bus today. And we'll do it again next weekend. And the next. For as long as it takes until we bring our student home."

Doucet takes the microphone again, summarizing the efforts of law enforcement and showing photos of Beth, Preacher, Ellie, and me on the screen. He explains our connection to Sarah.

"He showed Ellie?" Raelynn fumes, expressing what I'm

thinking. His footage violates our private struggle. Posting Sarah's photo on air is helpful, but broadcasting my daughter's tearful face is another thing entirely. Especially when he tells the world that Ellie was her designated buddy of the day.

"The churches are sending vans too," Preacher says, focusing on the good. "They're leaving straight after today's service."

"I can't believe how many people are helping," Beth whispers. Exhaustion is about to conquer her. "You haven't slept at all, have you?" She clutches my shoulder, as if it's me she's worried about. We've been searching nonstop, both Friday and Saturday nights. Now we're trying to refuel with the strongest coffee we can find.

"I saw Vivienne," Beth adds. Viv is my friend, a fellow clinical social worker who shares a therapy practice with me. "She drove down by herself, to offer support."

"Yeah. She's canceled my clients. Said to take as much time as we need."

"Ma'am?" The lead investigator with the Louisiana State Police has arrived. He greets Beth first, then shakes hands with Preacher and Jay. He's ready to give us the update we've been waiting for. Law enforcement organizers have charted a grid and given us precise instructions on how to spread out. He reviews our timeline. "We've got dive teams on the river now. Another team searching the canals."

Beth stares at the agent, her eyes swollen and red. It's common knowledge that divers usually come for recovery, not rescue.

"We'll find her," I say.

Raelynn, too, does her best to revive hope. "Today. I can feel it." Despite her knee pain, she's walked every step of this search with us, never complaining.

Jay reminds us that sheriff's deputies from three parishes are helping, and the police have placed checkpoints on all the roads running in and out of New Orleans. "We're watching the bus stations. The docks. Amtrak too."

The state trooper adds his support. "We've got every arm on this case, Mrs. Broussard. Our guys, the sheriffs, NOPD. If need be, we'll bring in the Feds too. We want to assure you, we're doing everything we can to find your daughter. Because of his ties to your family, and because the case involves the Livingston Parish School District, Sheriff Ardoin will be our coordinator. He's your go-to guy for anything you need. Anything at all."

Louisiana's unique Napoleonic Code gives him a lot of authoritative power, so putting Jay in charge makes perfect sense.

As the state investigator provides precise instructions for Jay, they turn to exclude the rest of us from the conversation. Beside us, the large television continues to show intermittent coverage of the search.

"It sounds as if no one has found a single clue," the CNN journalist says on TV. With her brash style, she's known for stirring up trouble and making a story bigger than it should be. In this situation, we're grateful for the international coverage. "No green field trip T-shirt, no green hair bow," she continues. "No witnesses. No signs of the angelic Sarah Broussard. This sweet, innocent preacher's daughter simply vanished with the fog. One minute she was in a popular café, laughing and playing rock-scissors-paper with her best friend. The next she was gone. The only clue we have is the black backpack she left behind in the restroom. That tells us that something happened. She didn't just get lost."

The reporter cuts to a tourist who is visiting the States for holiday. "You say you have a piece of information that could help solve the case?"

This gets our attention. Preacher taps Jay's back. We all watch the screen.

"Yes." The woman speaks with a heavy accent. "I have try to call police but they do not take me for serious. Maybe we try this."

"We're all committed to finding Sarah Broussard. Anything we can do," the reporter says. "What information do you have?"

"Well, I look through my photograph from café, and I find one. Time-stamped 1:47. It show a woman leave café with another person who you see in costume. What if Sarah Broussard in that costume?"

The television screen fills with an image. In it, a young woman is shown to be walking through the restaurant. Maybe in her early twenties, at most. There is nothing eye-catching about her. She has plain brown shoulder-length hair, not too dark, not too light. She's about five foot five, and she's neither too thin nor obese. I'd guess a size eight, maybe a ten. She doesn't look stressed or anxious. In fact, her expression reveals no emotion at all. Everything about her is ordinary. The only odd thing about her is that she is holding the hand of a shorter person who wears a mask, the rubbery kind that completely covers the hair and face. This tops a long black robe of sorts, one that easily could have been pulled over Sarah's clothes to disguise her completely. As the reporter continues, we tune in to every word.

Jay makes a phone call directly to CNN. "I want to speak to your guest," he says. "Have her call my cell phone. And can you please put me on the air?" Within seconds, he has stepped outside to find a CNN correspondent who immediately puts him through with a live feed. From the lobby, we watch Jay on TV.

"I encourage anyone who was in this area Friday, October 29, to contact the Livingston Parish Sheriff's Department," he says. "If anyone has photographs or video, we want to see them. Tips? We want to hear them. If anyone knows the woman in the photograph you just aired, we want to speak to them." The screen divides to post a toll-free number.

As Jay continues to answer questions, the trooper pulls Beth and Preacher to the side for a private conversation. Raelynn and I collapse into two leather chairs perched near the sofa where Ellie is sound asleep. I stare at the photo on-screen.

"Why would Sarah put on a costume and leave with some stranger? It doesn't make sense."

Raelynn shakes her head with equal confusion. "You really think that's her? I can't imagine Sarah doing that. Ellie, maybe. She's the follower." She looks down at my daughter, who dreams deeply on the lobby sofa.

"Ellie would never even talk to a stranger, much less go off with one," I explain. "Sarah's always been much more outgoing. She's grown up behind the pulpit, eager to reach out to everyone. No fear of people."

Raelynn nods. "You should have sent Ellie home with Nate. Heard from Carl yet?"

"Finally found a charger." I hold up my phone. "He got a chopper out, but he needed to go home first, get a few things. He was on the causeway when I called him. Should be here any minute. How's your knee?"

"Been better." She slides back against the club chair, as if she may join Ellie and take a little nap right here. Around us, media and tourists crowd the breakfast bar while desk clerks manage the morning checkouts.

"I still can't seem to accept this. I've talked my clients through trauma so many times. But now that I'm the one facing the crisis, I understand. It's weird what the brain will do."

Before I can get too deep in thought, Jay returns. He looks at Ellie, sound asleep. "Y'all should go up to your room. Get some rest."

"This could be the lead we've been waiting for." My words slur from fatigue. "Any information come in? About that woman in the photo?"

"Nothing yet, but we're on it. Listen, Amanda, you're so tired at this point that Sarah could walk right past you and you'd never see her. You all need a break. It's been a long few days."

"Carl's almost here. We'll take shifts with Ellie."

"He'd better let you have first nap," Raelynn pipes.

Jay reaches for my empty cup. "More coffee?" He takes Raelynn's too. "We'll head back out in twenty minutes." Just as he turns for the coffee station, Carl enters the lobby, suitcase in hand.

I rush to the door, greeting my husband with a tight hug. He pulls away before I am ready. "Where's Ellie?"

"She's crashed," I say, leading him back to the sofa where Raelynn stands guard.

"Reporters everywhere," he complains. "I barely made it inside."

Jay returns, handing off coffee before shaking Carl's hand. "We're about to head out. You coming?"

"Nah, I'm beat, man. I'll probably head on up with Ellie. Sleep it off."

Raelynn rolls her eyes.

I offer a tired smile. "I'm just glad you're here." I give him a kiss, but he shifts away and it lands on his cheek. "I'll help you get Ellie up to the room."

"It's all right," he says. "Y'all go on. I'll call you when we wake up."

"Stay right with her, okay?" My exhaustion puts an edge to my tone that I don't intend.

His voice rises in volume, defensive. He must assume I'm

doubting his ability to be a father, telling him what to do. "Of course I'm going to stay right with her, Amanda."

What I hear is *I'm not the one who lost a kid.*

People in the lobby are staring. Beth and Preacher too, as if they're just coming to terms with the fact that I am the one responsible for all of this.

"Let's go," Raelynn says, standing with defiance and pulling me away from Carl. Jay leads, and the three of us leave the lobby, where my daughter still sleeps.

Chapter 7

Friday, November 5, 2004

I WAKE TO A LOW-VOLUME RING TONE, THE ONE ELLIE SET FOR ME. It's her voice, teasing with exaggerated inflection. "Your phone is ringing. Answer the phone, Mom." Her quiet command pulls me from deep sleep, and before my brain is fully awake I've hit the Answer button.

"Gloopy?" It's Jay, the only person who calls me by the silly nickname. I earned it back in kindergarten, when we fought for the Elmer's glue while making our first-day-of-school badges. He pinched me. I pushed him. And before all the students had even arrived, Jay and I were wrestling on the floor in tears. When the teacher leaned over us, we were both red-faced. She pulled us apart, ruining her Lee press-on nails, and she never forgave us. We ended up sharing a carpet square the rest of the year as punishment, and whether she intended it to work out that way or not, we've been friends ever since. As a result, he's always called me Gloopy, teasing that he'll stick with me for life. "You up?"

I roll toward the bright-red numbers on the alarm clock, rubbing my eyes. "It's after eight?"

"You were sleeping?" He half laughs. "You're usually up with the sun." Then he adds, "Sorry I woke you."

"It's okay." Beside me Ellie sleeps on, undisturbed. I yawn as I explain she's right here with me. I feel safer that way.

"I'm glad y'all got some rest," Jay says. "You needed it."

"Mm-hmm." I'm barely processing this conversation.

He laughs for real this time. I stir myself to life and shake away the slumber as the clock numbers change, a reminder that time keeps moving. It's Friday. One week since Sarah went missing.

"I'm hoping Ellie will go back to school Monday. She's already missed a week."

I pull myself from the bed, my legs still clumsy. Ellie doesn't stir. As Jay fills me in on the search, my brain spins, rehashing the trauma, still trying to process our new reality. *What if it had been Ellie? What if I were standing here looking at an empty bed? What must Beth be waking to this morning? How can we bring Sarah home?*

We have cried and prayed and searched and questioned. We have retraced our steps a million times. We have gone through every possible scenario, every potential nightmare. And still no answers.

"You going back to work Monday too?"

"I'm not sure yet. I want to be out there with Beth and Preacher. I can't focus on anything anyway. I just feel bad leaving it all on Viv, canceling my clients."

I leave Ellie sleeping and move to the back porch.

Jay finally gets to the point of his call. "I'm heading out to Gator's. Need you to ride with me."

"Why? What's wrong?"

"He's having a rough time. Last Friday he dropped the kids back at school, drove the bus to his house, and never returned it."

"He still has the bus?" I hold the phone with my shoulder while I sweep the porch. Seven days away. Bugs have claimed this turf. I brush their webs and brittle casings over the low concrete ledge into the grass.

"Yep. The district has a couple extra buses, but they asked me to go out there. Have a talk with him. I thought you might come. To help. He needs it."

With the porch halfway clean, I dust off the wooden swing and relax into a soothing sway. Our calico, Beanie, jumps up to join me, purring and rubbing her head against my waist. I scratch behind her ears. "Is he still listed as a person of interest?"

"I don't think anyone really suspects him, but the investigators sure have given him a hard time. His record was a flag for them."

"What's on his record?" Gator looks sketchy, with his redneck vibe and his backwoods way of life, but I never would have suspected him to be a criminal.

"Just a few things in his early years. Nothing unusual. Fight or two, some petty theft. Mostly stuff he got caught up in with his cousins. You know they're trouble."

"To say the least." Thinking of the expansive clan of outlaws gives me the quakes, and I start to wonder if Gator could have anything to do with Sarah's disappearance. "Jay? You don't think—"

"Oh, no, Gloopy. Gator's not involved. I know him better than that."

"You sure?" Beanie climbs into my lap and curls into a nap, a fuzzy lump of patchwork fur.

"I'm sure. And you know it too. He's different, but he's not sick."

"You're right. It's just . . . I can't figure it, Jay. Nothing makes sense. Anything could have happened."

"Yeah, I know. But the stress is about to do him in. He's as innocent as you are. And he needs our help."

"*As innocent as you are.*"

"Jay? Do you mean . . ." I struggle to say it. "Do you mean they're pointing a finger at me too?"

He says nothing. Then, "You coming with me or not?"

"Carl's back offshore. I can't leave Ellie here without me."

"Bring her with us. I'll pick y'all up. Two hours?"

I roll my fingers through Beanie's soft fur and stare out into the neighbor's cluttered yard. It's filled with muddy bikes and well-worn sports balls, tangled kites and toy guns, Hula-Hoops and Hot Wheels. Her three children are all in school today, but their tracks remain. Signs that suggest we are fortunate to live in a world where kids are safe. Where they can play in their yards without fear. With no risk of being taken.

"Okay," I say. "We'll be ready by ten."

Jay arrives to find me cleaning the house. "Sorry, just trying to catch up." I welcome him inside, moving supplies out of his way. "I vacuum when Carl's not home. He hates the noise, but he hates the mess even more."

"How long's he gone this time?"

"I'm not sure. He posted for a position at the plant. Talking to his boss today and putting in applications for land jobs."

Jay makes himself at home, sitting on a stool. I move to join him in the kitchen, sliding a platter of blueberry muffins across the counter. "Still warm. Want some?"

I offer him a plate and pour him a glass of milk.

"Delicious." He takes a second bite. "Thanks. So he wants regular shift work? That doesn't sound like Carl."

"I don't think he wants it. He says it'd be better for Ellie and me. To have him home more. At least until we find Sarah." I go back to the living room and resume dusting, trying my best to keep life good for my family.

"Probably right." He refills his glass with milk. "You mind?"

"You know I don't."

"I can't see Carl working regular hours. It'll be interesting to see how that plays out."

I hold up my wedding photo, dusting the frame. Carl and I both young and naïve, staring into the camera, all smiles and nerves. "I don't know. He tends to like things to be predictable, routine. He might surprise us. Maybe he'll love it."

Jay raises his eyebrows but doesn't answer.

"Ellie's still in the shower. Could be awhile. Want me to brew some coffee?"

"Nah. This is good." He takes another long gulp of milk. "Tell her I've got Boudreaux with me. That'll get her to hurry."

"True," I admit. There's no greater lure for Ellie than an animal—especially Jay's loyal yellow Lab.

I continue dusting family photos in the living room while Jay enjoys his breakfast. As I work I feel the warmth of his stare on the back of my neck.

He breaks the silence, talking from the kitchen. "Gloopy? Are you okay?"

Am I okay?

He leaves his second muffin on the plate and moves toward me. Then he draws me into his arms and holds me, the way a big brother would try to comfort a grieving sister. With strength and protection, his steadfast heart pulsing against my own. "It's not your fault, you know?"

He moves my hair behind my ear. His fingers brush my neck. Jay's fiancée was killed in a car wreck back in college, so he knows loss. He's able to care. Nothing more than that.

I pull away, holding my tears. "I'm fine. I'm sorry I let Ellie sleep so late. I didn't mean to make you wait."

"Not a problem. I would have let her sleep too." Jay returns to his muffin.

"Have you talked to him? Gator? Since Friday?" I'm determined to switch the focus off of me.

"Yeah. He's pretty shaken up. I thought I might send him out with my river patrol. Figure if I can get him in the boat he'll come back to his senses. It'll settle him down to be on the water."

Ellie joins us, drying her hair with a towel. "Hey, Mr. Jay."

"Ellie!" He cheers her name, trying to keep her life as normal as possible. Then he gives her his seat. "I saved you a muffin."

She smiles and accepts both. He pours her some milk while I put away the last of my cleaning supplies.

"I brought Boudreaux," Jay tells Ellie. "He's out there waiting."

As predicted, this is all it takes to get her moving. She grabs a second muffin and rushes out to share breakfast with her favorite canine companion.

Within ten minutes we're in Jay's white Ford F-250, the unmarked sheriff's vehicle he prefers to drive. Boudreaux and Ellie share the backseat as we bounce down a complex maze of rutted back roads, wending our way to Gator's house. These are moss-draped routes, the kind where people come to drop empty beer cans, unwanted dogs, and dead men. We pass a small camper trailer with an oversized

Confederate flag across the front. A hand-painted sign in the yard reads *God, Guns, and Glory!* Beneath the trailer, part of the floor has fallen through to the ground, but no one seems inclined to fix it.

We've had a fairly dry week here in Walker, so Jay's truck kicks up a cloud of dust. We pass long stretches of litter and mobile homes where rusty cars are parked, half hidden by weeds, in the overgrown yards. One vehicle is hanging from a tree. The entire car, a cardinal-red Ford LTD, is suspended in midair, dangling from a giant chain like a big, ripe apple. Its engine rests nearby on a sawed-off stump, a stub contrasting the old-growth hickory, elm, and ash that tower around it.

Each time the road forks I try to remember which direction we'll need to return. There are no street signs and no significant landmarks, only trees, trees, and more trees. The farther we drive, the less anchored I feel.

We round one final curve and finally reach Gator's claim, marked with more than a dozen large *No Trespassing* signs. This doesn't give Jay any pause. When we come to an unbalanced cattle guard, I get out and open the gate. A sheet of plywood reads *Enter at Own Risk*, the last few letters squeezed together as if the writer failed to plan appropriately for the limited space. Additional signs warn about aggressive dogs; one reads *Pit Bulls Bite*.

After Jay pulls the truck across the rusty guard pipes, I close the gate behind him and climb back into my seat. I have known Gator all my life and have never had reason to suspect him of any wrongdoing. But now, as we approach his property, I shudder. I hope Jay's instincts are right.

We drive another half mile or so past a timber clearing before a final trailer comes into view. The Livingston Parish School Board bus is parked alongside it. This home belongs to Gator. More threatening messages, including a large white sheet that flaps against the aluminum panels of his doublewide. In red letters: *Trespassers will be shot and killed. Not the quick and easy way.*

"Interesting." I point to the offensive warnings.

"Yeah, he's had some media out here the last couple days." Jay parks in a white dirt patch under a shady oak tree, and the dust settles around us.

"I'm surprised they'd come out here. Takes guts."

Jay laughs. But as he gets out of the truck, he adds his .40 caliber Glock 22 to his hip. I'm not sure if this gives me more comfort or less.

Gator waves from across his property, rifle in hand. He's at the edge of his pond, feeding a congregation of alligators. He's known for catching small ones from the rivers and bringing them back as pets, a habit that earned him his nickname.

"Are those his gators?" Ellie asks, holding her hand above her eyes to block the sun.

"Think so." I count at least fifteen of them scattered across the bank, their spiky spine ridges narrowing against the water's murky edge. They range in length from three feet to ten, and there's no doubt the larger ones could share a dog or two for dinner if they ever got hungry enough. The scaly reptiles lunge and snap their sharp jaws against air, battling for the final cut of meat Gator tosses their way.

As they crawl into the muddy pond, their toothy profiles sink out of view. Gator shuffles toward us with a gruff laugh. "How you like my decoratin'?" He points to the sheet suspended from the trailer's roofline. "Gotta do somethin' to keep them bloodhounds away."

Jay smiles and shakes Gator's hand. "Could be a little overkill."

"Nah." Gator roars with laughter, coughing a harsh smoker

hack. "Next time they try to mess with me out here, I'm gonna start firin' shots. You got my back, Sheriff?" He grins at Jay while moving to give me a happy hug. "Good to see you, Mrs. 'Manda. What kinda trouble you been gettin' into?"

I try to keep him laughing. Like most of the people I know in Louisiana, humor is his comfort zone. "Oh, you know me, Gator. I stay in trouble."

"Better not turn your back on a woman like this one, Sheriff." His brittle gray ponytail pokes out beneath his tattered ball cap, a faded orange Nascar lid with a fishing hook attached to the rim. He turns to Ellie and says, "Follow me. I'll put you to work."

Curious, Ellie obeys.

Jay and I trail behind, leaving Boudreaux safe in the backseat— the windows rolled down enough to give him air. Across the dirt lot, nearly fifteen pit bulls are chained to pine trees. Each dog has been assigned a bright-blue plastic barrel for shelter, sanctioned behind a metal fence to keep the gators at bay. A few growl and groan, stretching their chains, so I am careful to stay between the dogs and Ellie. Some seem eager to charge us if needed.

Gator opens a metal feed bin, causing the lid to clang loud, tinny echoes against the trees. Then he stacks a set of plastic bowls and shows Ellie how to dole out Solo-cup portions of food for his pack of dogs. Dry bits roll against the plastic, and like Pavlov's study, the canines salivate beneath the pines, each one pacing circles across the bare earth. Once she fills the bowls, I hold Ellie back, insisting Gator can handle the rest of the work. We watch, mesmerized by the way he pulls each bowl a safe distance with a rake, not daring to go within chain's length of his own dogs.

When he finishes his chores, Ellie is full of questions. "Why don't you let them off those chains?"

Gator laughs, leading us up his steps and struggling with the climb. "You don't see those scars?"

The three of us take a second look at the pit bulls, now noticing a few missing ears and thin patches where fur no longer grows. One has only three legs.

"Gator, please don't tell me you're fighting those dogs?" Jay looks back toward Boudreaux. He is taking this seriously.

"No, no." Gator chuckles a bit. "I don't go for none of that. I rescued them fellas. From the pits."

"So why are they still on chains?" Ellie tilts her head.

"It's not like you can just reach your hand into a fightin' ring and pet one of them boys. What you think would happen if I tried that?"

"They'd bite you?"

"You bet they would. They don't know I'm tryin' to help 'em. They know only one thing—survive. They've been trained to fight to the death. Yours or theirs."

"But you said they don't fight anymore," Ellie challenges.

"Yeah, but they don't know that. I just got these guys a few weeks ago. Trust don't come easy once you've been in the ring. Love don't either." He taps his temple and says, "In their mind, everybody's out to get 'em."

"Will they have to stay chained forever?"

Ellie's question brings me back to New Orleans, where the fortune-teller's sparrow stayed locked in its cage, singing behind bars as the beautiful green Quaker parrots flew free around him.

"Depends on the dog." Gator opens his front door, revealing a tattoo on his forearm. Inked in standard army green, the letters read *POW*. He sees me looking. "Some never do find their way to freedom."

"But some do," I tell Ellie, trying to reassure her.

Gator rubs his scruffy chin, repeating, "Some do."

Near the porch is a falcon. He rests on a branch, surrounded by thick wire fencing. As I lean in for a closer look, our rough-edged friend offers a stern warning. "Watch your fingers. He'll snap 'em right in two."

The dogs quiet behind us, chomping their daily rations, and the bird eyes me with a broken stare, as if he wouldn't have the energy to chew my fingers even if I gave them to him. All hope has been caged right out of him. *"What good is it to have feathers if you don't fly?"*

Jay holds out his arm, gesturing for Ellie and me to enter the trailer. He follows. Inside, the thin paneled walls are lined with prized hunting mounts. An entire row of deer, each a twelve-point or larger. And in between, a turkey, a bobcat. Even a wild boar, his tusks chipped and yellowed, proof he never would have gone down without a fight.

"You like to hunt?" I tease.

"Nah. I like to eat." He laughs, coughing again. "Only thing I ain't caught me yet is a loup-garou."

"You catch that, you'll be set for life," Jay joins in. Stories about the legendary werewolves of the swamps have given Louisiana children nightmares for generations. But so far, no one has ever been able to prove they exist.

"You think they're real?" Ellie asks.

He gives her a wink.

"Trust me," I tell Ellie. "If a loup-garou were out there, Gator would have found it by now." This makes Gator laugh again, exposing a missing molar.

Beneath the stuffed bobcat rests a set of clear plastic drawers, two rows of six, each sealed tightly and heated with insulated bulbs. Muted patterns of grays, browns, greens, and yellows press against the faded plastic fronts.

"What are those?" Ellie asks, curiosity getting the best of her again.

"Snakes," Gator says. "I breed 'em. Got about six different kinds. Go on, open 'em up. They won't bite."

I give Jay a wary glance and he steps in. "Venomous?"

Gator snickers, as if we're the biggest fools he's ever seen. "Boas. Ball pythons. King snakes. You tell me." Then he teases that we can't possibly be from LP if we don't know the answer. "They're safe. Same ones I've brought to school a hundred times. You remember how to handle them?"

"Yes, sir." Ellie beams.

"Have at it." With this he moves into the kitchen, inviting us for lunch.

Ellie wants a better view of the reptiles, opening one drawer at a time before pulling a yellow serpent from the bin. The snake is about as long as her arm, and she wraps it around her wrist before lifting it high for observation.

"Good choice," Gator tells her from the stove. "She's a banana. Ball python. Sweet little thing."

I try not to squirm as the snake slithers against Ellie's elbow. It's the first time I've seen her smile since the field trip. Once I'm certain she's safe, I leave her to enjoy the harmless serpents and join the men in Gator's kitchen, still fully in sight of Ellie. The room is small but tidy. In fact, there isn't a single speck of dust to be seen anywhere. In contrast to the cluttered yard, Gator keeps a spotless house, clean and organized, which helps me feel a little better about all his feral pets.

Gator serves us heaping helpings of the fried catfish, hush pup-pies, and corn maque choux he's been keeping warm on the stove. The rich aroma tempts Ellie to leave the snakes and join us in the kitchen.

"Wash your hands," I tell her, setting the table for four. Jay offers a quick blessing, and we begin. As we gather, our minds are miles away in New Orleans, where we sat on Gator's bus counting kids and discovering that Sarah was no longer with us.

"Gator, you're an incredible cook," I tell him. "Best catfish I ever had. Where'd you catch it?"

"Right there in that pond," he says, nudging his head toward the window.

"I see you've still got the bus out there." Jay eases into the con-versation we've been avoiding.

Gator lifts his eyes and gives Jay a haggard look.

"You know they need it back, Gator," Jay persists.

"They want it? They can come get it. I ain't never gettin' behind that wheel again. Not as long as I live." Gator takes a swig of sweet tea.

Jay tilts his head, nudging me to take the lead.

"I don't blame you, Gator," I say. "I've been a wreck all week. I don't want to look at that bus, much less go inside it. But we have to get it back to the school. So what should we do?"

He stares at his food for a while before answering. "Some folks are acting like I'm the one who took her. How could I have done anything? I was with the bus the whole time." Gator looks at Jay, pleading his case. "I swear, I didn't do it." Then he looks at me and at Ellie, repeating, "I didn't do nothin' wrong."

Do I believe him? He lives on the fringe of society. He looks for opportunities to be around children, driving the school bus, visiting the classrooms. He's a bit of a loner, preferring to associate with his own relatives back here on family land. In a way, he's exactly the kind of person who could do something like kidnap a child.

It suddenly dawns on me that we should look around Gator's place. *Sarah could be right here and we'd never know it.*

"We know you didn't do anything wrong, Gator." Jay sounds sure.

Calm down, Amanda. I talk myself back to sanity. *You've known Gator all your life. He's never given you any reason to doubt him. And neither has Jay.*

"I always bring the same number of kids home as I bring out. Leave no child behind." Gator's hands are shaking. "They questioned me. It don't look too good that I got a record."

I try to reassure him. "They have to look at every angle. It's their job." I steady his hand. "They've questioned me many times. People probably suspect me too."

"They do?" Ellie questions, surprised to think of me in this light.

"I'm sure they do, Ellie. I was the last one with her."

Her eyes grow wide and she says, "No, Mom. I was."

This reality hits hard, and the three of us stumble over one another's words, trying to convince Ellie that no one blames her for Sarah's disappearance. But I've said the wrong thing, and there's no changing Ellie's mind. The fault, she now believes, is hers.

After lunch we move back outside, where Gator tinkers with his four-wheeler and ignores Jay's requests to drive the bus back to Livingston.

"I told you, I won't touch it. I'll die before I ever drive that bus again." Gator runs his hand across a frayed wire beneath the gas tank of his ATV.

Jay leans against his truck, petting Boudreaux. "Well, I was hoping we could follow you to drop off the bus and then maybe swing by my office. Let you go out with the river patrol. Get away for a while. Somewhere the media won't find you."

This elicits no response. So Jay continues. "Or maybe I could drive the bus back for you."

"Gator?" I intervene. "That's a good idea. Ellie and I can follow in Jay's truck. We'll get it back for you, and you won't have to look at it every day. That'll help, don't you think? Out of sight, out of mind?"

Gator wanders off toward the woods, and I follow. "Gator?"

He keeps walking, and I match his pace. Ellie keeps up. "I know you love your job. Driving that bus. You don't have to quit it, you know?"

No reply.

"How can we help you, Gator? What can we do to make this easier for you?"

He finally comes to a stop in an open glade. The noon sun streams into a dome of light, gleaming through the evergreen canopy that circles us. When he turns to face me, his eyes are red and watery. He inhales.

"Just get it out of here," Gator says. "Take it. I'm done." He spins again and heads deeper into the woods.

"Gator?" I chase after him, Ellie at my heels. "We know you didn't have anything to do with it. In time everyone else will too."

Again, no reply.

"People will beat you down as low as you will let them."

Finally he slows down, then turns. "That's the thing, Mrs. 'Manda. Everybody ain't nice like you."

I pull Ellie against me, wrapping my arm around her shoulders. "This is hard for all of us, Gator. We're being tested, and some people will be cruel."

He nods.

"But we have to remember the real one suffering here is Sarah. She's the victim. The rest of us are on the edge, trying not to let the horror pull us under. We can't let that happen. Because if we give up, then who's left to fight for the truth? Who's left to fight for Sarah?"

He wipes his eye and gives me a look that could melt my bones.

"It's up to us," I tell him.

He lets this sink in. Then he gives a quick nod before turning to Ellie. "It's up to us."

Part 2

For the Lord is the Spirit, and wherever the
Spirit of the Lord is, there is freedom.

—2 CORINTHIANS 3:17

Chapter 8

Thursday, November 25, 2004
Thanksgiving Day

"GOOD MORNING, SUNSHINE." AS ELLIE ENTERS THE LIVING ROOM, I drop a kiss on the crown of her head.

She carries her favorite quilt to the sofa and lies back down without responding.

"How should we spend our Thanksgiving? It's not too cold. Want to go to Jay's camp? Get away from it all?" I don't say what we're both thinking. *How is Sarah spending her Thanksgiving?*

Ellie pulls the blanket over her head. "I'm tired."

No matter how many counselors try to help her, she hasn't been the same since Sarah went missing nearly a month ago.

"How about we take a little walk then. Get some fresh air? Just me and you." I sit at the end of the couch, and she puts her feet in my lap. Outside, the sound of a hammer pounds in pulses. "Your father's already working on the shed. We could help him."

From beneath the cover she mumbles, "I'm going back to sleep."

I sit for a while, letting her socked feet rest against me, wanting more than anything to take my daughter's pain from her. At twelve years old, she should be laughing and having fun with her friends. Or at least excited about being out of school for the Thanksgiving holiday. Something.

I pick up the remote and flip on the TV. The voice of an NBC announcer breaks the silence. ". . . live from New York City with our telecast of the 78th Annual Macy's Thanksgiving Day Parade." Katie Couric and Matt Lauer wish the world a happy Thanksgiving from Herald Square. Performers stand around them wearing patriotic outfits, waving red, white, and blue. Then the screen switches to a drum line, where jolly Al Roker is reporting from uptown.

In our previous lives, before what we now call The Day, I'd already be in the kitchen, basting a turkey and preheating the oven. The counter would be filled with ingredients for stuffing and pies, casseroles and cookies. Mom would still be alive, walking in with deviled eggs and green bean casserole, the kind using cream of mushroom soup and dried onions. She'd joke about her gourmet cooking skills, and we'd all give her grief for it. With love.

Carl would likely be in the attic, hauling down the Christmas decorations, and Ellie would be watching the parade on TV, making her Gratitude List. She would read it aloud later in the evening, when we'd join Beth and Preacher at the church reception hall. After counting our blessings, we'd open the doors to anyone who had nowhere to go for the holiday feast. Every year the seats would fill. But not today.

This year new volunteers are hosting the dinner while Beth and Preacher search soup kitchens, hoping to find Sarah.

I should be helping them, but instead I'm here with my own daughter. Still in my nightgown, I stare at the screen. Someone cuts the oversized red ribbon, announcing the parade route officially open. Brass bands begin to march across the set, and giant helium balloons are carried down 77th Street by a team of paraders handling the strings.

"Look, Ellie. The balloons." She has always enjoyed seeing the floating characters, but this year the magic is gone. She's sound asleep as the massive toy soldiers float by, tethered against the blue. More than two million people line the New York City sidewalks, eager to enjoy an unusually warm November day. Normally the classic American tradition excites me too, bringing out a sense of patriotic pride. But not anymore. The tubas and trumpets, the costumes and revelry—they all bring me back to New Orleans and to The Day.

Mom's voice echoes from years of gentle guidance: *Find the good, Amanda. Learn the lessons you are given. Embrace the pain.*

But this is different, Mom. I can't find any good from this pain.

As soon as I think it, the guilt surges through me. I know I should listen to my mother's advice as she returns to me in memory. Plus, it is Thanksgiving and I refuse to drown in despair, so I turn off the television and sweep away my grief, grabbing a notepad from the end table. I uncap a pen, scribbling to draw ink to the tip, and force myself to list all the blessings in my life. Not what was good in my life before The Day. Not what I hope will be good in my life after we find Sarah. I focus instead on what is good right now. Today. Just as I have taught my clients to do as they navigate their own sorrows.

I stare at the notepad, my scribbles a jumble of scratches. No matter how hard I try, I only see emptiness. Blank space. Loss. But as Ellie stirs, I manage to write my first gratitude.

1. Ellie (my whole world)

From there, the items come one at a time, dragging slowly across the page.

2. Carl (fifteen years of marriage, more good than bad)
3. Friends (Beth, Preacher, Raelynn, Jay, plus Viv, the perfect business partner)

4. Our health (and insurance coverage for Ellie's therapy)
5. Our home (and our land where we plan to build)
6. Our church (and the support they have offered since The Day)
7. Our community (and the support they have offered since The Day)
8. Our jobs (especially the flexibility that allows me to be a wife and mom)
9. Finances that meet our basic needs (food, shelter, health care, communication)
10. Faith (fragile as it is now)

As I read back through my list, I am able to exhale for the first time in a month. Despite the gaping holes where Sarah and Mom once belonged, I still have much to be grateful for. Many people would trade places with me if they could. Right now. Today.

I lift my eyes. *Thanks, Mom.*

With Ellie back asleep, I ease my way from the sofa and out to the porch where I call across the yard for Carl. He comes around the corner, and I smile. "Happy Thanksgiving. You plan to take a day of rest?"

My husband doesn't bother answering. We both know he never stops working. But he does give me a quick peck, his lips salty from sweat.

"We weren't going to celebrate this year, but maybe it'll do us good to have Thanksgiving dinner. Keep tradition for Ellie's sake. Just something small. What do you think?"

"Sure."

"I'll run to the store before they close. We'll keep it simple. Just the three of us."

"Okay." It's clear he's not listening. He's probably calculating dimensions in his head, counting the number of two-by-fours he'll need to finish the shed.

"How about we just go with a chicken? Sweet potato casserole. Maybe asparagus, pecan pie. Any requests?"

"That works for me."

"Carl?" I wait for him to connect. "I love you."

He gives me a second kiss and says, "Love you too."

Hello Sparrow,

Can you hear me? I hear you singing. And tapping my window. Are you trying to tell me something? Stay with me, please. I'm listening.

Love,

Sarah

Hello Sparrow,

The Lady gave me notebooks and a pen. She said I have to "keep them hid real good." Then she pinched my mouth and warned me not to tell The Man.

That's what I call them. The Lady and The Man. The Man is mean. I don't know why he is doing this to me.

Keep singing, please. I'm listening.

Love,

Sarah

Hello Sparrow,

I know my letters are stupid. I shouldn't write to a bird, but you're the only one here I can talk to.

Can you find Mom and Pop? Tell them I want to come home. And I'm sorry.

Thank you, Sparrow.

Sarah

(The Man calls me Holly. My real name is Sarah.)

Hello Sparrow,

Today is Thanksgiving. I've been here almost a month. It feels longer. Sometimes I can't remember things. So I'm going to write about my real life. The one I'll go back to someday.

In my real life, I make a Gratitude List. So does Ellie. That's what our moms call it.

Things I Am Thankful For:

1. My sparrow (that's you)
2. My notebooks
3. My pen
4. Turkey and mashed potatoes (even though they were cold)
5. The Man didn't come see me today
6. The Lady is nice sometimes

7. I don't have to stay in the box anymore
8. I am still alive
9. God is with me ~~(I think)~~ I know

Saturday, December 18, 2004

As we pull into the first truck stop, I gather our supplies. I carry a tote bag filled with fliers and magnets, staplers and pushpins, tape and markers. It's been a month and a half since Sarah went missing, and this has become our standard action pack. We've gotten this process down to a precise method, and we attack it as if it's a job— the most important task of our lives: finding Sarah.

Preacher, with his giant heart, walks the darkened section of the back lot, knocking on doors of tractor-trailers, holding out hope that one of these men will have his daughter. A couple truckers have wired Christmas wreaths to the front grills of their cabs, and this particular gas station has carols playing over the speakers. A happy voice croons, "It's the most wonderful time of the year." I squeeze my hand into a fist around the bag's handles, trying to reduce my rage. It's as if the Fates are taunting us, laughing at our pain.

Any other year we'd be at Beth and Preacher's house, enjoying their famous Christmas decorations alongside hundreds of locals. But this year their holiday lights are boxed away, their yard remains dark. Their living room is without a tree, and no stockings hang from their mantel. Our church youth group is celebrating the holidays without their annual bonfire, and families will have to drive to Baton Rouge to visit Santa.

Tonight, as Preacher talks to truckers, Beth and I make our

way beneath the light of the Exxon sign, seeking out the station attendant to explain our search. Most of these people know us by now. Even the new hires tend to cooperate. Who would tell someone they can't hang up fliers about a missing child? But regardless of how polite and sympathetic the employees are, they never have the information we need. No one has claimed to know Sarah. No one has brought her home.

"The news coverage is dying down, Amanda. People are forgetting all about her." Beth tapes another flier to a window while I hand one to a couple passing by.

I don't know what to say. Beth is right. Two months have passed and most people have moved on with their lives, especially now that Christmas has everyone so busy. The media buzz is gone, and the school superintendent suspended the weekend caravans to New Orleans, explaining, "Following the advice of legal consultants and with the discontinuation of organized searches by law enforcement, we can no longer provide transportation at the expense of the district. We are still committed, as individuals, to finding Sarah, and we will continue to support the Broussard family in every possible way." Soon after the school's announcement, the churches canceled their caravans too.

"Has Jay found any more information about that woman? The one in the photos?" I ask this as we make our way back to Beth's car.

"Nothing you haven't heard. Bridgette Gallatino. She's got a criminal history. But nobody can find her."

"Yeah, Jay mentioned something about drug charges, robbery, and—"

"I know." Beth interrupts before I say "prostitution." "They've got undercover guys looking for her too, but—" She stops midsentence and then begins again. "I don't know, Amanda. How hard can it be to find somebody like that? I don't understand why no one has seen her. Or Sarah. It's as if they've both vanished. Up in smoke. Either people aren't paying attention, or they're afraid to get involved. Or they . . ."

Her lip quivers, and she bites back tears.

I give her a hug. "Beth, listen. We're going to find her. If she really did leave the café with that lady, at least she's got a young woman with her. That's a good thing. Someone to mother her. She's probably taking care of Sarah right now, watching over her." I try to convince myself this is a reasonable possibility.

"I can't understand. Forgive me, Amanda, but why weren't you there? With them? In line? I'm not blaming you. I just need to know. Why'd you leave them? It's not like you." Beth begins to cry, repeating, "I don't understand."

With each heart-wrenching syllable, my denial gives way. I lost Sarah. I lost my best friend's daughter. I lost my daughter's best friend. I turned my back when I was supposed to be on guard. I am the one responsible for all of this. And no matter how hard I try, I can't fix it. Sarah is gone.

Chapter 9

Hello Sparrow,

It's Christmas Eve! The Lady brought me some math workbooks and a new pen. She found them at a garage sale. She's got short blond hair now and she wears big sunglasses when she goes anywhere. She wants me to do my schoolwork so I won't end up like her. I never thought I'd be happy to do math!

Hello Sparrow,

Last night I heard firecrackers. The room turned colors, so I bet they were pretty. We always pop them for New Year's Eve and Fourth of July. I write my name with sparklers. Ellie likes Roman candles. Nate likes Black Cats and bottle rockets. Those hurt my ears.

I hope the noise didn't scare you. It sounded like bombs. Mom used to say, "Don't be scared. Then you can see how pretty they are."

That's what I'm trying to do now. I'm trying not to be

scared here, so I can find something pretty about this place. You know what I found that's pretty? You!

Hello Sparrow,

When I was in the box, I could only *hear* you. I didn't know what kind of bird you were. I thought you might be a sparrow because my grandmother taught me birds. Plus, the palm reader had that sparrow. And her bird sang a song like yours.

Are you the same sparrow I held that day? Did you come to get your feather back? I still have it. I've been guarding it, just like the palm reader told me to do.

I like it when you sing to me. Like my grandmother used to say, "Softly sings the sparrow."

Hello Sparrow,

The Man doesn't make me stay in the box at all anymore. So now I can see every time you come to the window. It's the best part of my day. The pretty part.

He did put a chain on my ankle, so I can't reach the window or door.

Fly to Mom and Pop, please. Tell them I love them. And I miss them. Tell them I'm sorry I went with The Lady at the café. Tell them I want to come home.

Friday, December 24, 2004
Christmas Eve

"I GUESS YOU'RE TOO OLD TO SET OUT COOKIES FOR SANTA AND carrots for his reindeer?" I ask, half hoping Ellie will burst into a fit of giggles and say, "No, let's do it!"

Instead, she rolls her eyes and plugs tiny white earbuds into her ears. *Where are you, Sarah?*

I get the hint and leave my daughter to her music. Then I head to the carport, where Carl is tinkering with his compound hunting bow. "Help me. Please. I can't get through to her no matter how hard I try."

"That's your problem," he says. "You try too hard." My husband doesn't look up from the fletching jig as he repairs several faulty arrows. I move closer, and he slaps my rear. "Mm-hmm! Nothing better than a woman who knows what she's made for." He pulls me close with hungry desire and leans me back against his workbench. "You ready to give me my Christmas present?"

I laugh it off, pulling away. "Sure. Right out here in front of the neighbors."

This seems to arouse him, and he pulls me close again, even more forcefully this time. He kisses my neck, and my body reacts with flame.

In the yard next door, children are playing.

"Carl, there are kids everywhere." Still, I cave in close against him, enjoying the way it feels to be in his arms. He's kissing my shoulder when Ellie comes outside, calling, "Mom!" as she closes the door behind her.

I pull away quickly. Frustrated, he spins his attention back to the arrows, as if I have no right to leave him wanting, even when our child needs me.

"Change your mind?" I ask Ellie. "Want to make Santa cookies?"

"I guess so." She says this with a flat tone, but I take it as a spark of hope.

"You hear that, Carl?" I can't hide my relief. "Wanna help us?"

He responds coldly. "No." Then he grabs his bow and heads for the full-sized foam deer in the backyard. He pulls an arrow from his quiver, nocking it in place while attaching his release to the string loop. The tense line snaps, the carbon arrow spins through the air, and the shaft slices the target with a loud, clean *pop*. We leave him to his fun.

In the kitchen Ellie and I discuss Christmas memories from years gone by. "Remember when you caught me hiding your new bike and I had to confess that Santa wasn't real?" I hand her the sugar, and she measures while she talks.

"Yeah, I was glad you told me the truth. One kid in my class still believed last year. I felt kind of sorry for her."

"I struggled with the whole Santa thing, actually."

"Really?" Sarah pours her scoop of sugar into the bowl.

"Yeah. I wanted you to have all the fun, but I didn't want you to be traumatized like I was when I learned he didn't really live at the North Pole with elves and reindeer."

She rolls her eyes again. "You're so dramatic."

"I never told you that story?"

She shakes her head and reaches for the flour. I point to the next step of the recipe, and she reads the measurements.

"Well, you know I was adopted, right?"

She nods.

"I found out about the adoption just before I learned the truth about Santa."

"Ouch," Ellie says.

"Yep. Hurtful stuff." I smile. "Seriously, there's no comparison between the two. But I was able to express my feelings about Santa Claus. I couldn't really talk about being adopted." I pass Ellie the baking soda and measuring spoons.

"How'd you find out? About Santa?"

"Friends at school. They'd been teasing those of us who still believed. Our teacher admitted it was all a hoax."

"Your teacher told you? That's harsh!"

"Yep. Second grade. I locked myself in the teachers' restroom and refused to come out. For hours. It only had an inside lock. Even the janitor was at a loss. They thought about taking the door from its hinges, but they decided to call my mom instead."

"No way."

"True. When she got there, I screamed at her through the heavy door, 'Why did you lie to me?'" I act out the part with extra flair.

Ellie laughs softly. "Like Dad says: Drama Mama."

"It really did upset me. I trusted those people to give me the truth. When I found out I had been fooled, my faith in them was broken."

"Oh, come on, seriously?" She rolls her eyes, stirring the dry ingredients.

"You have to understand. In the span of one week, I had learned my mom and dad weren't my real parents. And that Santa didn't exist. Took me a long time to learn to trust again. And right when I was beginning to do so, my father left us. That was that."

Ellie steals a few chocolate chips before adding them to the dough. "But you trust Dad, right?"

"Of course. Can't have a marriage without trust."

"So what finally got you out of the teachers' restroom?" Ellie asks.

"Easy. All my mom had to do was offer chocolate chip cookies." I smile, and we continue working together in the kitchen, making our favorite dessert. Mother and daughter. Ellie and me.

Friday, December 31, 2004
New Year's Eve

> Hello Sparrow,
>
> I'm trying to get The Man to like me. Then maybe he'll let me go home.
>
> I'm scared of him, but he brings me food and water. And he takes me outside to use the bathroom. I have to keep a pillowcase over my head out there. And my leg feels weird without the chain. I think I got used to the heavy.
>
> The other girls have to stay chained, but I'm his favorite. That's what he says. I don't know the other girls. I only know The Lady, and she says I ask too many questions.
>
> The Man says he'll keep giving me food, water, clothes. Even an iPod. As long as I'm good. He says I shouldn't be scared. But I am.

Julie Cantrell

Saturday, January 1, 2005
New Year's Day

Hello Sparrow,

Happy New Year's!

I bet Mom is cooking black-eyed peas and cabbage. She says they make us healthy and wealthy. They really just make the whole house stink. She's probably making cabbage rolls. I always hold my nose while I eat those. But now I miss Mom so much, I'd eat all her cabbage rolls and never complain.

I bet The Lady won't cook cabbage. She seems to be as scared of The Man as I am. I asked her why they would want to take someone else's kid. She said, "Asking why won't change nothin'. You might as well get that through your head."

Sarah's New Year's Resolutions 2005

1. Go home.

Hello Sparrow,

The Lady said we're in a place called Chalmette. I don't know where that is. Sometimes I hear cars go by, so maybe I could run for help.

I'm in a shed. There are holes in the floor, but all I can see is dirt. There's one lightbulb hanging from the ceiling, like in our attic at home. Sometimes The Man keeps it on all night. Sometimes he keeps it dark for days. I like it to be on, but he won't let me touch the switch. If The Man wants the light on, it stays on. If he wants it off, it stays off. He is in charge of everything. Even The Lady knows that. She says, "What LeMoyne wants, LeMoyne gets."

LeMoyne is what she calls The Man. I don't call him a name because he won't call me mine. He doesn't call The Lady a real name either. Just *Baby* or *Woman* or the really bad B-word, depending on if he's in the mood to be nice to her or not.

The walls here aren't finished. Pop would laugh and say, "That's what we call a stud. Like me." I like to help Pop build things. But now it feels like none of those things ever happened. I don't want to forget who I really am. So I will keep writing everything I remember.

Hello Sparrow,

I like to look for patterns in the ceiling, like when I was a little kid. I find elephants and tigers. Even dinosaurs. My favorite is a nest of birds. I pretend you're in there, but I'm glad you're outside instead, flying free.

The nest makes me think of our field trip. Miss Henderson showed us pelicans on the Louisiana flag. She said the mama pelican didn't have anything to feed her babies, so she let them drink her blood.

Miss Henderson told us that we should always think of that mama pelican. And that we should know our parents would do anything to save us. Mrs. Amanda said, "That's true. Anything."

> The Man says my parents don't want me. That they
> aren't looking for me. But I don't believe him.

Monday, February 14, 2005
Valentine's Day

"Happy Valentine's Day." I snuggle against Carl's warm chest, drinking in the woodsy smell of his aftershave. It makes me want to curl next to him in a flannel sleeping bag beneath a world of stars. I try not to let my mind drift away to Sarah, the search. "I have a surprise for you."

"Let me get my coffee." He shuffles into the kitchen, and I trail him, laughing, holding his mug.

"I already fixed it, honey. Set it down by you? When you were shaving?"

He takes the warm cup, a tacky souvenir from our summer road trip out west. It shows a picture of Hoover Dam with shiny black letters that declare *I took the dam tour*. We spent the night on a houseboat, sleeping in the middle of Lake Mead. One of my favorite vacations. I can still picture Ellie plunging into the clear, cool waters of the lake. She felt so proud.

Carl pulls the sugar bowl from the shelf and adds another scoop, stirring with hard, rapid clanks of his spoon.

"It's not sweet enough? I put two. How you always like it." He ignores me, so I try another approach. "You ready for your surprise?" I add a flirtatious tilt at the hip, trying to give Carl my undivided attention. He's grown weary of the emotional roller coaster this trauma has caused all of us, telling me again and again that life goes on.

He ignores my mention of a gift, asking instead, "What's for breakfast?"

"I should know better than to talk to you without feeding you first. Let me fix an omelet."

"Forget it. I'll make sausage."

"Or sausage. No problem."

"I got it!" he says, opening the fridge with a jerk.

I pull a tea bag from the drawer and put some water on to boil.

"We're out of sausage?" He settles for a pack of bacon and slams the door. It's hard to tell if he's angry or just moving through the world with force. With Carl, a simmering undercurrent of rage rests just beneath the surface.

Don't take it personally, Amanda. He's hungry.

And then my mother's voice: *A good wife never lets her husband go hungry.*

Carl fries the bacon, adding two eggs to the grease. Then he fills his plate, leaving a couple slices for Ellie and me. He moves to the counter. I lean in from the opposite side, trying again for conversation.

"You're off today, right?"

He nods.

"What's the plan? Want to take a picnic? Hit the river? Maybe go out for lunch or something?"

"I need to work on the car. Change the oil. Swap out the brake pads. I'll probably clean the gutters too and knock down that old mailbox."

"Need help?" I have no interest in cars or gutters, but I want to spend Valentine's Day with my husband if I can make that happen.

"Sure, Amanda. You handle the brake pads. I'll tackle the oil." He laughs as if I'm the most pathetic person on the planet, completely useless.

Half of me wants to call his bluff and march right out to the carport with the maintenance manual in hand. But he's right. I have no idea how to install new brake pads. So he wins. Again.

I leave him to his daily tasks and don't bother telling him he has a new Stihl chainsaw wrapped in the utility room. I figure he'll find it eventually. If he got me a gift, he doesn't mention that.

Happy Valentine's Day, Amanda.

Hello Sparrow,

It's Valentine's Day. We always go to the father-daughter dinner at church. Last year Pop played guitar and sang a song for me. Some people started crying. It was one of his favorite songs. "My Darling," by Wilco.

When he finished, he asked the dads to teach their children what it means to be a "good guy." Then he listed ways we could tell if somebody was a good guy. He said the girls should write it down for our brothers. Only I don't have a brother. So I told Nate.

I can't remember all the things Pop said, but here's the important part.

My Pop is a Good Guy because:

1. I've never been afraid of Pop, and I don't think Mom has either.
2. He's always on our side and he'll stick with us for life. No matter what happens.
3. He doesn't lie, cheat, or steal.
4. Pop always tries to make the right choice.
5. When he does mess up, he says he's sorry and he means it.
6. If we're hurting, he's hurting more because we are hurt.
7. I can talk to him about anything, as long as I'm nice about it.

Pop is the best guy I know. He always says if Mom and me don't know how much he loves us, then he's doing something very wrong. He comes home every day and kisses Mom and tells her thank you for being his wife. And then he kisses me and tells me thank you for being his daughter. And then he says he's the luckiest man on the planet because of us.

Chapter 10

Sunday, March 27, 2005
Easter

"HAPPY EASTER, HONEY!" I WAKE ELLIE WITH A GENTLE BACK RUB, hoping to bring a little holiday magic to her morning. I know she's too old for the fantasy, but I want her to feel joy again. "You've got a basket of treats in the living room. Come see?"

"Don't tell me. You sprinkled flour in the shape of bunny tracks." She rolls her eyes. "Or left a pile of half-nibbled carrots on his trail? Or wait, let me guess, he pooped jelly beans in the yard again."

"Yep. All of that." I laugh, grateful she has held on to the memories.

"At least I have a new outfit." She leaves the bed to examine the spaghetti-strapped sundress we bought last weekend from Urban Outfitters, her favorite store. She steps into her closet to change, pairing it with a grungy pair of Converse sneakers she's decorated with various shades of Sharpie markers. Gone are the days of smocked cotton dresses and sweet spring sandals.

"I'm sure everybody's gonna think I'm crazy for wearing this to church."

"Who cares," I tell her. "Shoes are shoes. As long as you're safe. And happy."

She looks down, eyeing the skull-and-crossbones she's sketched across the rubber toe guards.

"Are you happy, Ellie?"

"Happy is a myth." She leaves me sitting on her bed, staring at her walls. They are covered in rock band posters and tween mementos. Next to her desk is a large bulletin board, pinned with photos of Ellie and Sarah. One is from an Easter egg hunt when they were about four years old. Ellie's tiny fingers curl around the wicker handle of her basket, and she stares up at the costumed bunny with full belief in her eyes. Sarah stands next to Ellie, equally in awe. Their baskets are filled with plastic eggs, candy, and stickers.

What I wouldn't give to turn back time. To cancel the field trip to New Orleans. To bring our girls back to a place of innocence. When happy was more than a myth.

Hello Sparrow,

It's Easter. I wonder what my family is doing.

The Man says I am never going home. That this is my home now. He works for a very bad boss who made him take me here. If I do everything The Man tells me to do, he'll make sure The Boss won't hurt me.

The Boss knows where Mom and Pop live. If I try to run away, he will kill them.

Every time The Man sees me looking at the door, he jerks my chin and says in a really mean voice, "Don't be stupid."

He says Ellie is here too, locked up like me. If I do everything he tells me, then he won't hurt Ellie. It's up to me. Because I'm his best girl.

I don't want him to kill Ellie. Or Mom and Pop. So I do whatever he tells me. What choice do I have?

Ellie, Carl, and I arrive early for Sunday school. I've agreed to help Beth place the Easter lilies. Ellie wants to give us a hand. As we enter the reception hall, Carl heads for the coffee station, where he bonds with the other men over sugar and sports. I walk past them, greeting the deacons as they down glazed doughnut holes. Half of them are talking about Tiger Woods and the upcoming Masters. Others swap baseball stats or hedge their bets for the NFL draft. Carl makes his rounds through each conversation, sounding off his predictions. The men circle him, eager for advice.

"Ellie?" Beth is in preacher-wife mode, focusing on the task at hand. "Why don't you take this into the sanctuary? You can start setting the flowers out. Anywhere you can find a place. We'll be right behind you."

"Yes, ma'am." Ellie pulls the cart filled with potted white lilies and makes her way to the sanctuary. Beth and I move into the church's small library. The room is stashed with flowers, wall to wall. In less than a minute, my allergies kick in. I sneeze. And sneeze. And sneeze again.

When I finally catch my breath, I ask Beth for any updates.

"None." She turns away and continues grouping flowers. "Unless you count the fact that Preacher wants to leave his job with the church."

I listen.

"The committee declined his resignation." She pulls one limp petal from a stalk and straightens a bow, looping the wired ribbon around her fingers for extra-wide volume. "I keep thinking he just needs a break, but he's sticking to his guns. The problem is neither of us has really been working since . . . since Sarah . . . The church has been very patient, but they've had to pay an interim, and they can't maintain Preacher's salary if he's not working. Plus, we've used so much money hiring private investigators, we're running out of savings. Something has to give."

"Does he have a plan? Another job in mind?" I take the flowerpot from her and set it on the cart. The fragrance makes my nose itch.

"His cousin. The one in Zachary. With the pool and spa business. Preacher has helped him out a few times. We figure he can do that for a while. At least until he makes a final decision."

"Might be good for him, Beth. Get outside. Sweat a little. Could help clear his mind."

"Yeah, I guess." After a silence, she opens up. "You know what I'm struggling with the most? It's Easter." She spins one of the pots in a circle, staring at the soil.

I load flowers onto a second cart and think of all the special Easters we shared with our girls.

"It's not the kids and their candy that's getting to me. You'd think that, but it's not. It's that I'm sitting here counting lilies. I mean, my daughter is out there, and we have no idea how to find her. And I'm sitting here counting lilies!"

She pulls a bloom from its long green stem and starts to cry. Not slow, quiet Beth tears, but a loud sobbing, an emotional outpouring. The kind I experience with my clients. The kind that means a heart is splintering and only darkness remains—a black pit where hope no longer lives.

I close the door of the library and move to Beth's side.

She yields, crying against my shoulder. This is what pain sounds like.

Between heavy breaths she says, "I'm supposed to be encouraging people to have faith. To believe in miracles and renewal and some Higher Power who watches over us. Who loves us." She laughs, looking up at the ceiling. "You call this love?"

Preacher opens the door just then, calling her name. Seeing his wife in shambles, he freezes, exposing his own anguish. Without another word, he steps back out into the hallway and closes the door behind him.

After skipping Sunday school, Beth and I have joined our husbands for the Easter service. Carl and I sit with Ellie midway back, while Beth and Preacher have opted for their regular place on the front pew. With only a few minutes left in the sermon, Preacher whispers into Beth's ear. Whatever he's told her causes her to frown. She's clearly questioning him. But then she softens, as if to grant him approval. With this, he rises and moves to the pulpit to shake Brother Johnson's hand, whispering to him as well. The reverend reacts with befuddlement, and a brief conversation ensues between the two men. Then Preacher takes the podium and delivers his news to the congregation.

"Today is Easter," he begins. "Many of you have spent the morning hunting eggs, opening chocolate bunnies, posing for photos. These are the kinds of days we look forward to. The special moments when we take notice of all the good in our lives. This year, as you know, Beth and I aren't dyeing eggs or filling baskets. But we take pleasure in seeing you celebrate this holiday with your loved ones. While we are suffering a great loss in our own lives, we do have many things to be grateful for today. Mainly, we are thankful for each of you. For the support you have shown our family in the last five months, and for the patience you have offered as I've been unable to lead the youth ministry the way I was called to do."

Preacher turns his attention to Beth and then continues. "Today I realized something. I realized that Beth and I can sit here in this pew and sing the hymns and say the prayers. But our hearts are no longer in it. We're broken. I don't know about Beth, but I can tell you something about me. I've got so little faith left at this point, I don't have enough to share anymore. I've decided to submit my resignation as your youth pastor. We appreciate your prayers as we continue to search for Sarah. Thank you."

May 2005

Hello Sparrow,

The Man scares me. He makes me do bad things. If I don't do what he says, he will kill Ellie. If I run away, he will kill my family. So I do what he wants.

He brought a guy here who gave me a tattoo. He told the guy to make it look like a dollar sign. It hurt a little when the needles went into my shoulder, but The Man told me not to cry. I am learning not to cry.

I wasn't crying because it hurt. I was crying because Pop always said that my body is a temple. And that I need to take care of myself because God lives in me. I hope Pop won't be sad when he sees the tattoo. Or when he finds out what else has been done to this temple.

One day, when I get out of here, I'm going to cover that dollar sign with something prettier. Maybe a feather.

"Can you believe it? Last day of sixth grade!" I hand Ellie a hand-written thank-you note with a gift certificate enclosed for one of Baton Rouge's nicest spas. "Be sure to give this to Miss Henderson. She's been so good to you."

Ellie adds the gift to her backpack. "She's not coming back next year. Did you hear?"

I nod. "This has been hard on everybody. You aren't the only one who blames yourself, Ellie. Miss Henderson feels like it's her fault for taking her class to New Orleans in the first place. I feel like it's my fault for not standing with y'all in line. Gator feels at fault for not getting you all back home safely. Mrs. Beth, for not staying the whole day. The restaurant manager has expressed guilt too. And Jay. He hasn't found her yet."

Ellie takes this in, and I hope, with all I have in me, that it eases her guilt.

"You going to the end-of-the-year party? With Nate?"

She shakes her head. No matter how much I encourage her, she has withdrawn from nearly all social interactions with her peers.

"Well then, how should we celebrate? Want to get a sno-cone after school? Go swimming? How about a movie? Just the two of us."

She shrugs. "To be honest, Mom, I'd rather come home and sleep."

"Are you sure? It's a beautiful day. What if we go shopping?

You need some new summer clothes. Could we go to that Asian restaurant you like? The one with the good spring rolls and sushi?"

"Maybe." She doesn't completely shut down this idea, so I stick with it.

"Perfect. I'll pick you up at noon for early dismissal, and we'll head straight to lunch and then to the mall." With this, I give her a hug and send her off to catch the bus. As she climbs the steps, I wave from the driveway, feeling an ache in my bones. No matter how hard I try, I can't give her childhood back to her.

"Morning." I enter my office in a rush and greet Vivienne. The two of us have shared a practice for the last ten years, and she hasn't aged a bit in that decade. "Can you at least have a bad hair day or something?" I tease. "That's all I'm asking. Some proof of imperfection."

Viv is toned and tanned, with the trademark Cajun beauty common in Louisiana. In addition to her good looks and petite frame, she carries the Acadian French lilt to her speech and moves through the world with graceful steps. "Oh please," she says, not looking up from her computer. "You're one to talk." She finally glances my way. "I'm registering for my first marathon."

"Of course you are." I smile.

"Turning forty," she sighs. "I won't go down without a fight."

I drop my purse on my desk and head for the electric kettle. I find it already filled. And heating. "Viv, you are so thoughtful!"

"Brought you some new kinds of tea too." She taps her keyboard. "In the cabinet."

"You didn't." I pull a box from the shelf where she's stashed three new cartons.

"They were in the clearance bin at Carter's. Apparently you're the only person who drinks that stuff."

I laugh and opt for something new, Oolong Pomegranate. "Want a cup?"

She declines, so I pour her some Community Coffee instead.

"I'm taking off early, don't forget. It's Ellie's last day of school, and we're going to celebrate."

"How's she doing?" She gives me her full attention as I bring her coffee.

"Honestly, I don't know, Viv. I'm still worried. All she wants to do is sleep. She's stopped hanging out with friends. She sits in her room listening to music and drawing. Just her and Beanie."

"How's Carl handling that?"

"Oh, you know Carl. He's not the kind to talk about things. He thinks she's fine. And I'm overreacting."

"Do you think you're overreacting?" She looks at me now as if I'm her client.

"No." I hold my mug in two hands, and the steam rises between us.

"Trust your gut, Amanda. You know a lot more about this stuff than Carl does."

"Maybe so, but that's the problem. He thinks I try to diagnose everybody. That I want to send everyone to counseling."

"What's wrong with that?" She laughs.

"Forty, huh?" I bow, pretending to worship her beauty. "I'm thirty-five and wish I looked half as good as you do. I honestly can't understand how you manage to stay single."

"I'm waiting for The One," she says with a smile. "I won't settle for less."

"But he won't stop. You don't understand." My client is shaking, wiping her eyes with a crumpled Kleenex that hangs in shreds from her hand. "I had to call 911. I had to run. He was going to kill me this time."

"Tell me what happened." I keep my voice calm, steady, and offer no judgment, although pieces of me want to rush from my office and nail her husband to the wall. Mrs. Evans is all of five feet tall and ninety-five pounds after a holiday feast. There's nothing about her that feels threatening, not her soft voice or her kind eyes or her fragile frame. For any man to use violence against her reflects the worst form of cowardice, in my opinion. It's hard for me not to tell her what I'm thinking. But I don't. I listen.

"He came home in a rage again. I was taking a nap because I'd been running a fever, just a little cold turned bad, but I never do that. I never sleep during the day. Only Monday, I did. And he came home early, and the kids were outside playing like they always do. They're old enough, you know. And I woke up with him carrying on about how lazy I am. He was screaming and shouting, going off about how he's out working and I'm home sleeping. Before I knew it he had broken everything in our den. Everything. Glass everywhere. Throwing everything he could reach. Throwing it right at me."

"He was throwing things at you?"

"Everything. Yes. The vases, the pictures. Everything he could grab. I was on the couch, just sitting there, covering my head, trying not to move."

"Did he throw his stuff too? Break anything important to him?"

She pauses. Considers. "You know? Now that I think about it, he broke everything around him except his guitar. It was hanging right there on the wall. He never touched it. It's got marks all over it, from glass and wood flying up and scratching it. But you're right. He didn't break his guitar."

I nod. "So he was more in control than you think?"

She takes this in. Then continues. "I know it sounds crazy. But I knew if I as much as looked him in the eye, I was dead."

"Can you tell me more about that? How you knew?"

"It's hard to explain. But I've never felt anything like that before. It was a bad feeling. A very bad feeling. You ever see those TV shows, about lions and stuff over there in Africa?"

I nod.

"Well, you can see it in their eyes, you know? Those zebras or whatever they're stalking, they know they're about to die. The lion is in kill mode, and they're the prey, and there's nothing they can do about it. But they run anyway, because what else can they do? Well, I was the zebra. Only I knew I couldn't outrun him. So I sat there real still, and I let him throw his fit. And I thought to myself, *I'm not going to look at him, or cry, or make a sound. I'm going to stay still and pray.* And that's what I did. I prayed. *God, I've got babies. They're right outside playing. They need me. And they need their daddy too. So please, God. Don't let him do anything crazy. Don't let him hurt me. Keep us safe. All of us.*"

I allow myself a little time before responding. Then I ask, "Do you believe God kept you safe?" I try not to sound snide.

"Yes." She says this without the slightest sign of disbelief.

I, on the other hand, have enough doubt for us both. No telling how many times a woman has prayed for God to save her, just before her head gets bashed in. I've seen these abusive relationships play out, and it's all I can do not to tell her it takes a whole lot more than prayer to survive them. I try to get us back to something real. "So how do you feel about what happened?"

"I feel scared. I'm scared he'll do it again, only next time I might not live to tell about it. It seems like he's getting worse."

"That's very serious," I tell her. "Most people don't feel afraid of their husbands. They aren't afraid for their lives. You should listen to that voice, Mrs. Evans. Maybe that's God's voice. Telling you to protect yourself. To protect your children."

She listens, stays quiet.

"What your husband is doing to you is wrong. You've told me this kind of explosion has happened more than once. That's not okay. It's abusive."

The word *abusive* seems to set her off. "I'm probably making it sound worse than it is." She defends him. "He's never touched me. I don't have a mark on me. See?" She lifts her arms, proving she has no bruises or scars.

"He threw things at you. He scared you. He yelled at you. And it sounds like he said some pretty awful things too."

She shrugs.

"What did he say to you?" I am taking notes. I've learned to document when a client tells me about violent episodes.

"Oh, I don't remember." She isn't comfortable with my pen. She leans and pulls another Kleenex from the carton. Then she wipes her eyes, collecting herself.

"Do you remember anything he said? Anything at all?"

With reluctance, she fills in the blanks. "I don't know. The kind of stuff he always says, how I'm lazy and stupid and insane. All that. It's mostly a blur now."

"You know, Mrs. Evans, it's not unusual for an abuser to manipulate his victim into thinking she's crazy. That's part of the emotional abuse." The word still draws resistance, so I lean closer. "Or it could be that he doesn't understand how you feel. And so he says you're crazy."

She gives me a pensive look, as if she's truly processing what I'm saying to her.

"But that's his problem. Not yours." I continue. "Think of it this way. Let's say you have a terrible pain in your ear. So you go to the doctor, and he runs every test available. They all show up negative. He scratches his head. He's got no idea what is causing your pain. So he decides there's nothing wrong with you. He can't understand it, so you must be crazy."

"It happens."

"It does." I sit back. Let it simmer. "It happens every day." Then I make sure it sticks. "You aren't crazy, Mrs. Evans. And what your husband does to you is considered abuse. You are in an abusive relationship. So let's talk about what you want to do about that."

By noon I'm waiting in line to pick up Ellie from her last day of sixth grade. As she comes to the front of the school, a few kids come running, chanting, "We survived! We survived!" They say this with smiles, eager for summer break, but the cheer brings tears from my Ellie.

Grabbing her backpack, I wrap my arm around her, trying to shield her from any more pain. We hurry to the car, where she collapses in grief. I drive away from the crowded campus as quickly as possible and pull into an empty lot where a concrete slab and driveway have been poured for a new home. At the moment no construction workers are on-site, and we find the privacy we need.

"Ellie?" I keep the car running, trying to combat the day's heat with air-conditioning. "Honey?" I reach for her hand, and she lets me hold it. "I'm listening. Please talk to me."

"She's not coming back, is she? That's what people say. They say Sarah's never coming back."

"They don't know that, Ellie. We are still trying our best to find her. We won't give up. I assure you."

"But what if we can't find her, Mom? What if she's dead?"

I sit in silence and let Ellie's sorrow find its way to the surface. She talks. I listen. And for the first time since The Day, we both begin to accept the truth.

"You know what I think, Mom? I think even if she does come back, it'll never be the same. So either way, she's gone for good."

July 2005

"We're heading out. Come with?" I tie my tennis shoes and try to convince Ellie to join Beth and me for a walk.

"No." She doesn't look up from the couch, where she's pretty much been camped since the end of school. She's got a pile of books to read, a glass of sweet tea, and the remote control. She changes channels faster than she can possibly tell what's showing.

"Come on, Ellie. You'll feel so much better if you get some fresh air with us."

"No." She says it louder, in a low monotone. Her message is clear. She won't join us.

"All right then. See you in a bit." I give her a kiss. Beth follows me out the door. "I still hesitate to leave her alone. I know I have to stop thinking that way."

"Is it better now? Since you cleared your summer clients to stay home with her?"

"I don't know. I mean, I feel better being here, but now she says I'm smothering her."

"Carl still won't let her get a dog? It might be just what she needs. Maybe a Lab, like Boudreaux."

"He won't budge. We're lucky he tolerates Beanie."

Beth says nothing, and I let it go. We walk in silence for a while, down our rural lane that runs long and flat like a landing strip between the open ditches. On each side, crawfish chimneys dot the yards, puffy white towers of mud where they've burrowed into the wet soil. As we pass the last of the small brick houses on my street, we turn onto a wooded trail. We're barely ten yards from the road when a large doe snorts loudly, a guttural warning to other white-tailed deer in the area. In response, Beth breathes deeply, as if she's glad to have something to distract her from grief. We continue walking, despite the mosquitoes, each of us working up a sweat. Last autumn's pinecones and sweetgum balls crunch beneath our feet as the bright summer leaves shine green. We weave our way through the sturdy, thick trunks of hickories and honey locusts, cedars and sycamores, until we come into a towering pine grove with a few thick-leaved magnolias tucked around the edge. The evening sun streams through the tops of the pines, turning the needled carpet a burnt orange beneath our feet. The air smells of barbecue, and I'm guessing one of my neighbors has lit their backyard grill for supper. To everyone but us, it's just a normal day.

"People like to say this is God's plan. That he doesn't give us anything we can't handle," Beth says as pine needles wave in the wind, the air whistling crisp notes between their wire-thin tips.

"I never like it when people say those things. Do you?"

"Truthfully?" The act of speaking seems to be taking all she has to give. "It's hard to hear. I'm still angry, Amanda. And the longer this goes on, the madder I get. Why would God let this happen? Not just to Sarah, but to anyone? To any child. I don't understand."

I can't give Beth the answers, so I stay quiet.

"Preacher and I always thought we could handle anything that happened to us. Our faith was unshakable. But now . . ."

I wait in silence, grateful Beth still allows me to be a part of her life.

"Back when we were in the early years of ministry, we met a young mother who had just lost all three of her children. It was a house fire," Beth says. "Remember?"

I nod. The family had not lived in Walker long before the tragedy, but it made the front page of the *Livingston Parish News*. "How could I forget?"

"And to make matters worse, it was her husband who had set the fire. He burned down the house with his own children locked inside. Didn't want her to have custody, so he killed them all. It was one of the worst things I've ever seen. Preacher and I were so young. We had no idea how to help her."

I shake my head. I can't imagine.

"We sat up with her all night in our living room. She cried out again and again, 'Why would God do this to us?' Preacher said, 'It's okay to be angry at God. He can take it. And it's okay to blame God. He can take that too.' The woman said, 'I do blame him. I do.' And what could I say to her? I wasn't even a mother yet. I couldn't possibly begin to fathom her loss. Everything I thought to tell her sounded so trite. I was afraid she was going to take her own life, right there in front of us. I've never seen anyone so broken, not before or since." She releases a gentle sigh and then adds, "Not even you and me."

I pull a palm-sized piece of bark from one of the pines. "What happened to her? The mother?"

"She moved back down to Grand Isle where her parents lived. But when Sarah disappeared she saw it on the news, and she reached out to us. She said there wasn't much she remembered about that night when her kids were killed, but one thing Preacher said had always stuck with her. Had seen her through the worst of it all."

I wait for Beth to explain.

"He told her, 'If you want to ask God, "Why me? Why my children?" that's okay. Ask him. Because his son was killed too. That's what the crucifixion is really about. God stands with us through our suffering. The loss. The pain. He understands.'"

"I guess I never thought of it that way," I admit.

"The woman said, 'Every time I start to feel hopeless, as if there is no longer a reason to live, as if God is against me and I'll never be okay again, I remind myself that life is not all we think it to be, that there is more to the journey. Much more than we can understand.'"

I look up into the straight, thin pine needles striped against the sky, their lines like ribs inhaling and exhaling with each pulse of wind. "Is that still what you believe? Since Sarah?"

Beth follows my stare to the heavens and exhales loudly. "I don't know."

Hello Sparrow,

I asked The Man if I could see Ellie. He hit me. He said I wasn't being good enough, and that Ellie was going to be put in the box because of me. I didn't cry, even though blood was all around my eye. He said The Boss is mad at me. I have to do everything they tell me, even when the other men come to visit. I have to stop fighting. I will try.

Hello Sparrow,

The day I was taken, we met a lady by the big church in New Orleans. She gave me a feather—the one I think might be yours—and she told me to guard it.

When we walked away, she shouted, "God's eye is on the sparrow." Mom and Pop taught me that in Bible times sparrows were sold for cheap. The verse means that even when other people don't care about us, God does.

I think the lady in New Orleans was saying God's eye is on me. That I'm worth caring about, even here, where nobody thinks I matter at all.

So I was thinking about God and the palm reader and the feather, and then I figured something out. Now when the men come, and when they make me do all those things I don't want to do, I leave the shed. I fly away. Just like the lady said. I fly right out of my body, and no one even knows I'm gone.

Hello Sparrow,

I learned a new trick today. If I fly all the way across the yard, past the willow tree, past The Man's house, past the other shed where he says he keeps Ellie, past the muddy palmettos, then I can see the water. I call it the ocean, but it's really just a swamp.

If I make it all the way to my ocean, I can let the men do whatever they want to me in here and I don't even have to know it. I don't come back until I hear them leave.

Can you see me flying out there by my ocean? There's a pretty blue crane and a bunch of doves. Turtles and snakes too. But the snakes aren't scary from way up high. I bet you know that.

The men come a lot now. More and more of them. Some come on their way to work at the plants. Sometimes they talk about their wives or kids. I don't know why they come here. Some of them use drugs or drink beer. Some don't. Some are mean. Some are not. One man cries when he leaves. I heard The Man call one of them a senator. He wore a suit, and when The Man left us all alone, the senator just sat in the broken chair and looked at me. Then he left.

Chapter 11

"Ellie, please don't fight me on this. Vivienne's been very helpful so far, and I think if we just stick with it—"

My daughter turns up her stereo, blasting Green Day over my voice. I stand at her bedroom door, waiting for her to turn my way. She doesn't. So I move closer, and she spins sharply toward me. "I'm not going!"

When I turn down the volume, she yells again. "Why can't you leave me alone?"

"Ellie, I'm just trying to help."

"Don't you see? That's your problem! You try to fix everybody. You want to save us all. You really want to help me? Then stay out of my life!"

Don't react, Amanda. These are Carl's words, not Ellie's. She's just repeating what she hears.

When she settles on her bed with Beanie, I leave her room. Then, while folding a basket of laundry, I make the call. "Viv? She won't come." I apologize for the last-minute notice. "Maybe she needs some breathing room. I don't know what more we can do."

"Of course," Vivienne says. "Just let me know when she's ready. Seventh grade is a hard year. Even in the best of circumstances."

"I'm at a loss, Viv. I feel like I can help everyone else I meet, but

I can't seem to reach my own daughter. She won't take calls from her friends. She won't go anywhere. All she wants to do is sleep. Theater's the only reason I could even get her back in school this year. She's really struggling."

"Do you think she might need an antidepressant? Just for a little while? Get her over the slump?"

"I don't know. Carl says no way. He thinks it's ridiculous. Meds. Therapy. All of it."

"With the right prescription, I've seen it make a big difference," Vivienne says. "Haven't you?"

"For some, yes. For others, it seems worse. Scares me a little, to be honest. She's just twelve."

"I understand." Vivienne waits through my silence and then says, "Amanda? How are you holding up?"

"I'm good, I guess. Just trying to keep the ship from sinking."

"Be sure you're giving yourself the care you need too. You know how important that is. In fact, why not use Ellie's time today? Come in for coffee? Even if we just go for a walk. I need it as much as you do."

"Oh, I don't know." I look down the hall toward Ellie's door. The music still blares from her room. "I'm hesitant to leave her alone like this. As much as I'd love to see you. Rain check?"

"Sure," Vivienne says. "I'll hold you to that, though. I'm ready for you to come back to work. I worry."

"Thanks, Viv. No worries allowed."

I hang up the phone and call Carl. He answers on the second ring, surprising me. "Hey. I figured I'd have to leave a message."

"Yeah, I was just about to call you. Got a hurricane near Florida.

They've been shorthanded, so I'm flying out to the rig. Helping with the shutdown."

"Think it'll turn our way?"

"Probably not. You know how it goes. We'll stop production. Ship everyone back home. And then it'll slow to a tropical depression. End up being nothing more than a thunderstorm."

"Well, be careful." After a pause I say, "Ellie's not doing well, Carl. She's refusing to go to school today. She won't see Vivienne, and she's really lashing out at me."

As soon as I try to talk to him about Ellie, his mood shifts. His tone becomes darker, angrier, and his words leave bite marks. "I can't do this right now, Amanda. I'm busy."

"I understand. I'm sorry." After another awkward pause I add, "It's okay. I know you're busy. I love you. Be safe."

He says, "Bye." And he is gone.

Hello Sparrow,

You are tapping fast and loud, trying to warn me about something. I think I know why.

I heard The Man say we're supposed to get out of town before the hurricane hits. But he thinks we should stay here in Chalmette.

The Lady says it's supposed to get bad. She knows where an empty house is. In Hammond. She says it never floods there.

Fly with me, Sparrow. Don't stay here in the storm.

"Knock, knock!" Raelynn walks into my house singing the words. She enters from the back carport, as any good friend would do, and finds me in the kitchen washing blueberries.

"You're off today?"

"Dentist. Figured I'd take a sick day. Brought y'all some étouffée. Hungry?"

I greet her with a hug and take the two warm Tupperware dishes, setting them on the kitchen counter. "Starving," I say, pulling out enough bowls and spoons to serve the three of us. "Would you mind asking Ellie to come to the table? She's not speaking to me. Maybe she'll be nicer to you."

"She's not at school?"

I shake my head, too sad to admit I can't get my daughter to leave her room. Raelynn accepts the challenge, making her way toward the back while I fill our bowls with scoops of rice and then smother them with her rich, roux-based crawfish sauce. The smells of sautéed bell peppers, onions, and celery fill my home. It's a combination folks here call the Holy Trinity. When mixed with just the right pop of seasonings, it really can bring a soul straight to heaven.

I've set the table and poured three drinks by the time Raelynn returns. "She won't come."

I sigh. Grabbing a TV tray, I carry Ellie's food to her room.

"Ellie?" I call through her closed door. The music is lower now, but still playing. She's moved from Green Day to the *Donnie Darko* soundtrack, playing "Mad World" on repeat. I've told my clients so many times, *If you want to understand what a teenager is feeling, pay attention to their music.* Now here I stand, with my daughter closed off from me, listening to the saddest lyrics I have ever heard.

I set the tray down and open her door. "Ellie? Honey, Raelynn brought crawfish étouffée."

She is lying facedown across her bed. Doesn't even acknowledge I'm in the room.

"Okay, well. I'll leave it here for you. Try to eat while it's warm."

I stand for a few seconds, wishing I knew how to reach her. "I love you. I'm here when you're ready to talk."

Back at the table, Raelynn has waited for me to join her. "You hear about that hurricane?"

"Yeah. Carl's on his way out to the rig. They needed extra help shutting down. Says it's just a Cat 1 though. Probably won't do much damage. He should be home tonight."

"I don't know. The news says it's gaining strength. Heading our way now. We could get a direct hit." She fills her spoon. "Might want to keep an eye on the weather."

I turn on the TV. Carl has set it up so that we can watch it from the dining room table, something I would normally discourage. But not today.

We watch the noon broadcast. The station's chief meteorologist tells us the hurricane is "rapidly strengthening" as it crosses the warm Gulf of Mexico. The storm has intensified to a Category 2. Named Katrina. Our governor, Kathleen Blanco, is already taking proactive measures by declaring a state of emergency for Louisiana.

"Hope Carl doesn't have any trouble getting home." I stir my étouffée and take a bite. "Delicious. Thank you. Just what I needed."

Raelynn smiles, enjoying hers as well. "The boys are going to be upset. My brother got alligator tags. Planned to leave after school for a weekend hunt."

I'm talking hurricane stories with Raelynn when my crisis

phone rings. Recognizing the name as one of my most at-risk clients, I excuse myself. "I need to take this."

"Mrs. Amanda?"

I step outside. "Yes, it's me. How are you, Brooke?" When she doesn't answer, I ask, "Are you crying?" I take a seat in one of our back porch rocking chairs, giving her my full attention.

"I'm sorry. I didn't know who else to call." She's definitely crying.

"You can always call me, Brooke. What's wrong?"

"I can't do this anymore. It's too hard. One year today. And I just can't handle it. I'm scared."

"Where are you?"

"Home."

"Are you alone?"

"Yes."

"Okay, is there anyone who can be with you? What about your sister?"

"She's supposed to come over later. I don't want to bother her. She's got two kids. She's busy," Brooke sniffles.

"She's not too busy, Brooke. She loves you."

"I know, I know. But she's tired of seeing me like this. Everybody is. I should be able to get over it. It's too hard."

"Brooke, this is a very hard day. But you'll get through it. Just like you made it through the other hard days. And think about all the good days you've had in between."

"I can't see the good anymore, Mrs. Amanda. That's the problem. You understand? Even the good isn't good."

"You're depressed, Brooke. You're having a difficult day. But it'll get better. I promise. It always does."

"Not this time. I keep staring at the medicine cabinet. Trying to find a reason not to swallow all those pills."

"Brooke, listen to me. That's not an option. You have too many people who love you and who need you here in this life. You're looking for a permanent fix, but this is not a permanent problem. It's temporary. You will get through this. And you'll feel so much better. You'll be glad you didn't swallow those pills."

"You don't understand."

"I may not understand how you're feeling, you're right. But I've heard too many people tell me how happy they are they made it through the hard part. And some of them barely made it, Brooke. They saw no reason to live. They felt just like you're feeling right this minute. But they hung in there, and now they're glad. Able to play with their kids, their grandkids. Go to the beach. Sometimes it's the littlest things they notice."

Brooke is crying louder now as a television blares from her side of the phone. "Like what?"

"Like crawfish boils. A good movie. A concert. Even a nice, quiet night at home. Alone. They don't see that as scary anymore, Brooke."

"I hate being alone."

"That's because you can't see the truth right now, that's all. Your brain is confused. It can only see the lies. But you're going to feel better. You are here for a reason. And you owe it to yourself to stick it out and see what this journey is all about."

"Mrs. Amanda, I want to die."

"Okay, listen. We need to find a way to get you through the next few minutes. I'm going to call your sister. I want you to stay on the phone with me and listen while I call her."

I carry my cell phone inside the house and dial the number on my landline. "You still with me?" I gesture, and Raelynn gives us privacy.

"I guess," Brooke whispers. I make the call, telling her sister to go right away and be with Brooke.

"Okay, did you hear? She's on her way. She loves you, Brooke. She'll be with you soon. Stay on the phone with me until she gets there."

"Okay."

"She's going to take all the medicine out of your home. Okay?"

"Okay."

"Do you have any guns?"

"No."

"I'm going to stay on the phone with you. We'll get you through this. I promise. You're not alone."

"Thank you. I'm sorry. Thank you."

She keeps repeating these phrases through her tears, again and again, until her sister arrives. "Brooke, listen to me. I've told your sister to call 911 if she thinks for a single second that you are in danger. I'm also going to call the sheriff and have one of his deputies come by. We're going to get you through this. I will call to check in with you every hour, okay?"

"Okay."

"And if you want to call me in between those check-ins, I'm here. You understand?"

"Yes. Thank you. I'm sorry." Her voice is a whimper now.

"Brooke, you have no reason to apologize. Thank you for calling me. Thank you for caring about me and your sister and all the people who love you and want to help you. Thank you for not hurting yourself, because if you do that, you'll hurt us."

When Brooke's sister assures me she's got things under control, Raelynn joins me again at the table. "I don't know how you do it," she says. "That job would really get to me."

I think for a few minutes and then I tell her a story. "When I was doing my practicum for my master's degree, I had a client who had survived a suicide attempt. When I read his file, I was expecting to meet a broken kind of guy. But he came in whistling. I remember my mentor said to him, 'You seem very happy today.' And the guy said, 'I am.' He said that the day he tried to kill himself, he sat in front of Walmart for three hours trying to talk himself out of it. He sat right there on the bench, almost in tears, and thought, *If one person smiles at me, I won't do it. That'll be a good enough reason to live.* But in those three hours, nobody did. You know how many people go in and out of Walmart in the span of three hours? But everybody walked right past him, looking down at their phones or off in the distance, pretending he wasn't there at all. He felt invisible. As if he were already dead. So he figured, what's the point? And he went home and he did it. And only by the grace of God did he live to tell us that story. So from that moment on, I decided I never want to be the one who walks by and doesn't smile. I want to be the one who makes everybody feel glad to be alive. To let them know they matter."

Chapter 12

CARL MAKES IT HOME AT ABOUT 3:00 A.M. I WAKE TO THE SOUND of the shower and wait for him to join me in bed. When he finally climbs under the covers, he stays on his side of the mattress.

I move closer, rubbing my bare legs against his, pressing my body into the curve of his own. "It's good to have you home," I say. He smells clean, carrying the floral undertones of soap and shampoo, and his muscular arms feel warm against me. I rest my head on his shoulder and breathe him in.

"You touched the thermostat? It's burning up in here."

"Of course not, Carl. You know I never mess with the temperature."

He sighs. "Don't lie."

I don't bother trying to convince him. "Was it bad out there?"

"Stronger than I thought it'd be." He jerks the covers down and moves away.

"Looks like a big one, from the radars. But still just a Cat 2, right?"

"Think so. Let's get some sleep." He rolls over, turning his back to me. I try not to feel rejected.

"Carl?"

He offers a half mumble, showing he's not in the mood to talk. I want to tell him about Brooke, how she came back to her senses and called to thank me for talking her away from the medicine cabinet. Instead, I say, "I hope you know how much we appreciate you, all you do for us."

I fall asleep trying hard to count my blessings.

Sunday, August 28, 2005

"This hurricane hit Category 5 as it strengthened over the Gulf," Brother Johnson says from the pulpit during early-morning worship. Only a handful of devoted families are here. The rest have stayed home on account of the storm.

He adjusts his glasses and clears his throat. "We're expecting winds of 120 miles per hour, with even stronger gusts. Plus, a surge of at least ten to fifteen feet of water along the coast. Some say higher. This is serious, folks." He peers out to the back pew. "To those of you who have joined us today from the evacuation zones, welcome to Walker. We'll do all we can to make this a home for you until you can return to your own."

A few unfamiliar visitors nod. The rest of us acknowledge them with welcoming smiles and even some handshakes from regulars near the back.

"We're expecting Mayor Nagin to announce a mandatory evacuation in New Orleans any minute now. It's the first time in history, so that should tell you something. The roads leaving the city have been bumper-to-bumper for days. And the interstates are now under contraflow order, so if you're thinking about heading east for any reason, scratch those plans. Hotels are overflowing. People are making camp in parking lots, under the overpasses, pretty much anywhere they can find a place to stop. We've announced that our church will serve as a sanctuary for anyone in need, and we ask that our congregation help provide food and shelter for these families."

Ellie scribbles on the paper bulletin and then draws a hangman with a row of blanks for me to guess her secret phrase. I write my letters, one at a time, and she responds by either filling in the appropriate blank or adding a body part to the noose. As the minister gives the podium over to the choir director, my letters begin to morph into words: I __OPE T_E STOR_ _ITS _S

I write the letters *H, M,* and *U.* As the small congregation finishes singing "How Great Thou Art," Ellie shows me the complete phrase, in all caps: I HOPE THE STORM HITS US.

When Brother Johnson returns to the pulpit, he gives us an update. "With the storm coming closer, we're going to dismiss early and let you all go on home. I'm sure you've already stocked up on extra food and water. Be sure to have reserve fuel for your generators and plenty of batteries for your flashlights. We could be without power and water for a long time, so have some candles and matches . . . a weather radio." Then he waves his hand. "Y'all know what to do."

Looking toward Carl, he then says, "Brother Salassi, would you lead us in the benediction. We could use a good one. This storm, Katrina, she's a doozie."

Carl stands and leads us in the closing prayer, and then we head out to our cars, shaking Brother Johnson's hand on the way.

Beth and Preacher meet us just outside the sanctuary. The wind is building strength around the steeple. Beth is frantic. "What if Sarah's been there all this time, Amanda? In New Orleans? What if she's evacuating? She could end up at a shelter. She could be parked at one of the gas stations right now. This could be our chance. We've got to go look."

"I was thinking the same thing," I admit. Carl stands with his arm around my shoulders, smiling and greeting other church friends. "Let me get Ellie home with Carl. Once they've eaten, I'll head out with you and Preacher. Sound good?"

"We're going now," Beth says, shaking her head. "I can't wait."

She shifts uneasily as I look at Carl. I hope he'll say he doesn't mind me joining my friends. That he won't be bothered fixing Ellie a sandwich and taking care of the storm preparation without me. But he says nothing, so I smile at Beth and hope she understands.

"Just call when you're ready, Amanda. I'll update you."

"Morning." Jay joins us, giving Ellie a handshake like she's one of the adults. "Did I hear you say you're going to the evacuation sites?"

"She could be there. Don't you think?" Beth's hopes are growing higher, despite the doubt in Preacher's eyes.

Jay's voice shows concern. "The weather could really get rough, Beth. Maybe y'all should stay here where it's safe. My guys will be out there, and we'll be keeping our eyes open."

"But I want to be out there too, Jay. I need to look with my own eyes."

Children run around the church grounds, squealing and tugging at their Sunday clothes, excited to be released. Ellie stands beside us, quiet, solemn, watching the sky. Women pass by, offering Jay flirtatious smiles. He thanks one of them for the casserole she brought to his house last week. No one reacts. He's been the town's most eligible bachelor for far too long, and we've all grown accustomed to the interest he draws.

He shifts his attention back to us. "Interstates are westbound only, Beth. Other roads will be at a standstill too. You'll spend hours stuck in traffic."

She turns to Preacher for support. He sighs.

"If it gets closer, they'll end up closing the roads completely," Jay says. "You could get stuck at one of those evacuation sites."

Carl pulls his arm a little tighter around my shoulders, drawing me closer into him with his chin raised high. "What'd I tell you, Amanda?" Then he speaks to the group. "Y'all know my wife. She doesn't always think things through." He laughs, as if it's a joke. As if I'm a joke.

I offer my daughter a half smile, hoping no man ever makes her feel like this. She stares at me, a hollow gaze.

"Tell you what," Jay says to the group. "Why don't y'all stay here at the church. You'll be safe, and who's to say Sarah won't end up here?"

"Jay's right," Preacher says. "I'll send an e-mail to all the pastors, asking them to distribute fliers at evacuation sites in their communities. And I'll make sure they keep their eyes open. Jay, can you do the same with law enforcement?"

"Of course," Jay says. "I'm on it."

"This makes sense." Preacher tries to sway his wife's stance. "At least until the storm passes."

Beth turns to the reception hall. A few families are already unloading sleeping bags and suitcases from their cars. Toting pet carriers and children, they make their way into the sturdy building. "We'll get her photos out to every site? Every one of them, right?"

Jay and Preacher both insist this can be done. And will.

After a long look to the sky, Beth reluctantly agrees.

"All right. Looks like y'all have things taken care of here," Carl says. "We'd better get home."

Beth hesitates, then gives in, offering me a long hug as I reassure her.

"I'll be a mile away," I say. "Call if you need anything. Anything at all."

With that, Carl pulls me from the group and gives them all a hearty farewell. Ellie trails behind us. "Mom, why are we leaving? If Sarah might come here, shouldn't we wait for her?"

My husband climbs into the driver's seat, unlocking our doors from his control panel.

"Carl?" I plead with my eyes. "These people are going to need help anyway. Someone will have to cook for them. And you can see Beth needs moral support. Why don't we go home, take care of a few things, and then head back here? Do our part?"

"Amanda, you know as well as I do, Sarah's not going to show up here. It's a waste of time. We've got our own issues to worry about."

"What issues, Carl? What issues do we have to worry about? Our daughter is with us. She's safe. We're not in the strike zone for this storm. Look at Beth and Preacher. Look at those families over there. We aren't the ones with any problems."

"Well, I live in the real world, Amanda. And in the real world, we've got patio furniture to tie down, windows to secure, and a utility room door to barricade. So if you want to sit around the church all day and convince yourself these people need you, then go ahead. Suit yourself. But I'll be taking care of our family. The one you seem to ignore more and more each day."

When we leave church, Carl drives to fill our extra fuel containers at the gas station. From here, we can see that the I-12 overpass is at a standstill, packed with refugees who have fled the coastal parishes. The two main gas stations in Walker have as many as twenty vehicles in line for each lane, and handwritten signs already declare *Empty!* on a few of the pumps.

"This is pointless. No way am I waiting in line." Carl turns the car around and we head home.

"Carl, there won't be enough rooms for all those refugees. We should go tell them they can stay at the church. They'll end up stranded."

"Refugees?" He looks at me as if I've lost my mind. "Do you know how much we have to do?" His word is final. He keeps driving. "I swear, Amanda. Why can't you ever just shut up and look pretty?"

My stomach spins into a tightened knot, but I stay silent, looking back to Ellie with a smile. I hear my mother's voice again. *He doesn't mean it, Amanda. He's got a lot on his mind and he doesn't handle stress well. It's not his fault.*

At home Carl turns on the television while I start a quick batch of dirty rice. From the living room, the weatherman's voice delivers stern warnings, reaching me in the kitchen as I chop vegetables, brown the meats, and boil water for rice.

"Hurricane Katrina . . . Devastating damage expected . . . Unprecedented strength . . . Most of the area will be uninhabitable for weeks . . . All gabled roofs will fail . . . All windows will blow out . . . Livestock exposed to the winds will be killed . . . Power outages for weeks . . . Water shortages will make human suffering incredible by modern standards . . ."

This last sentence brings me to the living room. "They're really starting to sound as if this could be a big one," I tell Carl. "Think we should board up the windows? Fill the tubs with water?"

"We can tape up, fill the tubs. But I'm not worried. It's their job to build hype."

I glance out the window. Nothing more than normal afternoon winds. "But did you hear what they said about water shortages? I've never heard them talk like that."

"'Human suffering incredible by modern standards.'" He imitates the news report and scoffs. "Makes a good headline."

On-screen a ticker scrolls at the bottom, flashing the words CATASTROPHIC HURRICANE EXPECTED.

Then they switch to a live feed of Mayor Nagin. Just as Brother Johnson predicted, he's announcing the first-ever mandatory evacuation of New Orleans and opening the Superdome as a shelter for those unable to leave the city.

As soon as the announcement is made, my phone rings. It's Beth. "Did you hear? They're telling people to go to the Superdome. Sarah could end up there. Amanda, this could be our chance. I can feel it."

"How can I help?" I ask, tossing in some cayenne, salt, and pepper as I sauté the bell peppers, garlic, and green onions. "I can send e-mails. Call the news stations. What should I do?"

"Take care of your family, and I'll keep you posted," she says. "Otherwise, for now, just pray."

"Looks to me like it's turning east," Carl says. It's been a tense day, but now that all the storm prep has been taken care of, he's finally able to relax. We climb into bed while the local weatherman tracks the storm on-screen. "It'll miss us completely. What'd I tell you?"

But the news reporters don't seem convinced. They broadcast from New Orleans, interviewing locals who have chosen to stay home despite the mandatory evacuation orders.

"I ain't for that leaving," says a middle-aged woman with a thick New Orleans accent. "I rode out Betsy, and I'm gonna stay right here."

The camera then shows footage from the early-evening broadcasts, with long lines of people going into the Superdome. "We're trying to spread the word," says the correspondent. "Many people can't evacuate. They don't have transportation or the means to leave. A lot of them are elderly or ill or they simply have nowhere to go. As you can see, many are coming here to the dome."

The camera zooms out for live footage within the Superdome. "We have food and water here. And if you look behind me, you'll notice the atmosphere is calm and peaceful. This building was designed to sustain winds higher than a Category 3, so it's a safe place."

Then the anchor asks a few questions, and the field reporter tells us the rains started around seven thirty tonight. They cut to scenes of empty city streets as locals have hunkered down, ready for the worst. Heavy rains and winds are shown, but the brunt of the hurricane hasn't yet reached New Orleans.

"This is the calm before the storm. Some parts of the city are six feet below sea level," the reporter says, reminding me of Miss Henderson's field trip lessons and The Day. "If the levees fail, waters could fill the city like a soup bowl. Especially low-lying areas."

The screen then returns to the woman who is refusing to leave her home in the Lower Ninth Ward, an area that has been known to flood. "Get prayed up," she says. "That's all we can do."

As the news shifts back to Baton Rouge, the local weatherman suggests we may get lucky, saying the storm will likely stay east of our capital city. "Nothing we can't handle," Carl says. "Now, come here and let me show you what a real storm feels like."

I laugh, letting him pull me close, glad his anxiety is waning. As the weather radars glow green in the background, I give in to every primal urge I feel when I am in my husband's arms. For the moment, I allow myself to leave the rest behind. The grief, the fears, the worries, all the hurts and scars and sinkings. I try to forget we've lost Sarah, and that a storm is pressing down on us, and that everything in our lives is being twisted from its foundation. Instead, I retreat to the safest place I know, Carl's body. And as we come together, I almost forget myself completely. There is no more worry. No more pain. No more me.

Chapter 13

Monday, August 29, 2005

Hello Sparrow,

Did you see us leave? Did you see what happened?

The Man packed up a bunch of boxes and told me to get into the back of his truck, under the camper top so nobody would see me. I asked about Ellie. I didn't want to leave her behind. He laughed and said Ellie was dead. I started screaming and I hit him, so he threw me hard against the truck and told me to shut up. Then he said, "You're so stupid. We never had your little friend."

So I asked him about the other girls, the ones in chains, and he laughed again and said, "Get it through your thick skull. We only have you." Then he shoved me into the back of the truck, piled a bunch of boxes around me, and closed the door.

Pop always says it isn't right to hate anybody, but I hate The Man. I really hate him.

Hello Sparrow,

I am going to try to find the good. That's what Mom always says to do. So the good news is this: I snuck my notebooks and math books here with us because The Lady gave me a big black trash bag for my things. The Man was so worried about packing his own stuff, he never noticed.

I figured he would stop for gas. I had a plan. But he drove us straight to this new place, and he never stopped. Cars were next to us the whole way. I could hear the traffic. But I couldn't reach the windows. I never found a way to get help.

Now we're in this new place, and The Man says we have to stay here until the storm ends. The Lady says we should stay here forever. She likes it better here. I do too.

Hello Sparrow,

Do you hear the rain? I used to think a dragon lived in the clouds. His growl was thunder. His fire was lightning. Mom and Pop used to let me crawl into their bed on stormy nights. They'd read stories to me and sing until the bad weather went away.

I will keep singing all the songs Mom and Pop taught me.

Hello Sparrow,

The Lady is letting me stay inside with her. She's scared of the storm. She likes when I sing. Pop always lets me help with things at home, so I asked The Man if I could help. He whacked my shoulder hard with one of the flashlights and told me to shut up.

The wind gets loud sometimes. It sounds like big eighteen-wheelers going by. When a tree limb falls I jump, and that makes The Lady laugh. I'm trying to be brave for her. I think I'm the only friend she's got. I told her that even storms happen for a reason. And that good things always come after the storm. That's what Mom and Pop say anyway.

The Lady said Mom and Pop sound like real nice people, and I told her they are. I told her if she would help me get home, maybe they could help her too.

She said, "For a smart kid, you sure don't understand much."

Our electricity is out. We're relying on the weather radio. It's been blaring alarm warnings about Hurricane Katrina since five thirty this morning: "extreme tropical cyclone" and "destructive wind warning." We haven't seen it get too bad here in Walker, however. Just a heavy dose of wind and rain.

While Katrina makes her way north over southeast Louisiana, we launch a game of Bourré. Carl shuffles the cards. "Ante up," he says, tossing in the loose change from his pockets.

After finding a bunch of coins in the junk drawer, Ellie and I add our own money to the pot and Carl deals us five cards each. Beanie watches from the sofa, curled safe from the storm.

"Sarah never plays cards with us. She thinks it's a sin."

It's the first time Ellie has mentioned a specific memory with Sarah, and I'm not sure how to respond. "Yep," I say. "But she loves Yahtzee."

Ellie laughs. "And Monopoly."

"That game takes forever," Carl adds, smiling, and the three of us reminisce about the girls' board-game competitions that would sometimes stay in play for weeks on end.

I surrender my lowest number cards and draw two replacements. Ellie stands pat, leading with the ace of spades. By about the tenth round of play she's managed to win the entire pile of change. "Beginner's luck," Carl teases her, and we're all laughing when the weather alarm sounds again.

This time the update announces the eye of Katrina is moving across St. Tammany Parish. "Sustained winds of 110 miles per hour with gusts up to 135." People in these areas, including Hancock and Harrison Counties of Mississippi, are advised to take shelter in an interior room.

"Far away," Carl tells Ellie. "Don't worry. I'll keep you safe." He gives her a confident smile.

As we continue to play cards, the wind snaps a long, heavy limb, tumbling it through the sky with as little effort as a child throwing a toothpick. Rain pummels the house. The yard fills with water as our ditches overflow. Pinecones hit the roof like grenades.

"Maybe we should have boarded the windows," I say. "Think it'll get worse?"

"You think I don't know how to take care of my family?" Carl snaps.

My stomach tightens. No matter how careful I am, something I do always seems to set him off. He thinks I'm against him.

"I'm just asking if the tape will hold," I explain. "The wind seems to be getting stronger."

Carl gives me the all-too-familiar death glare and then speaks to Ellie as if I'm not here. "It's already heading into Mississippi. Nothing we haven't seen before. Your mother's crazy. You know that, don't you?"

Ellie laughs, and Carl eggs her on. They tease me for making a big deal out of things. I tune in to the warnings that continue to stream from the radio. Reportedly, the communications hub in New Orleans has suffered massive power outages, so the alerts now have more to do with Mississippi than Louisiana, but again and again warnings are issued, many for microbursts churning from Katrina's eye wall. We learn Bogalusa has been hit hard by spin-off winds. That's the town near the Pearl River where Beth's mother lives.

"I should call Beth." I reach for my phone and Carl reacts, shooting me his death glare again. With one look he manages to make me feel stupid. As if I'm his biggest problem. I leave the phone alone and return my full attention to Carl, as he demands. *Beth will call when she needs me.* I try not to feel guilty that I'm sitting at home with Ellie and Carl while my friends are sitting out the storm, worried about Sarah.

Hello Sparrow,

The Man caught me writing in my notebook. He didn't say anything. Now I don't have to be scared when I write to you. Yay!

The storm got bad last night. Gravel was hitting the windows. One of the big trees fell down.

> We still don't have electricity, and the only food we have
> are cans of beanie weenies. At home Mom always went to the
> store before a storm. She made sure we had water bottles
> and snacks and good fruit. And Mrs. Raelynn had hurricane
> parties so we could use up her freezer food.
>
> I told The Lady about that. She laughed. When I asked her
> about the storms when she was a little girl, she got all quiet
> and left the room.

Tuesday, August 30, 2005

We made it through Monday night without electricity. We're using the generator to run the refrigerator, which leaves us no air-conditioning. The heat and humidity are intense, even with the windows open. We're soaked in sweat.

"We could go to the church." I fan Ellie with a piece of cardboard. "They've got a bigger generator there. We need to help anyway."

Carl's not having it. He shoots me his look. I cave again into silence, but Ellie stands her ground. "Let's go." She grabs a few basics and heads toward the door, not giving her father a chance to argue.

Somehow this works, and within the hour, we're at the church. The parking lot is packed, and we enter the reception hall to find a crowd. Tables and chairs have been arranged so that families are sectioned off, eating, drinking, talking. No one seems particularly upset or anxious.

Except Beth.

Ellie runs straight to one of the box fans as Beth greets us, her fingers pressed against her scalp. "I've been trying to call you. Cell towers are out. Lines are jammed. No Internet either. Have you heard?"

I shake my head. "We haven't heard anything since we lost power," I explain. "Just the weather radio. Told us it had turned east. And that Bogalusa got pummeled with winds. Were you able to reach your mom?"

She pulls us outside, whispering after the door has closed. "It did go east, and yes, she managed to get a call to us. Said she's okay but her house isn't. Two trees crashed through it. Thank goodness my uncle is there with her. Chimney bricks were rolling down the roof like they were nothing but pinecones. Crazy. But they're both safe."

I settle, relieved, but Beth stands tall and serious. "Now listen," she says. "It's awful. Aunt Betty just got through to me too. Took her four hours. I'm telling you, communication has been tough. She's up in Memphis, watching it all on the news."

"What's she know?" I ask.

Carl stares blankly, waiting for more.

"It's bad, Amanda. Biloxi, Waveland, Gulfport. All destroyed. Nothing left. Entire stretches of the Mississippi coastline wrecked, right down to the slabs. That's all you can see for miles. Entire neighborhoods are gone. Just gone. Sarah could be out there." Beth's eyes fill with tears, and she stutters as she speaks. She's no longer the poised diplomat, polished and ready for front-pew politics.

"Remember what you said at first, Beth. Remember? This is our chance to find her." I try my best to calm her nerves. "She's at a shelter. I'm sure of it."

"No, listen. I haven't told you the worst." She steadies herself against the church door, then continues. "The footage showed the storm as it was hitting New Orleans. If Sarah's there . . ." Beth stops again, trying to regain composure. She dabs her eyes before continuing. "There were roofs peeling back like plastic wrappers, Amanda. Much worse than what we saw here."

Around us, limbs and leaves have been strewn in every direction, as if Mother Nature threw a frat party and we've arrived the next day to find the mess. Beth follows my line of sight to the debris, reading my thoughts. "Yeah, see what I'm saying. Even here the traffic lights were spinning and the houses were shaking. But there, all those high-rises. Shattered glass flying everywhere. Curtains ripping from rooms. She said it looked like a war zone."

As Beth talks, her emotions take over. Carl seems more annoyed than concerned. I push this to the back of my brain and focus instead on Beth's story.

"Even parts of the Superdome blew apart. It was raining in the dome. All those people, sleeping on the floor. They had to move up into the seats and hope the rest of the roof wouldn't fall to pieces. Can you imagine? All I can think is where is Sarah? Do you know how scared she must be?"

I listen. Carl does too. All night we've stayed by Ellie's side. Sleeping in the same room together, comforting her as the branches broke and the wind howled. Surely he must feel something.

"And it's worse than that," Beth continues. "The levees. In New Orleans. They didn't hold."

"Serious?" Carl questions.

"I can't imagine it either, but Aunt Betty says the news keeps showing water up to rooftops. They think a barge got blown from its anchor. Slammed through one of the concrete walls or something. That's all it took."

Carl wipes sweat from his brow. "Seems a stretch."

"They think there's more than one breach." Beth keeps going, despite Carl's resistance. "The canals are overflowing. Some of the pump houses aren't working." Speaking faster now, she is near panic. "The water flooded in so fast it even came up from the drains, snapping those manhole covers off. Like popcorn. People are dying, Amanda. They're dying."

She starts crying harder. I pull her to me and try my best to offer comfort.

"Sarah won't be in those places, Beth. Listen. I'm sure she's at a shelter. We'll find her. Have you talked to Jay?"

"No. I'm telling you. I can't get a call through to anyone. I'm clawing at my skin. I need to get out of here. I need to get to New Orleans."

"Okay. Let's think this through." I try to slow the pace, help her mind settle. Give her a few solid plans to cling to.

"The news is showing dead bodies. In the streets, Amanda. My child could be—"

Carl has had enough. "I'm going to find Preacher."

"Beth, listen." I brush the hair from her wet cheeks as Carl goes back inside the fellowship hall. "The media exaggerate. Rumors get out of control. It can't be that bad."

"The water came in so fast. Some of those people couldn't swim. They were grabbing two-by-fours, beer kegs, coolers. Anything that would float. And some couldn't get out, Amanda. They had to claw their way to the attic, break through to the roof. Think of the ones who couldn't break through!"

I hug her. "It's all right, Beth. Sarah knows how to swim. And this could be her chance. Stay with me, okay?"

"Aunt Betty said people are stuck out there waving their shirts. It's almost a hundred degrees. Think of how hot those shingles are. The metal roofs."

"If she's in that area, then she'll be on TV. Someone will recognize her. This is good."

"No. That's the thing. No one is rescuing them. 911 isn't even taking calls anymore."

"I'm sure the Red Cross is there, Beth. And the National Guard. This is Louisiana. We know how to deal with storms."

"This isn't just a storm, Amanda." She pulls away, exasperated. "You're not hearing me. The mayor said there could be as many as ten thousand people. Dead!" Her voice reaches an alarming pitch.

"Hurricanes don't kill ten thousand people." I speak slowly. "Your aunt exaggerates sometimes, doesn't she?"

Beth exhales. Then she says, "Well, yes, she does."

"There's no way the entire city is flooded. Think about it. And 911 would never stop taking calls. Tell you what. We'll keep trying to get in touch with Jay. He'll know something. And in the meantime, let's get a TV hooked up in here. See for ourselves."

Chapter 14

Wednesday, August 31, 2005

Hello Sparrow,

　　We finally got our power back on. It's been HOT! The Man is in a very bad mood. The Lady thinks he's gonna "have himself a heatstroke." The tree didn't land on the house. We got lucky. I hope you got lucky too, Sparrow. I'll be watching for you.

　　They're still letting me stay in the house with them. I'm glad. We have some chairs and an old mattress. I sleep on blankets. I brought them from Chalmette.

　　It feels like The Man and The Lady are starting to think of me as family. But I already have a family. I want to go home.

Hello Sparrow,

　　The Man found a TV, but he can't get any channels. That made him mad, of course. He's always screaming about something. Mom says somebody who acts like that is a little kid on the inside. Throwing a fit, trying to get their way. She says they don't know how to handle their feelings. I think that's what's wrong with The Man. He doesn't know how to handle his feelings.

The Lady is mad about the TV too. So I told her how we have "No TV Sundays" at our house, and how we play charades and tell stories. She said, "You didn't have to watch TV because you had a TV family."

I think she means we have a family like the kind you see on TV. I asked her what kind of family she had, but she didn't answer. So I taught her how to play charades.

When the lights flicker back to full brightness and the air conditioner roars to life, the reception hall fills with laughter. Someone starts singing "This Little Light of Mine," and another boosts spirits by yelling, "Clap it up!" Soon everyone joins in. As their voices rise, hopes rise too. Even Preacher and Beth are smiling.

When the song ends, Preacher draws everyone's attention to the front of the room. "There have been a lot of rumors about what's going on down in New Orleans," he says. "I know you're worried and communication has been difficult. We've got this TV now, so hopefully we can get a better idea of what's really happening."

The families hurry closer, and Preacher gets busy connecting the set. Carl helps, and together they find a way to tune in to a static feed of a public station.

About a hundred of us gather, eager for news. When the images begin to flash across the screen, a stunned silence fills the room. A reporter narrates, and we piece together bits of information, slowly coming to terms with what has occurred.

"Remember," the reporter says, "Monday night we were all focused on the Mississippi coast, the strike zone. Everyone was saying we had dodged a bullet here in New Orleans. But when we woke up Tuesday morning, the streets were filled with water. It was as if we went to sleep on land and woke up at sea."

As the footage shows clips throughout the Crescent City, the refugees gasp and cover their mouths in shock. Some begin to cry.

"The last two nights, the only lights have been from police cars and cameras. It's become a dark, eerie place. We've heard gunshots and helicopters. Tension is beginning to build."

The anchor chimes in. "And no help has arrived?"

"None. It's hard to believe. The people here at the dome—they are not the looters. These are people who followed the rules, did as they were told, and have been waiting for nearly three days for help. It's ninety-seven degrees with full-blown humidity. Sweltering heat. You can see, tensions are rising. People are afraid."

The camera shows countless refugees, each experiencing emotional extremes. Anger, fear, sadness, grief. The common expression is hopelessness. As Beth watches the screen, she wears the same sad eyes as the storm survivors.

The reporter continues exposing us to truths too surreal to believe. "There are dead bodies being lined up in the street."

The camera shows images of corpses, some sitting in wheelchairs, some lying in the gutter. Their faces have been covered with towels, sheets, ponchos. Any piece of cloth people have managed to salvage.

"These are old people. Sick people. Babies."

The anchor says, "We're told more than a hundred thousand people could be stuck in the city. What do they need right now?"

"Water and food. Diapers and baby formula. Many of them

need medication. And they need a way out of New Orleans. They need transportation, and they need somewhere to go. The trains all shut down before the storm. Buses aren't running. No one seems to be coming to help. Just locals with their boats, pulling people from their homes. No one seems to be in charge."

As scenes flash across the screen, someone behind me yells, "The bridge!"

"That's I-10!" yells another. "Lake Pontchartrain." Entire sections of the twin-span interstate have collapsed into the water.

Beside me, a woman holds her head in her hands. "I can't believe this. I can't believe what I'm seeing."

"We're showing footage from the helicopters now and it's devastating. Not only the Mississippi Gulf Coast, where nothing remains at all, but in New Orleans, where the floods have caused significant damage. We're talking an area the size of Great Britain. Destroyed."

The clips show children floating in old refrigerators, shirtless men pulling women from flooded houses, and elderly people walking neck-deep in filthy waters, some holding babies above their heads. One civilian rescuer says he just helped five children.

"She ran out of oxygen," he explains as the camera shows a woman's body, stiff and swollen, in her bed. "They've been sitting in this house with their dead mother for nearly three days. None of them can swim." He's crying as the lens closes in on a boatload of shell-shocked children being carried away to dry land.

"That's Circle Food," a woman near the TV says. The neighborhood grocery is shown with water at least halfway up the front door. "That's not by the lake. It never floods. What is going on down there?"

As the scenes continue, people call out recognizable locations, identifying landmarks in St. Bernard, the Lower Ninth Ward, and New Orleans East. All underwater.

"There's a lot of frustration. Fear. Rumors," the reporter continues as the images are shown. "We've had a total breakdown in communication. Even city officials are unsure of the facts."

On-screen, people lean from upper-story windows waving string mops, flags, anything they can find. Those on rooftops also signal for help. Below them, locals boat from house to house, pulling survivors into pirogues, bateaus, and airboats before hauling them out to bridges and overpasses, anywhere they can wait for transport out of the city.

"They're calling us the Cajun Navy," a local boatman says into the camera. "But I'm a veteran. Served twelve years in the US Navy. All over the world, helping everybody. And now we can't help our own people?" His face reddens, and his voice gets loud. "You hear me, Mr. President? Call in some help. What are you waiting for? People are dying down here."

Thursday, September 1, 2005

"They're busing people to the River Center," Beth says. "Who's coming with us?"

Ellie and I don't hesitate to follow Beth and Preacher, but Carl doesn't budge from his spot.

"You coming?" Preacher asks Carl. "We could use two cars. Split up and cover more area."

"Of course," he says. "I'm right behind you." As soon as Preacher turns his back, Carl shoots me a hateful glare, but I ignore it and keep moving.

It takes us more than an hour to drive from the church to the downtown performing arts center in Baton Rouge, a trip that should only take half as long. We arrive to find a scene unlike any I've ever witnessed. There's a long line of charter buses, church vans, school buses, even RVs. They each wait their turn to drop the caravans of shell-shocked survivors at the designated entrance.

"So many people," Ellie says. "They all lost their homes?"

Exhausted Red Cross volunteers seem as stressed as anyone. They do their best to keep things organized, checking in each person and striving to provide some sense of community for the displaced. They assign refugees from specific neighborhoods to camp together in various conference areas, a simple gesture of compassion that seems to be giving hope to those who arrive.

A large board has been set up behind the registration table. It's being used to track the locations of those who are seeking someone. We join a few distraught refugees who are carefully searching the board for names of their missing loved ones.

A volunteer approaches us. "Are you here to help?"

Preacher introduces himself by his occupation, and this causes the volunteer to retract. "I'm sorry, sir, but we can't allow any religious groups inside the shelter. You're welcome to help outside if you'd like. It's policy."

Beth turns white. "We're looking for our daughter!"

I pull the volunteer to the side and explain the situation. Once he realizes why we are here, he apologizes profusely. "I'm sorry. We have rules. I had to turn away a group of nuns this morning. I'll let you come in. Just don't tell anybody you're with a church."

Preacher waves it off, without offense, and shares more about Sarah. "Can we add our names to the board?"

"Sure." The volunteer looks to be in his seventies, and his tired eyes suggest the stress is wearing on him too. He turns to Ellie. "Is Sarah your sister?"

"No, sir. My friend." She stares at the crowds. "What's gonna happen to all these people?"

"Good question," he says with exasperation. Then he leaves us to our search.

I tack Sarah's flier on the board of missing people. Beth and Preacher add their contact information to the chart. Then we split up and begin searching for Sarah. Carl stays at the entrance, watching new arrivals. Ellie and I head to one of the conference rooms where people are given their own eight-foot square of America. "You see this?" a haggard man says to us while claiming his spot on the floor. "A blanket, a toothbrush, and the clothes on my back. That's all I got to my name."

"Did you lose your home?" I ask. Ellie watches the exchange.

"I lost it, all right. Had me one of them old wood homes. Sat up on cement pilings, you know? Down in Chalmette. Water come in, carrry my house away. Last time I saw it, it was bobbing like a fishing cork. Who knows where it ended up. Probably sitting in a cow pasture somewhere."

"Thank goodness you weren't hurt."

"Yeah, boy. Take my house. Take everything. It's just stuff. Never felt so happy to be alive. I tell you that. Only thing I can't replace was my dog, Heisman. He was like my son." The man's eyes get watery and he looks away.

"You'll find him," I say. "He's probably sitting on the porch, in the middle of that pasture, wondering where you are." This makes the man smile, and a few others around us too.

I pass each person a flier and ask them to be on the lookout for Sarah. A couple people say they remember her kidnapping. Others nod. They do too.

We continue this process from room to room, working our

way through the massive complex. Some groups have written the name of their subdivision on a poster board and taped it to the door. Others have gathered according to town or ward, school, or church, anything that can give them a sense of home. Most people have only a blanket or a towel. There is a shortage of cots, but no one complains.

Those coming out of shock are beginning to talk about their experiences. Others listen, blank-faced and numb.

"I saw a dead cow. Twenty foot up in a tree," one man says. "I'm not lying."

Another chimes in. "I believe you, man. I ain't never seen nothin' like it. Until you live through it, you just can't know."

An elderly woman nods, her dentures missing. "I been on this earth eighty-seven years, and I'll tell you, that was the longest night of my life. Stuck in my attic," she says. "All those snakes and nutria climbing in. I was thinking, *God, what else you gonna throw at me? Survive the winds. The water. Still gotta survive the snakes?*"

"She's not kidding," the woman's sister adds. "Worst part was, we could see boats all out there. But we couldn't find a way to get to them."

One room at a time, Ellie and I distribute fliers and search for Sarah, hearing story after story of survival. By the time we make it to the main floor, it's almost lunchtime. "One meal per ticket," a volunteer says, walking down the long line to repeat the instructions.

"What do you serve?" I ask him.

"Depends," he says. "For now, we're passing out MREs, but we'll serve three hot meals a day."

From the line, another man says, "We're grateful for whatever we get."

Ellie and I make our way through the large space and into a

smaller room. At the back, a middle-aged woman sits alone. She asks me if my phone is working. I let her try to reach her missing son, but it goes straight to his voicemail. Others ask for a turn, and we pass the phone around, hoping someone will hear good news. The fifth caller is an elderly lady whose arthritic fingers are bent at the knuckles. I help her dial the number. When her sister answers, we all cheer. It's the first reunification for the room, and spirits are lifted.

When she ends the call, she looks at Ellie and says, "See there? Never give up."

Friday, September 2, 2005

As we crawl through the traffic, I turn up the local NPR station and listen carefully for updates. "Tens of thousands of refugees have fled to Baton Rouge and surrounding parishes," the reporter announces. "The infrastructure can't handle the numbers, and we've got LA-level traffic jams." In typical NPR style, they add background sounds of car horns and diesel engines.

Another journalist says, "Baton Rouge is about an hour west of New Orleans and has sometimes been referred to as its country cousin. Tell us about that city."

"The population of Baton Rouge was about 400,000 before Katrina. Latest estimates show as many as 250,000 evacuees have made it to this area, and let me tell you, people here are welcoming them with open arms. The response of the community has been overwhelming."

"In what way?"

"We've seen people invite strangers into their homes. They

have been volunteering at various shelters, helping with disaster cleanup, taking in pets. There's been some chaos, but people here in Louisiana really are trying to look after their own."

"Have people been able to get into New Orleans to help?"

"You have to understand, people here had no power. No Internet. Cell phones have been useless. Even radio coverage has been sporadic. They didn't know what was going on down there. They weren't able to see the news like people in the rest of the country. But despite all that, yes, many went to help. They were there on the ground, in their boats, leading man-to-man rescue operations."

"And now that the coast guard and others have taken charge?"

"I just came from New Orleans. The streets are filled with Humvees. Restricted access getting in, but I'll tell you, getting out was almost more difficult."

"How so?"

"They've set up checkpoints. Before I could exit the disaster area, my vehicle and all my belongings were searched. Anything that could potentially carry disease had to be left there."

"Did you have to leave anything behind? In New Orleans?"

"My backpack. A Styrofoam cooler. If it could hold bacteria, it had to stay. I admit, it was a tad disconcerting to see people in Hazmat suits after I'd been knee-deep in those floodwaters for days."

"I'll bet!" The correspondent sounds as shocked as I am. "So the hundreds of thousands who have been able to get to Baton Rouge, where are all these people staying?" She wants details.

"Everywhere," the reporter says. "Universities. Churches. Some students at Southern have let their families move into their dorm rooms. School administrators seem to be turning a blind eye. What can they do? Every hotel room has been occupied. There are approximately five thousand people at the River Center."

"I'm assuming the surrounding towns are absorbing a lot of people too."

"Absolutely."

"What about the hospital patients? We've heard conflicting stories about available medical care in New Orleans."

"LSU has set up trauma and triage hubs, so the hospitals in New Orleans are sending patients here for treatment now. The university also set up a shelter in the Ag Center. They're taking care of stranded pets."

"What about storm damage in that area?"

"It wasn't too bad in Baton Rouge. Just typical trees and roofs. Nothing these folks can't handle." Outside the car, the storm damage is exactly as the reporter describes. "Now that power is being restored, people who had evacuated are starting to see the news coverage. They are devastated. Many have tried to go home and have not been allowed in. People are beginning to realize this is no temporary situation."

"Surely they can't keep occupying dorm rooms and hotel suites. Where will they stay long term?"

"We are hearing that asked again and again." Then he introduces a city official who discusses plans to bus people west to San Antonio and Houston, where he says many refugees have already found shelter. "There simply isn't room here for all the people in need," says the politician. "This is a disaster of catastrophic proportions. We'll be relocating people across the US and these could very likely be permanent relocations. Most of these people will be starting their lives over from scratch. With nothing. They thought they were leaving home for a day or two. Now they have no home to go back to at all."

The reporter takes over again. "In the meantime, locals are trying to get back to their normal routines, but there's nothing normal right now about their city. Gas stations have sold out of fuel. Grocery store shelves are empty. It's starting to sink in that Baton Rouge will never be the same."

Carl turns off the radio. "We'll never get through this traffic." We've been stalled for ten minutes at least. Beth and Preacher are a few cars ahead of us, trying to reach the next shelter. "You do realize how ridiculous this is, don't you?"

I lean my head against the window and sigh.

Ellie speaks up from the backseat. "What if it were me instead of Sarah? Would it be ridiculous then?"

This silences Carl for a minute. Then he looks in the rearview mirror with soft eyes and says kindly, "I'm glad it isn't you."

Hello Sparrow,

You found me! I have been praying ever since we left Chalmette. Miracle!

Our old place got flooded real bad. We'll stay here now, and I can stay in the house. As long as I keep behaving.

The Lady told me, "It's a good thing you weren't locked in that shed when the levee broke. You'd be dead right now."

See? God got me out of that shed. And he'll get me out of here too.

I know people are sad about the hurricane. But Mom taught me to Be Grateful, Never Hateful. So here's why I'm glad the storm came:

1. Now I know that Ellie is safe at home.
2. I don't have to sleep in the shed anymore.
3. No men have been to "visit" since the storm. NONE!
4. Even though we have electricity again, we have not been making films.
5. The Lady is being nice to me, and I think The Man is starting to like me more too.
6. We are in Hammond now, not too far from Walker. Maybe Mom and Pop will find me.
7. You found me!

See, Sparrow? Good things do come after the storm.

Chapter 15

Wednesday, September 7, 2005

BETH AND I WORK TOGETHER IN THE CHURCH, WASHING LINENS for the families who are now calling our Sunday school rooms their temporary homes. I add a towel to the basket. "We've closed the clinic all week. Still too many clients without power. Or taking care of relatives from evacuation zones."

"Yeah," Beth says with a monotone voice and a stare to the side. It's clear her thoughts are elsewhere.

I try to draw her back. "How long do you think people will need to stay here?"

"Months, maybe. The ones who have insurance are getting the runaround. Can't move home. Can't afford to start over. Some are trying to get trailers from FEMA. In the meantime, they're stuck." Beth folds a fitted sheet while I tackle the flat one.

"How do you do that?" I tease her. "Martha Stewart couldn't fold a sheet better than you."

She shrugs. "Mama taught me." This tugs my heart. I remember my own mother teaching me to do the laundry.

"My mother always thought of you as the model wife. Said you were the poster child for Proverbs 31."

Beth's forehead wrinkles and she shakes her head.

"It's true," I tell her. "I should be more like you."

Now she laughs. "You know Proverbs 31 is taken the wrong way. It's not supposed to be a bullet list defining how to be a good woman."

"I know that. You know that. But Mom didn't know that. She was terrified I'd end up in her situation. Divorced. Poor. Single mom."

"She was a wonderful mother. And wife. It wasn't her fault he left."

"Again, we know that. But she didn't. One of the last things she told me before she died was that I should always try to be the perfect wife, no matter how hard it may be. She was so afraid I'd end up alone."

Beth's entire demeanor has been flattened since Sarah went missing, but now, as she looks at me, her facial muscles sink. A sadness moves through the room. "Amanda, you are the perfect wife. And mother. And friend. Just as you are. You don't have to try."

I've lost Beth's daughter, and she's telling me I'm the perfect friend. I'm overwhelmed with emotion, but I don't let it show. Instead, I stack a folded sheet atop the pile of fresh linens and pull another towel from the dryer, eyeing the board of photographs. "Hard to believe so many people got separated from their families. Just from a hurricane."

"Yeah. There's a mother here in the nursery. Arlene. Did you meet her?"

"The tall one? With the PhD?"

"She's only got three of her four kids with her. Her husband passed away last year, and now she's got no idea if her oldest daughter is dead or alive. She's sixteen. Left the house with friends after the storm. But then the levees broke. Arlene hasn't heard a word since." Beth points to the board. "Thankfully, she had a photo we could share."

I shake my head and stare at the faces, each one tagged with a name, age, and contact information for the person hoping to reconnect. "Just look at all those pictures."

"Hard to imagine, isn't it? All those other moms out there, feeling just like me. On account of a storm. Never imagined anything like that could happen."

"I never imagined any of this," I admit. "Yet here we are."

Beth touches a photo of her own daughter. Portrayed in color against the wall of Katrina's missing. "Here we are. But where is Sarah? It's been nearly a year."

"We'll find her, Beth. Her photo is everywhere."

"You saw those shelters. So many people coming and going. You know as well as I do, Sarah could be anywhere. Lost. Scared—"

I interrupt. "And all those people are taking time to look at the photo boards. They're paying attention. This is good."

After a long sigh, Beth lifts her shoulders and slides the laundry basket across the counter. "Ready?"

"Ready."

With that, we head to my car and spend the rest of the day driving from shelter to shelter, looking for Sarah. Never mentioning that tomorrow is September 8, the day both our girls were born thirteen years ago.

Thursday, September 8, 2005

I bend to light thirteen turquoise candles, each one tall, twisted, and thin, as Carl and I sing "Happy Birthday" to Ellie. Carl records her on video as she closes her eyes and makes a silent wish. Her candles light the dining room, lining the wall with shadows as she leans over the heart-shaped cake and blows. One by one the tiny lights give way and darkness descends. I hurry to flip the switch, brightening the room to serve slices of her favorite dessert: butter cake with chocolate-marshmallow icing, a gooey recipe from my own childhood birthdays.

We are keeping the party small and quiet this year. The mutual understanding is that we'll have a big bash when we find Sarah. Until then, we use every candle to wish her home to us.

Adding a second scoop of Blue Bell ice cream to her plate, Ellie shows signs of youth again. "Homemade Vanilla. Yum!" Then she turns her attention to the pile of presents. I've wrapped each one with sparkling papers, bright curly ribbons, and oversized bows, but there's one gift I've kept tucked under the table, saving it as a final surprise.

Before she can finish her cake, she's already tearing into her gifts. I take over the video camera as she opens a new iPod nano, jumping and squealing with delight. It's the first time I've seen her this happy since The Day. Hope is seeding.

She thumbs through the playlists. "Weezer!" A few seconds later, "The White Stripes! Ohmigosh! Feist! This is awesome!" I've spent hours compiling her favorite artists, and it's a hit.

After she has opened a few more gifts, taking time to comment on each new outfit and piece of jewelry, Carl pulls the final present from beneath the table and passes it to Ellie. I work the camera.

She rips ribbons from the box and lifts the lid. "What is this?" She sets out a stack of videos, each housed in a plastic shell, organized and labeled according to date.

"We hired a guy to transfer our home movies to DVDs," I explain. It may be too sentimental, but I hope watching hours of happy family footage will help heal us all, remind us of the good times. "I was thinking we could have a family movie night."

Ellie smiles at the camera, hiding her new set of braces with one of the DVDs. "O-kay." She pronounces it as if she's unsure, adding a little teenage angst.

"Don't look at me. This was your mom's idea." Carl holds his hands up, clearing himself from the bad gift. But then he turns and puts his arm around me. When I lift my chin, he kisses me for the first time in days. Just a quick brush of the lips, but still it's something. My body reacts.

I turn off the camera and return my focus to Ellie. "Oh, come on. It'll be fun. Grab your quilt. I'll make popcorn. We'll settle in early tonight." I begin to clear the dishes and ask her to choose a disc.

She sorts through the stack, shouting over my stream of water. "Disney or Destin?"

"Hmm . . . both sound good to me."

With this, Ellie bounds down the hall in search of her favorite blanket, a patchwork quilt my mother made for her when she was little. Carl sets up the DVD player while I finish the last of the cleanup. We meet in the living room where Ellie curls into the corner of the sofa. I sit near her. Carl finds his La-Z-Boy and hits Play. The memories begin.

I adjust my own blanket as a six-year-old Ellie skips across the screen singing "Oh! Susanna, don't you cry for me." Carl is in the background building her swing set.

Next, the three of us are on the beach in Destin. Ellie beams in Carl's arms. He protects her from the ocean's forceful churn, turning his back against every wave, jumping as Ellie squeals with delight. "We've had the best vacations."

"Every one of them," Carl says. Then he smiles at me, and for a moment I see the Carl I fell in love with. The teenage boy who danced with me in a field at midnight, our song playing from his car door speakers. The young man in a hard hat who spun me through the air when he got his first real paycheck. The new father who cut Ellie's umbilical cord and ran through the hospital shouting, "It's a girl!"

With every white-capped wave on-screen, all the love comes washing back over me. And I see my husband as I first saw him. Strong. Steady. Stable. That was before life got complicated. We were good together as long as we stayed on the surface. But eventually couples have to navigate deeper waters, far away from the shallows.

I fear we've lost sight of shore. We've been drifting for years, farther out into the deep, dealing with a series of undertows and storms. Mom's illness, then her death. Carl's career frustrations and the fractured relationships in his own family. Financial pressures and the stress of owning the clinic. Sarah and the immeasurable grief. We can't catch our breath.

The film skips to another scene, a bit later in time. We are on vacation in Colorado, renting horses for a trail ride. Ellie waves to the camera. She's wearing two French braids and Western boots. "The white one," she says, pointing to the youngest, most skittish horse of the lot.

"You always have been drawn to animals." I give her leg a gentle pat.

She keeps watching the TV, but smiles. When the guide straps the saddle for her, the young-voiced Ellie argues her case. "Indians don't use saddles."

The trail guide sets her straight. "Rules are rules. Even I use a saddle."

Carl, still a young father, gives his daughter a wink and helps her climb into the stirrups. He holds the reins, but she thinks she's leading the feisty mare all by herself. By the end of the trail, the guide has been worn down enough to give Ellie a chance at bareback. She rides the steadiest paint through a field of flowers as the guide keeps one hand in the mane.

"I always wanted to live in the mountains," Ellie says from the sofa. "And have a horse."

"We still plan to get you a horse." I look to Carl, but he says nothing about building the new house. It's been months since we discussed it, and with so much focus on finding Sarah, it's been the last thing on my mind.

"A white one!" Ellie imitates her six-year-old voice. She's giggling!

The next DVD shows her older, at church camp, taking a brave leap from the high dive. Then riding her bike with no hands. Backflips on the trampoline. A long series of cartwheels across the length of the yard. She stands at the end, dizzy, spinning back down to the ground with pigtails and a belly full of laughs.

"You were fearless. Remember when you climbed the tree at school and the principal had to call 911? The firemen got you down. Wish we had that on video!"

Ellie laughs. "I was only afraid of people. As long as I didn't have to talk to anybody, I was fine."

"That's why I'm surprised you love theater so much. Painting the backdrops is one thing, but I never thought you'd want to be onstage, talking in front of everybody. You're a natural."

"Yeah, but onstage I don't have to be me."

By midnight Ellie and I are both still awake, but Carl is snoring in his oversized chair. We've watched hours of recordings, drawing us through laughter and tears. At times Sarah would appear on film, laughing and dancing alongside Ellie as if she were right here with us. In those moments we would all grow silent. In other times, the innocence of Ellie's childhood would return to a scene on-screen, and we would exhale with relief.

If only it could be that easy. Hit a button. Go back to good.

Hello Sparrow,

Today is my birthday. I'm thirteen!

The Lady gave me one of those pens. I can write green or red or blue or black. It's the first time she's gotten somebody a present. Nobody has ever given her one. Her birthday is in June.

Ellie and I always give something funny. One year I gave her a can of those snakes that jump out when you open the lid. She got so scared, she punched me.

Another year I got Mrs. Amanda to put trick candles on Ellie's cake. She got me back. When I fell asleep, she covered my walls with glow-in-the-dark eyes. She woke me up, screaming, "Help! Help! They're attacking us!"

The best was last year. Mrs. Amanda helped me fill Ellie's room with turquoise balloons. That's her favorite color.

I wonder what Ellie is doing for our birthday. I hope someone gave her a funny gift.

Hello Sparrow,

I got to go outside today. Just The Lady and me. We walked all around the yard. We sat in the grass and looked at clouds. I almost felt free again.

I watched you fly. That made me think about the birds at Mardi Gras World. The painter said that when we see a bird, we should remind ourselves not to ever be a slave. I want to fly free.

Hello Sparrow,

That day in New Orleans, the fortune-teller put this feather in my hand. I've been keeping it safe. She said that feathers are strong. They can bend a long way before they break.

I'm going to remember that. When The Man gets really mean, or when I get scared, or when I start to think I'll never go home. Or when The Boss comes and I have to make those films. I'm going to remind myself that I can bend and bend. No matter how bad things might get, I will never break. Because I'm stronger than they think I am.

Wednesday, September 14, 2005

"We found Arlene's daughter," Beth says enthusiastically, referring to the family we've been hosting at the church. "She was in Houston. They're driving her back."

"That's incredible," I say, closing my office door. "I forget, how old is she?"

"Sixteen," Beth answers. "Can you believe they sent her to Houston all by herself?"

I flip through my appointment book, checking my schedule.

"She got separated from her friends when someone rescued her from a rooftop. Left her on a bridge, and she ended up on a bus to Texas."

"Gosh, Beth. She's lucky. Imagine if the wrong person—" *Think before you speak, Amanda.*

When Beth stays silent, I change the subject. "I finish at two today. I'll head that way after work. Need me to bring anything?"

"Just come when you can," Beth says. "That's all I need."

At two I head straight for the church, where Beth is busy cleaning dishes from the group lunch. She excuses herself and leads me down the hall to the nursery where Arlene's family is housed. The door is open, and we find her teen daughter being reunited. The family members are huddled close together, crying. Arlene looks up to us, whispering again and again, "Thank you. Thank you."

The scene overwhelms me, and I walk away, giving the family privacy.

Beth follows, reaching out for me as I catch my tear. "Amanda, do you realize what this means? If Arlene's daughter was sent to Houston, maybe Sarah's there too."

Chapter 16

Saturday, October 29, 2005

WE HAVE SPENT A YEAR PACING DARK CORNERS OF THE CRESCENT City, showing Sarah's photo again and again, hoping someone would give her back to us. A full year of searching every face, every set of blue eyes, every news report. We extended the search across to Texas after Katrina, visiting shelters and working with every volunteer agency we could find—begging them to be on the watch. And yet, as the anniversary hits, we have not found Sarah. Nor have we found the woman from the tourist's photo, Bridgette Gallatino.

"Today's the twenty-ninth," I tell Carl. "I can't believe it's been a year."

"Don't tell me you're sinking again."

"What does that mean, Carl? Sure I struggle with it sometimes. But I haven't sunk. I think I've stayed very strong."

He snorts.

"Would it hurt you to show a little compassion every now and then?" I regret my sharp tone, but I don't apologize. "You're not the one who lost her. You're not the one whose best friend can't look you in the eye."

I am ironing his shirt for tonight's graveyard shift at the Shell chemical plant in Geismar.

He stares at me with a look of warning. The kind a dog uses to say *Don't come any closer.* I give him his space and keep ironing, determined to prepare a perfect shirt. *A man with wrinkled clothes is a man who isn't loved. Yes, Mom. I hear you.*

"Just tell me you're going to work today."

When I don't answer, his jaw tightens, as if all chances of reasonable communication are done. If I really were interacting with a canine, he'd be hunched and growling, eyeteeth long and exposed. But this is no dog; this is my husband. His lips are pinched against his nose in disgust. "You think I like working the night shift? I wanted to work the rigs. Now I'm in the plant, and I hate it. But that's what we do, Amanda. We grow up. We go to work. Even when we don't want to. It's been a whole year. We can't keep putting our lives on hold."

This stings. Maybe the anniversary has me edgy, but for some reason I can't keep my thoughts in any longer.

"How can you say I've put my life on hold? I've worked myself to the bone trying to keep up with my practice while managing all of Ellie's extra needs, and trying to help search for Sarah, and still making sure you have what you need. You and Ellie have suffered because of me? I run in circles trying to keep you both happy. Not that you've noticed. Or offered to help."

I set the iron down, fold his collar carefully, and begin to steam the crease. Sarah's disappearance has left us living on a fault line, with frequent tremors rising up and shaking us to the core. There's never any warning. One minute we're able to live a semi-normal life, baking cookies, watching Ellie in the school play, ironing work shirts. The next, something triggers a mind shift and we're right back in that café, coming to terms with the fact that Sarah has never been found.

Carl reaches for his shirt, eyeing the few small wrinkles. "You expect me to wear this?"

I shift from fight to flight, moving to the first escape hatch I can find, the master bathroom. My back is turned when the iron flies by my ear. It crashes through the wall, mere centimeters from where I stand frozen in place. I turn to see Carl, red-faced and yelling. "You can't even get your mind right enough to iron a shirt!"

The familiar fear rises in me. I hurry into the bathroom, slamming the door. He is throwing things. I slide into the dry tub. I cover my ears. *Stay strong, Amanda. Don't fall apart.*

Then my mother: *You should have known better than to push him like this. You knew this would happen.*

In the bedroom Carl continues to rant. Ellie is down the hall. I can't get to her. And this is the worst of it. I know he'd never hurt her, but of course she'll wake and hear every bit. Of course she'll hate the both of us for all the tension and anger and hurt in her life. Of course she'll blame me for not keeping him calm.

"Don't you understand what you do? Why can't you just go to work? Do your job. Come home. Take care of your family. Why is that so hard?"

His fury builds. I begin to sway back and forth in a subtle soothing rhythm, the way my mother used to rock me in her lap when I was a little girl. It's pathetic, but in this moment it's all I can manage. Just as I did when I was a kid and my father would yell and throw things and threaten my mom. No matter how many times I tell myself to stand my ground, I cave. So here I am, curled in a ball, rocking away the pain, crying until I go numb. One simple word swirls inside my mind. *Disappear.*

"You think we all need Perfect Amanda to swoop in and save us. Well, guess what? Nobody needs you. Nobody even wants you. What we want, what we need, is for you to either grow up and pull yourself together, or stay out of our lives. Leave us alone. Stop running around in circles trying to fix everything. You mess things up, don't you see? You can't even iron a shirt!"

Don't listen to him. It isn't true.

But I can't hear my own voice. All I hear is Carl. "You have some fancy college degree and you think that makes you so smart. Think you know everything. You can't even help your own daughter!"

Another crash, this one against the bathroom door. I pull my head between my knees and shield myself like a schoolkid in a tornado drill.

Carl continues. "Want to know what our problem is? It's you! You're our problem! Solve that!"

"Stop!" I yell, pounding my fist against the tub. "Stop, please stop!" *Get a grip, Amanda. He's pushing all your buttons. Don't let him break you. You're stronger than this.*

He's at the door, yelling through the thin wooden panels. And then he kicks it, and his boot comes right through. I jump to my feet, grabbing the first tool I can find to defend myself. It's a hairbrush. Nothing makes sense. I don't say anything. I don't move from my place. I don't open the door or yell or fight or flee. Instead, I freeze. And this is how I stay until I hear the front door slam.

After some minutes of quiet, I am finally able to get control of myself. I make sure the bathroom door is locked. Then I run the shower water, letting steam fill the room. I undress and step under the steady stream, turning the dial almost as warm as it will go. As I yield to the roar of white noise, I think, *The problem is me? I'm not the one who just threw an iron.*

My mother speaks again: *He's just a man, Amanda. They get angry. It's normal.*

And then, from somewhere deep inside me, another voice:

Normal people don't try to hurt their wives. Normal people don't destroy the ones they love. Nothing about this is normal.

By the time the water turns cool, I find my footing. I take my time getting dressed. Then I exhale and I re-press his shirt, smoothing the lines that triggered his outrage.

The hole in the wall reminds me how close he came to hurting me. How many times have I warned a client about the dangers of domestic violence? How many times have I sat in my office listening to stories like this one, wondering why in the world a woman would stay in such a relationship? *How did I end up in this situation?*

I bring the shirt to the living room. Carl has returned to sit in his favorite chair and watch the morning news. Now that things are calm, I try again to communicate. *Don't show emotion. Don't go too deep.*

"Can't you understand? It's my responsibility, Carl. It's the anniversary, and Beth and Preacher will be out there looking. I need to help them."

Carl takes his shirt out of my hand with a rough tug, but speaks with a quieter tone now. "Face it, Amanda. Sarah's gone. All the fliers in the world aren't going to change that. If she were still out there, someone would have found her."

Of all the hurtful things he's said this morning, these words throw the hardest punch.

"Mom?" Ellie grumbles into the den, rubbing her eyes. "I don't feel like going to school today."

Carl cuts her a look, now taking his anxiety out on her, something he's never done. "What's new? Nobody wants to go to work. Nobody wants to go to school. Why don't we all just call it quits? Life's too hard."

The bite in his voice is too much. He knows today is the anniversary. Even Carl can't be this cold. To me, yes, but never to Ellie. Mom speaks again: *Maybe he's just tired. Three night shifts at the plant would wear on anyone. Don't react, Amanda. He can't process emotions the way you do. He's stressed. It comes out as anger.*

I hold back my words and move to feel Ellie's forehead, pressing the back of my palm under her long brown bangs. "No fever." Then I kiss her, a motherly peck to offer compassion and care.

"You're going to school, Ellie," Carl says sharply.

I try to ease the blow. "You have the haunted house fund-raiser. Only two more nights of it. Then Halloween. If you miss today, you won't be allowed to participate." I turn to Carl. "Ellie's been helping her theater group raise money for their summer competition in New York. Remember?"

"Of course I remember, Amanda. You think you're the only one who knows what's going on around here?" Such hate in his voice. He gives me his death glare. The one that reminds me to stay in my place. I cast my gaze toward Ellie, trying not to shake the boat.

Still in her pajamas, she eyes me, half listening, so I take advantage of her attention while I've got it. "You've been working so hard on the set. Who will be the Grim Reaper if you don't show up?"

She shrugs, struggling to care about the haunted house today no matter how much fun it will be. I move to the kitchen and pull canisters from the pantry, trying to maintain a normal life for my daughter. "Pancakes?"

She nods sluggishly while Carl switches off the TV and heads to the shower.

I heat the griddle and whip up a batch of batter, finally able to breathe now that he's left the room. *What do I really have to complain about? Beth would trade places with me in a second.*

It's times like this I am hit with the unfairness of it all. Not only that Beth's daughter is missing, but that Sarah was her only child. Beth suffered two miscarriages right alongside my own. Our lives ran parallel in nearly every way imaginable, until The Day. When my daughter returned from the restroom and her daughter did not.

"Can I go with you?" Ellie fumbles with a newly printed stack of fliers on the counter.

I whisk a half-dozen eggs in a glass bowl. "I'll be going to some pretty rough places."

Ellie holds one of the fliers in her hand, tracing the colored photos with the tip of her finger. One shows Sarah at age twelve, how she looked when she went missing. The other is an age-progression image, portraying how she might look today at thirteen. Beneath the pictures we've printed a toll-free number, still hoping someone may call with all the right information.

I have no words to soothe my daughter's aching spirit. Her pain is as real as my own. There's only one way to make it better. Bring Sarah home. In the meantime, I serve Ellie a warm batch of buttered pancakes and pass her the maple syrup. I'm dashing salt and pepper into the scrambled eggs by the time Carl comes back to the kitchen, freshly showered.

"You used all the hot water."

I don't reply. Instead, I scoop eggs onto a plate and add a stack of pancakes, handing it off to him as he sits next to Ellie at the counter. He shoves the fliers out of his way and says nothing. I pass him some silverware and pour his coffee, stir in some sugar. He stays silent.

As soon as he finishes his breakfast, he announces, "I'm going to bed. One of us actually works around here."

"Carl?" He waits as if it's the biggest inconvenience of his life. "It's a hard day. For all of us. Listen, please. Since you've been working the night shift, we do well to cross paths at all. Why don't you call me when you wake up, and I'll come home. Maybe we can do a late lunch before you head back. Talk some things through."

He grumbles something I can't hear and then closes the bedroom door behind him, not bothering to kiss me good-bye.

Ellie and I continue our morning routine and head out for the day. By the time I turn into the carpool line at the middle school, the cheerleaders are holding spirit signs at the entrance, sharing enthusiastic grins as they try to boost excitement about tonight's big game.

"I still can't believe you're a teenager." I touch Ellie's long, soft curls and she retracts.

Leaning her head against the passenger-side window, she stares at the cheerleaders, who giggle and wave near our car. "I wonder if Sarah is in school somewhere." She speaks from a haunted place, as if the weight of the world rests on her tongue.

Second-guessing Carl's insistence on sending her to school today, I inch the car closer to the drop-off point and offer an alternative. "Maybe we should have a mother-daughter day. Spend time together, just the two of us."

"We're already here. I might as well go."

I touch her knee. "Ellie?" I wait for her to look my way. "I know I've said this so many times, but you need to know—what happened to Sarah is not your fault."

She sighs and turns back to stare out the window.

"Remember what all the counselors have said. And your grief group. It's normal to be feeling overwhelmed, even after a year. Especially on days like today, the anniversary. But it's not always this bad, right?"

She doesn't respond.

"Ellie?" I try again to get through. "We may never understand what happened to Sarah. But it had nothing to do with you. And to be honest, I have often wondered . . . what if you had been with Sarah when it happened? What if we were out there looking for you too?"

She turns now and looks me in the eye. Every inch of her is drawn down, depressed. "Don't you get it, Mom? I wish it had been me."

Her words gnaw at my bones. "Ellie, listen to me. I couldn't make it through a single day if something happened to you. I really don't know how Beth and Preacher manage. I don't have that kind of strength."

"And I don't have this kind of strength."

"Oh, Ellie. Honey. You do. You are stronger than you think."

"No, Mom. I'm not. I hate this. I hate that Sarah's gone. I hate that I'm still here. And I hate that everybody blames me."

"Nobody blames you, Ellie. Nobody. I assure you."

"You don't see the way they look at me, Mom. Like it's all my fault."

"Who looks at you like that? Everybody loves you, Ellie. You have tons of friends. The entire town has supported you. Nobody blames you at all. I promise." It's time for Ellie to get out of the car, but I'm not ready for her to leave. Not like this.

"Whatever," she says, opening the door and grabbing her heavy backpack from the floorboard. "I'm staying late for haunted house, remember?"

"Okay, sweetie." I smile through my worry. "What time should I pick you up? Seven?"

"Seven thirty." With this she closes the door and makes her way through the crowd. Several girls rush to join her, tucking in at her side. If only she could feel how loved she really is. I don't know how to help her see that. I pull my car to the side and watch her weave her way through the world, wishing more than anything I could ease her pain.

Chapter 17

BEFORE I HEAD TO THE OFFICE, I PULL INTO THE OLD FINA STATION
to refill my tank and give Beth a call. Once upon a time we were
meeting here as teens, trading cigarettes and wine coolers, chasing Carl and his older friends. Beth served as the designated driver
and constant lookout to ensure we wouldn't be caught. Now a long
blank space spreads between Beth and me. No matter how many
times she and Preacher insist they don't blame me for what happened to Sarah, I blame myself.

She answers on the second ring, and I speak with a soft voice,
acknowledging the weight of today's anniversary. "Beth? I've got an
eight-thirty client, but I've cleared my schedule for the rest of the
day. I'll be heading out with fliers. I just wanted to see if you might
want to go with me? Or we can go for a walk? Grab some coffee?
Anything you need."

"Thanks, Amanda."

There's a pause, and I'm not sure how to fill it. If either of us
speaks, we may burst into tears. So we steep in the silence until Beth
takes the lead. She tells me their plans for the day include a few television interviews.

"We've just finished the local morning shows. We're trying to
keep Sarah's pictures out there so people won't stop looking."

"I'm glad they're giving you air time."

"We go in to talk about trafficking. No matter how much we hate it, we've been given this platform. We're trying to make the most of it. Even if it doesn't bring Sarah back to us, maybe we can at least help other missing children."

I take a deep breath. My lungs fill with the harsh fumes of gasoline.

"You think she's being exploited?"

"It's a possibility," Beth says. "Preacher's convinced."

"I'll target the typical hot spots again today. I keep thinking there's something we're not seeing. Something right in front of our eyes."

"Thanks, Amanda. As soon as we finish up here, we plan to spend the afternoon out at Jay's camp. Just the two of us."

"I'm sorry, Beth. I'd do anything to fix this. To bring her home."

As I say the words *fix this*, Carl's criticisms come rushing back, and my hands begin to shake. *What if he's right? What if what they really need is for me to leave them alone?* I set the fuel pump and clasp my hands together. The chemical scent clings to my fingers.

"We don't blame you, Amanda. We really don't. It's . . . it's all too hard." Her sigh lasts longer than any I've ever heard. For the first time since The Day, I sense she is losing her final bit of faith.

We end the call, and I cap my tank just as Jay pulls his truck to the opposite side of my pump. He smiles and exits the cab. "You still fill up at the Fina? Who does that?"

"Too sentimental for my own good."

"Yep. Loyal to a fault." He laughs. "Where are you headed?"

"Work." We talk around fumes as cars rush by. "Just one client. Then off to post more fliers. It's been a year. Today."

"I know," he says. "You holding up?"

"Ehhh. What choice do we have?"

"Right."

I move to his side of the pump. "How did you get through those days, when we all relied on you to be the strong one?"

"Somebody's got to do it." He shines his trademark grin, a bit of a crooked hook to the right corner, with the kind of perfect white teeth that make every girl dream of being kissed.

"I'm serious. It has to get to you."

"Of course it does, Gloopy. Just don't tell anybody." Another smile. As Raelynn likes to say, Prince Charming has nothing on this man. But I'm not one of the many who fall for that charm. I'm his friend. He can't butter his way through truth with me.

"Jay," I challenge.

"Gloopy." He slides his credit card into the machine, selects his fuel, and begins to pump.

"Get real."

He pulls back a second before lowering his guard. "Okay. Truth is, I learned it the hard way. Right after I was elected. One of the worst things I ever had to do. I had gone out to a wreck scene. One of my deputies was killed. Remember?"

I nod. I do.

"I had just hired him. He wasn't on duty when it happened, but still. I felt responsible. Having to go to his house and tell his wife. She was standing there, pregnant, holding another kid on her hip. All of twenty-two years old."

"Horrible."

"It was." He returns his debit card to his wallet and leans against his truck. It's shiny clean, with a fresh coat of wax.

He doesn't mention his own similar heartache. I can still picture Jay's beautiful blond fiancée, Riley. She was a girl he'd met in college. He'd brought her home a couple times from Lafayette, once to announce their engagement. Her death was awful. Those invitations all stamped and ready to mail, strewn across the highway from the crash. There's no doubt, delivering that kind of news to his deputy's wife brought it all to the surface for him. But I don't mention Riley. And neither does he.

"So I figured I sure wasn't going to last long in this job like that. I had to learn right then and there. When it starts to get the best of me, I walk away. Separate from it. If I need to cry, I go off and cry. And then I come back and take charge again."

He opens up to me and I listen. In all my years counseling families, I've never heard a man be so honest about his emotions. Not here in Livingston Parish, where boys are taught to be solid, tough, almost brutal. And yet here's the strongest man in all of LP telling me he cries. And he owns it.

"It's like my grandfather always said, somebody's got to be the leader. That's what I was hired to be. But how am I supposed to help anybody if I'm a wreck myself? Simple as that."

I enter my office and move straight to the calendar. I've got all of ten minutes before Mrs. Hosh arrives. It's been years since her son's suicide, and she's finally scheduled her first official appointment. She begged to come today, and I couldn't dare tell her I was taking the day off.

As she enters, I stand to greet her, hoping I can give her what she's come to find.

"I'm not sure why I'm here," she says, nervously fidgeting with her purse as I offer her a seat. She stays on the edge, straight-backed and guarded.

"It's scary the first time. Everyone feels that way. What can I get for you? Water? Tea?"

She accepts a cup of cold water from the Kentwood tank and begins to ease herself against the back of the upholstered chair, one of the few pieces I took from Mom's house after she died. At Carl's insistence, I left the rest behind for the new tenants. No easy thing for me to do.

"So how does this work?" she asks.

"Well, in all my years as a therapist, with all those families, I've learned I'm not here to give people advice. I'm here to listen."

There's a pause here. Then she says, "I was hoping you would have something to say. And I could listen." She laughs nervously and fidgets with her hands.

I take a seat in the chair next to her. "I do have a few tricks I can teach you. Might help you cope with the pain."

"Yes." She relaxes a bit and takes a sip of water. "That's what I need. It's been nearly five years, and I still have what you would call panic attacks. I fall apart at random times, when something brings it all back to me. A smell. Something I see. It's crazy. I think I'm going crazy."

"You're not going crazy. You're dealing with a terrible tragedy. Losing a child—that's one of the hardest things anyone could experience. The fact that you're sitting here with me today proves how incredibly strong you are."

She sighs. Spins the paper cup in her hands.

I stand and grab a cardboard shoe box from my shelf, pulling it to my desk. "Some of my clients have found this helpful." I give her the empty box, and she sets her water down on the end table. "They like to think of it as a tool."

She opens the lid but says nothing, so I explain this as a way to compartmentalize her pain.

"I'm not sure I understand." She closes the box and sets it in her lap.

"Well, sometimes it helps to move through the steps. Are you willing to give it a try?"

She shrugs, eyeing the box suspiciously. "Okay."

"What is hurting you most? Right now? The first thing that comes to mind?" I give her time.

"Today is his birthday. Ryan. He would be twenty-three." She doesn't cry when she says this. It's as if she's telling me what to get from the grocery store or what size shirt to order.

"This must be a very difficult day for you."

She doesn't nod or say a word. The answer is in her eyes.

On an index card, I write, *It's hard to deal with certain days like birthdays, holidays, and anniversaries.* Then I hand her the paper. "Go ahead and put this in the box."

She does as I ask, and we continue the exercise. She tells me her hurts, and I record them.

"My husband won't go to the cemetery with me. He won't talk about Ryan. He acts as if we never had a son at all."

I write on the card. When I hand it to her, she reads and nods. Then she puts it into the box.

"Anything else?"

"My daughters say I'm stuck in the past. That I can't let go of my son. It's the worst. I love my children. All of them."

"Of course you do." I write on the card, and she adds it to the box.

"What else is causing you to feel hurt? Anxiety, anger?" I let her process each emotion.

"My parents. It's almost as if they blame me. They tell me . . . they say I didn't raise him to fear God. That we weren't Christian enough."

I listen as she fights tears.

"But I did my best," she continues. "I brought him to Mass every Sunday. We rarely missed. We prayed together before every meal. I don't know what more I could have done." She's crying hard now as she moves her right hand in the shape of a cross.

"That's the thing about suicide. It's an irrational act."

"Yes. It is." She nods repeatedly.

"People don't know how to make sense of it. We try to frame it around our traditions of faith."

"That's true."

"And anytime a child makes an unfortunate choice, people tend to blame the parents. Usually the mother. It's how we convince ourselves it could never happen to us. What happened to Ryan is not your fault."

"I know. But sometimes I feel like it is."

"From what you've explained to me, it's clear your son was suffering from depression. Would you agree?"

She nods again. "Yes, that's what the doctor said."

"So it sounds to me as if he didn't take his own life to hurt you." I pause here. She waits for more. "Ryan wasn't enraged or seeking revenge. He was suffering. And he couldn't find any other way to end the pain. It's as simple as brain chemistry."

"I know, I do. Because I know Ryan. I know my son's heart. But how can I make everyone else understand? They think I'm making excuses. That I can't face the truth."

"But that is the truth. Your son had an illness. No different from cancer or diabetes."

She sighs.

"Maybe it will help to think of it this way. Let's say you have a disease. You live every day in pain, suffering, even in your sleep. You could be in this kind of pain for the rest of your life. No way to numb it. This is not a bearable pain. It's the unbearable kind. The kind that makes people want to pull their own abscessed tooth."

"Exactly. Yes." She holds the box with two hands, as if she's guarding a treasure.

"That's what his mind did, Mrs. Hosh. It pulled the tooth. The only difference is, in Ryan's case, the root of the pain was his own brain. An imbalanced chemical reaction. It had nothing at all to do with how many Sundays he sat in those pews. It was an illness. He died from that disease just as others die from cancer or pneumonia."

I write on another index card: *People's cruelty and criticism.*

When I pass it to her, she reads it out loud and then puts it into the box.

"Anything else?" I pass the cards and the pen to her, and she accepts.

She writes another card, reading it to me as she adds it to the pile. *I am ashamed of my weight.* Then a second. *I am afraid my husband is about to leave me.* And another. *I'm not sure I believe in God anymore.*

As she drops the final card, she looks to me and asks, "Too many?"

"No such thing," I assure her.

She stares into the box. "I think that's it. For now, anyway."

"Okay, let's close the lid."

She does as I suggest.

"Now, what do you think the point of this might be?"

I wait, letting her think it through. When she says nothing, I explain. "I want you to learn to control your pain instead of allowing the pain to control you."

She sits up, intrigued.

"From this point on, you are the only one who can open this box. You control when you open it, where you open it, how you open it. Only you can release these thoughts. When it's not an appropriate time to face them, you keep them locked away. When you need to process another part of the pain, you confront it. But on your terms only. Make sense?"

"Yes, actually. It does." She laughs a little at the absurdity of it all.

"Now I'm ready to listen. You can pull out a card and talk about one of those hurtful issues, or you can keep them locked away and talk about something else entirely. You are in charge."

With this, Mrs. Hosh pushes the box under her chair and says, "As silly as it seems, you just set my mind free for the first time in years." She moves her purse to her lap and pulls out a mini photo album. "How about I show you my new puppy?"

I lean to see.

"His name is Milo. We call him our holy terrier." She laughs and shows me the pictures, each one depicting a scruffy Jack Russell being loved to bits.

We talk about the puppy, the joys of expecting her first grandchild, and the plans to surprise her husband with a deep-sea fishing trip for his fiftieth birthday. By hour's end, she picks up her shoe box and says, "I'm going to beat this. I'm going to fight for me."

Chapter 18

By the time I pick Ellie up from her theater practice, I still haven't heard from Carl. I called several times between truck stops and hotels, but I've had no better luck finding him than I've had finding Sarah. So now, as Ellie and I arrive home after this long and difficult day, I'm surprised to see his truck parked crooked under our carport. Walking past, we notice it's full of boxes. He comes out of the house, hang-up clothes in hand.

"Carl?" My voice trembles.

"What are you doing?" Ellie asks.

"I'm leaving." He shows no emotion.

"Carl, honey?" a woman's voice calls from the kitchen. "You want these glasses?"

I fall straight to the ground, slamming my knees hard against the concrete.

"Who's that?" Ellie yells, running into the house.

"How can you do this to us?" I whisper, looking at my husband, the man I have loved since I was a teen. In a flash I am ten years old again, screaming at my own father as he packed his things into the trunk of his car and left my mother and me crying in the driveway. "We're your family, Carl. Your family."

He puts the clothes into the cab of his truck and hurries back inside. I am unable to follow him. I can no longer feel my feet. My knees are bleeding, and my legs fail to hold me.

I'm still on the ground when Carl returns with a young woman by his side. He is holding her hand as Ellie runs behind him, screaming, calling him terrible names. I've never heard my daughter curse, but now she uses all the words we've declared off-limits, and I don't stop her.

"Get in the truck," he tells the woman. She obeys, climbing in from the driver's side.

I cannot move. Instead, I sit on the concrete, watching it all play out around me. "How long have you been with her?"

"Six months," he says. "Her name's Ashleigh. We've got an apartment in Baton Rouge."

He moves back into the house and comes out quickly, holding his guitar. An acoustic six-string. I gave it to him, a gift for our twelfth anniversary. "Why are you doing this?"

Ellie stands in front of his truck door, arms crossed, defiant. "You aren't going with her," she says. "You're my father. You can't up and leave us."

"I'm sorry, Ellie," Carl says flatly. "Your mother can tell you why this is happening. Talk to her."

I pull myself to my feet. "What do you think I know? I don't understand this at all. We have everything."

"Amanda, stop pretending. Our marriage has been dead for years."

This knocks the wind from my lungs. "What are you talking about?"

I look at Ashleigh. She's not all that much older than Ellie, early twenties at most. About the age Carl and I were when we said our vows.

Ellie opens the truck door and starts to yell. "He's my father! My father! What right do you have?"

I'm not sure what I would expect someone to say in this situation, but the words I hear are the last thing I'm prepared to process.

"He loves me," Ashleigh says, shrugging. As if it makes perfect sense.

"You'll understand one day. When you're older," Carl says to Ellie. "Your mother and I, we're very different people. It was never a good fit." He might as well be asking her to feed the cat.

I look at the girl in his truck, Ashleigh. So young. "Who are you?" I ask.

"Don't blame me. You didn't give him enough attention." She looks at me as if I should have known better.

Without another word, Carl cranks his truck and leaves Ellie yelling after him in the driveway, crying and chasing him out to the road. Exactly as I did when my own father drove away.

And just like that, he is gone.

"He did what?" Raelynn yells with an intensity that causes me to drop my cell phone. I fumble to pick it back up as she continues. "I'm on my way. Don't do anything stupid."

Ellie slams doors and yells. She's releasing every pent-up emotion she's banked for the last year. I don't stop her. I am beaten down, a mess.

Within minutes Raelynn is at my house. "I'm packing you a bag, and we're going to Jay's camp. He's on his way to meet us there. Ellie?" She gives my daughter instructions, and Ellie obeys.

"What about your boys?" I follow Raelynn to my bedroom,

where she pulls a suitcase from my closet and begins to fill it with clothes.

"Not a problem. They're with my brother. I'm getting you out of this place."

While Raelynn and Ellie pack, I sit on my bed, trying to understand. "Of all days for him to do this to us, Raelynn. He had to choose today?"

"I heard a story on TV last summer," Raelynn says. "*The View* or *Regis and Kelly*, I don't know, but there's this lady who sees a snake in the road, right? It's been run over, but it's still alive. Writhing on the blacktop. So she stops and she goes over to save the snake."

Raelynn pulls socks from my drawer and adds them to the luggage. Then grabs a pair of jeans. "So the lady, she did all this work to save the stupid snake, and you know what the snake did? After she saved his life and took care of him and nursed him back to health and all that?"

I shake my head.

"He bit her! He did. And then the woman started crying and was all upset and she asked the snake, 'Why'd you bite me? I saved your life. I took care of you. I loved you.' And you know what he said to her?"

The hum of the refrigerator grows louder than Raelynn's voice.

"He said, 'You knew I was a snake when you picked me up. What'd you expect?'" She pulls a couple shirts from my closet. "You married a snake, Amanda. A snake."

We hit the highway in Raelynn's minivan. The moon is covered with clouds, and a delicate drizzle begins to fall, just enough to slick the blacktop. It seems to make her hurry faster, determined not to let anything stop us from reaching the river.

We head down Highway 447, where water tops the ditches. Tucked tight behind the trenches are beautiful homes, most built in traditional Southern style with massive front porches. In many of the yards, mobile homes are perched next to the larger house—a typical LP scene as families share their acreage for generations, adding trailers onto random parts of their land until younger relatives can afford to build a home in their designated spot.

Cutting left at the 16 T, we head through Port Vincent and on toward French Settlement, the original river village founded by a group of Acadians that included Raelynn's ancestors. Some of them later ended up staking claims a little farther north, in Walker. As soon as we take the turn, the parish vibe shifts to nearly all Cajun. The land changes too. Houses are now built on piers to withstand rising floodwaters. Many of the wooden homes have raised porches, high slanting rooflines, and outdoor ladders characteristic of Acadian architecture.

Beside me, Ellie starts to cry. Her pain carves canyons in me, a shift of my soul. *Is Carl really a snake, as Raelynn believes?*

We are now in black—no moonlight, no stars, and a steady rain. The highway is flanked here with even steeper, deeper ditches on either side, and only a few porch lights shine. Halos. Like a kid, I pretend they are angels guiding our way, and that no harm will ever come to Ellie again.

Oh, how I want to believe!

As we near the river, the rain becomes a downpour, blocking visibility. Raelynn navigates the bends, focusing intensely as she drives over the narrow bridge and through the long stretch of homes being built along the Diversion Canal. I roll my hands together, trying to ease my nerves.

I knew from the start he had a troubled past. A hardened heart. An abusive family. But my father wasn't much better than his. Who was I to judge? I thought my love would heal him. And I bet my future on it, believing that, together, we would make it.

We reach the launch at Head of Island, and Raelynn finds a place to park in the gravel lot. "We should wait out the rain in the van," she suggests.

"No," Ellie insists, crawling out of the vehicle as quickly as possible.

Jay is waiting for us in his jeans and ball cap, pacing beside his unmarked Ford, soaking wet. His headlights shine, turning raindrops to white as he steps back and forth, breaking the beams.

He rushes to meet me, but I cannot look him in the eye. Carl's words resurface. *Nobody wants you. You're the problem. Our marriage has been dead for years.* And Ashleigh's. *You didn't give him enough attention. He loves me.*

Jay wraps me into his arms, holds me close. "Let this be the last time he hurts you."

There's nothing I can say. I just let him hold me long enough to gain my footing, long enough to catch my breath.

Then Jay returns to his truck, ready to launch his Bass Tracker into the water.

I guide him with hand signals from the canal's dark edge as Ellie waits anxiously, her hands keeping rain out of her eyes. Raelynn unloads the van, complaining about the weather. After pulling the empty trailer back to land and locking his truck, Jay heads our way again, this time with Boudreaux on his heels. The loyal Lab jumps right into the boat. Raelynn joins us, bags in tow, and we all hurry to board.

Jay drops the luggage in his dry storage seat, where he finds a stack of ponchos. Then, shining a Golight across the black face of the water, he takes the captain's chair as I pull one of the wraps over Ellie's head. Raelynn and I cover ourselves too, and Jay takes us to his camp.

With the storm and the night, the Diversion is empty of people. Normally a hot spot for party crowds, the riverfront bars sit silent, clinging together in the dark like shunned mistresses exposing their bruises and scars. No music blares from the balconies; no hired-help repair boats near the pier; no bikini-clad beauties flirt with beer-bellied outdoorsmen. Just rain, pecking the pontoons and pounding the waters that circle the fueling station.

Jay steers the craft out through the canal as the rest of us huddle together in our seats. Even in the dark, the grand estates with their screened-in pools and outdoor kitchens loom heavy over the water, their lanterns blurring through the rain. On the opposite bank are quaint cottages. If it weren't pouring, we'd find people on both sides equally happy to sit on their swings enjoying the moonlight. No one here bothers to waste concern over haves and have-nots. They are as content as I have always been. As I wanted to believe my husband to be. *What does he mean it was all pretend?*

By the time we exit the smooth canal and reach the more rugged route of Blind River, I am cowering beneath the sky fall. I hold our ponchos tight against the wind, trying to shield Ellie from the rain, but the flimsy wraps flap like crazy. When I try to lean over her, to shelter her from the storm, she pulls away.

Jay navigates the river without a map, and despite having been here with him countless times, I become disoriented. I am soaked and shivering.

"Told you we should have waited it out in the van," Raelynn grumps, raising her voice to be heard over the growl of the motor.

Deep in the dark, the Golight catches the yellow glow of eyes scattered across the swampland. Alligators, nutria, opossums, and coons monitor our movements, reminding me that the whole wide world is one dark and dangerous place.

In contrast to the newer, more expensive homes back on the canal, we now pass river camps with no electricity, no running water. Some serve as permanent residences, but most consist of barely more than a wooden frame and a mismatch of salvaged materials. With the land accessible only by boat, getting construction items out here is no easy task, so rubber tires serve as stepping-stones, scrap wood and duct tape work as doors, and plastic tarps wrap rooflines—especially on the camps that have suffered storm damage.

This is a world on water, but I understand why people choose to come here, leaving behind the outside world, opting for the hazards of nature over the malice of man.

As we make the final turn, blasts of air whip against my face, thrashing my hair into a wet, matted mess not so different from the Spanish moss that drapes the cypress boughs around us. By the time we reach Jay's camp, we all look as if we've fought the devil. And lost.

As Jay pulls the blue-and-white Bass Tracker into a slot next to his bateau, Raelynn jumps out to tie the bowline to the cleat.

Once settled, Jay guides us with the Golight. We step beyond the pier to a set of mud-soaked rafters. They stretch end-to-end to form a shoddy walkway through the low-lying land. At his front door we remove our ponchos and shake water from our clothes before entering. We also leave our shoes on the covered porch, a practice that could attract all sorts of critters in search of dry quarters.

Inside, Jay hurries to connect the generator. It roars to life, and I flip a lamp switch while Ellie turns on the kitchen light. Raelynn plugs in a space heater, and we all crowd around the warm, orange glow. I offer my daughter another hug. "We made it." The dark rainy night, the rustic fish camp, the hard-knocked crew of survivors— our lives may not be a fairy tale, but here we are, all together, out of the rain.

Jay gets to work and hands us a stash of towels. After we pat ourselves dry, I brush dust from the sofa and offer Ellie a seat. Boudreaux lies at her feet, and she gives him plenty of attention. Then I pull a blanket from the closet and cover my child. She wraps herself into it and falls back against the couch, looking up at me the way she did as a little girl when she would catch a cold and ask for popsicles or milk shakes to soothe her sore throat.

"This was a good idea," I tell my friends. "Just what we needed."

"I'll bring the cooler in once the rain dies down." Jay looks out the window. "Your luggage should stay dry in the bin."

We settle in as Raelynn entertains us with stories about wild adventures at her brother's camp. Outside the rain begins to slow and the sky starts to fill with stars again. After about an hour, Jay flips the switches to dim the cabin. With the curtains open, he points outside and says, "And then there was light," urging us to watch the transformation taking place beyond the panes. Over the river, the moon shines white and the world is renewed.

Now, as the stars burn across distances too far to fathom, aging billions of years beyond belief, I am reminded of an old Sunday school lesson. The simple one from Genesis that taught us as children that God created the entire universe in the span of one week.

"It's funny, isn't it?" I say to the group. "We tend to get so caught up arguing over details such as days and hours and monkeys and rib bones, we miss the whole point of the story."

"Which is what?" Raelynn challenges.

"That in the beginning, God made light. It was waiting on us when we arrived."

Then I turn to Ellie. "We weren't brought into a world of darkness. Left to stumble around on our own. We were given flame. One that would outlast us all."

She huffs, but she hears.

"Sometimes we start to lose sight of it, don't we? Times like tonight, it felt as if we were lost in the dark. Not a spark to be seen. But that's how this great big world is designed, Ellie. It was made this way for a reason. Again and again we spin into darkness, but the sun is always there, waiting to rise again. It never leaves us. And if we can manage to hold on long enough to make it through the night, then we'll be given a brand-new day."

I pull her still-damp curls from her face and begin to braid them, as I did when she was young. "That's what we have to remember. Light defeats darkness. Never the other way around."

Chapter 19

Wednesday, February 22, 2006

Hello Sparrow,

It's been way more than a year since I was taken. Most people would give up by now. But not me.

Do you know about Daniel? In the lions' den? Daniel was a good guy, and some bad guys locked him in a room with lions. They wanted to prove God wouldn't save him. That God did not exist. They wanted Daniel to turn mean and his heart to turn hard—like them. They wanted him to die.

But Daniel prayed, and God saved him.

Maybe that's what this is, Sparrow. Maybe I'm in the lions' den. Maybe the bad guys don't just want my body. They are trying to take my heart too.

Pop always says if my heart belongs to God, then love wins. So here's what I'm going to do.

1. Pray.
2. Trust God.
3. Be strong.

And then one day, he will get me out of here. Just watch.

"I can't get enough of this weather," I say, looking up at the beautiful blue sky as I walk with Vivienne toward the Tammany Trace. It's an old railroad route that has been renovated to guide hikers and bikers through five quaint Northshore communities. Each month we schedule one planning day, during which Viv and I tackle the logistics of the business and take time for some much-needed "self-care." Today we're determined to soak up some sunshine and make the most of these warm temps. "We'll hit the eighties. Can you believe it?"

"I'm so glad we don't live up north. All that snow? I'll take bugs and hurricanes any day, thank you very much." Then she switches subjects, diving straight for the one topic I'd rather avoid. "So how are things at home?"

As we hit the trail, I reply with an embarrassed grin. "I already know what you're going to say."

"Really?" Viv calls my bluff. "What am I going to say?"

"That it's time for me to face facts. That the man who vowed to love, cherish, and honor me never really cared about me at all." I don't play victim. I'm determined to get past denial.

She makes a buzzer noise. "Not even close. I was going to say, with almost sixteen years of marriage, you've made it longer than most."

I step to the edge of the path, allowing room for a cyclist to zoom past me.

Viv continues. "Amanda, I need you to hear what I have to say."

I look up, my eyes still red and swollen from another sunrise. It's been almost four months since Carl packed his bags for greener pastures, and I have cried every single day. In that time, he's moved back home three times, only to leave again. And again. Just when I start to let go, he comes back, asking me to give it another try.

"You have been living in an abusive relationship. Do you realize that?"

I stop walking. It's the first time someone has put this label on my marriage. *Abusive.* She said it out loud.

"You do know that, don't you?" Viv seems surprised by my reaction.

I shake my head. Now I understand how my clients feel when I say this to them.

"Come on, Amanda. You aren't blind to this stuff. You've been a clinical social worker for years. How many women have you helped work their way out of unhealthy situations? You're one of the best, teaching people to set healthy boundaries for themselves. Coaching couples on how to behave respectfully, how to communicate, how to rebuild trust."

When I stay silent, she prods again. "You have to see the patterns in your own home." Her pitch lifts a bit. "Don't you?"

We start to walk again, but it takes me longer to answer. "I don't equate my own marriage to abuse, Viv. It's nothing like the stories I hear in my office."

"Then why did the truth hit you like a stone to the chest?" She looks at me as she says this, hurling a hard and heavy thought my way. "Forgive me, but I'm going to get real for a minute. From what I can tell, Carl has shown a complete lack of empathy throughout the entire search for Sarah. He has been cold. All those controlling acts, complete disregard for your feelings or needs. He thought he owned you, Amanda. The minute you started stepping outside of the box, he couldn't handle it."

I argue, defending Carl's character. Telling her how it's not as bad as she makes it sound. She's only heard my side of the story, and I haven't represented him fairly. "I never should have told you those things, Viv. It's wrong to let someone into my marriage like that. You're not getting the big picture."

"Stop, Amanda. Please. Listen to yourself. I'm no fool. He puts on a good show, but I hear how he treats you behind your office door. I've bitten my tongue for too long. Every time you tried to be his equal, he pushed you down. I've watched the slide. It's clear what he's been doing to you. For years."

I can't look at her. I keep my eyes on my shoes as they hit the paved trail. Slow steps.

"He's done whatever it takes to keep you beneath him so he could feel better about himself. It's classic abuse. You know this. And when he could no longer keep you down by yelling or calling you names, belittling you or criticizing you, manipulating and gaslighting you, he started getting violent. He had to scare you back into place."

"It's not like you think, Viv. It's what he was taught. That's all. Carl's got a short fuse at home, but he's harmless. It's just a safe place to let off steam, and I let him. We all need to vent sometimes."

"Violence is not the same as venting, Amanda. You're not seeing clearly."

"I know how it sounds."

"Do you?" My argument draws a deep sigh from her. "You know how many people sit in my office and say these things? You've heard them too. I know you have. 'He loves me. He just doesn't know how to show it.' Or 'He doesn't mean to hurt me. He can't help it.' You're smarter than this, Amanda."

I look up, out, through the trees. Anywhere but at Viv. She's right. I do sound like our clients. I try again. "You know Carl's background. He went straight from a rough home to working the rigs. And now the plant. He's in a hard world. He thinks this is how to be a man. Deep down, he cares."

"But that's not your problem, Amanda. He has to do better than that. At least in how he treats you. Sure, it started with a broken bowl, a slammed door, a few holes in the walls. But when that didn't stop you from looking for Sarah, or helping your clients when a crisis came up, or going on calls with Jay, he got meaner. He had to make sure you were there, serving his dinner the way he wanted it, ironing his clothes without a flaw."

I nod.

"I know I'm not in your home, but I've watched from the outside for years. Tell me if I'm wrong, but it seems to me that Carl has a skewed belief system. He honestly thinks it's your duty to give him 100 percent, all the time. So if you give any of your time or energy or focus to anything other than him, he sees it as his job to teach you a lesson and make it sink in. No matter what it takes. You walk the line, or you pay."

I listen. But I feel as if she's talking about other people. Not Carl and me.

"So when his bullying tactics stopped working," she continues, "he became a terrorist in his own home. Terrorizing you so you would be too afraid to stand up for yourself, to stand up to him, to stand up for what is right. You quit going out on calls with Jay, didn't you?"

I nod again. "Yeah, but that's because Sarah went missing. I was using all my spare time to look for her."

"Well, what about Sarah? You still help with the searches?"

"Yes."

"Only now that Carl's not home. Am I right? He wouldn't let you go anymore. Would he?"

I look down, embarrassed.

"Same with seeing your friends? Why did you always wait to return my calls when he wasn't around?"

How can I admit the truth? Carl didn't like me to use my phone. Or see my friends. Or volunteer. Or do anything outside of family when he was off work. Viv is right. I never even realized it was happening. I just kept trying to keep him calm. Trying to keep him happy. Trying to love enough. Be enough.

"It's all right. You don't have to admit it. I know. The bottom line is this: Your husband wanted to be your god. Bow to no other gods before him. Period."

"Viv, please." I roll my eyes. "You're acting as if I'm on the run for my life. That's a little extreme, don't you think?"

She follows behind me, getting worked up. "Throwing things at you? Shoving you? Beating down doors while you cower on the other side, shaking in fear because you know he might hurt you?" Now she gives my arm a gentle tug, insisting I look at her. "That's not love, Amanda. That's abuse."

No matter how much sense she's making, I can't bring myself to say she is right. To admit my husband does not value me.

But Viv isn't backing down. "It's clear you love him. I know you do. But right now he's not capable of giving that kind of love in return. You have to stop thinking he has the ability to care about you the way you care about him. He's not like you. The truth is your husband used you. He abused you. He lied to you, and now he's betrayed you. He hurt you and he hurt Ellie. At a time when y'all needed him most. Unless he manages to go through some significant personal growth, I'm willing to bet he'll do the same with this new girlfriend of his. He's got real struggles, Amanda. But there's nothing you can do to change him. That's up to him. You can only change what you are willing to accept from him. You can only change yourself."

***

I have been pacing for nearly an hour, phone in hand, trying to will myself to dial Carl's number. I've talked myself into a frenzy by this point, circling around the pros and cons of returning his call. I listen to his voicemail one more time.

"Hey. Call me."

That's it. Three words. They have hooked into the bruised and broken pieces of myself, the parts that were just beginning to heal.

So here I am, sitting on my bed, staring at my phone, trying to find a rational reason to call Carl, a man who could be, as Viv insists, completely incapable of caring about me—the woman who wore his ring, who birthed his child, who loved him. I'm still trying to absorb the truth—Carl doesn't care about me and maybe he never did. Now I have to pay the price for my poor decision. For choosing, as Raelynn says, to care for a snake.

The problem is, I still don't think of Carl as a snake. Not at all. I see him as a man, flawed and struggling, but still a man. With love tucked deep inside him. I've seen glimpses of it. And I still have hope he will see himself as I see him—as a good person, a hurting person, a person who was never really taught how to love and be loved, but a man who deserves to be loved, no matter how hard he makes it at times.

I press my keypad, and the phone begins to ring. Carl answers immediately. "Amanda?" He says my name like it's a life preserver and he's clinging to me for dear life. My mother speaks again: *You need to help him through whatever crazy stuff he's fighting through.*

"Carl? What's wrong?" *Stay strong, Amanda. Steady your voice.* I stand and straighten a framed photo on the wall. It covers the place where he sent the hot iron through the Sheetrock. It's a trick I learned from Raelynn. Hang a few pictures and mirrors, and just like magic the scars disappear.

As he talks, I remove the photo. It shows a picture of Ellie hiking a wooded trail during our Rocky Mountain vacation. But just behind the fantasy, the gaping hole remains. I hear Viv's voice: *He was aiming for your head. That's not love, Amanda. That's abuse.*

We're barely into the conversation when his tone shifts to hints of frustration, then anger. "I haven't seen Ellie in weeks. She won't return my calls. I don't know what you've been telling her, but it's not fair to turn my daughter against me."

"That's absurd, Carl." I almost laugh, but I know better. "I haven't told her anything negative about you. Not one word."

"You expect me to believe that?"

"Of course I do. In fact, I've been trying my best to keep y'all connected. She needs a father, Carl. She needs you."

"Sure, Amanda. Tell yourself that. You know as well as I do, you have always wanted to be a single mom, just like your mother. No clue how to take care of a man. This is what you always wanted. Total control."

Do not react, Amanda. Don't let him beat you down.

"Carl, I'm sorry you believe that about me. It was very hard for my mother to raise me on her own. You know that. And you also know that nothing matters more to me than my family, giving Ellie a stable, happy home. This is the last thing I wanted in my life. Especially for Ellie." My emotions get the best of me now. As my pitch peaks, Carl reacts with more hate.

"Stop yelling at me! You love to fight, don't you!"

"I'm not yelling. I'm crying. Listen, Carl. I would never try to come between you and Ellie. She needs you. She needs to know you love her. She's questioning that now, of course, and that will leave a lasting scar. Trust me. I know."

"Of course you do!" He is being sarcastic now. "You're the great Amanda Salassi. You know everything."

"She needs to trust that we will never abandon her. That there are two people in this world who are here to love her no matter how hard life gets. We are those people, Carl. If you want to leave me, that's one thing. But you can't leave Ellie. That's not how it works."

"That's why I'm taking her for the weekend. I made reservations in New Orleans. For Mardi Gras. We'll go down for Endymion on Saturday, stay through for Bacchus on Sunday. One night away."

I grab hold of the kitchen chair. Images of Ellie and Sarah come back to me. They are laughing and bowing in their costumes at Mardi Gras World, waving their hands like queens of the carnival. "Carl, you can't be serious. New Orleans? This time of year? After what happened with Sarah?" I hear him laughing. "I'm sorry, but I can't let you take her down there. Not for Mardi Gras."

"I knew you'd make a big deal out of it. Always overdramatic. Like we live in a soap opera or something. They're hardly even having the parades this year. Everything's still wrecked from Katrina. It'll be a bunch of locals catching beads. Don't make it a problem."

"Sarah was taken on a regular Friday afternoon," I argue. "In one of the safest parts of the city."

"What do you want to do? You want to lock Ellie in a cage? Don't you get it? You're doing more harm to her than if she was kidnapped."

I cannot find the strength to counter. He senses blood and goes for the kill.

"We'll pick her up Saturday morning. Around ten. Have her ready."

"We?" I ask, my voice a whisper.

"Ashleigh and me. You can't keep my daughter from me, Amanda. Don't fight me on this, or I'll file for divorce and demand full custody."

He hangs up the phone, and I'm left with my head spinning. I hurry to the bathroom, where I bend over the toilet just in time. When nothing remains, I wash my face, brush my teeth, and feel my way down the hall to Ellie's bedroom, crying.

"What's wrong? Mom? Tell me, what's going on?"

After all these months of staying strong for Ellie, refusing to break, being the container for her grief, I finally lose it. I crawl across her bed and cry until my heart is empty of pain.

Ellie sits beside me, watching me. "I'm sorry," I say, again and again. "I'm sorry."

Get a grip, Amanda. Don't throw this on Ellie. She's the child. You're the mother. Be strong.

I sit straighter, catch my breath, and then it comes rising up again. "This is all so unfair," I sob. "Why is he doing this to us?"

"I called Ms. Raelynn," Ellie says. "I'm worried about you, Mom. You're not okay."

"You're right, Ellie. I'm not okay. I'm not okay!" I explain Carl's plans for Mardi Gras. "I never wanted anything more than a happy home . . . a good family for you. And I tried so hard to be perfect, keep him happy. You deserve better."

"Mom, don't worry about it. I don't want to go to New Orleans." Ellie hugs me. "Besides, I'm not an idiot. I know he isn't doing this for me. He's just trying to look good in front of that Ashleigh lady. That's all he cares about now. Her."

"Oh, Ellie. He loves you very much. He's just confused. It happens to men around this age . . . a midlife crisis. It's very common. They get kind of lost. This isn't who he really is."

As I say this, Raelynn arrives, rushing into the bedroom. "What on earth is going on?"

Ellie answers for me. "She can't stop crying."

"What'd he do now?" Raelynn doesn't shield Ellie from her thoughts about Carl.

Again my daughter answers. "He threatened to divorce Mom and fight her for custody if she doesn't let him take me to New Orleans for Mardi Gras with that . . ." Ellie describes Ashleigh using words I've never said in my life, and Raelynn's eyes grow wide, but not because of Ellie's swearing.

"He did what?" She is a ball of fire. "Get up, Amanda. Get up!" She pulls my arm, and I claw my way from Ellie's bed.

"Ellie, you are not going to New Orleans. And, Amanda, you are not losing custody of our girl." She gives my daughter a strong, confident look, assuring us both she's got this all under control. "Here's what we're going to do." She hands me my phone. "You're going to call Carl right this minute. And you'll tell him there's no way on God's green earth Ellie will step foot in New Orleans for Mardi Gras. If he wants to file for divorce, then he can go right ahead. He owes you a favor anyway."

Hello Sparrow,

It's Mardi Gras, and The Lady brought us a king cake. I call her Bridgette now. It hurts her feelings if I don't. She got the piece with the baby, and she started dancing. She said she'd never won anything.

I told her the baby means good luck. That made her happy. She had never thought of herself as lucky before. I said, "Well, now you are."

I told her about the three wise men and how the baby is supposed to be Jesus. She said it didn't make any sense that Mary was a virgin, and I told her lots of things don't make any sense. She said, "Ain't that the truth."

Hello Sparrow,

I can't sleep. I keep thinking about a girl I knew who got pregnant. She was thirteen. Like me. Her name was Rose, and it turned out that her uncle was the father. She ended up having twins.

Rose lived with us for a while, even after the babies were born. She lived in the room next to mine. Then one day her uncle came to get her. They took the babies too. Never even said good-bye.

I told Bridgette this story, and she said, "Figures."

I asked Bridgette why Rose would go back to the man who hurt her.

She sat real quiet for a long time. Then she said, "Maybe she loved him."

Hello Sparrow,

I learned something about The Man and Bridgette. They aren't married.

My parents' anniversary is in March. I want to mail them a card, but Bridgette said, "I don't know how many times I gotta tell you. We're your family now."

Every year Mom and Pop would say their vows, like they were getting married again:

From this day forward, I will be your home.
My arms will shelter you, never hurt you.
My words will soothe you, never defeat you.
And my love will strengthen you, never betray you.

Then Pop would turn and say them to me. He used to tell me there was nothing I could do to stop him from loving me. I hope so. Because I've had to do a lot of things he wouldn't like. That's for sure.

Chapter 20

THE GYM IS PACKED FOR THE ANNUAL MIDDLE SCHOOL FUND-raiser, where coaches and town leaders square off. They ride donkeys while playing basketball, and the noise is deafening. Between the pounding of the basketballs, the roar of the buzzer, and the cheer of the crowds, I have to lean close to hear Raelynn's story about her family's latest hunting adventures. Ellie sits with Nate and his brothers, playing a game on her phone and pretending she doesn't know anyone here. During halftime Raelynn glances toward her and says to me, "At least she came."

"She's only here for Nate, you know. She'd never leave her room if it weren't for the school plays. Since Carl left, she just keeps sinking. I've tried everything."

"Give her time." The buzzer announces the start of the third quarter, and we both turn our attention back to the court. Raelynn cheers loudly for Nate's favorite coach, and the rest of us clap along when he scores. I watch the cheerleaders and wonder where Sarah is now. "Have you talked to him?" She's asking about Carl.

"I've tried. A million times. I can't get through to him. He won't let me finish a sentence."

"What do you mean?"

"He shuts down every conversation. Tells me all I want to do is fight, or that I'm crazy, or that I never wanted to be married in the first place."

"Where'd he get that idea?" Raelynn laughs. "I don't know anybody who was a better wife than you. Except maybe Beth. But even I could be a good wife to a man like Preacher."

"Carl should have married you." I laugh. "You'd give him a reality check."

"Ha! He'd be dead by now!" Then, after a pause, she adds, "I never would have married him. His true colors were showing way back from the start."

"Not really, Raelynn. It didn't get bad until Sarah was taken. That's when things changed."

She sits upright and widens her eyes. "Are you serious, Amanda? Let me remind you, this is the very same man who pushed you out of the car on prom night. Left you crying in the mud as he sped away. Remember? You called Beth and me to come get you. We found you with your dress torn. All covered in mud."

"Let's watch the game."

But Raelynn continues. She's ready to tell me all she's held in for years. I tune out, focusing instead on the donkeys and this ridiculous sport, wishing I could go back in time. Make different choices. Protect Sarah. Save my marriage. Fix these problems in Ellie's life.

". . . And remember when you caught him cheating on you with that girl from Live Oak? He stormed through your mama's house and punched holes in her doors like a madman. What were you, fifteen? I told your mom that day, I said, 'Carl doesn't really love Amanda.' And I was right. I knew it even then. You just never listen to me."

"We were kids, Raelynn. We all did stupid things. Let's not talk about Carl. Okay?" I turn toward Ellie, ensuring she is safely out of earshot. There's nothing I can say. Raelynn's right. While there were plenty of happy moments throughout the years, I should have known better than to believe Carl's violent temper would quell over time. That I could make him happy. Keep him calm.

"Move on, my friend. It's time." Raelynn swings back around to watch the game. Then she leans closer. "I'm not trying to be mean. I just know how it goes. It starts off as a cold look, a hurtful word or two. Soon you're living in constant fear of criticism, attacks. You think you can handle a few broken mirrors and plates, but before you know it you've got broken bones too."

"He never broke my bones, Raelynn."

She lets out a long sigh and says, "He didn't have to."

Raelynn keeps her eyes on me, making sure this sinks in. I respond as I always do, trying to defend Carl. "I just keep thinking he'll wake up and realize what he's doing to our family. To Ellie." I look at my daughter and fight tears.

"You think he'll go to counseling?"

"Probably not. He actually agreed last week. I even found someone neutral, a therapist I didn't know. But Carl never showed up. I sat there, humiliated, with the counselor trying to fill the gaps." I laugh it off. "But I have to try, Raelynn. I may not be able to save this marriage, but if the time comes to let it go, at least I'll know I gave it my best shot."

"You've given it more than most would give." She sighs. "I guarantee."

We're less than a minute into the fourth quarter when a man in a suit and tie walks up to us. "Mrs. Salassi?"

"Yes?" I question as much as confirm.

He hands me a legal envelope and says, "You've been served." His eyes offer apology. Then he leaves me sitting here, stunned. I pull open the envelope to find a petition for divorce.

Leaning over me as I read, Raelynn shouts, "What the—" Then she tugs the papers from my hand. "You've got to be kidding me!" Somehow her voice calls out louder than all the other noises in the gym. People turn and stare. Even Ellie looks up from her phone, embarrassed.

From across the room, Jay watches the scene unfold. He leaves the group he's been talking to and heads our way.

I take the papers back from Raelynn and stuff them into the envelope, out of view.

Jay approaches, smiling, teasing Raelynn. "Ladies, I'm sorry to tell you. Someone has filed a complaint about a disturbance of the peace over here. Some woman with crazy red hair and too many tattoos keeps making a bunch of noise. Know anything about that?"

"Not now, Jay." Raelynn jerks the envelope from my hands again, passing it to our friendly sheriff. "Look what this idiot has done now." She turns back to me, growling, "I'm gonna kill him one day, Amanda, I swear."

"What is it, Mom? What happened?" Ellie moves in closer, trying to understand the commotion.

Jay opens the papers, then gives us both a heartbreaking sigh of sympathy. I don't answer Ellie. And I don't respond to Jay. I am no longer here with either of them.

Hello Sparrow,

Something happened today. A new man came to visit. He paid The Man extra to leave us alone. "Privacy," he said, and he locked the door. I thought he was like all the other men who come to visit. But he wasn't. He whispered, "Is your name Sarah Broussard?"

I don't know what happened. I got scared. I sat there, looking at him.

He asked me again, "Are you Sarah Broussard?"

What if The Man sent this guy to test me? What if he was working for The Boss?

I didn't say a word. When he asked me the third time, I said, "My name is Holly."

He gave me a weird look, and then he told me what he wanted me to do. When he was finished, he left. I think it was a test.

Hello Sparrow,

Bridgette and The Man got into a bad fight today. He was throwing things at her and yelling. I hid in my room and prayed he wouldn't hurt her. She was screaming and throwing things too. They were arguing over what to watch on TV. I don't know how anybody could get that mad about TV.

After that, Bridgette came into my room and was yelling at me. She was so mean.

It made me think about something Mom told me. We were helping at a homeless shelter. One of the guys there didn't want the blanket we gave him. He didn't like the cot. He was mad about the pizza. He kept knocking things over and fussing. Pop took him outside because the other people were scared of him. I was too.

When Pop came back, I asked why the guy was being so mean. We were only trying to help him. Pop said, "Maybe that's why he's mad. He knows he needs help, and he's too proud to take it."

Then Mom put her arm around me and she said, "It's hard to understand, Sarah. But if you try to pet a dog who has a broken leg, he might bite you, just to make sure you don't hurt him worse.

It's 3:00 a.m., and I am jolted from sleep with another nightmare. The same one I've had countless times since Sarah went missing.

I'm running through the dark alleyways of New Orleans, chasing Sarah. She's ahead of me, just out of reach, and she's racing away, laughing. The alley walls are filled with colorful metal birdcages, like the one that held the fortune-teller's sparrow.

In the dream, I run for long stretches, calling out to her. "Wait!" I yell. "I'm coming!" I'm almost close enough to grab her when a man jumps from an alcove and attacks me with his knife. He stabs me again and again from behind. I fall to the ground, bleeding, and then I see his face. The man is Carl.

Only this time, the dream has something new at the end. Carl stands over me, knife in hand. He says, "I never loved anybody."

Just as I take my last breath, the cages swing open and thousands of sparrows fly free.

Sunday, May 14, 2006
Mother's Day

"Happy Mother's Day!" Ellie wakes me with a card and a vase of fresh wildflowers.

"Oh my goodness, Ellie. These are beautiful!" I ignore my allergic itch and give the blooms a deep inhale. "They smell so good!"

"Got them in the pasture at the end of the road." She smiles proudly. "Open the card."

I sit up and blink a few times to give my eyes a chance to wake up. Then I tear open the powder-pink envelope to find a handmade card. "Ellie! You drew this?"

She nods, grinning broadly.

The velvety-soft construction paper brings back a swarm of memories. "Gosh, this makes me think of all those art projects we used to do together." Hours spent painting, coloring, glittering, never worrying one bit about the mess. "I'm so lucky I get to be your mom. Best thing about my life. No doubt." I give her a gentle kiss on the forehead, and she accepts.

On the front of the card she's drawn a beautiful sketch of a feather. It's dark blue and deep purple with tones of turquoise peeking through. "This is gorgeous," I say, opening the folded paper to find another work of art inside. Here she's inked a mother and a girl.

"That's us," she says.

"I can tell." I offer a proud tilt of my head. The sketch really does resemble the two of us. Our arms are outstretched, depicted as wings, and we are soaring high above the rest of the world, which sits miniaturized below. We're both smiling peacefully. A halo of light catches the colors of our feathers, almost as if we glow. "This is the most amazing drawing, Ellie. You have so much talent. Thank you. Best gift ever."

She beams. At the bottom of the card, she's written: *The emancipation of you and me.*

"Tell me about the picture." I pat the bed, urging her to come cuddle beside me. She does.

"It's supposed to show us being free."

"I like that idea. Free from what?"

"Just free," she says. "Completely free. Free from our sadness. Our anger and our fears. Free from what we're supposed to do and what we don't want to do. Free."

Trying not to cry, I hold Ellie against my heart, her drawing in my hands. Out my window, the morning gifts us with a golden arch of light. Looking at the sky, I whisper, "You've always been so smart for your age. Such a deep thinker. When you were little, you used to stare into the clouds. You said the sky was the wild blue yonder."

She smiles. "I wanted to know what was up there. I wanted to fly."

"What do you say we get in the car, and we start driving, and we don't stop until we get where we're going?"

Ellie laughs. "Okay. Where are we going?"

"I don't know. Somewhere we feel free."

In less than two hours we've reached Gulfport, a navy town on the Mississippi coast, known more for its working seaport than its beaches. In these parts, the barrier islands keep the inner waters brown and unappealing. Katrina has done a number on the entire stretch, but by taking Captain Skrmetta's boat from the yacht harbor out to Ship Island, we'll reach white sands and dolphin waters that aren't all that different from Florida's Emerald Coast, our preferred vacation destination.

With swimsuits and sunscreen, we load our small cooler onto the *Pan American* just in time for the nine o'clock departure. The boat is crowded with passengers equally eager for surf and sun. Temperatures are supposed to reach ninety today, and the warmth is good for us both. Ellie stays close to me as the boat pulls from its dock and heads out toward the open sea.

Neither of us says it, but I imagine we're both remembering the ferry ride from Algiers, when Sarah stood on the deck shouting at the wind, "We're free! We're free!" It's one of the last images I have of Sarah. Her arms stretched like wings, her head tilted toward the sun, her smile shining with delight. Wherever she is now, I hope she's somewhere feeling free.

The captain thanks us all for returning, explaining how tough it's been since Katrina. We're one of the first voyages out to the island since the company resumed business last month.

"You won't believe it now, but that Friday night before Katrina, it looked like the Normandy invasion with all those boats coming in. They were trying to stay ahead of the storm, get upriver. But the forecasts were saying it would hit Florida. We didn't start tying boats until twenty-four hours before landfall. That's not enough time. It was every man for himself."

He continues to tell us about the extensive damage done to East Ship Island. With nearly two-thirds of it being lost to the storm, the channel known as Camille Cut was significantly widened. He assures us West Ship Island, our destination, fared much better. Then, with a sailor's spunk and a survivor's grit, the third-generation ferry captain blows the ship's horn with a celebratory howl. A signal to all: the worst is over.

Ellie turns her back to the wind and asks, "Think we'll go to Destin this year?"

"I'm not sure yet, honey. Let's just enjoy today."

Ship Island sure isn't the Emerald Coast, but it's the best I can do without Carl's help. He hasn't contributed a dime since he moved out, and I've been struggling to keep up with all our living expenses on my salary alone. Any little kink, like the new tires I had to buy last month, or Ellie's theater costumes the month before, can send me looking at my credit cards, a place my mother taught me never to turn. If it weren't for the rental income I get from her house, we'd be in trouble.

As the waves lick the ship, I'm betting that Carl and Ashleigh will be enjoying a week's vacation in Florida this summer. They may even invite Ellie to go with them. And of course she'll want to go. Why shouldn't she?

It takes about forty-five minutes to complete the eleven-mile journey to Ship Island. As the vessel docks, I point east and challenge Ellie with a bit of trivia. "Did you know there used to be another island out there—between here and Horn?"

She shakes her head and carries the mini-cooler from the ship. The sand is already warm, but it's not yet too hot for bare feet, so I kick off my flip-flops and hold them as we walk along the beach. Ellie does the same.

"Supposedly the Native Americans who lived on the coast—some of them your ancestors, by the way—used to talk about an island that would appear and disappear."

She gives me a strange look, as if she's way too old for fairy tales.

"Seriously," I tell her, "it would be seen for years at a time, and then it'd be gone again. Only to come back many years later. Some sailor found a dog that had been stranded there, washed in during a hurricane. So they named it Dog Island. It was on maps in the early 1800s, disappeared before the Civil War, and then came back again around the end of the century."

"Cool." Ellie chooses a spot to sunbathe and arranges her towel across the sand. I do the same, claiming a space beside her. The beach is long, with plenty of room for families to spread out, so we find a patch of privacy. And peace.

"I think at one time there was a big casino on the island. Back during Prohibition, when people had to come way out here to drink. They called it the Isle of Caprice, and they would bring boatloads of gamblers in to party. They even bet on swim races. People would swim all the way from the coast to the island. Twelve miles across the Gulf. Supposedly it was a pretty fancy place, with all kinds of imported furniture and luxurious carpets. Can you imagine? The Roaring Twenties." I say this with flare, prissing like a flapper.

"What happened to it?" Ellie pulls out her iPod, hinting this could be the final conversation we have for the day. I try to make it last.

"What do you think happened?"

"It disappeared?"

"It disappeared!"

Just before inserting her earbuds, Ellie looks out to the endless green sea and sighs. Then she says, "Nothing lasts forever."

Julie Cantrell

June 2006

Hello Sparrow,

I would be going to eighth grade if I wasn't stuck here. I always liked school. I miss it.

Bridgette brought me more books today. She'll keep buying them as long as I read to her. I don't think she knows how to read.

One of the books is called *The Little White Bird*. She says books shouldn't be written about places she "ain't never been to." I told her that's what's so magic about books.

She told me to read this one by myself. Here's my favorite part: "The reason birds can fly and we can't is simply that they have perfect faith, for to have faith is to have wings."

See? I believe.

Hello Sparrow,

Bridgette asked me why I'm always writing. I told her I like to journal. She said I'm weird.

I didn't tell her it helps me remember who I am. If I couldn't write it, I might forget all about Sarah Broussard. I might start believing I'm nothing more than Holly. The girl in the back room.

Sometimes, when I have to do the things I have to do, I remember the story about Gomer. Pop said it's about a girl who nobody thought was any good.

I think Gomer was kind of like me. They paid her to be

with men. But Pop says that all of us are born to love and to be loved.

I told Bridgette about Gomer. She said, "You know, not every story's got a happy ending." And I told her, "Mine does."

Hello Sparrow,

Bridgette says I talk about God too much. That if he's real, then why do bad things happen? I told her it's because God lets people make their own choices.

She said that God should make everybody be good. "He does make us all good," I said. "But some of us don't want to stay that way."

Then I asked her why she does bad things, and she said because she's a bad person. I said, "No, you aren't. God made us all the same. So why did you take me, and why do you keep me here?"

That made her mad. She hasn't talked to me since.

But today is her birthday. She's 23. I want to give her something special—my gold cross pin. Maybe then she can learn that even the worst story can have a happy ending.

Hello Sparrow,

I gave Bridgette her present. She cried. I told her I was sorry I made her mad with all my stories, and she said she wasn't mad. I gave her a hug, and she cried some more. Then she asked me why am I so nice to her. I told her I'm nice to everybody. That made her laugh.

I'm glad I gave her the pin. I think she likes it.

Sunday, June 18, 2006
Father's Day

I pull shepherd's pie from the oven just as the Parmesan begins to turn gold atop the mashed potatoes. "My favorite," Carl says, pouring himself a glass of iced tea as if he still calls this house his home.

I let the casserole cool while fixing glasses of water for Ellie and me. Carl waits to be served. Ellie joins us, accepting his hug. "Happy Father's Day." He gives her the attention she craves, asking about her summer.

"I can't believe you'll be in eighth grade this year." He hands her a wad of cash to buy some new school clothes.

"It's nice to have you here," I say, a nervous tremor to my voice as I carry the hot pan to the table and sit for the blessing. The three of us hold hands and Carl says grace, just as he has done for years.

After the amen, thirteen-year-old Ellie looks at her father and asks, with all the hope of a little girl, "When are you moving back home?"

Carl sits taller, puffing out his chest a bit. "I guess that's up to your mother."

This takes me aback. Ellie looks to me for the answer, fidgeting with the cloth napkin in her lap.

"Let's enjoy our meal," I say. "We'll talk about it later." The last thing I want is for Carl to get Ellie's hopes up again. He's played this card before, showing up unexpectedly, full of kind words. But as soon as I start to cave, he builds his walls back in a hurry and bolts for something safer—Ashleigh.

"Ellie's got a performance next week. A preview of the play they'll perform in New York."

"You're coming, right?" Ellie pleads with arched brows. "I got you a ticket."

"Of course I'm coming. Tell me about it. What play is it? Do you have the lead?"

Ellie sinks a little. "No, not the lead."

"But it's a big part." I jump in. "She's been studying her lines for weeks. And she's got a solo."

"You do?" This piques his interest.

Ellie nods. "Scary, huh?"

"You've nailed it every time," I tell her. She rolls her eyes and slumps down. I defend my claim. "You're doing a great job. It'll be incredible."

"I'm sure you'll be the star," Carl says, adding salt to his dish. "I'll be there. Front and center. Count on it."

After dinner Carl and I go outside to talk on the back porch. "How's the car?" He eyes my Honda, moving to look under the hood. "You put a lot of wear on it, searching for Sarah. You changing the oil? Every three thousand miles?"

"Yes. I get it done. It's been fine."

After checking the fluids, he closes the hood and moves to look over our one-acre lot. "And the yard? Mower holding up okay?"

I nod toward the freshly cut lawn. "Not a problem. I always did like cutting the grass. Ellie helps sometimes. It's manageable."

"You should clean out your gutters." He taps the aluminum shaft, pulling out a fistful of leaves still there from fall.

"Yep. I probably should."

"And did you call the exterminator?" Kicking the bricks, he adds, "That's got to be done once a year, you know?"

"I know. Already done."

With nothing else to worry about, he finally takes a seat in one of the rocking chairs. I choose the swing. The excess links of chain clang against the taut stretch as I begin to sway.

"You're doing good, Amanda. Better off without me."

I take this in. It's been eight months. *Am I better off without him?*

"I guess this is what you wanted all along, isn't it? Run the ship. Be in charge of everything."

"Carl, do you hear yourself?"

He sneers. "What, what'd I say? Here we go again. We're out here for two minutes and you're already attacking me." He rocks faster, with force. "Rude!"

I don't bother adding fuel to the fire. I pet Beanie and watch the neighbor's rambunctious crew of kids as they play in the sprinkler. They send plastic balls and Frisbees up in the high-pressure stream of water, trying to run beneath them without letting the toys fall to the ground.

"Remember when we made Ellie that enormous Slip'N Slide? You brought home a giant sheet of Visqueen and we soaped it down with Dawn? It was so slippery the kids couldn't stop at the end. They'd go sailing way off the edge into the grass every time. Remember?"

Carl smiles. "Yeah. We did have fun together, didn't we?"

"What went wrong, Carl?" I look at him now with soft eyes, trying to understand his choices. Something about him still gets to me. His strong jaw. Dark eyes. That scar below his eye from wrecking a dirt bike when he was a kid. I turn away before I become putty in his hands again.

"I don't know, Amanda. You couldn't be happy. Nothing I did was ever enough."

I sigh. "I wasn't the one who wasn't happy, Carl. I wasn't the one who went off looking for something better. This family was everything to me. Still is."

"Yep. I should have known you'd do this to me. You can't ever let anything go, can you? Always bringing up the past."

"The past? You're living with Ashleigh right now. We're still married, Carl. You show up every couple months, telling me you're sorry and want to move back in. This is not the past. This is today."

"Then sign the papers, Amanda. Let's be done with it."

Chapter 21

August 2006

"First day of eighth grade! You ready for this?" I wake Ellie with a kiss and give her a tall glass of ice-cold chocolate protein milk. She props herself up on her pillow as I move to open the blinds. "Look at this beautiful day. Must mean good luck."

She yawns, stretching before drinking her milk.

"I'll make a spinach tomato omelet. Any other requests?"

She shakes her head.

I hand her the outfit we bought for the big first day. She could hardly go to sleep last night, she was so nervous about her last year of junior high.

"I think I want to be homeschooled."

"You'd be bored by day two. And can you imagine me teaching you algebra? Not pretty."

"I'm serious, Mom. I hate going to school without Sarah. It's not the same."

I sit beside her and hold her hand. She lets me.

"We were always together. Like sisters. Stuff like this isn't supposed to happen, Mom. Kids don't just up and disappear. Not from a field trip."

"Does it make you feel unsafe?"

"Kind of. Yeah. I'm always looking around, wondering if someone is about to take me too."

"I sensed that when we were in New York with your theater group. I was scared too. I think that's a normal reaction, given what we've been through."

"Yeah, but I always wonder who I can trust, who might be dangerous. And the sick part is, half the time I wish they would take me. I know that's crazy, but it's so I could know what happened. I just want to know. Where is she? When is she coming back? Is she coming back at all?"

We don't cry. It's been nearly two years since Sarah disappeared, and we can talk about it now without a complete meltdown, but the wounds are not healed and the pain remains, even on our best days.

"I'm not like the others, Mom. All they care about are stupid things like spirit contests and pep rallies. None of it matters. Not to me. Nothing matters."

I sit quietly, letting Ellie release her thoughts, knowing there's not a word I can say to make this better for her. I listen.

"Ellie didn't want to go to school today." I pour Viv a cup of coffee and fix my tea. Then I move to her desk and deliver the caffeine.

She smiles. Accepts. "First day jitters?"

"I'm worried it's more than that. I know it's been nearly two years, but honestly, she hasn't ever come back from all of this with Sarah. And with Carl leaving. It's been too much. I'm afraid I'm losing her."

"Therapy helping?"

I shake my head. "Not really. We've tried everyone I know. Brother Johnson too. And teen groups. I think it's such a unique situation. No one else can really understand what she's going through. Most of the kids in her group are there because of drugs, alcohol. Or self-harm. Some have been abused. Some even have criminal records. Ellie's not them."

"I can see that."

"It's kind of like, one day she's a happy teen, joking with her friends, blowing us away onstage, or hanging out at parties. The next day she's dealing with survivor's guilt again, struggling to see the point of anything. That's how she was this morning. It scares me when she starts thinking like that. Like there's no point to staying alive anymore."

"Did the antidepressants help?" Viv sips her coffee.

"Not really. They numbed her grief, but they numbed everything else too. Turned her into a zombie. Everything alive in her just kind of disappeared."

"Maybe the wrong dose? Wrong prescription?"

"Tried a few. Psychiatrist said we may want to go without. At least until her head can clear. I'm hoping our new 5K training can get her balanced again. It's no marathon or anything . . ."

I smile at Viv, and she thanks me for cheering her across the finish line on her fortieth birthday.

". . . but I'm running with her every evening. It's been good for both of us." I blow on my tea to cool it and finally take a sip.

"I guess I can't help thinking that if Carl was home . . . if our family was intact . . . then maybe she would feel a little more protected or something. She must not even feel safe at home now—the one place she should never be afraid."

"Have you met with an attorney yet? About the divorce?"

"Oh, Viv. Come on." I blow on my tea again, then stir it with a spoon, adding a little lemon. "Let's get happy. You still dating that fireman? Mr. Hottie?"

She laughs. "So corny."

"That's me!" I head to my office and she follows.

"Seriously, Amanda. If Carl's really going through with this divorce thing, you need to be careful. I'm sorry, but I have to ask. He can't touch the business account, can he?"

I take a seat and she does too.

"No worries. I'm sure the business is off-limits."

"That's what the attorney says?"

"Well, I haven't actually talked to an attorney, but Carl's name isn't on this account. So it's safe. Don't worry. He wouldn't do that anyway."

Viv gives me a look of disbelief. "You have got to see an attorney, Amanda. Please. I don't put anything past Carl at this point. I hate to sound cold, but I have to protect our clinic. This is my business too. He's already opened his own accounts, transferred money without asking you. If you don't call a lawyer, I will."

"Honestly, Viv, I just keep thinking he'll wake up. He can't seriously want to marry that girl. She's young enough to be his daughter. She was four years old the day we said our vows."

"See why I don't put anything past him?" She sits back now, settling into the plush chair. "What makes you think he's really going to change, Amanda? Has he given you *any* indication of that? In any way at all?"

I rearrange papers on my desk and lock my purse in the bottom drawer. "I don't know. Yeah. He still says he wants to come back. And that he loves me. This just isn't like him. If I can give him enough time."

"Time?" Viv scoffs. "He moved out nearly a year ago."

"Yeah, but he's moved back in a few times since then."

"For what, a week? Two at most?"

"I know." We both turn our attention out the window, where my first client is parking her car in the lot. "It's not the typical situation, Viv. This whole thing with Sarah. It's been really hard on all of us. I still can't seem to get past it. My mind is never fully with Carl. I'm a million miles away most days, reliving it all, trying to find the clue we aren't seeing. And before that I was taking care of Mom through all her treatments. Hospice. Then her death. I wasn't the wife I needed to be."

"I don't feel sorry for Carl. You've always been there for him, for everything he needed. And he left you at a time when you needed him most. Not okay."

I grab the file for my nine o'clock session. "It isn't that simple, Viv. I left him too. Maybe not physically. But mentally, emotionally. It's not all that different really. What's important is that we have Ellie. And she needs us to be together. I have to believe it will all work out. So I'm sorry, but I'm not meeting with an attorney. I'm trying, with all I have in me, to save my family. That's all I can do."

"My blazing-hot fireman has a friend, you know." She stands and lifts her eyebrows as if she's waiting for an answer.

I shoo her out of my office, rolling my eyes.

"He's divorced. No kids. Wife simply wanted more money. Left him for a surgeon in Baton Rouge."

"I've got a new client. Need to get a few things together." I close the door, ignoring her prompts about the fireman.

"Don't forget," she hollers through the door. "Getting my hair done after lunch. Lock up when you go to carpool. If you have any trouble, call 911! He's a first responder." Her laughter follows her trail as she goes to begin her day.

Sunday, October 29, 2006

It's been two years since Sarah disappeared, and I've spent another anniversary of The Day looking for answers. The digital numbers glow red from my nightstand: 10:07 p.m. Another day in which I have not been able to give Beth, Preacher, or Ellie what we all need most—Sarah.

I set my alarm early for tomorrow morning, having packed my schedule with clients to make up for today's search. Then I head across the hall to give Ellie one more kiss good night. She rolls her eyes and says, "Mom, seriously?"

"I know, I know," I tell her. "You're getting too old for this. But I'm going to steal as many kisses as I can, as long as you'll let me." I brush her hair from her shoulders and pull her into a hug before planting a final kiss on top of her head. She smells like jasmine bubble bath, one of the birthday gifts we gave her in September when she turned fourteen.

"I loved going through the haunted house rehearsal tonight. It's a lot scarier than I thought it'd be. So much fun!"

"We messed up. You'd think we'd know how to do it. Three years of the same old thing."

"Seemed perfect to me. Thanks for letting me come."

She stares at the ceiling and doesn't respond.

"How'd you get all that makeup off? I could barely recognize you, especially with the black lights. You were glowing."

"It wasn't hard." She's obviously in no mood for chitchat, so I tuck her in beneath her bright new turquoise comforter, another birthday gift she received as I helped her redecorate with a more mature theme. The pastel décor was no longer cutting it. I switch off the overhead light, but she keeps the lamp on to read.

"Still obsessed with John Green?" I ask as she leans to pull *Looking for Alaska* from her bedside shelf.

"He's my favorite." She settles against her pillow and opens the book. "Mom?" She catches me watching her, thinking how thankful I am that she wasn't kidnapped along with Sarah that day.

She shifts for emphasis and repeats, "Mom?" This time, a genuine question. "I know I'm supposed to believe she's coming back. That we'll find her. But I don't believe that anymore. Dad might be right. What if Sarah's gone for good?"

I listen, wishing I had answers.

"In a way, I kind of think I might be gone for good too. None of us came back from New Orleans, did we? We all got lost that day."

"I know it feels that way sometimes, honey. But we're here. And Sarah is too. Somewhere. It's only a matter of time before we find her. I believe that."

She gives me the saddest look I've ever seen. A long, deep stare, as if I'll never understand anything.

"I love you, Ellie. From the sky to the mud." It's what she used to say when she was little. "I wouldn't change one single thing about you. And even if you weren't my daughter, I'd think you were the coolest person I've ever known."

"I love you more." She says this as if she's never told me before. As if it's the last time she'll ever say it.

I close her door, grateful to have her home. Safe.

After finishing the supper dishes, I settle into bed alone and listen to the evening news. On my dresser, the divorce papers sit waiting for ink, but I still can't bring myself to sign them. No matter how long Carl is gone, I can't get used to this empty bed.

As the anchorman breaks for a commercial, I hit Mute and turn my attention to the Baton Rouge *Advocate*, which still waits wrapped in a rubber band from the daily delivery. I've just popped the elastic beyond the paper edge when I hear a strange sound from Ellie's room. Almost as if she has kicked an empty cardboard box. As soon as I hear it, a fire spreads through my veins and I know. Somehow I know she has done no such thing.

I drop the paper on my bed and run to Ellie's room, calling her name. I open her door. My knees buckle. My voice scrapes across tense vocal folds, barely catching wind. "Ellie! No!"

My daughter is still in bed, but she has changed positions since I tucked her in. Her limp legs now dangle across the side of the mattress, and blood soaks the fabric. Carl's hunting shotgun leans against her chest, one of the few things he left behind and the one thing I begged him to take.

For a split second, Ellie seems to be smiling. Some part of my brain wants to believe it is a cruel joke. That she's poured ketchup on her sheets and is testing out a costume for the haunted house fund-raiser. That has to be the explanation. "Ellie," I say sternly. "Sit up. It's not funny." I can't bring myself to step closer.

I try to get my bearings, looking across the room to anchor myself to some specific place and time. Splattered around her newly painted walls, splashed across her favorite pen-and-ink sketches, and caught between the woven carpet fibers are tiny pieces of my daughter's brilliant brain, bloody strands of her beautiful brown curls. Her entire life, shattered into fragments, breaking all the promises we made—that we would always be here for each other, no matter the pain.

"Ellie!" I scream now, falling against her bed, grabbing her arm. *Girls don't use guns. Especially Ellie. She hated guns. This isn't how this happens. This can't be real.*

The smell of death consumes me, its ancient, acrid attack burning a hole right through me. "No. No! No, no, no . . ." My daughter, my beautiful, beloved daughter.

Somehow I will myself to call Carl. My fingers are numb and I can't feel the phone. I move to use the landline, but even with the larger buttons it takes four tries before I'm able to dial the right number. He answers by saying my name with hostility, aggravated I am bothering him.

"Carl . . ." I can barely talk. "It's Ellie."

"What? What's wrong with Ellie?" His tone shifts to concern. "Where are you?"

"Home. Come, Carl, hurry."

"Is she okay?"

"No. Please hurry." These are the only words I can form. My brain refuses to shape facts into sentences. Saying the sounds would make death real. And more than anything, I don't want it to be real.

"What happened, Amanda? Tell me!"

Carl needs more. I owe him that.

"She . . . shot . . . your gun." I can't do it. I can't tell my husband our daughter is dead.

"Is she alive, Amanda? Tell me, is Ellie alive?"

"No."

I hold the phone to my ear long after Carl has disconnected the call. A loud buzz tone breaks through, pulling me from the distant haze of shock. I shake my head and try to gather my wits. I struggle to dial 911.

Then I call Raelynn. She calls Beth, Preacher, and Jay. Within minutes, my house is filled with first responders, police officers, the coroner, our pastor, friends.

I feel only fear. I hear shattered sounds. Syllables bounce around me, out of sync. Nothing makes sense. Everything is broken. The words, the room, my world. All broken.

When Raelynn puts her arm around me, I break too. Beth catches me as I fall, pulling me to the sofa to ease me against the faded cushions. She is here with Preacher, whispering something I can't quite make out. She holds me close, passing me a tiny blue pill and a plastic glass of water. "Take this. It's from my doctor. It'll help."

The pill lands on my tongue, hard and small against the roof of my mouth. I tilt the cup to my lips, its bottom an eternal void. I want to disappear into it and never raise my head again. Into the black I go. Through silence and whispers and well-intentioned hugs and prayers, all is darkness.

A part of me has followed Ellie right out of this world, and the slender sliver of my spirit that is still alive is being pulled by the dark arms of death. A loud, horrible moan fills me. My blood becomes thick with the sound. I hear it. I feel it. I look down to see my heart pounding in my chest, throbbing against my rib cage, as if my very soul is banging to be set free.

"Where's Carl?" I ask no one in particular. *I need to see Carl. I need him here, right now.*

"He's with Jay," Preacher says. "In the back." He points toward

Ellie's bedroom. When I try to stand, my body stays slack against the sofa. I peel away from it. Suddenly I am in no pain at all. I am consumed by light. I float outside myself, across the living room. *Am I dead?*

I move without my body to Ellie's bedroom, where Carl and Jay are tucking Ellie's fingers into the long black plastic bag. Carl kisses her before pulling the zipper shut. His hands are covered in blood. And my heart is scarred forever.

"No!" I want to scream. "She's my daughter! You can't have her! Where are you taking her?"

But no words come. I'm nothing but air as the men from the funeral home move beneath me. Their black shoes march in sync. Left. Left. Left, right, left. A battalion of bizarre betrayals. A war against reason. Against all that is good in the world.

The bag is zipped, her body removed. Downward stares avoid me as I float suspended above them all. I begin to understand the truth. My daughter pulled the trigger. Ellie did this. Ellie, my only child. The one with a pitch-perfect singing voice and a laugh that could light up the night. Ellie, who rode bareback in fields of wild-flowers and swore she'd never leave the mountains. Who dared to jump from the high dive at camp, ride her bike with no hands, and do a backflip on the trampoline. This beautiful spirit who called me Mom . . . she is gone. Ellie is gone.

In a flash I am outside the house, where yellow crime scene tape flaps in the wind. The men are carrying my daughter's lifeless body out of our home. They slide her into the back of the hearse and take her away into the cool October wind.

If I were in my own skin, if I had bones and muscles and lig-aments to move me, I would run full speed after the taillights. I would scream, "You can't have her! You can't have her! She's my daughter. She's mine!" But I am nothing here, above the living. Trapped in a dark realm, the in-between.

As the lights fade into the autumn night, there is a snap. I am inside my body again. Feeling it all. The noise, the pain, the weight. *No, no. I don't want to come back. Take me with her!*

There's Carl. *I need you, Carl. Come be by my side, Carl. Come!*

Instead, my husband walks past me as I sit on the sofa surrounded by friends and church members.

The people. Who are these people? Why are they here? Whispers and hugs. And Brother Johnson with his prayers. Disappear! Disappear!

Carl looks right through me. *Can't you see I need you?* He moves to the patio, leaving the door wide open. Nothing but cold, damp air to fill his space.

Under the pergola he built for us with his own two hands, he lights a cigarette. He hasn't smoked since high school, but now he's bummed one from a friend and taken a long, deep inhale before sending a cloud of smoke against the carport light.

I know the truth. I know the truth. I'll walk among the dead now. Too broken for this life.

Chapter 22

Monday, October 30, 2006

CARL SITS IN THE DRIVER'S SEAT OF OUR FAMILY CAR. I'M TO HIS right, his passenger, but we're going nowhere. His door is open and the engine is off. "Take Beth with you. Or Raelynn. I can't do this, Amanda. I'm sorry."

"Carl, we have to do this. We don't have a choice. You can't make me go there without you."

"Choose something nice. Simple. Don't let them swindle you into spending a lot of extra money." He fidgets with the keys.

"Please, Carl, don't make me do this alone." I barely finish my sentence before he drops the keys in my lap and leaves the car.

"I'm sorry," he says again. Then he heads for the house.

I sit in shock for a few minutes, certain he is not really leaving me to plan our daughter's funeral without him. When he doesn't return, I move behind the wheel, start the engine, and head down Walker North, trying to reach Beth and Preacher.

"Beth?" I call as I drive. She responds with concern. "Carl won't go with me to the funeral home. I can't do this by myself."

"Of course you shouldn't be by yourself. I'm coming to meet you."

"I'm driving your way now," I explain. "I'll be there in a few minutes."

248

By the time I turn off the highway onto Beth's gravel driveway, she is already waiting outside, purse in hand, ready to go. "Let's take my car. You shouldn't be driving."

Without resistance, I pull to the side and park in the large space made for visitors. Before The Day, the Broussard home was frequently filled with guests, either teens for youth group activities or families coming to view their famous Christmas light display. Now a weathered Merry Christmas sign rests against a pear tree. Its letters were once painted to spread holiday cheer, but that was before. Before I lost Sarah. And my husband. And now, my own child.

"Thank you," I tell Beth. As I climb into her car, it's all I can say.

Beth brings me to Seale Funeral Home, where she's friends with the owners. Time has warped again, and I am immediately drawn back into the memory of planning my mother's funeral just a few years ago. But that was different. She and I sat down together and decided every detail in advance. It was difficult, but it was nothing like this. Now, as the funeral director shows us the room filled with caskets, asking me to choose one for my daughter, it is all I can do not to scream.

"Unfortunately, my insurance doesn't cover suicides." I can hardly say the word. No matter how many times I've gone out on call with Jay, counseling survivors of suicide, I never imagined I'd be in their shoes.

The director says nothing. My insurance is not his problem. I'll have to pay him either way.

I stare at miniature color samples for satin pillows, trying to get my brain to choose a permanent resting place for my only child. Despite his best efforts to be considerate, professional, the salesman might as well be pushing a used car. It's clear he has never known this kind of loss. I choose something simple, with a soft cream interior. *This is nothing I should have to do. Just as printing out missing-child fliers is nothing Beth should have to do. Yet here we are, the two of us, and both our girls are gone.*

Next we sit at a polished wooden table with a bowl of mints in the middle. The room is cold and quiet. The man checks his calendar. "Will the services be held here or at your church?"

"Here," I say.

Beth reacts with open-eyed surprise.

The man nods, and we set the wake for tomorrow, five to nine, despite my concerns about trick-or-treat. Other parents will be ringing doorbells, collecting candy with their costumed children. I'll be burying my daughter.

"That's fine." I feel nothing. "I guess we'll bury her here too."

"Not at the church?" Beth questions. "Next to your mother?"

The whispers come back to me now. As I sat in my home last night, surrounded by loved ones, one woman, a neighbor I never knew very well, asked Brother Johnson if Ellie would be allowed to be buried in the church cemetery. "Suicide," the lady said, questioning his rules. I can't tell Beth. The lady doesn't even go to our church, but if she was thinking it, others will be too. I can't deal with that kind of hate. Not now.

"Here is fine," I say, and the man follows us out to view the vacant plots.

I choose a shady spot at Evergreen Memorial Park. Then Beth drives me over to Edrie's, where the florist asks me what kind of flowers Ellie liked. "She likes wildflowers," I say, unable to talk about my child in the past tense.

The lady isn't sure how to respond. So Beth points to a photo and suggests, "How about all white?"

"That's always lovely." The florist appreciates Beth's guidance.

Then, not knowing the details of Ellie's death, she gives us two price quotes—one for an open casket, one much more costly if closed.

"Closed," I say, handing her a credit card. I've never done anything more difficult in my entire life. Paying for my daughter's funeral expenses on credit. If I didn't feel dead inside, I could be consumed with hate for Carl right now. *Why didn't he take his gun?*

Leaving the florist, Beth sits with me in the parked car. "Amanda, you know it's a lot less expensive if you have the services at the church. We even have men to dig the grave. You don't have to pay all that money."

How can I tell her? How can I explain how I feel? I shake my head and say, "This is fine."

Tuesday, October 31, 2006

I have spent all morning staring at Ellie's bedroom, trying to ignore the smells—a putrid mix of cleaning supplies, blood, gunpowder, and candles. Now I sit in the family room of Seale Funeral Home and confess to Jay, "I don't know what happened. Did someone call Clean Scene? I'm sorry, it's all a blur for me. I don't know who to thank."

"I called them, but I had to cancel the order," he says. "Raelynn's brother took care of it before the cleaners could arrive. And Gator. He helped too."

This leaves me speechless. I've seen this happen when we've gone out on call, especially in more rural locations, out in the country where people are used to taking care of their own, but it's usually relatives. Kinfolk who stick together. I have no family here, and yet Jay says these men cleaned my daughter's room for me, going so far as to haul the mattress out to Gator's woods and burn it all to ash. There is no way to measure that kind of love.

Jay sits beside me on the sofa. He wears the pin indicating he is family. No one here is related to me. But these are the people who love Ellie. The people who love me. Carl is nowhere to be seen.

"Ms. Salassi?" the funeral director whispers respectfully.

I look down at my hand. I still wear my wedding ring.

"Mrs.," I correct him.

"Sorry, ma'am." He clears his throat. "Would you like to see your daughter one final time?"

Jay helps me stand. "I'll go with you."

"No," I tell him. "Just me." I don't mean to sound sharp, but I feel a fierce protective urge to guard my time with Ellie.

We enter the room. The funeral director closes the doors behind us. Now here we are, with the open casket. The space between my daughter and me feels eternal, and yet it's nothing I can't bridge. In a few minutes this man will lower the lid and Ellie will be gone forever.

I don't know how I manage it, but somehow I leave the director at the door and make my way to the casket. My child's casket. Ellie.

I feel only loss. Absence.

Her face is wrapped completely. There is nothing for me to touch but bandages. No sweet brown curls. No smooth, soft olive cheeks. *Stand up, Amanda. Do this.* I am determined not to lose this time with my baby. My girl.

I touch her arm, a stiffened, painted version of the daughter I love.

I fix her dress, straighten the folds, feel the pull of the cotton around each turquoise blue button. Her first-day-of-school dress. The last special occasion outfit we bought together. Laughing as she came out of the dressing room with a twirl.

Behind me, the director clears his voice and speaks softly. "Excuse me, Mrs. Salassi. It's time."

I stand looking down at my child, trying not to blink as he closes the lid, wanting every last second with Ellie, resisting the letting go.

The director places the white floral arrangement into position, but no part of me can accept what is happening.

As I follow him back out of the room, the family is asked to gather for prayer before they open the main doors for the wake. Carl is still not here.

"Have you heard from him?" Beth asks, a tenderness in her tone that only Beth can offer.

"Not a word," I whisper.

Jay stands beside me. "I've been trying to call him. No answer."

"Should we start without him?" The funeral director seems unsure. It's obviously an uncommon situation.

I give one last quick glance around the building, hoping to see Carl. "I guess so."

Brother Johnson leads us in prayer. Then we make our way to the now-closed casket, covered in beautiful white blooms, exactly as Beth requested. In fact, the entire room is filled with sprays of fresh flowers, every color and kind imaginable. *Why didn't Ellie know she was loved?*

When they open the doors, people are lined up waiting. Throughout the evening, the line continues to extend, out the doors, into the parking lot, and around the corner of the funeral home. The wake lasts longer than planned. Beth, Preacher, Jay, Raelynn, and even Vivienne stay by my side through it all, shaking hands and greeting the hundreds of visitors who have shown up to offer sympathy and support.

"I can't imagine having to stand here alone," I say. Again and again I thank my friends, but no words will ever suffice. People are kind and compassionate.

"It could be us," several say. Another couple admits, "Our son is on antidepressants. We worry every day." A choir member confesses, "I tried to take my life once. Don't think for a second that she didn't love you." Another community friend says, "My father was in treatment for six months. We're sorry for your loss."

Hundreds of my clients have come too. They offer hugs and condolences, telling me again and again that I saved their lives or the life of someone they love. Brooke arrives, along with her sister, and she clasps my hands in hers. "Mrs. Amanda, I was going to do it. I'm here only because you got me through it."

Mrs. Hosh and countless survivors hold me close, assuring me I am not alone. "We know," they say. Or "I'm here." Their comments touch me in ways I am not yet ready to process, but I hear them. Every one of them.

It takes hours for the line to wind down, and even then the pews are filled with friends and loved ones. Teenagers have gathered in clusters, sharing stories about Ellie. Trying to let me know her life mattered, that she was loved.

Nate leads the pack, talking about Sarah and Ellie. "Remember when they dressed as identical twins for Crazy Day at school? They wore wigs!"

Another chimes in. "Or when they set off the church fire alarms trying to roast marshmallows on the stove?"

"What about when Ellie raked up a giant leaf pile and jumped off Mrs. Beth's barn?" The room fills with laughter.

"Remember when she wrecked that four-wheeler? Trying to race Nate?"

Nate is crying. The stories flow, and the laughter does too. With each memory, I cling to the life of my daughter, hoping all of these people will never forget the light she brought to our world.

Wednesday, November 1, 2006

Brother Johnson begins the service, thanking the overflowing room of loved ones for showing up in support of the Salassi family. Carl is finally present, but only because Jay drove out to his apartment and convinced him to attend the funeral. While I'm glad he's come, he's brought Ashleigh with him. I can't bear to look their way. They sit at one end of the row, while I sit at the other. Beth, Preacher, Raelynn, and Jay bridge the gap, with Raelynn's brother and sons on the row behind us. Vivienne sits at their side with her handsome firefighter boyfriend.

A church member sings Ellie's favorite hymn a cappella. The lyrics say, "I surrender all." Then Brother Johnson delivers one of the most beautiful sermons I have ever heard. At one point he looks to the teens in the back of the room and says, "Young people, I want you to know this was not your fault." Then he looks at me and offers me the same release. "This was no one's fault. Ellie was loved. By so many people. And what I want you to know is this. The way a person dies does not have anything to do with where they spend eternity. It matters more how a person lives. And Ellie, well, she was a girl who lived with love."

Chapter 23

Sunday, November 5, 2006

"PEOPLE HAVE BEEN SO KIND AND COMPASSIONATE," I TELL BETH and Preacher. They are here at the house, helping me sort through the paperwork. I've ignored it as long as I can. As we read through the names of all who attended the services, trying to write my way through thank-you notes, the doorbell rings. It's the lady from down the road. The one who whispered the night of Ellie's death, questioning Brother Johnson's stance on allowing my child to be buried in the church cemetery.

Before I can protest, Beth welcomes her. She is carrying a fresh batch of banana pudding, and I try to give her the benefit of the doubt. She offers Preacher the bowl. On the front, her name is marked in thin black Sharpie across a strip of dough-colored masking tape. Preacher peeks beneath the wrapper, eager to dig in.

"I don't know how you stand it, Amanda." She gives me a hug as I greet her. "Knowing your daughter is in hell."

Stay strong, Amanda. No one can be this cruel. Surely she didn't say what you think she said. Maybe you're being too sensitive again, as Carl always claims.

The woman doesn't flinch. She shakes her head and delivers an extra dose of shame. "I always thought you were the perfect mother. What happened?"

I don't reply. Instead, I move back to the kitchen table and Beth joins me, lifting my hand into hers. We sit quietly, letting Preacher lead.

He opens the dessert, serves himself a heaping scoop onto a paper plate, and takes a bite. "Best banana pudding I ever had." He smiles at the woman, offering servings to the rest of us. We decline. "This reminds me of the time I stole a pie from my mother's kitchen."

"You stole it?" The lady's eyes open wide.

"Aww, I was just a kid. And trust me. If you ever tasted Mother's pecan pie, you would have stolen it too."

Beth says, "Don't worry. She forgave him." Then she smiles at her husband and adds, "Just like I forgive you for all those little white lies you tell me."

"Me? Lie?" He laughs. "Never."

"Ha. Just this morning you told me I looked good in that dress. I almost left the house in it. Good thing I looked in the mirror. You had lied." Beth is working hard to keep spirits up. It's one of her gifts. A trick that's kept her going since Sarah vanished. I'm too sad to smile, but I don't mind her trying.

"Have you ever told a lie?" Preacher asks our guest.

The woman blushes. "Only when I don't want to hurt someone's feelings."

"That's all right," Preacher says, taking a bite and yumming with delight. "God forgives us for those little white lies. Just as he forgives us when we eat too much banana pudding." He takes another bite and winks.

The woman is charmed. "Ask and ye shall be forgiven," she jokes. Then she gets serious again. "That's why you can't go to heaven if you kill yourself, right? You can't repent. That's what the Bible says."

"Hmm . . ." Preacher pauses. "Is that what it says? I've never read that part." The woman has no way of defending herself. He lets her off the hook. "Ma'am, forgive me, but I'm going to get a little preachy. That okay?"

She shrugs.

"All right then. Your faith seems to be important to you."

"Yes. Very."

"So you believe Jesus taught us about God's grace?"

"Of course that's what I believe. I'm a Christian." She stands stiff-shouldered and pious.

"And wasn't he hardest on the Pharisees? The group of people who judged everyone else as being unworthy of that grace?"

She seems unsure of his point, so he continues.

"What about the woman at the well? She had been accused of terrible sin. Do you remember that crowd? The ones who felt so confident and virtuous? They actually believed God loved them more than he loved that woman." Preacher simplifies. "I guess what I'm trying to say is that, well, sometimes we tend to get God mixed up with Santa Claus."

The woman laughs a bit, uneasy. "Santa?"

"Keeping a list and checking it twice."

Beth gives my hand a gentle squeeze, but my stomach remains tight.

Preacher continues. "I'd like to think he's not up there keeping score, calculating rights and wrongs. We mess up, we learn, we grow. That's the point."

The woman crosses her arms, indignant. "It's a good thing I don't go to your church. Are you saying it doesn't matter what we do?"

Preacher finishes another bite of pudding. "No, ma'am, that's not what I'm saying. Every choice we make matters. Every single one of them. I'm simply saying God knew and loved Ellie. He understood her struggle. And he would never turn his back on her. Or on any of us."

"But she killed herself, Preacher. That's murder. It's one of the Ten Commandments."

"That's right. And there are nine others. Have you ever broken any of those? Stolen a pen from someone's desk? Done a little work on Sunday? Said false things about your neighbor?" He looks at me now, and her anger increases.

"Don't you believe there's a right and a wrong?" She stays indignant.

"Ma'am, with all due respect, my daughter is missing. Do you think I haven't held a gun to my head? But I'm an adult. I'm halfway in my right mind, and I can understand the impact of my choices. I can talk myself through the consequences and weigh my decisions on a different level than Ellie was able to do. She was just a kid. We can't forget that. And even if she was old like me, I think God could handle that too."

Now I am crying. Beth pulls me into a hug, and Preacher gives me a gentle, supportive look from across the room. The woman sighs. Surely she's beginning to see through a different lens.

Preacher doesn't quit. "Do you really believe God would want to punish Ellie, after all she's been through? After she fought for two years to stay strong for all of us? Ellie had more faith than I do. Because I'll tell you, I've blamed God at times. Yes, ma'am, you'd better believe I've questioned him. But Ellie never stopped loving God, and God never stopped loving her either."

Tuesday, November 7, 2006

"Wake up, Gloopy. Please?" Jay stands at the foot of my bed, insisting I come back to life.

"I'm tired, Jay. It's been a long week. I'm sorry. I can't do it today." My eyes are swollen and dry. My head is pounding. I'm still wearing my clothes from last night.

He sits at my side, and then he looks at Beth. She's standing above me, holding a cup of hot tea. "You've got an appointment," she says. "To choose Ellie's marker."

I sit up. "I know."

"Come on. We'll go with you," Jay says.

"It's after eleven, Amanda. You haven't gotten out of bed in two days. You know this isn't healthy." Beth again.

My friends have stayed with me round the clock since Ellie died, too afraid to leave me. And they're right to fear it.

Get up, Amanda. It's pathetic to lie here with everyone feeling sorry for you. I pull the covers down and force myself to rise. *Be strong.*

"Take a shower," Jay says, with not a hint of anything but kindness in his voice. "You'll feel better once you get dressed."

"I'll make you a sandwich." Beth heads to the kitchen and Jay follows.

I do as they ask and take a shower. Then I dress and join them at the counter. "Now what?" I ask, unable to think for myself.

"Eat," Jay says. He places a grilled cheese sandwich on a plate for me, along with some grapes. Beth fixes me a cold glass of water. Then they each grab a plate for themselves and join me.

"Remember when Preacher and I served in Ghana?" Beth asks.

I nod.

"We met a lady who lived in a tiny home all by herself."

I nod again, trying hard to stay focused.

"Lost her entire family to the rebellion. She was the only survivor. She always fixed her famous stew, using all kinds of vegetables we couldn't name. And she'd invite us to eat with her. She used to say, 'No matter what happens, never eat alone.'"

"I like that idea," Jay says, enjoying his sandwich and trying to lighten the mood.

Together they keep up the chitchat while taking their time through the meal. But it's all I can do to take a bite of my sandwich. The rest of my food sits untouched.

Afterward Beth and I tackle the dishes. I go through the motions, trying not to be a burden. When we're done, Jay grabs his keys. "Okay, Gloopy. Ready?"

"No." I'm not ready.

Beth gives Jay a look of surrender, and he takes charge. "Well, that's all right. There's really no reason you have to do it today. But there is something we want to show you."

With reluctance I follow them to Jay's truck. He drives us to the old Walker Junior High building where Ellie would be in school. Before I can protest, I realize what they've brought me here to see. Out front the chain-link fence is filled with turquoise ribbons, each one tied against the wind. Students have left cards and flowers, stuffed animals and band posters.

"All in Ellie's honor," Beth says. "They knew her favorite color."

"They've tied ribbons to their backpacks too," Jay adds. He parks and leads us to the memorial. The teens have written hundreds of letters and poems for my Ellie. Beautiful lyrics and messages, all expressing their love.

"I'm not sure how I feel about this," I admit. "I don't want the kids to think suicide is a good thing. I don't want them to follow her example, expecting to be honored somehow."

"Vivienne agreed," Beth says, reminding me that Viv is heading the grief counseling here for the students. "So she has the kids sign a pledge before they can get a ribbon."

"A pledge?"

"Yep. They have to promise Ellie that they'll learn from her mistake."

"That's a good idea," I admit.

Beth nods. "They pledge that every time they start to think life isn't worth living, they'll think of Ellie and the promise they're making to stay alive. To not waste one single second, and instead to live as if they're living for both themselves and for Ellie. Every step they take, they can think, *This is for Ellie.* Every challenge they tackle, they can think, *I'll do this for Ellie.* They're promising to choose life, Amanda. Every one of these ribbons shows they're choosing to live."

I can no longer hold back my tears. I lean into Jay, and hold Beth's hand, and sob.

We've spent a couple hours at the school, reading the cards and letters, accepting sympathy from Ellie's friends, and thanking the handful of grief counselors who have been brought in to help the teens cope with this terrible loss. I explain again and again that the last thing I want is for the kids to think of suicide as a viable option, a way out that brings glory. Thankfully, the counselors are setting the students straight about that, reminding them of how many people are hurting today because of Ellie's choice. They are advising that taking your own life is never the right decision.

Leaving Viv at the helm, I finally give in to Beth's urging and head for the funeral home. With clear skies and temps in the seventies, I wish Ellie could see this beautiful day.

I try my best to do as expected, but choosing Ellie's tombstone proves to be the hardest decision of my life. I shiver as the hollow tones of the funeral director's voice echo through the parlor.

"What would you like the inscription to read?" He points to a wall of sample plaques, as if the choice should be easy. Like buying a toothbrush or a pair of socks.

How can I possibly sum up my child's life with a few purchased lines? I want to tell him to place a solid boulder at the grave, plain and unmarked, to prove no words will suffice. No standard quotation or polished phrase will do. Nothing I say will ever be enough to measure my love for her. To show the worth of Ellie's life.

"I'm sorry." I shake my head and hold my hands in the air. "I can't do this." I turn and walk out of the funeral home as quickly as I can. Jay follows. Beth joins us a few minutes later at the truck.

"It's too soon," I tell them, apologizing for my behavior. "I'd rather plant wildflowers than put some generic marker in that space. I just can't do it."

"No reason to rush," Jay says, starting his truck and driving us back to my house. "We'll be here when you're ready. Take your time."

Jay drops us back at home, where Beth stays with me until Raelynn swings by after school. I scrub banana pudding from the aging mint-green Tupperware. The label crinkles and curls beneath my sudsy sponge, but no matter how hard I wash, the damage has soaked too deep. The woman's words can never be erased: *"I don't know how you stand it, Amanda. Knowing your daughter is in hell."*

Her cruel confrontation crawls through me. I can stand no more. I fall to the floor, dropping the bowl and splashing the soapy water across my chest. This is how Raelynn finds me, curled on my kitchen rug. The faucet is still running.

"I can't stand any more of this pain, Raelynn. I can't."

She scoots down to the floor and sits beside me, holding me as I weep. "What have I done? What have I done to deserve this?"

My mind spins with ways to end the hurt.

"Amanda. Look at me."

I do as I'm told. Once Raelynn's got eye contact, she hands me a pill. "This is from Dr. Martin. Take it." Then she stands and gives me a glass of water. I swallow it down. "It's going to help you sleep. Get us through the night. I'm not leaving you alone."

"You told me, remember? You said if your boys ever did anything like this, you'd have to follow them out. You couldn't live through it. Remember? You said it. You understand, don't you? It's so hard, Raelynn. I can't do this."

I'm crying again, and Raelynn convinces me to move to the sofa.

"Why'd she leave me, Raelynn? Why'd Carl leave me? Why does everybody I love leave me?" As I say these words, my entire life flashes before me. All the abandonments. Every one of them.

Raelynn takes my hand. "I'm not leaving. I'm right here. And so are Beth and Preacher and Jay. We're all here, Amanda."

"Maybe Carl's right." I continue spewing my deepest hurts. "Maybe all I ever do is make things worse. Maybe their problem was me. That's what he told me, Raelynn. All along it was me. Maybe if I had just left them alone . . ."

"Amanda. That's a lie. And you know it. He's filled your head with lies."

"But what if I drove my own husband away? What if I pushed Ellie into this? What if it's my fault? And Sarah too? It's all my fault!" I am heaving, gasping for air. And then, just like that, I am asleep.

Hello Sparrow,

The Man is yelling again. We're stupid, Bridgette's fat, I'm too skinny. He makes fun of our hair, our makeup, our clothes. But the worst is when he says nobody is looking for me anymore. That everybody thinks I'm dead.

What if he's right? Mom and Pop may not even live in Walker anymore. For all I know, they went off to be missionaries again. Somewhere far away. Maybe they adopted some kids and started a whole new family. What if they forgot all about me?

If I close my eyes, I see my mom standing in the front yard. The Christmas lights are on. She's holding a plate of cookies, telling me to hurry home.

Thursday, November 30, 2006

"Your clients keep calling," Vivienne says over the phone. "It's been a month. They miss you. So do I."

"I'm sorry, Viv. I don't have it in me anymore." Beanie gives me her hungry meow, so I stand to fill her bowl.

"You have to come back, Amanda. Your clients need you."

I rub Beanie's neck as I give her the food. This draws a purr. "There's a professor over in Hammond. She's expressed interest. I'll give you her number. Maybe she'll want to buy me out."

"Amanda, you're not hearing me. I don't want another partner. You can take it slow at first. But come back. Please. Be here."

"I know you care, Viv."

"More than you know," she counters. "Besides, it's how you're wired, Amanda. You help people. That's what you were born to do. You know as well as I do, healing others is the best way to heal yourself."

"Listen, Viv, please. I can't be responsible for another person's life. Never again."

"Well, you can't sit around all day in that house either."

"Jay has a friend with a real estate business, off Sherwood. He said I can work in the back. They need somebody to handle the paperwork. No stress. Just a way to keep my mind busy and bring in a paycheck. I can't go much longer without one of those." I am feeling more and more resentment toward Carl.

"Okay." Viv sounds unconvinced. "I'm not sure that's the best job for you, but it's better than sitting alone all day. Know this, though. I'm not going to look for a new partner. We're a team."

Hello Sparrow,

It's been more than two years since Bridgette took me in New Orleans. I've been thinking about Ellie and Nate. I wonder what I would be like if I could be a regular kid in school with my friends.

This makes me sad. So I'm going to count my blessings.

1. I have my sparrow. (Thank you, Sparrow!)
2. I have never gotten pregnant.
3. Bridgette brings me clothes and helps me fix my makeup.
4. I am learning to cook. And she's buying better groceries now.
5. I can go outside in the yard now, even when no one is with me.
6. I can listen to music.
7. She still wears the gold cross pin. Maybe she'll help me get out of here one day.
8. My feather hasn't broken.

Hello Sparrow,

When I go home, I will do all the things I miss.

1. Swim.
2. Ride my bike.
3. Jump on the trampoline.
4. Have a crawfish boil.
5. Put up our Christmas lights and decorate the tree and hang our stockings.
6. Try out for cheerleading and basketball and choir.
7. Study hard and make all As.
8. Go to all the LSU games—tailgating!

9. Get a puppy. Maybe a golden retriever.
10. Climb trees.
11. Go to Mr. Jay's camp.
12. Water ski.
13. Make cookies with Mom.
14. Build stuff with Pop.

I'll keep Ellie and Nate with me all the time. There are so many things I can't wait to do.

Hello Sparrow,

Guess what? Bridgette surprised me today and gave me a Bible. She didn't understand why I was crying, so I told her I was just so happy. That made her laugh.

I showed her my favorite verse, from when I was a kid. I'll write it here for you too.

He will cover you with his feathers. He will shelter you with his wings. His faithful promises are your armor and protection. (Psalm 91:4)

Here are some of my new favorite verses:

Don't be afraid of those who want to kill your body; they cannot touch your soul. (Matthew 10:28)

For I can do everything through Christ, who gives me strength. (Philippians 4:13)

After you have suffered a little while, he will restore, support, and strengthen you . . . (1 Peter 5:10)

Part 3

*The light shines in the darkness, and the
darkness can never extinguish it.*

—JOHN 1:5

Chapter 24

October 2007

AFTER RUNNING A QUICK BRUSH THROUGH MY HAIR AND SLAPPING
on a smudge of Chapstick, I head for Baton Rouge. I am numb as I
navigate the congested interstate route I've taken every single work-
day for nearly a year since Ellie died. Other commuters manage
coffee cups and cell phones while they drive. They seem stressed,
worried about things that mean nothing to me anymore. I join their
Monday-morning crawl all the way to Rod and Reel Realty where
I park my fuel-efficient Civic between the rows of oversized four-
wheel-drives. Once inside, I get right to work, managing the phone
lines as callers hope to find their dream hunting and fishing prop-
erties across our bayou state.

Five days a week I enter this glass-walled office and become
nothing more than an anonymous voice, directing calls to the
agents and listening in as they wheel and deal. I leave them to their
reindeer games while I file MLS information, plug each home into
the database, and upload photos for online viewing.

The job is low-stress but it keeps my brain busy, and that helps
me avoid the constant cognitive cycle, a mind gone mad with trying
to reason it all. How one minute I was a doting mother, a faithful
wife, and an idealistic social worker who believed wholeheartedly
I could make this world a better place. And in a blink, I woke up to

find a cheat as a husband, a child in the grave, and a low-paying job that barely makes my mortgage. I never thought my story would come to this. But here I am, closing myself off behind the glass.

Since Ellie died, sleep has become a challenge; long nights and bad dreams toss and turn me through the lonely hours. Today I can barely stay awake. I answer phones and watch time tick. As soon as the clock signals lunch, I head outside for a dose of fresh air, hoping to walk myself awake.

Usually I avoid the tiny park across the street, all those playful mothers and happy children. But for some reason, today I turn toward the swings.

Sure enough, there's a playgroup having a picnic under the pavilion. Kids run around rambunctiously while their mothers pull grapes and sandwiches from Ziploc bags. One of the moms looks up from a wicker picnic basket to notice her young son climbing the monkey bars. "Wait!" She's on her feet, rushing beneath him, just in case he falls.

That's what mothers do. We promise our children we will be there to catch them, to get them through their weaker moments and build their confidence until they are strong enough to go forth alone.

A child's ball crosses my path, and I grab it before it hits the street. Tossing it back to a girl in braids, I smile and watch her bounce away with her friends. Maybe we should have moved to another state and started over. Maybe I shouldn't have been so set on searching for Sarah. We could have found a brand-new life. We could have focused on healing, not staying stuck in place. Carl never would have met Ashleigh. Ellie would have been a regular kid. We would all be together. As a family.

My lunch break flies by. I spend the rest of the afternoon filing property information. At the five o'clock mark, I leave the office to find Jay standing by my car. "What's wrong?" I hurry toward him. "Is everybody okay?"

"The gang's all fine. I just got a call. Suicide. Over in Watson. I've been in meetings all day here in town, so I figured since this was on my way, I'd see if you might want to go with me."

"No, Jay. I can't do that." I unlock my door.

"It hasn't been long, I know, but you can help this family. You know what they're going through. It makes a difference." He circles his scant set of keys around his index finger. "Ride with me?"

Viv's words come back to me: *"Healing others is the best way to heal yourself. You help people. It's what you were born to do."*

I look out toward the afternoon traffic and exhale. "Who is it?"

"Young guy. New to town. Left behind a wife. She's not from around here either. Her family hasn't made it in from Georgia yet, so she's got nobody. She really could use your help."

It's been almost a year. You've seen other survivors come out to the scenes that soon. Even sooner. They do make a difference. If they can do it, you can do it. Be strong, Amanda.

"Okay," I sigh. "I'll try."

Jay nods and smiles. Within minutes, we are on our way to the couple's home in Watson. He fills me in on the details. "Twenty-four years old. His wife found him. And the gun." He switches on his hazards and drives as quickly as he can, especially once he's crossed back into Livingston Parish.

"Kids?"

"None yet. The wife is pregnant."

He says this as he pulls up to a well-maintained home off a quaint country lane. Deputies have already draped yellow-and-black crime scene tape across the shaded driveway, and a female officer stands guard at the front door. She greets me by name and steps aside to let me in. I've become far too familiar with this scenario. With this despair. *Stay here, Amanda. Be present.*

Jay and one of his investigators work the scene, snapping photos and taking notes in collaboration with the coroner. Within minutes, funeral home workers are carrying the man's remains down the hall, zipped tightly closed in the plastic body bag, while others in the room pretend it isn't happening.

I take my time, looking for the young woman who was reportedly the first to find her husband's body. The living room and kitchen are filled with unpacked boxes, fresh from the move. Folks are gathered, whispering. I assume them to be curious neighbors, probably some church members or coworkers. I don't see anyone with the familiar haunting half-dead stare of a suicide survivor. These people are talking quietly, shaking their heads and making assumptions about the events leading up to the act. But no one is pale or in shock. No one here seems to have left the world of the living.

I ease my way toward the minister, and he seems relieved to see me. We know each other from past calls.

"I'm glad you're here," he says. "We can't get her to respond. Maybe you can help."

I follow the humble pastor into a back bedroom, where a woman is lying on the floor of her closet. Her long hair covers her face in loose tangles. She wears a substantial diamond wedding ring on her left hand. She is dressed in jeans and a sweatshirt, but both feet are bare. Her face is tucked tight against her swollen belly, her unborn child likely kicking inside, and her hands are held against the crown of her head, covering her ears. She is doing all she can to disappear. I know this strategy.

With a soft, calm voice, I call her name. She doesn't answer.

The minister shakes his head and says, "We've tried everything. She won't respond."

"Any family members here?"

"They're on their way. She's pregnant, you know?"

I nod. "When is she due?"

"February."

This draws a moan from the closet as the woman begins to rock back and forth. I count in my head. She's about five months along. Maybe the child will give her reason to live.

I've been on calls with Jay many times, but not since Ellie took her own life. Not since I wrapped my hands around my own ears and sobbed, wanting death to take me away. But now that I know this walk, I begin by taking off my official social worker hat and being present as nothing more than a survivor. I show my own scars, something my license would never allow.

"My daughter committed suicide," I say softly. "Almost a year ago. She was barely fourteen. I was alone when I found her."

She may not hear what I'm saying, but I trust the right words will find their way to her at the right time. That's all I can do.

"The night she died, I was home with her. I walked into her room. She was on her bed. Just lying there. She used a gun too." I continue, detail after detail, letting her know that not only do I care, but I understand. I've been there. I'm still there.

When I say, "She was my only child," the woman stops rocking and moaning and pulls her hands away from her head. As she looks at me, I say, "You will get through this. I promise. I'm here to help you. Lots of people are here to help you."

She reaches for my hand. I repeat this message in various ways, again and again. It finally begins to sink in. Twenty minutes later, she crawls out of the closet and leans against the bedroom wall, her arms curled tight around her belly. Her eyes connect with mine, as if I'm all she has to believe in anymore.

"Stay with me," she says. The fact that I'm still here, that I somehow survived my daughter's suicide, is enough to get her to the next inhale.

Hello Sparrow,

Today I was reading to Bridgette. The story about Moses. I was at the part when his sister hides baby Moses in a basket and puts him in the river. That's when Bridgette got real serious and said, "I don't get it. All this time, and you're still believin' God's gonna show up. Why's he lettin' all this happen to you? Explain that."

Monday, October 29, 2007

Today's The Day, the third anniversary of Sarah's disappearance and one year after Ellie's suicide. This year, instead of helping Beth search for Sarah, I have come to my daughter's grave. I am here to focus on her life, not her death.

I still haven't ordered her marker. Instead, I placed a cement bench near her grave. It's a quiet spot beneath the oak. A place for me to examine my emotional shoe box, confront the piles of pain.

I set down a thermos of tea and begin to flip through photographs I've brought with me. They show Ellie through the years, from the moment she was born, wrapped in a striped cotton blanket at my breast, to a red-cheeked toddler at dance lessons, wearing a sequined costume and shiny tap shoes, then tutus and ballet slippers. Sarah is beside her in nearly every pose. Photos show them earning Girl Scout badges, pitching a tent at church camp, singing in the choir. With each page, memories surface, and I become more and more convinced that we gave our daughter a good life. A happy life. A life with love.

Some of the photos show Carl, Ellie, and me together, roasting marshmallows over a campfire, cutting a Christmas tree from a wild stand of pines, bringing Beanie home for the first time. Ellie holds the tiny kitten up to her mouth, kissing her. Beanie lived up to the love. A constant companion, curling atop homework pages and purring Ellie to sleep each night.

I laugh to myself now, remembering Ellie's protest. She slept on the porch with Beanie that first night, insisting that if the cat couldn't come in then she wouldn't either. That lasted all of two hours before Carl gave in. I admired her stance. She had a fire in her that I believed could never burn out.

"You survived so much, sweet girl." I talk to her now. "You were brave. And strong. And you never let your hurts make you mean."

I start to cry now as I tell my daughter what I need to say.

"Ellie, honey. I'm so sorry.

"I'm sorry I let you down. I'm sorry I lost Sarah. I'm sorry I couldn't keep our family together, and I'm sorry I couldn't stay as strong as you needed me to be.

"When your dad left us, I fell apart. I relied on you. That never should have happened. You were the child; I was the mother. I should have done better. I wish I could go back and make different choices. I'd do anything, Ellie, to save you."

I wipe tears and continue.

"I wish, more than anything, that you had known how much you were loved. How much you were needed here, in this life, with us. I wish you had not done this, Ellie. Every day is hard. I miss you. And . . ."

I can't finish my sentence. I lie down on the bench, photo albums in hand, and I curse the sky.

Nearly an hour later, the sound of my cell phone stirs me awake. It takes me a minute to realize where I am. On the third ring, I take a look. It's Carl.

"Hello?" *Please let him say he's sorry. Please let him show he cares.*

"Amanda?" When I don't reply, he continues. "I just wanted . . . I know it's been a year today. And . . . well . . . I guess I just wanted you to know. That's all."

"How are you?" I ask.

"Fine." He doesn't ask me in return.

"Have you been to the grave?" I ask him. "Did you see the bench?" We haven't talked in months.

"No." After a length of silence he adds, "I'm sure it's nice."

I don't bother asking him to help me pay for it. Every month, as I pay my credit card bill, I swallow the bitterness I feel toward Carl. It would do me no good to hate him.

"I haven't heard from you in a while. You still at the plant?"

"Yeah. But I'm going back offshore soon. I never liked working dogs."

"That night shift must be rough. I'm glad you'll be happy." I say this with kindness, but apparently that's not how Carl receives it.

"There you go again. Why do you think I never call, Amanda? All you ever do is attack me."

I set the phone on the ground and lie back down on the bench.

Carl's muffled voice continues to launch the same old accusations, but I no longer listen. Eventually he must realize I'm not there. He hangs up the phone.

I'm nearly asleep again when the sound of a truck draws me to a seated position. It's Jay, pulling up near Ellie's grave. He parks and heads my way, flowers in hand.

I rise and offer him a hug. He holds me, for the longest time, and then we sit together on the bench. "Wildflowers," I finally notice. "Her favorite."

Jay gets up and lays the fresh batch of blooms across her unmarked grave. Then he spends the rest of the afternoon with me, sharing memories and stories of the good times.

"I almost forgot," I tell him. "I brought a balloon."

The sun is beginning to sink beneath the tree line as we walk to my car. He helps me carry the photo albums, and I trade my thermos for the turquoise balloon. "Her favorite color," I say. He nods and eyes the note on the seat. I grab it and explain. "I wrote her a letter. Last night."

I loop the letter with string, attaching it beneath the helium balloon. Standing at my car, out from under the oak tree, I look skyward, hoping the heavens will get my message to Ellie and that she'll feel my love. Jay puts his arm around my shoulders and we release the string. Together we watch the message wave in the wind, and then we light a candle for Ellie's grave, leaving her not in darkness, but in light.

The narrow route home from the cemetery is flanked by deep ditches. Thick woods creep right up to the edge of the water-filled trenches. For years, these dense stands of timber were broken only by an occasional home, with plenty of privacy for those who opted to live in Walker. But since Katrina, clear-cut neighborhoods have been dropped in between the miles of rural acreage, cluttering the landscape and pressing neighbors together on small lots for maximum profit. Now, as we near Election Day, political signs have been tacked onto wooden stakes and stuck in the ground, creating a special kind of chaos, especially combined with the decorations people have set out for the upcoming night of trick-or-treat.

I've neglected to leave a light on. Without streetlamps, darkness slips in, surrounding me. I feel my way to the back door, but I don't enter quite yet. Carl and I constructed this small brick ranch-style home as our starter place, perched on an acre of scrub land. The parcel was originally a cattle farm, then a pine flat, before the owner sold the timber and divvied out one- to three-acre sections for new construction. We had never planned on staying here long. Instead, we had commissioned an architect to design a four-bedroom Acadian. "My dream home," I had bragged to Raelynn. It was to be built on a ten-acre spread north of her place, overlooking a fish pond and a horse pasture and a large backyard with shade trees and plenty of room for Ellie to roam. The house, the horses, the hopes . . . distant memories now.

Tonight I stand at my back door, letting my eyes adjust to the dome of darkness around me. The swoop of bats merges with the roaring rumble of insects. "Hush," Carl used to say, holding baby Ellie in his lap as he rocked her on the porch swing. "Listen. It's the call of the wild."

I listen now, standing here alone. "Where are you, Ellie? Where are you, Sarah? Do you know you are loved?"

I move into the house and go through boxes of Ellie's school mementos. One of her best school projects, a science presentation on feathers, earned her an A++. On the front of the report she drew a beautiful feather, edged in iridescent green. We searched three different craft stores trying to match the hues of the wild Quaker parrots that had first caught her eye during the field trip. She had bent low to collect the feather from the ground after Sarah went missing, and carried it with her the entire week, clinging to it as we spent full days pacing the grid, searching for her friend.

Nearly two years later, Ellie pulled that feather from her bulletin board and began researching the natural habitat of Quaker parrots, discovering they are not from Louisiana at all.

I am taken back now, as Ellie's voice comes through to me. "Mom, did you know they didn't migrate to New Orleans? They were living in South America. Wild and free. People would capture them and sell them as pets. That's how they ended up here. In cages."

The very idea makes me clutch the feather to my heart. She's here with me. In this room. "Some of the birds got loose. They were free, but they couldn't go all the way back to South America. They don't migrate. You'd think they'd die, right? If their owner wasn't feeding them? But they didn't die. They found a way to make a new home, right there in the middle of New Orleans, building big nests in the palm trees and on the power poles. After Katrina, some of them ended up on the west bank. People call them Katrina parrots now. Like the hurricane chickens we had in our yard for a while. Remember those?"

I give in to the magical thinking, as if Ellie were really right here with me. In this space. Alive and teaching me about the parrots. "Did you know, Mom? They have some green feathers and some that are kind of turquoise too. See?"

I look at the drawings she's made, capturing the bird's unique hues.

"That's why you chose this project?" I ask her. "Because of the turquoise? Your favorite color?"

"Of course!" She laughs. My daughter laughs! I reach out, as if I can still touch her, longing to feel her hair in my hands.

"But, Mom, here's the coolest part. Some of the feathers aren't actually blue or green at all. They only look that way because the light moves through them. Like a prism. It's an illusion. That's what the scientists say. They found out peacock feathers are like that too. They aren't blue or green or turquoise like we think. They're really just brown. Kind of grayish. So how can I say this?" She twirls her pen through her ponytail. "They don't have pigment in them. It's actually their structure . . . how they're made . . . and the color only really comes through when it finds light. Birds, butterflies—they were made for the light."

Hello Sparrow,

It's been three years. Three YEARS! I will not give up hope. I will not give up hope. I will not give up hope. I will not give up hope. I will not give up hope. I. Will. Not. Give. Up. Hope!

Chapter 25

January 2008

"HAPPY NEW YEAR!" I PLACE A SLICE OF POUND CAKE ON VIV'S desk and head for my office.

"I'm glad you're back," she says, following me to my desk. "It's been way too lonely without you."

"It was time," I say, unpacking my bag. I add a fresh batch of ink pens to my favorite container. It's a piece of terra cotta pottery Ellie made for Mother's Day way back in first grade. Her fingerprints are stamped around the circumference, painted to look like flower blooms. *I will not cry today.* "What'd you do for New Year's?" I ask Viv.

She holds out her left hand for me to inspect a bright, shiny diamond ring.

"No way!" I cheer. "Is this for real?"

She's blushing and giggling like a schoolgirl. "Took me forty years, but I finally found The One."

"Viv!" I hug her. "I'm so happy for you. Tell me everything. How'd he propose?"

"Had the whole unit involved," she explains. "We had gone out to eat at Don's down in Denham. Nothing fancy, you know, just good food. Good people. And anyway, we were at the table with his family. They'd all met us out, so I should have known something was up, but I really was clueless. And then this lady started choking back in the corner booth. All of a sudden the restaurant was swarming with first responders. All his firemen. He made chief, you know."

I nod, smiling. My friend is radiant; a light surrounds her. So much joy.

"I'm thinking, gosh, this is a big deal. I mean, they were all rushing in to help her. And then . . . music begins to play, and the whole restaurant, everybody, they all get up and start singing my favorite song."

"Don't tell me."

She's laughing. And we sing in sync, "Holding Out for a Hero."

"Perfect! He's perfect for you!"

"I know, right! I mean, what kind of man is going to coordinate a flash mob to 'Hero' in the middle of Don's Seafood?"

"Your one true love, that's who!"

She laughs, and I give her a hug. "Pictures. I need pictures."

"Don't worry. They got it on video. You'll see. He got down on one knee and everything. I was bawling like a baby. A total mess. I wish you could have been there. You'll love him."

"I already do." I hug her again and give the ring a second look. "It's beautiful, Viv. You have a date set yet?"

"Well . . ." She hesitates, grinning guiltily. "I've been waiting forty years. I don't want to wait anymore. We're too old for a big wedding anyway. We're going to the justice of the peace this week. And then we're leaving next Monday. Flying out to the Greek islands and calling it good."

"Monday?" I'm shocked.

"Monday." She can't stop smiling.

"I'm so happy, Viv. I've never seen you this excited. Look at you. You're glowing."

"I know. It's crazy. I mean, all these years I've sat here listening to horrible, hurtful things people do to one another, and I still want to believe in happy-ever-after. It's kind of ridiculous."

"Not at all," I tell her. "I still believe in it too."

"So I do have this little fantasy." She grins. "Have I ever told you about it?"

I perk my head, intrigued.

"It goes like this. Someday Jay will come swooping in here, wearing those jeans and cowboy boots that make him look killer. And he's going to put a big diamond ring on top of an Elmer's glue bottle. Just stick it right there around that orange twisty cap. Then he'll bend over your desk and give you a huge kiss and he'll say, 'Stick with me for life, Gloopy?'"

I roll my eyes. "*That's* your fantasy?"

"Yep. And then you'll say yes and y'all will live happily ever after." She gives me a more serious look and adds, "You deserve it, you know. The happy-ever-after part."

"I can't get engaged without a flash mob and a theme song. What fun would that be?"

She smiles. "I already thought of that. 'Brown-Eyed Girl.' Because one day Carl came to pick you up. Your car was in the shop or something, I don't remember, but anyway . . . you probably never knew this." She waves her arm and says, "Maybe I shouldn't tell you."

"I'm sure it's nothing I haven't heard from him before. I can handle it." I smile for extra assurance. She finally tells me the story.

"He was looking at a magazine, waiting for you. He made some kind of comment about Cameron Diaz and her sexy blue eyes. And then he said, 'Nothing worse than looking at a woman's eyes and thinking about a pile of poop.' Only he didn't say it with that much tact."

I laugh. "I'll bet."

"Then he pointed to your office." She imitates him, mocking his harsh tone. "'Look at my wife in there. Dirt-floor hair and eyes like poop. And she can't even be ready when I come to pick her up. See what I have to deal with?'"

I smile, but what I really want to do is close my eyes and bleach my hair.

"So one day," Viv continues, back in her own voice now, "I want a man to look at your beautiful brown eyes and your long, dark hair and I want him to see your worth, Amanda. Something Carl could never see." Then she raises her mug and says, "Here's to happy-ever-after."

I tap my cup to hers and add a second toast. "True love."

"He's left me." My client spins her gold wedding ring around her left finger, tugging it up to her knuckle and back down again as she works the words through her brain. "Thirty-seven years, and he up and leaves. Just like that. How can I tell the kids? We've got grandbabies now. Where will they stay when they visit? How will we handle Christmas? And birthdays? This isn't how it's supposed to work."

I listen, wishing as I always do that I could ease my client's pain. Viv's right. We sit here day after day, witnessing the hurts people cause one another. Serving as a catch basin for all the grief and loss and heartache life can deal. "Thirty-seven years," I say.

She nods. "Why would he leave me now? When I'm too old to start over? Look at me."

"You're beautiful," I tell her.

She doesn't believe me.

"You are. Tell me, how would you describe your marriage? Have you been happy?"

"Yes, yes. Very much so. We were the couple everyone else wanted to be. That's what makes no sense. We rarely argued. We took great vacations as a family. We hardly had any real problems. Not like our friends. He loved his job; I loved being home. We shared the workload, managed our money, got our kids off on solid ground. They're doing great—all three of them—married, successful. I wouldn't change a single thing."

"What do you think happened?" I sit back, ready for a story.

"I don't know. I can't explain it. He started getting depressed after he retired. Spending more and more time up at the golf course. Or fishing. Just alone. And then last Tuesday we're sitting at the breakfast table, drinking coffee, reading the paper, as we have done every morning for almost forty years, and he doesn't even look up from the sports section. Just says, 'I'm going to file for divorce.' It didn't register at first. I said, 'What did you say?' And he repeated it, this time looking directly at me. I laughed. I thought he was joking. But he wasn't."

"You haven't told your children?"

"No. I haven't told anyone." She touches her hair, feeling to make sure it's set in place.

"Would he be willing to come to counseling with you? Or by himself?"

"He doesn't believe in counseling. Says it's a waste of money and time." Then she tilts her head and says, "Sorry. That's not what I think, of course."

I wave my hand to assure her I'm not offended. "Are you financially secure if he leaves?"

She nods. "Money's not the problem."

"And you're healthy?"

"Oh yes, for now anyway." She knocks a few times on my wooden desk.

"And you have your children as a support network. Friends, I'm betting."

"Yes, yes. All that. I'm luckier than most. But . . ."

I wait while she gathers her thoughts.

"I love him. I never imagined myself without him. I gave my whole life to him, and now we get to the really good part, and he quits." She tosses a hand in the air as she says it. "That's it! That's the thing that's really pinching me. I chose him above all the others. And you know why? Because he wasn't a quitter. He's got a stronger work ethic than anyone I know. There's not a half-finished shed on our property, no vehicle in need of repair. He finishes what he starts. Yet here he is, quitting on me."

Hello Sparrow,

One time, in second grade, we went to see the circus. I wanted to be the lady who rode the elephants. She had long black hair, and her costume was shiny gold. Her boots came up to her knees. They were made of glitter. She sparkled.

The elephants marched in a big circle, holding on to each other's tails, while the lady walked across their backs.

Mom told me someone has to train an elephant to be tame like that. First, they catch her in the jungle, and then they chain her between two trees so she won't run away. They beat her until she stops trying to escape. By that point she's so thirsty, all she can think about is getting some water. She doesn't want to die.

Just when the elephant is about to give up, the owner brings her some water. And then some food. She knows he's a bad guy, but he's the one who feeds her. And he gives her water. And he talks nice to her sometimes. So she tries to stay on his good side. No matter what it takes. Because he's keeping her alive.

This goes on for a long time, until she is "broken." That's what they call it.

The other elephants have already been broken. They teach her how to do her new job. Eventually she learns what she's supposed to do, and she finally gets off the chain.

"So then she runs away?" I asked Mom. "Back to her family?"

"Nope," Mom said. "The chains are gone, and she's not even fenced in, but the elephant stays right there, trying her best to make her trainer happy."

I asked Mom, "Why wouldn't she stomp the man and try to escape?"

Mom said it's because they have a bond now. A strong one. "Sometimes, Sarah, the chains around the heart are the hardest to break."

Yesterday Bridgette took me to the grocery store with her. It was the first time they let me leave the house. I could have run, Sparrow. I could have told someone in the store that my name was Sarah Broussard. I could have gotten help and gone home.

It's all I wanted to do. But The Lady said, "Don't be stupid. He'll find you. Cut you into a million pieces. He's done it before."

So there I was, Sparrow. Off the chain. No fence. But too afraid to do anything.

Chapter 26

Sunday, June 15, 2008
Father's Day

"I'M GLAD YOU'RE HERE," I TELL CARL. I'M ALSO GLAD HE CAME
without Ashleigh, but I don't say that. It might trigger a fight. I navigate the conversation as if I'm walking a minefield, the way I've done throughout our entire marriage. Only this time my stomach isn't in knots and I don't carry the burden of blame. He planted those mines. Not me. I finally accept that his deepest wounds are not my fault, and that his anger has nothing to do with me either. What *is* my fault is that I served as his emotional punching bag for nearly twenty years, allowing him to take all his resentment out on me. *Set the mines. I'll walk them for you. Blow me to bits again and again. I can take it. Because I love you. And you're worth it. No matter how much it hurts.*

Well, no more minefields, Carl. Enough is enough.

"I've made copies of the photo albums and DVDs." I hand him the box of memories. "Ellie always liked this sort of stuff. She was so sentimental."

Carl says nothing as he puts the box to the side and takes a seat at my kitchen table.

I set a stack of papers in front of him. "I've signed them. We can go forward with the divorce whenever you're ready."

He looks at me, and for the first time in years I get a glimpse of the man I married. The one he buried deep beneath defensive layers, protecting his heart to the point he could no longer love. Or be loved.

"What changed your mind?"

"It's taken me awhile, Carl, to work through it all. I think you had been preparing yourself for years before I ever knew. I needed time to catch up with you. I couldn't give up."

He nods. "What about the house?" He looks around the kitchen, examining the simple window valance and the expensive stand mixer, as if he's seeing it all for the first time. "When do you want to list it?"

I'm not prepared for this. "Sell it? Carl, I don't know if I can leave my home."

He looks down the hall toward Ellie's bedroom, the place where she died, and he says, "I'm surprised you want to be here."

I move to the window, looking out into the yard at the long-forgotten swing set. "This is my home. It's where Ellie took her first steps. Learned to ride a bike without training wheels. She did her first backbend out there in the grass. And look . . . that swing is where she learned to pump without a push. All those memories, Carl. Her whole life is here."

"Then you can buy it out from me. Is that what you want?" He stares toward the box of photos but remains matter-of-fact.

"Honestly, I need some time to think about it."

"More time? It's been almost three years, Amanda. How much time do you need?"

I lean in. "Can you give me a month? The lease is ending soon at Mom's place. I need to weigh my options."

"Whatever." He sighs, but he doesn't draw any reaction from

me. Instead, I stand at the window for what feels like a very long time. Outside, the pecan trees are green and thick with leaves, growing their fall crop of nuts. The neighbor's children race their bikes through a homemade obstacle course, and Beanie sits on the swing, watching the commotion. Carl stays seated at the table in silence.

"I wish I could understand, Carl. Why did you leave us?"

"I'm not doing this, Amanda." His voice gets hard. He stands with fast aggression, and the chair scratches across the floor. "Let it go."

"Carl, listen." I stay soft, slow. "We don't have to talk about it. I'm healing. It will be okay. Besides, I've decided to look at it in a different way now."

He simmers down a bit. "How's that?"

"Before, I saw our marriage as a failure." He stiffens. "My failure, Carl. I had failed to be a good enough wife. But I don't believe that anymore."

He waits, and I speak slowly. "Viv said something that has shifted things for me. Instead of looking back on our marriage as a failure, myself as a failure, or you as a failure, I see a lot we should be proud of."

"You do?"

"I really do. We had almost twenty years together. Way more good than bad. I mean, look." I point to the photos and videos I've prepared for him. "There's a whole box of memories there to prove it."

His mouth relaxes into what could almost be called a smile.

"We were kids when we started out together. And look how far we've come. We've gotten each other through some tough stuff. Really tough stuff."

"Don't you know it." He nods, agreeing with me for the first time in years.

"And you know what else we did together? We brought one amazing little girl into this universe, and we gave her fourteen years of love and laughter. She had one heck of a good life."

Carl's hands begin to shake.

"We just grew apart. It happens. We went different directions. I didn't know how far you had strayed, is all. I thought you were right around the corner, waiting for me to catch up to you. I've been chasing you down for years, believing if I could just reach you again then we'd finish the journey together. But I get it now, Carl. And it's okay. I understand. I forgive you."

"You forgive me?" Defensive again.

"Yes, I do. And I'm asking you to forgive me too. For not being able to reach you in time. For not being aware of how much you were hurting and for not knowing how to make you feel loved enough here in our home. You were loved. You just couldn't see it."

Tears well up now, for both of us. It's the first time I've ever seen Carl cry.

"You were a good wife, Amanda. You always were. I didn't deserve you."

These words . . . these words.

"I couldn't be who you needed. All that with Sarah. Then Ellie." He cries harder now. For the first time, he doesn't turn to some mundane task to release emotions. He doesn't pick up a hammer or work on the car or mow the lawn. Instead, he holds his head in his hands and he sobs, finally mourning our child with raw expressions of grief.

I move to touch him, place my hand on his shoulder, lean over and kiss his head. He is still the man I love. Despite it all.

"I wasn't good to you, Amanda. I know I wasn't. I'm sorry."

"Carl." I wait for him to look at me. "I'm letting it go. All of it."

He cries for a long time here in our kitchen and then on the couch. It all rises from within him, the anger, the hurt, the darkness that has tried so hard to drown his light.

As the sun begins to set, it's time for Carl to leave. I walk him to his truck, and we say good-bye. I offer one final wish. "I want you to be happy," I tell him. "I want you to know how it feels to love someone with your heart wide open. I want you to know you are loved."

The minute I tell Raelynn about Carl's visit, she's rushing over here to vent. I think I've touched a nerve about her own abusive marriage, a wound for which she's never found closure. She needs to let off some steam. Carl is an easy outlet, so I give her room to blow.

"Remember back in school, that time he punched Jay? For no good reason. Just didn't want him to look at you. And the time he threw a tire iron at an old man for taking too long at the gas pumps?"

I don't bother arguing. The list of things Carl has done is endless. I spent years making excuses for him, apologizing to everyone he insulted, trying to convince everybody he was not as bad as he sometimes seemed. Especially during our younger years, before he learned to target his rage at me and present a polished surface in public. Now I have nothing to say. But Raelynn does.

"You sold yourself short, you know?"

Reverting back to old habits, I begin to tell her what a hardworking person Carl is. How good he was at handling money, taking care of the house, the yard and cars. How much fun he was as a father, playing with Ellie almost like he was a kid himself. But this time the words won't come.

"Now Jay, on the other hand . . ." She fumbles with her purse and pulls a stick of spearmint gum from the pocket, popping it into her mouth. "I don't know what you're waiting for."

A rise of heat blushes my face, and I can't hold back a smile.

"Aha! So there is something going on between you and Jay!" She says this with such volume, I jump.

"That's ridiculous. I'm finally free. The last thing I want is another man."

"This is Jay we're talking about. You're the one who got away." She's relentless. "His first love. From way back in kindergarten."

"Okay, now you really have to stop. You've been reading way too many trashy romance novels. It was Riley he loved." Truth is, I've often wondered what might have happened if Jay hadn't gone off to Lafayette for college. What if he had gone to LSU instead of leaving me here to marry Carl?

"That was a long time ago, Amanda. Trust me. Mr. Long and Strong is back in the game and ready for action. Has been for a while now."

"Jay's a friend, Raelynn. Nothing more." I straighten the curtains and open the windows.

"Good to know." She sits in Carl's old La-Z-Boy, pulling the lever to recline. "Then you won't mind if I go after him."

"As opposed to the way you flirt your skirt off with him already?"

"Oh, believe me. If I thought I had a chance with Jay Ardoin, I wouldn't hold back." She hums.

"How about that UPS guy who comes by your office all the time?" I ask. "The one who looks like he could bench-press a tiger. He'd be a good one."

She roars. "Married."

"Honestly, Raelynn. I don't get it. After all you've been through with that ex of yours, after all we've learned searching for Sarah, seeing what disgusting animals men can be, how in the world are you still thinking about landing one?"

"I don't know. I guess . . . here's the thing. If I start to believe all men are monsters, then that means I'd have to give up on my own sons. And I won't do that. No way, nohow. So I choose to believe some good ones still exist. You should too."

Hello Sparrow,

The Man has been buying me and Bridgette a lot of nice things.

He puts our movies online now. People pay to watch them. I don't want anybody to see that stuff. But I'm trying to find the good. If people can see me, then maybe Mom and Pop will find me.

Hello Sparrow,

The Man has been making lots of money. He says we don't need The Boss anymore. We can do it on our own. He says we're getting a big house. One with a swimming pool.

I asked Bridgette if The Boss will hurt us when he finds out we moved away with The Man. She said yes. He will.

Stay with me, Sparrow. Follow me to the new house, just like you did before. I'm scared.

Hello Sparrow,

I'm so glad you followed us here! I like the new house. I have my own bedroom and bathroom. It's very big.

The Man said we don't have to worry about The Boss or anybody else ever again. I don't even have to hide anymore. The Man said to tell people I'm his daughter, and we'll be fine. He said I belong to him now. Just like Bridgette. And that's how it will always be.

He lets me watch TV now too, like a regular family. I watch the news sometimes, but I never see anything about me being kidnapped. Maybe The Man is right. Maybe everybody thinks I'm dead.

He said more girls might come here to live with me, like sisters. I always wanted a bunch of sisters. If I don't think about the films and the men, it's not too bad.

Hello Sparrow,

The men who visit now are rich. They are not like the men who came to the shed in Chalmette. They wear nice clothes and drive cool cars. They never chew tobacco or smell like sweat.

"You don't know how lucky we are." That's what Bridgette tells me. "We've got the best pimp in the game."

The Man makes me call him Master now. I don't like that. When I was little, I learned a Bible verse that says, "No one can serve two masters."

Bridgette said, "You only have one master. LeMoyne." That's what she calls The Man. "God is his master."

And I said no. Money is his master. And I told her the other part of that verse. "You cannot serve both God and money."

"Well, God ain't givin' us no fancy clothes and car and house," she said. "So I'll take LeMoyne."

Chapter 27

Saturday, November 1, 2008

SUNRISE ON THE WATER IS AS HOLY A SIGHT AS ANYONE COULD ever see, even for someone who hardly believes in holy anymore. This morning makes me feel as if God is right here with me. The simmering mist rises hip-high against the smooth, dark currents, brewing a mood that is almost mystical, beckoning me back to a foundation of faith.

All around me, the faint fog is broken only by weighted, dew-soaked leaves. They drip into the silken surface of the river, forming ripples. Mosquitoes and swamp flies dart low near the water's black face, tempting hungry fish to bob for breakfast. Blue herons swoop against tapered trunks while gators and turtles slide out to sun between weathered cypress knees. The morning air is still. A few determined fishermen cast hoop nets, pull catfish jugs, and race to their honey holes, whipping fine lines across the sky to snag a biting bass.

I have stepped away from Jay's raised walkway, choosing instead to sink at the edge of the camp's soft bank. As the lapping water splashes against my jeans, my old tennis shoes sink deep in mud. I am tempted to let the swamp swallow me whole, pull me down below the thick, green growth and bury me under the giant salvinia.

Jay draws near. I acknowledge him with a subtle lean, not yet ready to quit the quiet.

The smell of warm chicory rises between us, blending with the muddy smells of marsh as he hands me a faded LSU mug. The inscription reads *Geaux Tigers*, with most of the letters rubbed off.

"Remember when we all had season tickets? Never missed a home game. Except maybe Vandy. Or Tulane."

"Those don't count," Jay says. I smile. He sips his coffee from an oversized mug: *I'd rather be fishing* spelled out in hunter-green letters.

"Think we'll ever do that again?" I cling to the hope that our lives will spin back to normal someday.

"Of course we will." Jay holds his mug up for a toast. "To the Tigers."

I tap my cup against his and salute. "Geaux Tigers."

The two of us stand side by side, sipping coffee, our eyes on the horizon. Like an arm, the river stretches, reaching and grasping for something far in the distance. A snowy egret flies above us, her bright-yellow feet in stark contrast to her black legs and white feathers.

"Two years," I say. "Hard to believe." I left Ellie's grave on Wednesday, the second anniversary of her suicide, and came straight here to hide from the world. Jay arrived this morning unexpectedly, to check for a pulse. He moves closer. Pieces deep within me react with spark, but I smother the flame before it can grow. Jay is my lifelong friend. He's here because he knows how it feels to carry watermarks on the heart.

"We'll get through this. I promise. We will." His voice is steady, calm. And he says *we*. This simple word offers the assurance I need. For this moment, with Jay in sight, I feel safe. In fact, I don't want to leave. I want to stand right here and watch the sun rise and set forever, far removed from all the ugly in the universe.

Downriver, the water reflects the sun in clipped waves, bending the morning like a mirror ball spinning at a disco. I'm reminded of Ellie's project about feathers. *Some things are made for the light.*

"Does it ever get to be too much for you, Jay? Your job?"

"I've seen stuff I never wanted to see. Stuff I wish I hadn't. But you've been right there with me for most of it. You know how it is."

"Not nearly as much as you. I read the crime reports. That pregnant mother stabbed the other day. How do you stay balanced?"

He thinks this through before responding. "People can do horrible things. I'll give you that. But give up hope? Start believing there are no good people left in the world? I can't do that."

"It's hard sometimes. Isn't it?"

"Sure it is," Jay says, eyeing the fishermen. "But look at those guys." Two bass boats point in opposite directions. "What do you see?"

I don't answer. I watch the boats floating slowly across the water.

Jay continues. "All right, then. I'll tell you what *I* see. I see good people, people who wake up and do their best to get through the day, to take care of the folks they love. Maybe even try to make the world a better place."

One of the fishermen waves his hand, and Jay returns the friendly greeting. Then he passes me the wallet-sized case that holds his sheriff's badge. "Here. Take a look."

I open its black leather cover to find the brass symbol he keeps with him at all times.

"See what I had them put on there? When I took office?"

The five-pointed star is draped with a red, white, and blue American flag and bordered by a symmetrical circle. Engraved on the top in bright-blue letters is *To Serve and Protect.* Below is

Est. 1832. Two inner circles show the Louisiana state seal with the brown pelican plucking her own breast—that old, familiar symbol of sacrifice and protection. Around the pelican, the badge identifies its owner as the Livingston Parish Sheriff. It's a beautiful badge, but I'm not sure what Jay is asking me to notice.

"See the bottom banner?" He eyes the emblem.

"Here?" I point to the numbers *13:4.*

Jay nods. "You know what that's for?"

I shake my head, feeling guilty for not knowing already.

"It's from Romans—13:4. 'The authorities are God's servants, sent for your good.' For your good," he repeats.

I offer him a smile. "You can be too idealistic at times. You know that?"

"Nah." He laughs. "No such thing."

After a few minutes I nod toward his Bass Tracker. "Mind if I take your boat out? There's a place I've been wanting to visit."

"Sure. I'll go with you." He walks down the dock, holding his empty mug.

"It's okay. I think I need to be alone for a little while."

He shoots a worried stare, trying to gauge my mood.

"I won't be long. I promise."

"Where're you going?" He asks it more from concern than control.

"That little chapel on the water. You know the one?" I step over the bow and move into the driver's seat, drying dew with my shirt.

"Our Lady of Blind River?" He lifts the frayed bowline with one hand and tosses it into the boat. "Sure I know it. Mr. Bobby Deroche built it for his wife, Mrs. Martha."

I take this in, surprised anyone would do something so kind. "That true?"

"So they say. Story goes Mrs. Martha had a dream one night. The Blessed Virgin told her to build a place where people could come and pray. Then she had a vision of Christ kneeling in the exact spot where the chapel is today. Word spread fast, and they ended up with something like twenty people to offer help. Built the whole place by hand."

I don't know what else to say. I'm finding it difficult to believe in miracles. After an awkward silence I continue. "I went there once, a few years back. Was thinking today might be a good day to pay it a visit." With that, I pass him my coffee mug and fumble with his floatable banana-shaped keychain before cranking the motor. It sputters to life, and he raises his voice over the churn.

"Be careful, Gloopy!"

I move the lever into reverse and give the throttle enough gas to exit the slot. Leaving Jay with a friendly wave, I head off to find the chapel.

With the sun rising higher now, the water shifts from black to brown. A white wake draws wide behind me. I pass thick patches of swamp grass, their firm, green bases stretching into brittle points that wave like flags against the wind. It might be fall-foliage season in other parts of the country, but down here in Louisiana, the leaves cling to green. The water is warm, with one side of the river lit golden from sun. The other half has gone to gray, still in shadow.

In between the yellow pulses of fading wildflowers, a new crop of Louisiana irises is emerging. Not yet budding, the strong green shoots carry the promise of violet blossoms. By spring they will pepper the riverbank, filling gaps between the shacks and fish camps. But for now it's November, so the wetlands offer no bright iris dance today.

I am alone on this broad stretch of open river, where not even camps clutter the landscape. Most of the trees have been crop-topped by storms, and moss forms a thick, gray curtain for waterfowl and squirrels, songbirds and insects. I much prefer this quiet, private span, without the brash company that clusters the canal all summer, parking boats side by side, maxing out their radios. I steer clear of the large lily pads. They dot the water's edge with massive lotus blooms, both white and pink.

Within a few minutes I turn the bend to spot a small shack sinking into swamp. Left to ruin, the small structure has been claimed by the elements. With each mile, more camps begin to flank the river. One pier home, no larger than an outhouse, is surrounded by elaborate decking and wooden walkways. Another holds long ropes suspended beneath a rusting tin roof. Buoys, traps, and nets all dangle.

Not every camp has been built for such serious angling. Some are geared for revelry, with plastic chairs stacked against the structures and fans ready to cool the guests. Oversized ice chests hold fish, beer, or both. Outdoor speakers sit silent for now, but at any moment they could begin to blare music beneath the year-round party lights that hang crookedly from rooflines.

I pass one place that is nothing more than a boxcar, pulled from a train and plopped onto bright-blue plastic barrels that have been strapped together beneath its sturdy base. Someone has attached a wooden platform to serve as a wraparound porch, more than doubling the square footage of the camp. They've also sawed spaces into the metal, adding a flimsy door and an aluminum window, both of which are sure to leak. A towel is tacked across the glass panes.

The banged-up shipping container has been roofed with a few flat pieces of sheet metal, and secured to the deck is a small pirogue, ideal for afternoon fishing trips or a ride to the deer stand. A savvy outdoorsman obviously engineered this camp with sustainability in mind, as rainwater collects in his rooftop garden before dripping down into a catch basin for additional use.

Beside this camp lies another, not much fancier. This one is a small trailer. Its porch holds a traditional wooden bench swing and a bright-turquoise slide that leads straight into the river. These two slapdash camps sit next to a larger, more expensive weekend home with an elaborate stone seawall protecting three pricey boats, each elevated by automated hoists. Also visible, a set of wave runners, a gazebo-covered hot tub, and pastel Adirondack chairs.

Another camp greets boaters with a hand-painted sign. It is written in French: *Bienvenue.* Air-conditioning units bulge from the narrow windowsills, and a rope swing is tied to a high cypress branch, set to carry children out over the water.

One thing remains constant. Whether expensive retreats or patchwork hideouts, the piers all share the same markings, stains from higher waters. Whether rich or poor, sinner or saint, we're all Louisiana and we all have to weather the storms.

After navigating a few miles of river, I see a sign reading *Slow Idle Area. Throw No Wake.* Attached to the nearby cypress trees, two more signs read *Welcome Visitors.* I pull my boat against a row of black rubber tires nailed to the dock of the Blind River Chapel. I kill the motor, secure the bowline.

Since its construction, Mrs. Deroche has always left the chapel open to welcome people from the river, to shelter them at the feet of Mother Mary. But I'm the only person here this morning. Even though there's a boat at the adjacent Deroche place, their well-maintained riverfront home is dark.

Careful to avoid the splintered latticework barrier, I make my way beyond the wooden bench and across the pier, where a large plantation bell stands silent. Admiring the craftsmanship of the quaint cypress sanctuary, the first thing I notice are three wooden crosses: a sturdy one that tops the steeple, a second perched along the eaves, and a third tacked beside the entry. Painted with the words *Our Lady of Blind River* is a sign hanging left of the aluminum door whose screen has already been replaced with glass for the upcoming winter season. To the right of the door stands a large blue painting of the Blessed Virgin. Typical of Catholic icons, her head is circled with a golden halo and bowed in prayer. At her feet these words are inscribed: *Do unto me according to thy will.*

Another flock of ducks flaps overhead, sending a thin, high-pitched *chit-chit-chit.* I squint, trying to identify the species the way Jay has taught me. They don't display the colorful green feathers of the mallards. Nor the long, slender, goose-like neck of the pintails. Instead, a group with black bellies and bright-pink feet fly overhead. Mexican whistlers. They squeal as they come to nest in a tree.

The chapel's exterior is layered with thousands of small cypress shingles, each one cut by hand to overlap the row below it. The shingles have been weathered for decades, their edges tattered by Louisiana's legendary heat and humidity; but the linear steeple points straight to the sky.

The main door, with its symmetrical stained glass squares, has been left wide open. Inside the small chantry, I give my eyes time to adjust to the dimly lit space. To my right, a spiral notebook sits on a simple wooden podium. I opt not to sign my name and turn instead to examine a brochure explaining how Bobby Deroche did, in fact, build this place for his wife, Martha, just as Jay claimed. He started Easter Sunday, 1982, and with the help of a few dozen friends finished construction in a mere three months.

It has been three years since Hurricane Katrina hit. Entire neighborhoods rest in ruins and "temporary" FEMA trailers can still be seen. I wonder what would have happened if they had put the Deroches in charge of reconstruction. Based on the looks of this chapel, I imagine the job could have been done right.

Here at the entry, an open Bible sits adjacent to a portrait of the Deroches and a porcelain plaque: *The Beatitudes of a Christian Marriage.* The words bring a sting, as I continue to struggle with the guilt of the D-word. For better or for worse, I was all in. I never considered any alternative.

I read the plaque to myself with a whisper, grieving the loss of my marriage.

Blessed are the husband and wife who continue to be considerate and affectionate long after the wedding bells have ceased ringing.

Blessed are those mates who never criticize or speak loudly to one another and who instead quietly discuss their disagreements and work toward solutions.

Blessed are they who thank God for their food and who set aside time each day to read the Bible and pray.

Blessed are they who love their mates more than any other person in the world and who joyfully fulfill their marriage vows in a lifetime of fidelity and mutual helpfulness to one another.

Near the plaque sits a basket of plastic rosaries and scapulars. I select one of each from the stash and walk the short length of the chapel, running my hands along the three parallel rows of hand-carved pews. Framed pictures of Jesus hang in mismatched frames across the paneling. They depict the story of Christ—his life, death, and resurrection. Because the small screened windows have been left open, a gentle breeze forms a cross flow. The battered air conditioner remains unplugged.

In just a few steps I reach the front of the chapel, where a life-sized Virgin Mary stands taller than me, resting against an enormous cypress trunk that has been crosscut to form the altar. The brochure explains how the men pulled this sunken beauty from the swamps and floated the majestic tree downriver before carving it specifically to fit this space. The result is a sacred iconic work of art.

Between the statue and the trunk a natural hollow forms around a knot in one of the cypress knees. Visitors have tucked handwritten prayers into the space, hoping Mother Mary will bless them with a miracle. Some claim she has done just that.

Today I pray she'll grant me one too.

I am not Catholic, but I have spent my entire life in Louisiana and am vaguely familiar with the finger rosary ring and the scapular pendant. I don't know the exact way to say the Hail Mary, but out of reverence for the devout Deroche family who built this holy space, I pray aloud, on my knees, in front of Mary.

I pray in the name of her son, the Jesus of my youth, the Christ I was taught to build my faith around. I know him now as a man born of humble beginnings, a man who dared to challenge the powerful authorities of his day. A man who performed miracles and taught a radical message of love and grace. A man who was killed for daring to offer such hope to a hate-filled world.

I think back to the Bible stories of my youth, most of which depict a dark and devious side to human nature. Is it so different now than in the days of Jesus? Have we managed to learn anything in these two thousand years?

"Mary," I whisper. "You know this grief. This pain. If I'm to believe the history, you lost your own child. How did you survive it? How did you keep faith? Help me believe."

Then I turn my heart to God and beg for mercy. For miracles. For grace. It's been a long time since I've been able to pray. At first, after Ellie's death, the words simply would not come. My spirit was so broken, I could only wail, *Help! Make it all go away!*

After that I hit a wall. Every time I turned to the heavens, a swell of anger would fill me. How could I possibly pray to a God who had taken so much from me? My message turned from *Help* to *Why, God? Why?*

But here, now, words come faster than I can speak them. I let them slide into the air, rising up from a clear, deep spring that has long been walled within me. Tears come with the words. Then anger. I breathe deeply. A part of me wants to toss a threat, shout to God: *You hurt me again, I'm done for good.* Instead, I try not to blame him for my suffering.

I stay here for a long time, my knees pressed hard against the wooden floor, the chapel door open wide behind me. Dawn is breaking fully into day. The room fills with birdsong and the wind moves between cypress needles, causing branches to creak. Above me, squirrels scamper across the roof, barking their signature warning calls.

There's something about the mix of the religious icons and the sounds of the swamp that convince me Martha Deroche was onto something when she insisted the chapel be built here. The site seems sacred.

Between birds and squirrels, wind and water, I listen for the voice of God. But once again I am left with no answers. No promises. Only my fragile faith, as I cling to the feet of Mary.

Like my daughter, Ellie, I was baptized when I was eight years old. With two pigtails and nervous eyes, I stood at the altar, chest-deep in lukewarm water, cloaked in a white choir robe with the pastor's hand placed firmly against my spine. My mother waited with a towel in the choir loft, smiling reassuringly as I offered a public profession of my Christian faith. Church members sat silently in padded pews while the pianist softly played "Just As I Am." But truth be told, at eight years old, I wasn't thinking about the Father, the Son, or the Holy Spirit. My thoughts were focused on two things only, and as I sent God a prayer, it was to ask him: *Please don't let my underwear show through the wet robe, and please don't let the water go up my nose.*

Before I could say amen, the preacher put his hand over mine and tilted me backward for the dunk. I pinched my fingers around my nose, held my breath behind tight lips, closed my eyes, and let my weight fall beneath the water.

In an instant I reentered the world of air and light, with my pigtails wringing wet and my mother standing in tears, waiting to wrap me in the warm, dry terry cloth. I hadn't expected to feel changed. But I had done it. I had proven I was no longer a little girl.

Standing there, I had an epiphany of sorts, if you can call it that at such a young age. With every Bible study and Sunday school lesson, every youth group meeting and choir rehearsal—it had all come down to this. I was loved. Not just by God but by these people, this community, this church. As they sang the hymn, they were telling me I mattered, that my soul was worthy of being saved, that I had a place to call home.

When I wiped water from my eyes and walked with wet feet

toward my mother's open arms, the congregation's voices rose in tune. Music swelled around me, and I promised myself I would never let them down.

But somehow I have done just that. I lost Sarah. I failed to keep my family together. I buried my child. And no matter how hard I try, I can't fix these broken parts of my life.

Now I remember that eight-year-old little girl, the one in pigtails whose faith could not be shaken. *I want to keep believing. You know I do. Please, God, show me how.*

I move to the small collection of ruby-red prayer candles. I open the cardboard matchbox. "Please hear the prayers of all the people who have come here to pray. Mine too." I strike a match.

First I light a candle for Ellie. I repeat the process for Sarah, taking time to focus my intentions. Then a third flame, lifting to heaven all the children across the world who are suffering. And another for the millions of adults who have somehow lost hold of their own souls, who prowl like predators, stalking every vulnerable heart.

As I place another burnt matchstick into the narrow chamber of sand, a sprawling shadow spans the chapel, and I turn to find a man in the doorway. Just shy of six feet, he stands against the cypress frame, a weathered camouflage cap in his hands. "You out here all by yourself?"

His accent is heavy Cajun-French, the clipped cadence that sounds like song. He doesn't threaten, but I've learned from years with my clients that eyes are the best way to get a true sense of someone's soul. With the sun behind his back and his eyeglasses blocking my view, I step forward to get a better look. Dark brown. Soft. Honest. I exhale.

"I was just about to leave," I announce, trying not to show any fear. He steps away from the door, allowing me free exit.

"Don't let me run you off." He sends a smile. Gray rubber boots reach his knees, with worn blue jeans tucked down deep into them. "I'm just doing my mornin' check. Where're you headed?"

I assume this must be one of the Deroche relatives. In these parts, it'd be rude to let on I don't know who he is.

"Just out lookin' around a bit." I offer a vague answer and switch to a more informal code.

"You got the sheriff's boat?" He eyes the craft.

I tuck the scapular and rosary into my pocket for safekeeping. "Yeah, I'm staying down at Jay's place. I'm Amanda."

He hums to acknowledge me as one of his own. As he shakes my hand, his suspicions seem to ease.

"My aunt and uncle built this place. My aunt Martha, she's got her a real deep faith. Talks about the Blessed Virgin nonstop."

I smile. "You think she really had a vision?"

"Oh, I don't know. I'd say it's smart to believe whatever my aunt tells me." Nothing sarcastic here. "She's got this unique way of thinking about it all."

"Really? What's that?" I rest against the wooden frame. It holds the heavy bell.

"You know how people say Mary was a virgin, or whatever."

I nod.

"Well, Aunt Martha, she likes to say God knew what he was doing putting that story in the Bible. Because it means a lot more than we think. God knew, if he really wanted to save the world, he'd have to rely on a woman. And he chose Mary because he wanted to make a point."

"Interesting." I chuckle a bit. "What point?"

"My aunt thinks God was trying to say that men had let him down too many times. So he turned to a woman. A virgin, who was not under the control of any man. And he made her a mother for a reason. And he gave her a son for a reason too."

I arch my brows, waiting for the moral to be revealed.

"It's so she could bring a new kind of man into the world, one who could teach men how to love again. We had forgotten."

As I motor away from the chapel, I eye a small wooden cross. It has been nailed to a cypress tree, right here, in the middle of the swamp. I pull Jay's boat closer and kill the switch. Despite the fact that it is shadowed by thick gray beards of moss and banked by the bald knees of the trees, someone has indeed taken the time to attach a cross to this weathered trunk.

The Blind River is a dangerous place. Many have died here. So I suspect the cross serves as a memorial. A tribute to a life lost too soon. As I sit in Jay's boat, the sun leans long across the river bend and casts a warm glow atop the wooden marker.

Here, in one of the most misunderstood places on earth, where predators prey and perils pervade, where a loved one's life was stolen, this grieving survivor chose hope. I imagine a woman, pulling her boat through the murky waters. She reaches out over the thickest depths and nails a cross to this tree, reminding us all that even in the deepest, darkest pits of despair, there is light. We are loved.

I return to find Jay at his outdoor sink, cleaning a fresh batch of fish.

"Where else can people live off the land like this?" He leans against the porch and looks down at his own mud-caked boots.

Boudreaux runs to greet me. I give Jay's devoted Lab a pet, and he responds with a hearty tail wag, nearly knocking me from the deck. As I reach to grab a post, it shifts, barely holding. "You ever going to fix this place up, Jay?" I laugh.

"What's the point?" He shoves the post back into place. "Good enough for my grandfather; good enough for me."

I can't hide my smile. "A man who doesn't want to toss the old, familiar parts of his life. Shows a sense of loyalty, stability. I like that."

Jay blushes a bit, nailing the post back into position. Then he says, "I wanna show you something. Come with me."

In less than a minute the two of us are paddling through prickly palmettos using strong, quiet strokes. It's a bit difficult to steer the pirogue along the shallow backwaters, especially with Boudreaux between us. I switch my oar from one side to the other, trying to maintain momentum. With each sway I fear we'll tip right over, and I am surprised by my own desire to stay afloat. I no longer want to sink to my death in the swamps. I want to paddle. I want to live.

I watch the low-hanging limbs for wasps and snakes while Jay clears branches from our path. The channel narrows and becomes more difficult to navigate. A few feet from the hull of the boat, an alligator slips beneath the murky surface. Swallows swoop from tree to tree, narrowly missing the tangles of Spanish moss that hang suspended in thick twists above us. Back here, the bayou is coated with green growth. Clear water laces behind us.

Every square millimeter of this place is teeming with life, all designed to fool the less observant. Nothing is what it seems. The ground itself breathes and moves. What looks like a twig is actually a living walking stick. A rock sprouts arms, becoming a turtle. That lily pad? The head of a gator. That mess of leaves, a snake.

But suddenly, between the muted, camouflaging hues of the swamp, a flash of pink sparks a few feet in front of us. I follow the splendor as a roseate spoonbill takes flight from behind the bulrushes. I point toward the sky and whisper to Jay who, like me, has turned to watch the bird lift. "Did you see that?"

He nods. He sees.

The bright, rosy feathers remind me of Sarah, who always declared pink her favorite color. I smile to myself, thinking again that some things were made for the light.

Every bark of a squirrel, every trill of birdsong, every breeze through the leaves seems to bring a smile to Jay's face. Through his eyes I take fresh notice of the marvels around me. The pulse of the paddle helps me relax, and I begin seeing the world with the wonder of a small child, each discovery a gift. *How long has it been since I've really appreciated a flower? A river? A tree?*

Geese, egrets, and herons dot the backdrop, calling out warnings to their feathered friends. Two nutria splash across soggy soil before climbing their mountainous dam of sticks. If they could lose those hairless tails, they'd be cute as beavers. Above us the blue sky is broken by an eagle in flight, one of the many who make their treetop nests in this wildlife management area.

As Jay and I loop our oars through dark waters, I lean over the edge of the pirogue and dip my hand into the lazy flow. Thick, green duckweed coats my fingers, and I almost laugh as I struggle to wash it off. Above us a redheaded woodpecker taps notes into a towering tupelo, a rhythmic baseline to the roaring hum of insects that still swarm nearly every inch of space around us.

An area of open water reveals a slim blue heron. Standing in the shallows, he fans his wings around his bowed head like an umbrella, blocking the sun so he can have a better view of the fish below the surface. His long bill takes a quick, silent dive and he snatches breakfast. As soon as he swallows, he cups his wings around to bend and begin again.

With each pull through the water, my burden lightens. I am reminded of the Bohemian fortune-teller in Jackson Square, years ago. The one who placed a tiny brown feather in Sarah's hand and told her she had been blessed with the ability to fly. In moments like this, surrounded by such beauty, I am half inclined to believe in miracles again, to believe my bones hold stems to feathers and that I, too, can fly free.

Thirty minutes in the backwaters, and I am at peace. We spin our craft around, but we don't yet begin to paddle back toward camp. Neither of us is in a hurry to leave this space. Without having to say it out loud, Jay and I take our own sweet time with the rowing. Sometimes life is a river; sometimes it's a swamp. But even with the heartbreak and the hurt, Jay has reminded me—this life is one worth living.

Chapter 28

I'M IN THE MIDDLE OF WINN DIXIE, STARING AT AN ENDLESS ROW OF potato chips and fighting another anxiety attack. Two years ago I packed Ellie's lunch on a Monday morning, dropped her off at school, and had no idea it would be the last time. No idea, as I flipped her pancakes that morning, I would never again share breakfast with my daughter. Just when I think I'm past the crying stage, something draws water from the well again.

"Amanda?" Raelynn breaks my daze. I've drifted away, completely forgetting I'm standing in the most public space in all of LP. "Mambi!" From the seat of Raelynn's shopping cart, her tot-sized niece, Kayla, struggles with my name. She lifts both arms above her head. "Up, Mambi. Up!"

I unbuckle the buggy's restraints and pull her close against my chest, breathing in the sweet smell of No More Tears shampoo, giving in to the dose of life only a small child can offer.

"Hanging in there?" Raelynn asks.

"Just got back from Jay's camp." I don't have to explain to Raelynn that this time of year is always the hardest. That I want to hide away and stay silent in my grief until the anniversary and the holidays pass me by. "I'm staying busy."

I pull a pack of Goldfish down for Kayla and let her eager giggle heal my heart.

From around the end of the display, a woman turns down our aisle and offers a smile. "Amanda? Amanda Salassi? Is that really you?" She's moving closer at such a speed, I'm unable to process who she is. I should have gone to Carter's, the locally owned store run by a lifelong friend. A safer space.

Raelynn cocks her hip and whispers behind her teeth, "No way. I haven't seen Tina in fifteen years. At least."

"Tina?" Thank goodness Raelynn recognized her. I never would've placed our old classmate. Tina tugs me into a hug and then pulls back to give me a head-to-toe. "You haven't aged a bit!"

Just being nice. Anyone who has ever buried her child knows a body carries the scars as much as a heart does. My hair has grown thin, my face falls in lines around my eyes, and the gray is too much to cover these days. I look twenty years older than Tina, despite the fact we shared high school graduation.

"You still living out west?" I ask. "Last I heard, you were working in sales or something. In California?"

She leans on one high heel and carries a vibe that is as Barbie as it gets—short pink skirt, legs tanned and toned, blond highlights down the full length of wavy hair. She's always been beautiful, but now she looks like a beauty-queen-turned-pharmaceutical-sales-rep, with her bright smile and bleached teeth. The kind of woman who could sashay through a doctor's waiting room with bribes for the staff and then walk back out with a hefty commission in her account.

"Yeah. I'm just in town for a few days. Daddy's selling off the last of the land, and he needed me to come take care of some paperwork. Can you believe we've all left LP? He was the last of the Mohicans." She finally acknowledges Raelynn, who is playing with her niece and pretending to ignore Tina—an impossible feat.

"Oh my goodness, Raelynn? I just realized who you were." She offers a hug, which Raelynn accepts reluctantly.

"It's me." A bit of a bite. Raelynn never did care for Tina. Thought she was uppity, driving her brand-new convertible Mustang to high school.

"So fill me in," Tina says, turning back to me. "How's Carl? Y'all have a daughter. Am I remembering right? Just one?"

This catches me off guard, as it always does when people ask if I have children or want to know about my family, just general questions that never mean any harm. Sometimes I tell the truth. Sometimes I don't. In this moment, I can't bear to tell Tina that my daughter is dead. I can't stand here in the middle of Winn Dixie and say my teenage daughter put a gun to her head. I can't try to explain that Ellie's life was worth so much more than what the word *suicide* brings to it. So I look Tina right in the eye and I say, "Ellie, yes. She's great. We all stay busy. You know how it is."

After a quick conversation, Tina has caught us up on her success stories before easing her way down the aisle. Almost at the end, she turns back to me and says, "Oh, Amanda. I meant to ask. You still friends with Jay?"

Raelynn rolls her eyes and mumbles under her breath. "Watch out for this one."

"Sure," I say. "He's sheriff now, you know?"

"I heard. And he's single, right?"

"I could've seen that one coming from a mile away," Raelynn says, turning her back to Tina.

I nod.

Tina smiles and rounds the corner before Raelynn has a chance to pounce.

"People are idiots. Stick with me." Raelynn pushes her buggy in the opposite direction of Tina. I put baby Kayla in my own cart and trail my friend through the store. As we reach the freezer section, Raelynn offers a dose of normal. "How was work?"

I give her the small talk she's after and return the question. "You still like being in school?" When I pretend to take Kayla's Goldfish for myself, the happy toddler giggles, reaching for the bag.

"Beats being in sales." Raelynn glances back toward Tina, who is turning heads at the cash register. Raelynn says *sales* as if she questions what service Tina is paid to provide. Then she gets serious. "Maybe you need something new to focus on." Her mind is racing. "Did you ever look into your adoption records?"

"No."

"Why not?" She's genuinely perplexed. "What if we can find your birth parents? Maybe it's time."

"Raelynn, I love you for trying. But those reunions don't usually go well. I'd be setting myself up for another blow."

She tosses a gallon of Blue Bell ice cream into her buggy. In contrast, my cart is nearly empty, a meager snag of fruits and veggies to get me through the week. It's clear I'm not shopping to feed a family. *Don't go there, Amanda. Breathe.*

Raelynn gives me the look, the one that says *I pity you*. And I give her the other look. The one that says *Don't you dare*.

Pulling Kayla from my arms, she says, "Bunco. Saturday. My place. You coming?" She doesn't pause long enough for me to give it any thought. Instead, she wraps me in a squeeze-tight hug with Kayla giggling in between and insists, "You're coming." Then she takes her niece and bounces away, full of life and confidence and joy. The way I used to be.

Saturday, November 8, 2008

"Y'all playing with us tonight?" I arrange Bunco supplies—dice, cups, pencils, and score pads—across the three card tables we've crowded into Raelynn's small home. Nate grins with boyish charm, revealing the remains of a left dimple. Then he opens a bottle of lavender lotion and gives it a smell. It's one of the prizes Raelynn has purchased for tonight's competition.

"Up the stakes and we're game," he says.

His friends chime in, naming things they'd be willing to Bunco for. A date with Jennifer Aydell makes the list; Nate claims, "She can tug on my line anytime!" The boys erupt in laughter, bumping fists while making crude comments.

"Catch and release, if you know what I mean."

"Jennifer Aydell makes you wanna kiss and tell."

Raelynn swats her son's shoulder. "Enough!" But the boys can't stop laughing. As they cut up, my mind slips away again. Ellie never had a boyfriend. Never had a first kiss. Will I ever be able to handle this void? *There's nothing you can do to change the fact that Ellie is gone. You have to find a way to let her go.*

Within twenty minutes the boys are back under the carport cleaning the batch of fish they've pulled from the river. They work the filet knives as Raelynn's house fills with women oohing and ahhing over her new hairdo.

Another friend shows off her latest pair of heels. I recall the shoe-box lesson I've used with my clients, teaching them to compartmentalize their pain. Now I'm on the other side of the trauma, and it's not always easy to "keep it somewhere."

Just count the dots on the dice, Amanda. Don't let your mind roam. Count.

We're barely five minutes into the game when the first "Bunco!" is yelled out across the room. While I mark the winner down for a prize, Raelynn nudges my buzzing cell phone. Beth's name is on the screen.

"Amanda, you have a minute?"

"Of course. You okay?" I step outside to escape the loud chatter.

From inside Raelynn's living room, the light slants yellow through bent aluminum blinds, reminding me of an old Emily Dickinson poem about winter: *Heavenly hurt it gives us. We can find no scar.* I used to read poetry aloud when Ellie was young. The cadence of the language seemed to soothe her. Those old verses tumble to the surface sometimes, usually when I least expect them.

"They found her, Amanda!" Beth's voice cracks as she tells me that after four long years of an agonizing search, Sarah has been found.

Beneath the amber glow of porch lights, my mind flashes a million different reactions. "They found . . . they found Sarah?"

"Yes! She's alive!" Beth sounds as if she can barely believe it herself.

My mind races. "Where is she?"

"She's okay. That's all that matters." Beth tries to reassure me, but I get the sense she's reassuring herself too. "Listen, they've got her up at Jay's office. Preacher's driving us there right now. We just wanted to be the first to tell you."

"I can't believe it." I brush my fingers across the rough surface of the bricks. *Am I dreaming? Sarah has been found? Alive?* "Where has she been, Beth?" *Breathe, Amanda. Breathe.*

"We don't know much yet. One thing's for sure. God's hand is in this. He brought her home."

A silence falls between us. Unlike Beth, I struggle to understand God's "hand" in all of this. How he let Sarah go missing in the first place, how he allowed my Ellie to pay for it. "How can I help?" I stand straighter, eager for instructions.

"Well, for now I can think of only one request."

"Anything. Anything at all."

She sighs. "We don't want the press to get hold of this. Not yet. So try to keep it quiet if you can."

I look through the window into Raelynn's lively living room. "You mean Raelynn?"

"I mean Raelynn." Cliché as it sounds, Beth reminds me how people in town joke that there are three good ways to send a message: telephone, telegram, or tell-a-Raelynn.

"I'm at her house now—Bunco."

Beth sighs.

"Don't worry. I'm on my way." Then I hurry to catch her before she hangs up the phone. "Beth?"

"Yeah?"

"I'm just so glad . . . I mean . . ." With this, the walls within me break. I begin to cry, and I cannot finish my sentence.

Beth listens patiently. I struggle to find words.

"I know, Amanda. I know." Then she adds, "What am I thinking? Absolute truth. Absolute trust. Go tell Raelynn."

I exhale and rush to find the third arm of our fleur-de-lis. Despite it all, we are still the three amies.

"It's hard to believe. Four years." Raelynn drives us to Jay's office in Livingston as I try to imagine what Sarah has survived. "Wonder what she'll be like?" Raelynn slings my thoughts through the air.

It's clear we are both trying to picture the innocent, kind-hearted little girl who vanished all those years ago.

"She was twelve when we last saw her." *That means she's sixteen now. Same age Ellie would be today if somehow I could bring her back to me.*

One second on the clock. That's what haunts me most. The irreverence of time. If I had not collapsed into bed during the news that night, and instead had gone to Ellie's room for a third time to wish her sweet dreams and remind her to say her prayers, I might have seen the gun before she pulled the trigger. I might have been able to stop her from believing her life was no longer worth the effort.

The what-ifs have stalked me for years, carving their way into every hour.

"All this time, I figured she was dead," Raelynn whispers, bringing me back from my own tragedy to Sarah's. It's what most of the townspeople have assumed. That Sarah had somehow fallen into the Mississippi. That the waters were simply too swift for her body to be found. That alligators and snapping turtles had discovered her, and that her bones had settled deep beneath the mud, waiting for the river to reveal those secrets in its own slow time.

Raelynn drums the steering wheel nervously while she drives. "I didn't want to believe the worst. None of us did."

"I don't know, Raelynn. What if this is worse?"

With a long sigh, she reaches for my hand. "I know you'd give anything to have Ellie back."

The thought leaves me aching deep inside. *Would I want Ellie back at any price? Would I trade places with Beth right this instant if I had the chance?* I pull my hand back and rub my temples.

"Maybe I'm wrong to wish it, Raelynn, but I do. I wish I had my Ellie in that room right now. I mean, it's not that I would want her to have suffered."

Raelynn stays quiet. I keep talking. "All that matters is Sarah's alive. She's here. And now she'll be safe."

I speak as if I'm trying to convince myself. "But honestly, I'm scared to see her, Raelynn. What will she say to me? After all these years?"

I'm gone again, fighting the familiar spiral. Sarah's disappearance, Carl's abandonment, Ellie's suicide. The events whirl into a mix of unfinished sufferings, my own inner storm. No matter how hard I try to put it in frame, to sequence the hurt into rational pieces and line it all up behind me, the story is still being written. Here. In the now.

Jay greets us outside his office, waving us toward the back of the archaic three-story courthouse that holds the sheriff's department. Weaving through the maze of historic hallways, he calls out his youngest deputy as the hero. "It was luck, really, and good work on Dex's part."

"Just doing my job." Dex shrugs off the praise. His rookie nerves are apparent as he tries a little too hard to look me in the eye. The poor guy is barely out of school, and I fear this entire experience could be too much for him. He knew both Sarah and Ellie from church. Back when he was a kid, he placed one of those store-bought lemon-flavored daisy cookies on Ellie's tiny finger, told her it was a ring, and swore he'd marry her one day. She was just a preschooler, and he was trying to be big and make her laugh. By the way he shuffles his feet now, I've got a hunch I may not be the only one remembering that playful promise. She dipped the ring in red Kool-Aid before enjoying every bite.

"Sheriff was always talking about Sarah. Insisting we keep our eyes open all the time." Dex gives Jay the credit. "He kept her photos on the boards, made sure she stayed on the Crime Stoppers list, all that. We had those age-progression pictures too, and that's actually what she looked like when I found her. That stuff really works."

Jay takes a sip of coffee. "I always emphasized that if Sarah was still missing, other girls were too. Maybe not from here in LP, but from somewhere." He leads us down the hall toward his office where Sarah is waiting with Beth and Preacher. "I made it a point to train my guys to watch for it. Young girls with older men. Stories that didn't add up. Teens hanging out at hotels, truck stops. That kind of thing. We did those cyberstings too, posing as underage kids online. You know all this."

I nod. "So is that what happened? You found her online?"

Dex shakes his head. "Routine traffic stop. That's all it took."

"Speeding?"

"No, ma'am," he says. "Broken taillight."

"You're kidding."

Jay offers his quick, matter-of-fact chin dip. Sheriff-speak for *I kid you not.* He continues to fill us in as we near his office. "But anybody can pull a car over for a broken taillight. The difference is, Dex was observant. He had a hunch something wasn't right, and he had the sense to pull Sarah off to the side to question her. If he hadn't done that, she'd probably still be in that truck."

"She didn't want to tell me who she was," Dex says. "I had to ask her five times. I kept trying to assure her she was safe, that she wasn't in trouble. But even then, she kept saying her name was Holly. So I told her how we used to go to church together. That the whole town had been looking for her. I said her parents loved her very much and that they'd kept her picture on TV, even after all these years. She started crying. That's when she looked at me and said, 'My name is Sarah Broussard.'"

The questions rise so fast. I want to know everything. "Trafficking?" I look at Jay, and he confirms our worst fears.

"From what we know so far, she was kept in a small room at first," he explains. "A shed. Down in Chalmette. Then it seems they moved up to Hammond. Apparently to escape Katrina. Good thing."

"Hammond?" My breath leaves me. "She's been thirty minutes from home?" Thirty minutes. *How many times have we searched Hammond, posting fliers, sharing Sarah's photo, knocking on doors? Was this a house we visited by any chance? Had Sarah been there— right on the other side of the door?*

"We're taking it slow," Jay continues. "Don't want to push her too fast, but we're eager to get our hands on anyone involved before they run. I need you to help us, Gloopy."

I'm still the forensic interviewer on contract with the sheriff's department, called in to investigate child abuse cases. But when I went through all that training, I never imagined I'd have to use these skills to help someone I loved.

I try to hide my hesitancy. "Of course. Anything you need."

Fear swells within me. "But she may not want to see me, Jay. I'm the one . . . I'm . . . It was all my fault."

I have expected Sarah to be irate, perhaps with signs of drug abuse or visible scars. But instead, we open Jay's office door to find her sitting quietly between Beth and Preacher. Her hair is dyed black, clipped short and clean. She wears a heavy dose of makeup and she's got a row of earrings on both ears. Other than that, she looks no different from any other sixteen-year-old girl in our town.

She seems reserved, staying in place on the office sofa. "Ms. Amanda?"

Her voice is soft, still childlike in a way. I glance at Jay, whose steady look reminds me to stay strong. As much as I thought I was ready for this, I'm not sure I can handle it now that I am here with Sarah. Nothing I say will erase her suffering. Nothing I do will make up for the lost years.

But I try.

"Sarah—" I move closer. She doesn't reach for me, so I give a gentle glance instead of a hug. Four long years I have imagined this moment, planning what I would say, but now that we're really here together in the same room, words won't come.

"I'm sorry about Ellie." Sarah's voice quakes.

I shake my head and reach for her hand. She doesn't retract, as I fear. Instead, she takes mine in hers and squeezes it tightly. I don't look at Jay this time. Or anyone else in the room. I say what I came here to say. To Sarah.

"I'm the one who is sorry, Sarah. I'm sorry for all of it. I'm sorry I didn't stay right with you and Ellie that day. I've relived it a million times, and there's no excuse. I shouldn't have let you out of my sight. Not for a second."

"You didn't." Sarah smiles now. It's sincere. "We had to beg you to let us go to the bathroom without you hovering over us. Don't you remember us calling you a helicopter?"

Her words begin to heal wounds in me I thought would never mend. I speak a little slower as a calm moves through me. I want to hear her say it again. And again. Forgiveness. Relief. "I hope you know how hard I looked for you."

"I know."

"I searched and searched, but I couldn't find you. Looked everywhere, asking if anyone had seen you."

Sarah, still dry-eyed, stands and pulls me into her arms. "It's not your fault, Ms. Amanda." My entire body reacts. Then she says it again. "It's not your fault."

No matter how many times other people have said these words to me, it is different coming from Sarah. Years of dammed-up guilt and shame come bursting through like floodwaters.

Sarah looks me in the eyes. The child-blue innocence is gone, but her gaze still holds true. "You told me to stay with Ellie, remember? I knew better than to go with a stranger, but I followed her anyway. Bridgette. She said Miss Henderson had chosen me to be her helper. I had to put on the costume and go with her. To be in her show, out in the street. She told me not to let anybody know I was under that costume because we would surprise everybody at the end of the skit. You see, Ms. Amanda? It wasn't your fault. It was mine. She tricked me. I followed her. And by the time I realized she was lying, it was too late."

Now she falls back onto the sofa, curling in close next to Beth and placing her head on Preacher's shoulder. It's clear their daughter is caught in a strange space, some stratum that exists for those who grow up too fast. She's become a sort of woman-child. A minute ago I was listening to a young woman, wise beyond her years. And now she's a sixth-grade girl again, in need of a mother, a father, and a belief that the world is a good and happy place. She doesn't yet know where she stands.

"Sarah," I whisper. "We're all here with you. You're not alone."

Chapter 29

Sunday, November 9, 2008

WE'RE SEATED IN FRONT OF THE SHERIFF'S DEPARTMENT. A ROW OF reporters record the impromptu press conference. When Jay moves front and center, the eager crowd falls silent. He confirms the fact that Dex rescued Sarah during a routine traffic violation, and he guarantees that every measure will be taken to investigate this case further so as to expose all those involved in criminal activity.

Then Preacher takes the spotlight, and the questions begin to flow. "Mr. Broussard, is it true Sarah has been rescued?"

"Yes, our girl is home! We sure are grateful for all of you who helped us look for Sarah."

"Will she be going through any kind of therapy? Rehab?"

"We're already working with professional counselors. We're taking this one day at a time. Of course Beth and I will do anything Sarah needs. Anything to help her recover."

"Is she planning to go back to school? Normal life?"

"Right now we want to give her some quiet rest. A safe place to heal. We'll reevaluate in a month or so, see what she's ready for at that time."

"We're told she was held captive and sold into prostitution. Is that true?"

I want to pull this guy's professional license, if there is such a thing.

Preacher gives the man a disappointed glare, and a few reporters shuffle uncomfortably. It's their job to ask the hard questions. Preacher handles it well. "The case is still under investigation. We can't share any details at this time."

"Anything else you want to say, Mr. Broussard?"

Preacher hesitates, then adds one final thought. "Yes. Again, we thank everyone who has worked so hard to bring our daughter home to us. Take this as proof. Miracles do happen."

Preacher and Beth have decided to take Sarah home, but Jay asks me to stick around to help him sort through the evidence. As he leads me back into the building, we both reach for the door, resulting in one of those awkward situations where I don't know if I should let go or not.

"Would it kill you to let somebody take care of you every now and then?"

Every cell in my body turns to velvet, and my heart folds in on itself. After all these years of trying to take care of everybody else, determined to stay strong and independent, I turn to mush the moment Jay says these words. There's no more denying the truth.

When it comes down to it, I do want someone to take care of me every now and then. Sometimes I want nothing more than to roll my head against a strong shoulder, wrap into somebody's safe arms, and let the worries of the world fall away, even if only for a minute or two. I'm tired of doing it by myself. It's all I can do not to say, "Yes, please, Jay, take care of me. Take care of me and I'll take care of you and we'll shelter each other. Now. Forever. Forget the just-friends arrangement. I'll stick with you."

But of course I don't say anything of the sort. Instead, I force myself to snap out of it, killing the theme music that is streaming through my mind. If there's anything Ellie taught me, it's that happy is a myth. And that includes happy-ever-after, no matter how much Viv wants a fantasy ending for this brown-eyed girl. As Jay waits for me to enter, I step against the door and insist he go first.

"The last thing I need is a man to take care of me," I declare. "I tried that once. Look where it got me."

Jay retreats with a sigh. "Amanda, maybe I shouldn't say this, but I'm tired of holding it back."

I can't bring myself to look at him.

"Everybody knows Carl wasn't good to you, but that doesn't mean somebody else wouldn't be."

Suddenly my body feels as if it belongs somewhere else. What to make of those words? Is Jay suggesting *he* would be good to me?

I don't know how to answer, so I choose the safest route—silence. When I don't reply, Jay heads toward his office and I follow. At the entrance, he puts his hand on my back to guide me into the room. Despite my resistance, the warmth of his touch sends a hum through my bones unlike any I've ever known. Never once has Jay's hand caused me to flinch or fear, but right now it does more than comfort me. It ignites me.

I don't quite know how to absorb such a gentle touch. I move away.

He drops a stack of spiral notebooks onto his desk and says,

"Read these." Each is wide-ruled with water stains and tattered edges. The colors range from green to blue to orange, with scribbles and doodles sketched across the cardboard covers.

As I begin to read, all I can see is the twelve-year-old, pony-tailed girl I chaperoned all those years ago. I imagine her sitting in that filthy shed, writing letters to a sparrow, hoping day after day that we'd find our way there to rescue her.

The earliest entries reflect her innocence, with little hearts forming the dots of each letter *i* across the page. It's painful to see.

I read about the men coming to "visit" on their way home from work, dropping in before driving home to their families. It's been more than three years since I learned the truth about Carl, his double life, and I still have trouble trusting people. I can't imagine how Sarah will ever believe in anything again.

I sit for hours, reading every word of Sarah's journals, filling in the gaps of her last four years. In bigger cities I probably wouldn't be allowed to help with this investigation due to my personal ties to Sarah. But here, resources are limited. We have learned, in efforts like these when we know the family, to separate ourselves from our emotions, to get the job done in a professional and confidential manner. But this is Sarah. So I cry my way through every page.

I flag some sections for Jay along the way, words or phrases he'll be able to use to build a case against the abductors. Some entries stand out more than others.

Hello Sparrow,

I'm so glad you're here. Some days I start to think God has forgotten all about me. But then he sends me a message.

Some kind of sign, like you, Sparrow, to remind me that he really is with me.

I thought miracles were big things, like turning water into wine or making a blind man see. But now I know miracles happen every day.

You are here with me. That's a miracle.

The Man only took me and not Ellie. That's a miracle.

I wasn't locked in the shed when the flood came. Another miracle.

I survived being kept in a box. And chained. And all the other things. Miracle!

Bridgette brings me books and pens and stuff. That's a miracle.

So maybe a miracle is anything that gets us through another day when life gets too hard.

Remember that fortune-teller who gave me this feather and told me I could fly? I think I finally understand. We all have a feathered bone. It's called hope. If we hang on to hope, if we don't let anybody break us or make us forget who we are, then we will always be free.

Hello Sparrow,

Today I asked Bridgette if she loves The Man. And she said, "Ain't no such thing as love." I told her I believe in love, and she said, "Don't be stupid."

I told her it's because Mom and Pop love me. My friends love me. God loves me. And no matter how many bad things happen to me, I'll always have that love inside of me.

She got real quiet, and then she asked me how I know they love me.

I told her they would never do anything to hurt me. Not on purpose.

She said, "But God's hurting you right now, keeping you here in this place."

"God's not doing this," I said. "You are."

She got mad and said she wasn't doing it either. That LeMoyne was doing it. Just like he had done to her. And then she told me a really sad story:

When I was little, my mama was always pimpin' herself out for a fix. I don't remember how old I was the first time she let 'em have me. We were in The Boss's stable, but what I bet you couldn't guess is that LeMoyne used to be in The Boss's stable too. Just like me.

Boss used to beat him so hard he'd stop breathin'. Hold him under water 'til his face turned blue. Mama said LeMoyne got it the worst 'cause he was always fightin' back.

One day LeMoyne tried to get away. Boss caught him. Poured a whole pot of fish fry right on top of LeMoyne. You seen his back, right?

But you gotta understand somethin'. Back then, Boss was still workin' under the big man, Sax. So Sax comes in, finds LeMoyne there–his favorite boy–all melted like a popsicle.

And he figures Boss needs a lesson too. He slams a big

ol' pipe against Boss's back. Snapped his spine, so his legs don't work no more. That's why Boss is in that wheelchair. You see?

That was the last time he forgot who was in charge.

Couple years later, Sax died. Boss took over and started making everybody call him Boss. And now LeMoyne works for him. Well, he did until we got this big house. Now I guess LeMoyne's runnin' his own show, and Boss ain't so big no more.

Jay finds me in his office. "We're bringing in the suspects now. Oliver LeMoyne and Bridgette Gallatino. Find anything yet?"

"She's mentioning someone they call Boss," I say. "He might be paraplegic."

"Yeah, we're following that lead right now. Think we've traced it back to a man in Algiers."

Chills run through me. "Jay, I saw him. The day of the field trip. He was on the ferry with us. Then I saw him again by the café. He was near a young woman. I thought she might have been a prostitute. There was a younger girl with him on the ferry, but she wasn't with him later. That had to be him."

"Would you know him if you saw him?" He scrolls through his computer screen, pulling up profiles.

"That's him." My stomach sinks as I point to the man's weathered and familiar face. The same cold stare that set my nerves on end that day in New Orleans.

"You sure?"

I nod. "He's in two of the photos I have from the field trip." Sweat coats my palms. "He's been right here all this time."

"We got him now," Jay says, lifting his phone to call the NOPD.

While Jay handles the search for the man known as Boss, I continue reading Sarah's journals.

Hello Sparrow,

I told Bridgette how God gave Adam and Eve everything they needed—plenty of food, good weather, a pretty place to live. But Adam and Eve ate the fruit that wasn't theirs.

They knew it was wrong. And they did it anyway.

They didn't even say they were sorry. Instead, Adam blamed Eve. And Eve blamed the serpent. They both got mad at God.

Bridgette said, "I bet God taught them a lesson."

I said yes, but not the kind of lesson she's learned from Sax and Boss and LeMoyne. God just wanted them to know that choices matter.

"That's the point of the story," I said. "Even when we make really bad mistakes, we still have the choice to do better. It's never too late."

Then I bent down close to her and hugged her, and I whispered to her. I said, "Bridgette, it may take me a long, long, long, very long time, but you know what I'm going to do? I'm going to forgive you. And I'm going to forgive LeMoyne.

And I'm even going to forgive Boss. And all the men who visit. Forgive all of you."

"Why?" she asked.

"Because," I told her, "if I let go of all that hate, it'll leave more room for love."

Monday, November 10, 2008

Maybe five foot five at most, Oliver LeMoyne is a short, pasty, red-haired man with a freckled face and a potbelly. A battered set of crooked teeth jut out beneath a wiry mustache, and his receding hairline stretches long behind a sickening set of weak brown eyes. Bridgette isn't much shorter but even in her midtwenties is heavier than LeMoyne, with bleached tips on the dead ends of her frizzy hair. Neither says a word. They both seem to understand they are no longer in control.

"But she was trafficked too," Sarah says, defending Bridgette.

"Don't worry," Jay reassures her. "We realize that and we'll be fair. Now, tell me one more time, Sarah. Is this the man who hurt you?" Jay speaks with a voice as clear and steady as any I've ever heard, as if the entire four-year walk through hell has led us all to this exact moment. A dance with the devil himself.

"Yes," Sarah says, pointing toward the one-way glass that protects her from the three abductors. "That's him."

"And this guy? Is he the man you know as Boss?" Jay points to a frail, handicapped man in a wheelchair, the same haggard passenger who boarded the ferry with us from Algiers all those years ago. How could we have known that the girl we assumed to be his granddaughter had been trafficked for years? That her face had been printed on the side of a milk carton, listed as a missing child. That slaves were, in fact, still being sold across that river.

I point to Boss's wheelchair and say, "Who would have imagined? A man like that running one of the largest prostitution rings in the state?"

"Chains of the heart," Sarah says. Then to Jay, "Yes, sir. That's him."

Chapter 30

JAY PULLS AN EMPTY BOX TOWARD HIS CHEST, HELPING ME PACK my belongings. "I think it'll do you good to move out, Gloopy. Get a fresh start. Someplace new."

"Yeah, I'm surprised both houses sold so quickly. I figured Mom's would sit on the market for a long time. Especially with all those newer homes that have been built around it since Katrina." I gather newspapers from the recycle bin and wrap a framed photo.

Jay fills his box with Ellie's old yearbooks. "I'm just glad to see you moving forward. I was beginning to wonder if Carl might break you for good."

I shudder, remembering the moment Raelynn saved me from taking my own life. "He almost did."

Jay stops working and looks my way. "You know he's not worth it, don't you?"

I don't answer. I just move closer to Jay, sit on the floor, and begin to pass family photos to him. One shows Carl, Ellie, and me at Disney World. Ellie wears pink polka-dotted Minnie Mouse ears and stares up at Cinderella with the kind of grin that only exists for those who still believe in magic. I'm kneeling next to Ellie, smiling nearly as big. Behind us, Carl is tall in the background, looking disconnected. The same way The Boss stared from his wheelchair in New Orleans that day. The words Vivienne told me back on the trace rise again—*"That's not love."*

"I still can't believe he moved out without talking to you about it first. Same thing with the divorce."

I nod. "I never saw it coming, Jay."

"I remember." His tone reveals his deep compassion, as if he'd fix it all for me if he could. "I was with you and Raelynn at the gym."

I struggle to remember who was around me when it happened. It's all a blur now. "Yep. Right there, in front of the whole town. It's been a slow bleed."

Jay listens as he pulls another box for the frames. Somehow he has a way of making me feel heard. As if my feelings actually matter. As if I matter.

"But worse things happen, right?" I don't bring up his fiancée's death, but the look he gives me makes it clear. He knows, as I do, what real loss feels like.

I straighten another family photo in a cracked frame. This one shows a happy threesome. Carl, Ellie, and me on the beach, sitting close to one another. It was a photo I kept on my desk. A client once saw it and said, "Y'all look like a cozy family." I smiled and said, "We are." I always believed we'd hold tight to one another through life's storms. Never had a doubt.

"But look," I say, showing it to Jay. "There were plenty of happy times too. I'm telling you, if someone had told me about Carl's affair, I wouldn't have believed it. I trusted him completely."

Jay raises his eyebrows.

"It's true, Jay. I believed with everything in me that Carl was faithful, honest. It was the reason I married him. Trust. That's what

I believed he offered me. It wasn't always easy with Carl, but I was grateful. I was happy."

We both look at my wedding photo, the one that shows me smiling in my long white dress and matching veil. I was so young, standing there full of girlish hope, building my life on the dream of forever. *If only I had understood what Viv has taught me—we marry to heal our childhood wounds.*

I hand off the last of the photos and let Jay help me back to my feet. He pulls me up, then nearer. I am caught off guard, but I don't move away. Instead, I allow him to hold me here, against his sturdy chest.

"Amanda." This is all he says. My name. And yet this one word is packed with meaning. And hope. When Carl said my name, it was in an accusatory tone, or yelled across the house because he needed something. And Jay has always called me Gloopy. But now he's said *Amanda*, and I have never heard anyone say my name with such tenderness. Not like this.

I lift my eyes to his, blue and clear and steady. I don't offer any spoken reply. Leaving my body pressed against his is enough. We stand together, our hearts beating double-paced, as if the whole world has left us here, together.

Jay bends, and I hold for a kiss. Not just any kiss, but Jay's kiss, the kiss I have skirted since we sat knee to knee on our kindergarten carpet squares. But just as he leans in, his cell phone rings. The unexpected buzzing brings an embarrassed smile across Jay's chiseled features. I am filled with desire, like none I have ever known. His phone rings again, and we both move away from the almost-kiss.

He answers the call, and I go back to packing, holding myself together despite the flurry of chemicals igniting within me. Maybe it's the natural howling of hormones, but all it took was one brief touch and this man set me afire.

To give Jay more privacy, I move to the back of the house and begin to sort items from my bedroom. I am gathering rarely used clothes for the charity box when Jay joins me, near the bed. "Everything okay?"

"No big deal. Jenny again. Called from her mom's so I didn't recognize the number." He shrugs as if the women chasing him are nothing worth worrying about. Tina, the West Coast Barbie, was one thing, but Jenny is another. Not only does Jenny live right down the road with no risk of ever leaving LP, but she's able to turn the head of any man in town with one quick flick of her wrist. Add her high-pitched giggle or her talents in the kitchen, not to mention her ability to never know the answers to the simplest of questions. She's a man's dream, the mind of an eight-year-old and the body of a teen, the culinary skills of Martha Stewart and the sex appeal of Marilyn Monroe. With Jenny after Jay, I don't stand a chance. *He's not Carl, Amanda. That's not the kind of woman he wants.*

I pull a sweater from my closet as Jay looks out my bedroom window, watching my neighbor's teenage son drag a crew of cousins around the yard. They are piled into a plastic kid-sized swimming pool, tied to the back of a four-wheeler. He's racing circles around the lot, trying to get them to fall out of the pool. One girl takes a tumble, twisting and turning across the rutted grass. The others look back as she drops, laughing and holding on for dear life.

Another crew is jumping as high as they can on the aging trampoline. With no safety screen, they try to steer clear of the springing metal coils. In the center a young girl curls into a tight ball, trying not to let the big bounces separate the hold she's got on her own bent legs. It's an old game called crack-the-egg, a backyard favorite Ellie, Sarah, and Nate used to play.

"How many kids do they have now?" Jay asks, unable to keep track of my neighbor's growing family.

"Only three," I admit, "but it's kind of like Raelynn's house. Constant commotion."

I move to get a better look, standing close to Jay. Even without touch, the warmth of his body meets mine. When he shifts his weight, our arms brush together. I don't pull away. Neither does he. Instead, he turns his body closer and places his hand on my waist.

"So tell me about Dex's promotion." I try to keep us in neutral, but Jay isn't having it. He pushes my hair back from my face with slow hands, and I am no longer a worn-down carton of grief. It's been too long since a man held me. With Jay's touch I become a spiral of stars, swirling through the atmosphere. I can no longer tell north from south, up from down. My skin begins to swim around my bones. It's as if Jay is a magnet, and each particle that builds me is racing wildly toward him.

"Amanda, what are we doing?" Jay no longer speaks sheriff. "You know how I feel about you, don't you?" He rolls his hand from my waist across my lower back. His finger slips beneath the hem of my shirt, skimming my bare skin. My spine shoots sparks. They explode within me. Around us. Between.

"Honestly, Jay. I wish I did know. How you feel." I speak softly, a nervous kick to my voice. I'm not even sure I remember how to kiss a man. It's been more than three years.

"How can you not know?" Jay laughs gently.

"How could I?" I counter. "For all I know, I'm just another Jenny."

Now Jay pulls his head back to look intensely into my eyes. "Amanda," he says. "You're not just another anybody."

These words erase the dull gray layers that have long settled within me. In this very instant, I am nudged from despair. He has extended the rope, and sound by sound, he pulls me from the mud flats of grief, the swamplands of sorrow. *"You're not just another anybody."*

His message echoes through me and I am free. Free.

I unroll a stretch of bubble wrap across the counter and begin to pack the final stash of kitchenware, one piece at a time. Raelynn reaches into the back of the cabinet and hands each glass to me, pretending again and again to drop a dish.

Beth and Sarah are in the bedroom, stuffing the last remaining items into boxes that Preacher and Jay will load into their pickups and haul to my new condo.

"Gettin' cold feet?" Raelynn empties the shelf and closes the cabinet, stepping over to help me with the final few wraps.

I shrug. "It's easy to feel overwhelmed by it all."

"You can do this, Amanda. Viv's place will be perfect for you. At least until you decide what you want to buy."

"I'm just happy to have somebody pay the note," Viv adds, walking in with more newspaper. "Since the wedding it's been sitting on the market and hasn't had a single bite."

"It's such a nice place." I hand a box off to Viv and start a new one. "I don't know why it hasn't sold."

"It's the price. I shouldn't have bought at the peak, but values were shooting up so fast after Katrina, I got scared and jumped headfirst." She sighs and adds, "Live and learn."

I smile and turn toward the kitchen window, where a tapping

sound has caught me off guard. The curtains and blinds have already been packed away, so our view is unobstructed. There, perched against the narrow sill, a small russet-and-gray bird drums its beak repetitively against the pane. With bold streaks down its puffy white chest, I recognize it right away.

"Is that a sparrow?" Raelynn asks, moving toward the window for a closer look. I follow.

"Raelynn," I whisper, brows peaked high. "You don't think . . ."

I call out to Beth and Sarah, urging them, "Come quick!"

They rush into the kitchen, and Raelynn points to the feathered friend. "Is that your bird?"

Sarah moves quickly to the window and presses her hand flat against the pane. The sparrow pecks its bobbing head, a gentle rhythmic rap. Sarah looks back at us, a smile that sparks the room. Then she moves to another window, this one in the living room. The rest of us stare, astonished, as the bird flies around the house and reappears, knocking again, singing.

"Softly sings the sparrow," Sarah says.

"No way!" Nate shouts, coming in for another load. Sarah turns and laughs. When she moves to a bedroom window, the sparrow follows.

Viv is in awe, calling her handsome fire chief hubby to take a look. "That can't be happening."

Sarah says simply, "But it is."

I hurry outside to find Jay, Gator, and Preacher. They won't believe us unless they see it for themselves. "Hurry," I call out to the men who are busy cleaning out my shed. "It's Sarah's sparrow."

Preacher rushes in to join the others, but Gator and Jay hold back. "That don't surprise me. It's her spirit animal," Gator says, as if there's nothing to be all worked up about. "Her guide."

"Spirit animal?" I question.

"God's way of talkin' to us. We just gotta learn to hear what he's sayin'."

"You believe that?" Jay asks Gator.

"Why not?" Gator hobbles over to see Sarah's sparrow.

As I start to follow, Jay calls, "Hold up a second, Amanda. I've got something to show you."

I will never tire of hearing him say my name.

He walks with me to his truck. "We got an interesting call at the office yesterday. Then this came by fax. This morning. I've been waiting for a chance to give it to you." When he hands me an envelope, he seems confused by my reluctance. "Don't you want to read it?"

I look down and shuffle my feet. My hesitancy is clear. The last time someone surprised me with paperwork, it was a divorce petition. "What is it?"

He nudges the folder farther into my hands. "Read it. You'll be glad."

With everyone else in the house marveling over Sarah's sparrow, Jay and I take a seat in two retractable lawn chairs. I open the envelope to find a slender stack of papers. On top, a handwritten salutation: *For Amanda Salassi.*

Dear Ms. Salassi:

I am sorry to inform you that your mother, Adelaide Landry, has passed away. While preparing to depart, she asked me to find you. It has taken me awhile, with the limited information I was given. I apologize for the delay.

Before she died, she wrote you a letter. I have enclosed it for you. I hope her words bring you comfort.

I will honor Adelaide's request and remain anonymous.

Peace be with you.

My stomach turns a flip. I put the letter down and look at Jay. "Is this from my birth mother?"

He smiles. "Keep reading."

I fumble to the next page.

Dear Amanda,

My name is Adelaide Landry, and I am your mother.

My parents kicked me out of their home when they found out I was carrying. I knew only one place to go. I was sixteen years old when I left Lafayette. I had no diploma, no job, no husband. My cousin was studying at LSU, and she said she'd let me stay in her apartment until you were born. But when her parents found out, they kicked me out of there too.

I had no one. Your father's name was Jared Cordero. He was a kid, like me. I believe we might could have made it, given half a chance. He's not a bad guy, Amanda. Maybe you can find him. Last I heard, he was living down in Lake Charles. He owned a few car washes.

You may not understand, and you may never be able to forgive me, but I met a man who promised to help me. He convinced me to move to New Orleans. I believed he would give me a job and a place to live. I had no other options, Amanda. I followed him. Worst mistake I ever made.

He did take care of me, at first. He even took me to the doctor. But as soon as I gave birth to you, things changed. He became violent. You were in danger, and we needed to get away. I called home from the bus station, hoping my parents would change their minds. They refused. My cousin could no longer be involved. She suggested the Sellers Home, a place for unwed mothers back in New Orleans.

An older woman there named Betty wanted to help. She convinced me the best thing would be to give you up for adoption. You were only a few weeks old. I begged her to find another way. But in the end I had no choice. I signed over my rights as your mother and returned home to my own parents.

As soon as I finished high school, I left Lafayette for good and moved to Chicago. I went to college and taught school until the cancer took over. I never married. I never had another child.

I have only one photograph of you. I have worn it in a locket, pressed against my heart, every day of my life, and I will wear it to my grave. Our initials are on the back. A. L.– Amanda Landry. I named you that on purpose. I wanted your name to stand for something. "Always Loved."

Forgive me, Amanda. I prayed every day that God found you the right parents, a life I was unable to offer. I did not abandon you. You were Always Loved.

I am in tears by the time I turn the page. And there's the photograph. A faded color snapshot of Adelaide Landry sitting on a park bench in the city. She is smiling, one hand on her locket, as the sunlight streams through the sparse row of trees. It's the face I've been searching for all these years. My same dark eyes, dark hair, the same crook in my nose. I pretend she is looking at me, saying, "Amanda, always remember, you are loved."

Chapter 31

Thursday, October 29, 2009

TODAY I VISIT ELLIE'S GRAVE ALONE. I WILL SPEND THIS ANNIVER-
sary with my daughter, shaded by swaying pine limbs and sturdy
oaks. A wild orchard of satsumas rests feet from her stone. Their
citrus fragrance draws bees and birds alike, as a few forgotten summer figs turn to pungent liqueur across the ground.

I place my stainless steel thermos on the bench and kneel in
the moist, cool grass beside my child. I replace the faded artificial
bouquet with a new winter spray of white roses, red holly. Then
I clean her marker, as I do every Sunday. I brush away leaves and
acorns, sweeping tiny twigs from her name and blowing dust from
the raised inscription.

ELLIE CLAIRE SALASSI
SEPT. 8, 1992—OCT. 29, 2006
FLY FREE

I am finally able to set the dates down in order along a line of
time. Today we are:

- Five years past The Day when Sarah was abducted.
- Four years past The Day when Carl walked out with Ashleigh.

- Three years past The Day when Ellie made her final choice.
- And nearly one year past Sarah's rescue.

Hour by hour, our lives are slowly spinning back to good.

Near the grave an area of grass is beginning to thin, so I transfer a patch of St. Augustine from a lusher piece of ground and push it into the soft soil, hoping it will take root. Then I trace the edges of her marker, pulling weeds from the perimeter, before placing a small token near the vase. Usually I choose something I find while I'm here: a smooth, cool pebble; a wiry mesh of Spanish moss; a fine and fangled stem of fern. Sometimes I pick wildflower blooms and leave them for Ellie: a velvet tab from shade-soaked lamb's ear; a palmetto spire, sharp as a blade; a bleeding heart, limp and delicate with papery skin; a bright, black berry, plucked gently from the forest's edge. Other times I leave songs in the wind and hope my voice can somehow reach her, the lullabies that once soothed a teething tot or the hymns that taught her soul to mend, or the edgy alternative hits that both inspired and built fire within her adolescent arteries. Today I place two golden acorns just above her name, one for Sarah and one for me.

The sun burns bright between the branches above, speckling the ground beneath me. I reach under the cement bench and scoop cool earth into my palm. The rich smells of the soil are coiled together. A mix of humus and decay, new birth from ruin.

As a child, I was taught to find comfort in the idea of being born again. Even now I like to imagine an eternal life, a state of existence where we are filled with only peace and love and light. That's where I picture my Ellie. She may not be floating around in some picture-book version of heaven, or waiting for the day of ascension beneath this stone. But I have to believe she's no longer in pain. Wherever that may be.

As the day begins to fold, tree-trunk shadows stretch like matchsticks, each striking the sun. I write a love song to my daughter, as I have done each anniversary. Black ink against a pastel page, loops and letters soon to be set free. I scroll the message, tied with string beneath a bright-blue bulb of helium, and kiss the words good-bye.

Within seconds the turquoise balloon crests high above the canopy of leaves, disappearing into the great beyond. I hope with all my soul that it finds Ellie up there, within the mystery, clothed in wonder. Flying free.

Saturday, December 5, 2009

Sarah doesn't walk in anger or with even a hint of revenge. Instead, she seems to glide through the Broussard family living room, almost suspended like a source of light. The cameras focus on her as she begins to speak.

"My name is Sarah Broussard. I was abducted from a school field trip in New Orleans. It happened five years ago, when I was twelve.

"I was rescued last November, at sixteen. I am now seventeen, and I am ready to speak.

"Many people were with me that day, but I want to make it clear. None of them were to blame—not my chaperone, Ms. Amanda; not my teacher, Miss Henderson; not my best friend, Ellie; not my bus driver, Mr. Gator. Neither were my parents or anyone else who loved and cared for me. I was tricked. I was tricked into following a lady out of the café. And it was no one's fault but the people who abducted me. The people I came to know as The Boss, LeMoyne, and Bridgette."

The room is completely still, as if the whole world has paused to hear this young woman's truth.

"I am here today to tell you my story. I will no longer be silenced. I will not be shamed. I will do whatever it takes to be seen and heard. Hopefully, by claiming my own voice, I can give voice to all the people who are living in chains. Whether they are physically, spiritually, or emotionally caged, we will fight to set them free."

Reporters grab quotes from Sarah's speech and agree to help her promote an upcoming fund-raiser to combat human trafficking.

Frank Doucet, our local correspondent, says to Sarah, "You were abducted during a field trip. Surely that started off as a happy day with your friends. What was one of the last memories you had from this part of your life? Was there something that carried you through all those years?"

Sarah thinks a minute, and then she stands taller. "Mr. Doucet, that's a really good question. I'm glad you asked."

Preacher gives the familiar newsman a smile, forgiving him for pushing too far in past situations.

"The day I was taken, our class had gone to Mardi Gras World. It was my first time there, and we were having a lot of fun, dressing up in costumes, eating king cake. My best friend, Ellie, was very artistic, creative, so it was exciting going somewhere like that with her. And yes, there was something from that experience that stuck with me all these years."

Reporters lean in, pens at the ready, cameras recording.

"One of the artists taught us that corsets were made with

whalebones. But then somebody started using featherbones instead. I thought about those corsets a lot, probably because I had to wear them sometimes. What really stuck with me was that we could take the most powerful animal of the sea and harvest his bones. Use them to build a cage, of sorts, and then force women to squeeze themselves into them."

Sarah gives a dramatic pause here as we all wait for more.

"But it didn't work! Because those bones from the biggest, strongest, most intimidating animal, they couldn't bend. Those whalebones broke. It took the lightest, most fragile bones of all—the featherbones of birds—to be strong enough to bend without breaking.

"That's how I started to think of myself. Like a feathered bone. I kept a little sparrow feather with me through the whole journey, and when I'd start to think I was going to break, I'd hold my feather and remind myself that I was stronger than I looked."

As the commotion begins to wind down, Preacher announces that he's given Sarah the honor of flipping on the Christmas lights. First time in five years.

"Let's do this!" Sarah shouts, leading us all outside for the display.

I stand with Beth as the Broussard home ignites. Within minutes, the entire scene is on sensory overload. Music, blinking lights, displays, dancing elves. Preacher jigs around the yard dressed as Santa, happy as a schoolkid, while visitors stand in line for family photos.

In the background, Frank Doucet sets up a live broadcast. "It's been years since the Broussard home was lit with Christmas lights, but tonight we are here in Walker where, as you can see, a large crowd is gathering for the celebration." Doucet provides a few more details about Sarah's story. Then he turns his attention to Jay and begins to question the status of the investigation.

"Sheriff, in the year since your deputy found Sarah, you've rescued six children and dozens of young women who were being trafficked through this prostitution ring."

"That's correct. They were based in Algiers and Hammond, two communities where people think this sort of thing would never happen. The victims were brought to both New Orleans and Baton Rouge to meet paying clients. We found Sarah during one of those transports."

"We've been told you have developed a list of Johns? And this list may include the names of politically powerful members of our community?" Doucet turns the microphone back toward Jay.

"We do have the names of numerous clients," Jay says. "We believe they paid for services either in person or online. We are working with the state police and federal investigators to build a solid case. That investigation will continue."

Doucet takes a turn. "I imagine that might have a lot of men shaking in their boots tonight."

"It should." Jay gives his sheriff's grin, suggesting he's got the whole thing under control.

Doucet then invites Preacher to step in front of the camera. "Mr. Broussard, tell us how it feels to have your daughter here with you tonight."

Preacher releases a humble laugh. "All I can say is God is good."

"You were a youth minister before your daughter was abducted. But you've been running a pool and spa business in recent years. Will you be returning to a position with the church now that Sarah has been recovered?"

Preacher smiles. "Actually, yes. I'll be the men's ministry leader out here in Walker. Everyone is welcome to join us." He gives times, location. "If church isn't your thing, then just come on out to our house and enjoy the lights. They'll be on every night through January 6, when we'll switch gears for Mardi Gras."

After Preacher's invitation, Doucet turns his attention to Sarah. He begins with this question: "Sarah, how does it feel to be celebrating this Christmas tradition with your family again?"

"It's awesome! It's one of the things I missed most."

"Can you tell us how you managed to survive those four years in captivity?"

"Remember what I told you, Mr. Doucet. I'm stronger than you think I am." Then Sarah looks to her parents and smiles. "But to be honest, I credit my mom and pop for that. It would have been easy to give up. To believe no one was out looking for me. I could have forgotten all about this life and the person I was before. But when I was little, my parents taught me a magic trick. That's what they called it."

"Well, what's the trick?" Doucet plays along.

"When I started to feel afraid, they taught me to repeat a simple saying. So after the kidnapping, I would repeat it again and again: 'I am loved.'"

Doucet repeats, "I am loved."

"Yes, sir. Simple as that. That's why I'm here today." She smiles at her parents. "Because no matter what lies those people tried to tell me, that prayer helped me remember the truth. I am loved. That's the real miracle, isn't it?"

As the camera lights dim, Sarah pulls Beth and Preacher into a family hug. Her sweater falls loose from her shoulder, revealing her revised tattoo. She is no longer marked with LeMoyne's dollar sign. A beautiful feather is now sketched in brilliant turquoise hues, a tribute to my Ellie. Beneath, it reads: *Some things were made for the light.*

I'm fighting tears as Jay tugs me to a quieter space. "Amanda?" He says my name as if I've got all the answers he'll ever need. Then he leans low and I hold my breath. *Is he finally going to give me that kiss?*

Seeing this, Raelynn starts cheering, causing me to pull away, blush-red. "I don't see any mistletoe," she teases.

"Hey, a guy's gotta try!" Jay holds his hands up, laughing. Then he turns to help Raelynn manage her sons. I find the hot chocolate tent while Jay brings the two younger boys to see Gator's reindeer. They're actually goats wearing fake antlers, but nobody seems to mind.

The crowd grows steadily, and the energy level is rising to near carnival mode by the time Viv and her hottie hubby arrive. They weave their way toward me, nudging among young families who cart wobbly toddlers past the animated snowmen.

On the rooftop Preacher and Jay have added a new surprise to this year's display. Using chicken wire and white lights, the flight pattern of a sparrow is depicted above the shingles, with separate sculptures showing each stage of liftoff. The lights have been programmed to turn on in sequence, so the overall effect represents a small bird coming out of its cage, flying away into the night.

In the bird's mouth is a flag. With each step closer to freedom, another set of letters lights up so that in the end, the sparrow soars away holding a flag that reads *Fly Free.*

"Did you see the roof?" Jay returns.

"Very thoughtful," I say, moving near.

"We liked what you chose for Ellie's marker," he says. "We salvaged those materials from Katrina debris."

I lean back into him. His hands warm around my waist.

"You know, Raelynn and I stood by the river, talking about how it was only a matter of time before the waters would break through and flood the city. That was the day of the field trip. Nearly a year before Katrina."

"Are you trying to tell me you and Raelynn can see the future?" He's pulling out all his charms.

"Yep." I laugh. "Fair warning."

"Well then, Madame Fortune-teller, tell me. When are you going to let somebody breach that levee around your heart?"

Jay lifts my chin, and he gives me the most tender kiss a man could ever deliver. Before I realize what is happening, music begins to blare, and all my friends surround us, singing. Raelynn's brother is capturing it all on video, as everyone I love starts dancing in sync and belting out the words to "Brown-Eyed Girl." Viv comes rushing up to Jay with a bottle of Elmer's glue. He pulls a ring from his pocket, pops it over the orange plastic cap, and drops to one knee. I'm a mess of tears by the time the music stops and Jay says, "Amanda, will you marry me?"

Chapter 32

Thursday, December 24, 2009

IT'S CHRISTMAS EVE. WE HAVE BROUGHT SARAH TO ST. JAMES Parish to celebrate her official reentry into life. "She's done so well handling the crowds at the Christmas lighting and the fund-raiser," Beth says. "I hope this isn't too much."

"It's time," Raelynn insists, smiling at Sarah.

As the sun begins to set, Jay and I climb the levee, working our way behind Raelynn's rowdy crew. She holds her niece, Kayla, on her hip while her brother cuts up with her three boys.

Reaching the top, we stop to look out over the Mississippi River, where the water rolls between the banks. Louisiana crafters have worked for months, carving willow trees to construct a long line of bonfires. They stretch from Lutcher all the way to Gramercy and beyond. Some are traditional fourteen-foot-high piles, uniform and precise like guard towers. But others are feats of impressive engineering and artistry, a true celebration of the creative spirit.

We stop in front of one that represents an alligator. Sarah asks a stranger to take a photo so we can all be in the frame: Beth and Preacher, Raelynn and her gang, Jay and me.

"Say 'Family'!" Sarah says.

"Family!" we cheer.

Around us, people enjoy their stroll, stopping to admire the elaborate log sculptures: pirate ships, army tanks, crawfish, and Mike the Tiger. With the darkness thickening, we head toward one pyre built to resemble a massive Mardi Gras float.

"I heard you're going to be queen," I tell Sarah. "For the Denham Spring Mardi Gras parade?"

"I can't wait." She smiles. "Ellie and I always said we'd be queen one day, remember?"

"I sure do. She'd be very proud of you, Sarah. You're the strongest person I've ever known."

"We bend, Ms. Amanda. We don't break." Then she looks at Jay and adds, "I'm excited about the parade, but I'm even more excited about y'all's wedding. Thanks for letting me be a part of it."

"Of course you're a part of it," Jay says.

Beth chimes in. "I've got the church reserved. Preacher will officiate. Need me to plan anything else?"

"Nope. That's perfect," I assure her. "Raelynn will bake a cake. Sarah and Nate can help with the wildflowers."

"Wildflowers?" Nate is confused.

"We'll give everyone a pack of seeds and ask them to plant them somewhere special, somewhere they feel most at peace."

"I love it," Sarah says. "Ellie would too."

I draw her into a hug. "I'm so glad you're home."

"Me too." Sarah smiles at Nate, causing him to blush in front of his brothers.

"You know what I don't get?" Nate asks. "Why didn't you tell Dex your real name? Why'd you keep telling him you were Holly?"

Sarah gets quiet for a minute. We gather closer to hear her response. "It's taken me a whole year to figure that out. But remember when we went to the animal shelter? With the youth group?"

Nate pulls his cap from his head. "Yeah. Fifth grade or something?"

"Right." Sarah smiles at Raelynn's middle son, a fifth grader. "Remember that dog they unloaded from the car while we were there? The big white one with all those sores?"

"I remember," Nate says. "She was bleeding. Could barely walk."

"She had been living in a dump. Sleeping in garbage."

Nate nods, and I lean closer to Jay. He's always had a soft heart for dogs.

"The people from the shelter brought some food to her at the dump. But she wouldn't let them get close enough to put a leash on her. Took a long time."

"Did she bite them?" Raelynn's youngest asks.

"No. She wasn't that kind of dog. But when they started to lead her to their car, she pulled away. She tried to go back to the dirty blanket where she had been sleeping."

"Why?" Nate's brothers ask in sync.

"Because she had been in that dump for a long time. The fear of leaving was greater than the fear of staying where she was."

Nate replaces his cap, giving Sarah a slow shake of his head.

"You see? No matter how horrible it was, I was surviving. I didn't know what would happen if I tried to leave. I was scared."

"That's not the Sarah I knew," Raelynn says.

"The Sarah you knew had forgotten something. Something Mom and Pop had taught me." She looks at Beth and Preacher now. "That I can let go of the fear. Rely on my faith. Trust."

"Yeah, but I would have been scared too," I admit. "Especially after what happened in the café. You trusted Bridgette."

"True," Sarah agrees. "But I had a bad feeling about her from the start. That's what I had to learn. Some people nudge us into the dark, others toward the light. We just have to be smart enough to know the difference."

The younger boys still look puzzled.

Sarah explains, "How do you know where the fish are biting? Where the alligators are hiding? Where to set up your deer stand?"

Nate taps his temple and smiles. "Instinct."

"That's what I'm saying. We already have all the tools we need to survive. It's up to us to learn how to use them."

After a time of silence, Nate's littlest brother tugs Sarah's shirt. "What happened to the dog?"

"Oh, right!" Sarah almost sings this. "That's the best part of the story. You'll never believe it."

I lean in, attentive.

"She became a rescue dog. When they bring in other animals who have been abused, they put them with her. She helps them stay calm. Teaches them all the things they forgot when they were trying to survive. How to trust, how to love. How to be loved. No telling how many animals she's saved."

Jay looks to me and says, "Just think . . . if she hadn't had the guts to step out of that mess."

At seven o'clock sharp, a fleet of boats let loose their hollow horns. More than one hundred fires are lit.

"You know why we do this?" The flames fly high as Preacher explains. "So Santa can find his way in the dark."

Raelynn's youngest laughs, not quite believing anymore. But Kayla perks up at the mention of Santa.

Jay takes my hand in his. Smoke drifts over the water, and the bright line of fire reflects orange across the ribboned river.

Maybe Jay and Sarah are onto something. Maybe I have spent

the last few years building a levee around my heart. So determined to protect myself from harm, I stayed frozen in a terrible place. But sometimes life brings a storm strong enough to break through the highest flood walls. Only after the clouds have cleared do we know we've survived.

Now this storm is over. And here we are, still standing. We have climbed to the top of this levee where bonfires blaze across the ridgeline. The pyres shine far and wide—so that love can come and find us, even in the dark.

As the embers rise, locals break out their guitars, accordions, washboards, and fiddles. We clap and sing along to the familiar tune "Would You Fly." Within the first few measures, hundreds are lifting their voices into the night.

In the warmth of these bonfires, silhouetted in their towering light, I am surrounded by those I love most in this world. The darkness is being kept at bay. And the music plays.

And the music plays.

A Note from the Author

WRITERS ARE FREQUENTLY ASKED, "WHERE DO YOU COME UP with your ideas?" While this particular story is a work of fiction, many things came together to inspire Amanda's tale.

First, the loss of my own brother to suicide when he was a senior in high school. I write this in memory of Jeff, whose light still shines. My brother was loved, and he lived a life of love. He is greatly missed. Every second. Every day.

Second, I have seen too many friends endure the tragic death of a child. I have mourned their loss and observed the struggle they face while navigating this horrific trauma. To each of you who has known this unbearable grief, my heart hurts for you, and I thank you for showing us such models of strength and courage.

Third, I was mesmerized by the story of Elizabeth Smart and her personal account of miracles and faith that kept her spiritually strong in the face of evil. Elizabeth, you inspire me and countless others. This story exists because of you.

Fourth, I am passionate about being the voice for the many women (and men) who endure emotional and/or physical abuse for the sake of keeping a marriage/family together, or because they are too afraid/too in danger to escape safely, or because this abuse is all they know of love, or because this is what they believe they deserve.

To you, I ask, what good is it to have feathers if you don't fly? You are worthy of being loved. You are worthy of being free.

Fifth, I long to reach the many teens who suffer from depression or despair and who feel misunderstood and hopeless in this great big world. To you, I promise, it will get better! Inhale. Exhale. Good things await. Please don't let the pain win. You are stronger than you think you are.

Sixth, I saw a 2006 documentary film, *The Bridge*, which was written by Tad Friend and directed by Eric Steel. This film explores Golden Gate bridge suicides and led to my alternative telling in this book about a suicidal man in front of Walmart who wanted one person to smile at him. I want to be the person who smiles. I encourage you to be that person too.

Seventh, I was at a low point in my own life when I saw a viral video that had been posted on December 12, 2013, by Hope for Paws. This emotional clip featured the story of a dog who was rescued from a terrible life in a trash pile and inspired the final scene of this book, during which Sarah compares the dog's experience to her own. I send a heartfelt thank-you to all of you who reach out a helping hand and who understand the fear that keeps a hurting soul in a place of pain.

Eighth, I've had the honor of meeting with many people who have been abused and/or trafficked in America. These survivors bravely opened their hearts to me and told me their truths. These are people you work with, study with, live near, worship with. People you would never know had endured such unjust cruelties in their lives. They are strong, and many of them believe they only managed to survive because of their faith in God. Whether or not you consider yourself a spiritual person, it is hard to deny someone who stands in front of you and says, "God was with me," when describing one of the most vile scenarios humanly imaginable. There is power in that kind of faith, and that's what I hope to have brought to the pages of this story.

All of these experiences combined to form a novel about the many forms of slavery and all the ways our souls can become trapped in dark places. *The Feathered Bone* is written for every person who has ever felt alone, unloved, unsafe, or unvalued. It is written to remind us all that we are loved, we have worth, and we are never alone.

Acknowledgments

IN LOUISIANA, THE BEST WAY TO MAKE GUMBO IS TO INVITE others to add to the pot. Many people touched this story as it was simmering. Please visit my website, www.juliecantrell.com, where I share more about the wonderful people who contributed. I could not have built this fictional world without them.

Thanks to Nathan Deroche and Pat Hymel of Blind River Chapel as well as Martha and Bobby Deroche, Val Amato, Charlie and Jimmy Duhe, Moise Oubre, and Tommy Zeringue. To river friends: Pam Brignac, Barbara and Steven Gallo, Earl Hoseth, Michael Dale Howze, Damon Miley, Dennis Rohner, and Rhonda Littleton Sibley.

To Louisiana State Police Lieutenant Chad Gremillion, Sheriff Jason Ard, his lovely wife Erica, and the entire Livingston Parish Sheriff's Department. To Anny Donewald of Eve's Angels; Prof. Richard Campanella, with the Tulane School of Architecture; and Dr. J. V. Remsen, with the LSU Museum of Natural Science.

To LP'ers Anjel and Stan Cain, Dean Coates, Tammy Palmer Crawford, Nicole and Mike Green, Stephen Paul Howze, Kay Palmer, the entire Aydell Family and the Walker Museum, Myra Streeter, and everyone who ever brought me fishing, frogging, crawfishing, skiing, boating, hiking, exploring, or "to da camp." To the congregations of both Walker Baptist and Judson Baptist Church, especially to Betty Marsh. To the teachers of the Walker public schools, particularly Linda Purcell. To Carolyn and Sonny Aucoin, who made the wild woods my own. And to New Orleans friends: Christa Allan, Marci Glascock Lichtl, and Stephen Lukinovich.

To Taylor Bellard and my OGH gang: Paula, Pinky, Tammy, and Vickie. To Kenny, David, Craig, Stacy and Randy, Connie and Bobski, Gail, Mike and Cora, Josh, and Jessie. To Glenda and Jimmy Bell; Judy and Billy Kaufman; Mary and Mike Nola; Brenda Pepitone; the Livingston Parish Public Library and the East Baton Rouge Parish Regional Library; *The Livingston Parish News*; *The Advocate*; Rick Wentzel and the Livingston Parish School Board; Austin Flowers; Don's Seafood; Kay Landry and the Rotary Club of Livingston Parish; Blaine Kern's Mardi Gras World, St. Louis Cathedral, Algiers Point/Canal Street Ferry and Café du Monde; and the Baton Rouge Crisis Intervention Center. And to my Holy Yoga friends: Amber, Brigid, Catherine, Jane, Joy, Julie, Kaci, Kristi, Laura, Laurie, Lorraine, Lucinda, Mandy, Rachel, Stacy, Tiffany, Wendy, and NICOLE—my soul sister.

To Texas friends: Ashely Tesar; Still Creek Ranch; and College Station's Busy Moms Bookclub, specifically Kelli Backstrom, Ginny Brown, Gay Craig, and Brenda Rogers.

To my agent, Greg Johnson. To my posse: Christa Allan, Kerri Greene, Carol Langendoen, Michael Morris, Larry Wells, and Lisa Wingate. And to Mary Ann Bowen—the world needs more people like you. To Katie Bond, Amanda Bostic, Elizabeth Hudson, Jodi Hughes, Daisy Hutton, LB Norton, and everyone at TNZ Fiction.

Thanks to the best mom in the universe, Cindy Perkins. And to my husband, Charles, and our children, Emily and Adam, whose spirits and spunk bring more joy, love, and laughter to my life than I could ever measure.

Finally, to every reader who gives this story a chance. I offer a great big heaping helping of gratitude for all of you. Merci beaucoup and bon appétit!

Discussion Questions

1. We begin the story with Amanda examining the movement of the river and the boats around her while describing herself as "landbound." How does this represent her life?

2. In an early scene, Sarah and Ellie pull on costumes for photos, displaying childhood innocence. Consider the deeper meaning of "disguising" or "masking" our true selves. How does this play out when Sarah is kidnapped, in costume, and called by a different name? How does she manage to stay in tune with her authentic self and not forget her own truth?

3. Issues of faith are presented early in the book. We learn about the religious traditions of Mardi Gras and then see the cathedral spires rise above the fog as we ferry across the river. What do these initial images tell about the role faith plays in Louisiana culture? Examine the contrast of light vs. dark that is explored throughout the story.

4. While in New Orleans, Amanda notices a prostitute. She feels compassion for the young woman but believes things like kidnapping and trafficking don't happen to "people like us." Discuss the factors that result in human trafficking and take time to learn about the impact on your local community. What

does it say about us as a people if we ignore the exploitation of human beings, especially children?

5. Hurricane Katrina is explored in Part II of this story. Examine the reasons people may have chosen to stay in the evacuation zone and weather the storm. Can similar constraints apply in situations such as trafficking, domestic violence, and abuse? Consider the parallels.

6. Amanda struggles with the childhood wound of abandonment. She has felt unloved her entire life, despite having been loved greatly by her mother, her daughter, and her friends. How might this wound have impacted her choice to marry Carl, the one person who did not love her in a healthy way? What does she learn to accept about herself? About her husband? Do you believe, as Amanda learns from Viv, that we marry to heal our childhood wounds?

7. Throughout the book, our characters each build defenses for various reasons. Some harden their hearts completely, too hurt to give or receive love anymore. Amanda has the choice to harden or to heal. In the end, she takes a chance and allows Jay to "breech the levee of her heart." Is this the core meaning of faith—to remove those defensive barriers and return to an open heart? What does the Bible say about love? (1 Corinthians 13:4–7; 1 Corinthians 13:13; John 13:34; 1 John 4:7; 1 John 4:19)

8. Discuss the symbolism of the feathered bone, the role of women throughout history, and the idea of birds flying free vs. being caged. What do you want your daughters and granddaughters to know about being a woman? What do you want your sons and grandsons to know about how to treat women? What do our characters learn?

Newly repacked –
JULIE CANTRELL'S
early novels!

About the Author

Julie Cantrell is the *New York Times* and *USA Today* bestselling author of *Into the Free*, the 2013 Christy Award–winning Book of the Year and recipient of the Mississippi Library Association's Fiction Award. Cantrell has served as editor-in-chief of the *Southern Literary Review* and is a recipient of the Mississippi Arts Commission Literary Fellowship. Her second novel, *When Mountains Move*, won the 2014 Carol Award for Historical Fiction and, like her debut, was selected for several Top Reads lists.

For behind-the-scenes extras, including Louisiana recipes featured in *The Feathered Bone*, visit Julie online at juliecantrell.com

Facebook: juliecantrellauthor

Twitter: @JulieCantrell

Pinterest: juliecantrell